1̲_____ *ıth*

"Strong focus, admirable prose, and a nifty story line."
— *Library Journal*

"Brave, if blithely arrogant, character Maggie Fiori [is] a thirty-something Oakland writer/know-it-all sleuth/Volvo-driving wife and mom who solves the murder of her boss, the urbane editor of a chichi regional magazine."
— *San Francisco Chronicle*

"If you are a Susan Isaacs fan, you will love Linda Peterson's journalist cum sleuth, Maggie Fiori. I couldn't put the book down."
—JACQUELINE WINSPEAR
New York Times bestselling author of the Maisie Dobbs mysteries

"Edited to Death is an exceptional debut. With an engaging protagonist and a likeable cast, Linda Peterson brings a fresh new voice to a crowded field."
—SHELDON SIEGEL
New York Times bestselling author of
The Confession and Final Verdict

"Heroine Maggie Fiori's love of trivia makes for a great detective. As any crime buff knows, it's the little things that count. This book is smart, fast, and funny—a mystery to remember long after the last page."
— TERRY RYAN
author of *The Prizewinner of Defiance, Ohio*

"An entertaining debut that crackles with snappy dialogue, a rich and textured sense of San Francisco, and an appealing heroine who is as witty as she is resourceful. Sit back and enjoy the ride."
—JONNIE JACOBS
author of *Intent to Harm and Murder Among Strangers*

Praise for *The Devil's Interval*

"Impossible to put down. Sparkling dialogue, references both musical and literary, and an offbeat cast of believable characters make the pages fly by." *Starred review*

— *Library Journal*

"A fast-paced, intelligent tale of intrigue that will keep readers guessing until the refreshing end." *Starred review*

— *Publishers Weekly*

"An intelligent and gripping novel. Maggie Fiori is a witty, feisty protagonist, and Linda Lee Peterson deftly weaves a compelling tale of how far a mother will go to save her child. *The Devil's Interval* is a roller-coaster ride through the streets and alleys of San Francisco that will evoke Robert Parker's Spenser novels with a dash of Janet Evanovich. Get out the flashlight. You'll be up late."

— ROBERT DUGONI
New York Times bestselling author of *The Conviction*

**Learn more about Linda Lee Peterson at
www.lindaleepeterson.com**

EDITED TO DEATH

By
Linda Lee Peterson

PROSPECT
·PARK·
BOOKS

PROSPECT
·PARK·
BOOKS

Published by Prospect Park Books
969 S. Raymond Avenue
Pasadena, California 91105
prospectparkbooks.com

Distributed by Consortium Book Sales & Distribution
cbsd.com

Library of Congress Cataloging-in-Publication Data

Peterson, Linda Lee.
 Edited to Death / by Linda Lee Peterson.
    pages cm. -- (A Maggie Fiori Mystery)
 ISBN 978-1-938849-34-3 (pbk.)
1. Women journalists--Fiction. 2. Murder--Investigation--Fiction. 3. San Francisco (Calif.)--Fiction. 4. Mystery fiction. I. Title.
 PS3616.E8434E35 2013
 813'.6--dc23
                          2013043248

Cover design by Howard Grossman. Layout by Renee Nakagawa.
Printed in the United States of America.

To Murray Winthrop,
who taught me to love mysteries

BEYOND BOOKS AND COOKS

Here's something I can count on: If the phone rings twice before nine on a Friday morning, neither one of those calls is likely to be from the California State Lottery.

It'll be some carpool rearrangement or the automated voice at Sears telling me that, at long last, that extra special drill bit is in. That's about as good as early morning news gets.

At our house, we've got the bell turned up to dangerous decibel levels in order to hear it over the early morning racket—plummy voices on National Public Radio doing stories about imperiled loons or loony voices doing stories about imperiled plums, the kids squabbling over the last onion bagel, dogs and cats complaining about breakfast—right here, right now, and make it snappy!— and Anya, our melancholic Nordic au pair caroling from upstairs, "Maggie! Have you black tights without runners? Mine are too holey."

A person could get a headache. But through the din one fine fall morning, I heard that *brrring! brrring!* and Michael shouting, "Let the machine pick it up. It's nobody good. I know it."

But I couldn't. Not in the morning. Could be the lottery. The first caller was my freshman-year roommate, Sara Jenkins. She lives in London now, with her brilliant-but-dithery investment banker husband. When I picked up the phone she whispered, "Maggie, it's me. I need to know something quick."

"Sara? What's wrong?"

"Listen carefully," she said. "What happens eight days after the Nones of each month?"

"The Ides."

"Thanks, you're great. I knew you'd know."

Through the transatlantic crackle, I could tell Sara had her hand cupped around the receiver. I pictured her, dressed in her respectable English matron sweater and skirt, huddled in a corner of their elegant but drafty Sloane Square house, making surreptitious phone calls.

"Why? Why are you whispering? What's going on?"

"We're entertaining some business chums of Richard's—all weekend. By teatime I'd run out of small talk, so we broke out the Trivial Pursuit. I'm supposed to be upstairs searching out a sweater—it's like Siberia in the house, as usual. I've got to go."

"You spent Richard's cold, hard cash to cheat?"

"To get a wedge? You bet." She giggled. "Richard's money? What kind of a feminist are you, Maggie? Besides, it's English money—it's not worth anything anyway."

And she was gone. Without looking up from the paper, Michael said, "What's wrong with Sara? Her hollandaise separating again?"

"Nope. She was cheating at Trivial Pursuit."

Michael lowered the paper and shook his head. "That woman needs to get a job. Take her mind off all this domestic competition."

"She said it didn't matter. English money isn't worth anything. Is that right? I thought it was our money or Malaysian ringgits or something that isn't worth anything."

Michael said, "Mmmm," and returned to the sports page. He looked like a man who should be reading the business page. Six feet of respectability, packaged as usual in a starched white shirt with French cuffs. Gray suit, red silk tie, and his father's watch on a chain. Of course, when he wasn't dressed like this—as he was every work day of his life—he looked like a not-very-successful panhandler. Threadbare blue jeans or cords and an unfortunate collection of ratty sweatshirts. Michael was a man who'd missed out on the entire retail concept of casual clothes. But he wasn't reading the business page; he was deep in some bloodthirsty recounting of an ice hockey game, wondering if it was still too late to try out for the San Jose Sharks.

But about Sara, he had a point. She thought nothing of picking up the telephone to ask me if making hollandaise in a blender would keep it from separating, or to read me Colin's sonnet for school so I could fix the rhyme scheme. Since my major accomplishment in life is accumulating useless bits of information, we talked almost weekly. Sara carries almost no peripheral information around in her head, preserving all that space for life on a higher plane. She volunteers for underfunded pacifist groups and tutors graduate students in calculus.

Half an hour later, I was enjoying five minutes of the kind of solitude and silence only mothers with young children can appreciate. Lunches made, arguments mediated, socks found, animals fed, family out the door.

Josh was in school, developing interpersonal skills, experimenting with spatial relationships, and learning an occasional fact about history or grammar on the side. When I was ten, I was busy trying to wrest the four-square court away from Elise McElroy, who outweighed me by twenty-two pounds. If I wasn't locked in combat with Elise, I was trying to figure out why Dick and Jane never watched television, the activity of choice among my peers. Josh is the worrier in the family. If something troubles his serene environment, he develops brutal stomach cramps or throws up, usually without warning. Just as well he's not wrestling to the death over four square.

Zachary, my darling youngest, was in kindergarten. It was Friday. That meant he was acting out his hostile fantasies about me with the fantasy facilitator who came in once a week. Of course, when I was five and foolish enough to act on a hostile fantasy, I got sent to my room.

Michael was off giving obscure and probably un-followable tax advice to the undeserving rich.

"A tax lawyer does God's work," he announced to the children many a morning over breakfast. "Especially if he's a Democrat." Since the boys weren't yet up to ambiguous antecedents, they never called him on whether the Democratic "he" was God or the tax lawyer. Nor, for that matter, did I. I like a certain amount of peace with my bagel. Besides, Michael took such pure, undiluted pleasure in cooking up tax dodges for his foundation and nonprofit clients, I figured he deserved to deliver a self-righteous soliloquy or two over the breakfast table. Plus, he dressed the part.

So was I enjoying the bliss of post-breakfast solitude? Of course not. I was fretting over magazine deadlines. Should I go up to the computer waiting in the den and finish the research on "The Literate Manager: Role Models in Literature for Contemporary Business People," do an outline for "Maturely Mozart: Learning to Love Amadeus Late in Life," write a book review on a promising, if inaccessible, first novel (lots of sentence fragments and nanotech allusions) or do a first draft on "Goldilox: A Guided Tour through the Bay Area's Lox-and-Bagel Emporia." Of the four, only the Goldilox piece really stirred me. But that was probably because my bagel and cream cheese cried out for a little company.

I sighed. There were some non-work alternatives. But they seemed like worse work than work; there were bulbs to plant, the checkbook to balance, and flea collars ready and waiting for our menagerie of three cats (Batman, Robin, and the Riddler) and a dog. Raider, a German shepherd, named for Oakland's silver and black football hooligans, came and put his head in my lap and whimpered. He was bored, too.

I looked around the sunny kitchen. It was too nice a day to do any of those things. Fall in Oakland is inspiring, as it is all over Northern California. Crisp, warm days, with just enough trees turning and shedding to give the place atmosphere. Not enough, on the other hand, to make even the most dutiful householder haul out a rake each and every weekend.

With all the shortcomings of our sixty-year-old, five-bedroom, permanently disordered house, there were beautiful views from every room.

I decided the choices needed further study, poured another cup of Ethiopian Mocha Harrar (to live in the Bay Area any time in the last quarter-century and not be into coffee was to risk treatment as a social leper) and settled down to an intensive study of the jumbled word game in the *San Francisco Chronicle*. I looked around for a clean spoon to stir with, settled for the handle end of a knife, and took a sip. I figured I had another hour of peace before Anya, our au pair-cum-art student, breezed in from her "Painter-as-Poet" class with still another insight about the references to textiles in Amy Lowell's poetry.

Then the phone rang again.

"Margaret?"

American-born and Oxford-educated Quentin Hart was the only person who ever called me Margaret. Of course, he was also the only person I've ever known who gargled with mineral water, honestly feared for the souls of people who wore manmade fabrics, and refused to wear contact lenses because they seemed spiritually dishonest. I was Quentin's "discovery." He was my editor at *Small Town* magazine—and my friend.

"Quentin. God, it's good to hear from you."

"Any particular reason?"

I looked around the kitchen, still cluttered with Peter Rabbit dishes, two sick philodendra that needed re-potting, and a week's worth of newspapers. Quentin lived in impeccable near-solitude. Having understood—and then transcended—the need to marry well, he had systematically divested himself of clutter, both physical and emotional. He and his wife owned *Small Town*, California's chicest city magazine. Actually, Claire owned the magazine, or almost; she stood to inherit it from her ghastly and ever-so-healthy Uncle Alf. Quentin, after a few years of laboring in the journalistic vineyards, married the owner's niece and settled in to editing the magazine, with minimal meddling from both Claire and Uncle Alf. His gift for finding and nurturing good writers with original voices had rescued the magazine from near-collapse. Under his guidance, *Small Town* developed style, and even a little substance.

Advertisers, shocked by finding a vehicle people actually read, responded with enthusiasm. The magazine grew fat with advertising pages that peddled spectacularly useless stuff to the privileged. Those of us who scribbled for *Small Town* were grateful.

Almost two years ago, Claire and Quentin separated. Quentin cleared every trace of Claire out of their flat, lived alone for a year, and then invited his companion/assistant/friend Stuart to live in. Most people assumed that Quentin and Stuart's relationship had sexual overtones; but as Michael once observed early in his acquaintance with Quentin, "How could that guy have sex with anyone? Surely he doesn't actually undress. Don't you think he just goes to the dry cleaners along with his blazers to get his carnal desires attended to?" I didn't respond to Michael's speculation. I saw nothing good coming out of a discussion about what I knew about Quentin's antiseptic-but-complex love life.

"Well, my dear, I'm glad you're glad I called," Quentin was saying. "Can you come by? I have a thing or two for the January issue."

"Terrific," I said, sensing rescue from the computer, the garden, and the kitchen. "You mean besides the lox piece?"

"How's that coming?"

"It's just fine. I have a first draft on the screen," I lied. "It's fun, kind of, um, salty," I improvised.

Quentin sighed. "You haven't started yet, I take it."

Feeling courageous, I pressed on. "Listen, don't you think I could do something besides books and food for a bit? I'm up to it—you know that."

Indeed, Quentin did know. He had discovered me, as he liked to insist when people accused the magazine of precious elitism. Some suburban cousin of his had shown him a piece I'd written for a parents' community newspaper on what was wrong with most children's books. "I read this piece," Quentin recounts, "expecting to see another paean to non-sexist personal growth platitudes in children's literature; and what do I encounter? Wit, vitriol, and downright nastiness. I knew right off that Margaret belonged in our magazine's little stable of contributors."

So Quentin tracked me down and lured me out of semi-retirement to write a piece for *Small Town*. I'd worked as managing editor of a trade magazine for nurses before the babies came along, and I'd just started itching to put words on paper again. Writing was much more fun than editing. Quentin gave me an irresistible first assignment—test driving sports cars. He'd titled the piece "June Cleaver Hits the Road." I had a memorable time, after a little coaching from the National Association of Professional Drivers. Slaloming through cones, cornering, taking "hot laps"—I did it all, and *Small Town* got a story with a distinctive angle. What's more, I rose miles in Josh's estimation. He still carries a photo of me in helmet and jumpsuit, taped to the inside of his lunch box, to show off to his buddies. That made up for the guilt I felt when Michael brought him to the track to watch me drive and he threw up the moment I crossed the finish line.

"Margaret," Quentin chided. "Books and cooks are two perfectly acceptable subjects. They represent my major passions—nowadays, at any rate."

"Come on, you know what I mean," I said, trying to sound more like Dorothy Thompson and less like Dorothy Parker, and not particularly eager to discuss Quentin's other passions. "Front of the book hard stuff, power plays in high places, chemical spills threatening sleepy suburbs."

Quentin interrupted, "When, precisely, was the last time *Small Town* investigated anything more toxic than badly made martinis?"

I conceded the point. "I don't really think the magazine ought to do that stuff. It's just that I've been watching too many reruns of *The Year of Living Dangerously*. I think I want to be a journalist where the action is."

"There's plenty of action here," said Quentin. "All the people in East Pumpkin Corner think this is the most dangerous place on earth. They think if you don't get AIDS from the mud baths in Calistoga or a hot tub in Marin, you'll get knocked off in the crossfire of some overdressed drug kings in Oakland or underdressed drag queens in San Francisco."

"You happen to be stereotyping the place I'm raising my children."

"Well, read the papers. I happen to think we live with more than an adequate amount of danger myself." For a moment, Quentin's arch tone had a new edge.

"What do you mean?"

"Oh, I don't know. We'll probably all die of raspberry vinaigrette poisoning in some stainless-steel, high-concept yuppie-teria next week. Listen, if you want to go cover war-torn nations and unstable dictatorships, do it. What are you waiting for?"

"Well, for openers, there's Josh and Zach. And, in my limited experience, war-torn nations rarely need tax lawyers."

"A point in their favor," said Quentin. "And that's exactly the issue. You want all your domestic bliss—and excitement, too."

I didn't respond. Quentin knew far too much about my dueling desires for domesticity and thrills.

He continued, "Life is choices, my dear. So make yours, and as you say to one and all, don't kvetch."

"You shouldn't pronounce both the k and the v with equal weight," I said. "On second thought, you just may be too WASPy to even use that word, Quentin."

"I'll bear that in mind," he replied dryly.

"Okay, I'm sorry," I said. "Last week there was a partners' dinner at Michael's firm, a bar association cocktail party, and I had to make cupcakes for Josh's class. I'm just feeling a little too wife and mommy-ish."

"You made cupcakes? You hate to bake."

"Well, actually Michael made them. But I had to frost them. Truly, I will stop kvetching. Tell me what you've got that's coming up. I'll even do a 'In Search of the Perfect Chocolate Truffle' story for Valentine's Day."

"Spare me," said Quentin. "Actually, it's quite peculiar, you raising this issue about stretching your usual repertoire. That's exactly what I've got in mind. Tell me," he paused, "what do you know about the Cock of the Walk?"

I snorted. "It's how my boys behave when they think they've pulled a fast one on me."

"Mothers," muttered Quentin. "Imagine how uninterested I am in the little darlings' psychology. So you don't know anything about the Cock of the Walk?"

I sighed, "Come on, Quentin, let's not play Twenty Questions."

"Usually you like games," he said.

I didn't want to encourage further discussion along those lines either. "Okay, okay," I said. "Sounds like a restaurant on Polk Street." Polk Street, which predated the Castro district as San Francisco's most notable gay neighborhood, featured restaurants, bars, and boutiques with relentlessly cute names that mined predictable veins—a local spirits store named Sukkers Likkers, for example.

"You're not far off the mark. It is a restaurant."

"Hey," I protested. "I thought this was going to be different."

"Patience, my pet. It is a restaurant, although not on Polk Street. It's in the Frog Pond."

The Frog Pond was the latest in a series of gentrified revivals of old buildings, à la Boston's Fanueil Hall and San Francisco's Ghirardelli Square.

"A review? You want me to do a review? What about Lisbet?" Lisbet Traumer was *Small Town*'s regular restaurant reviewer, a woman who thought capital punishment was an under-reaction to overcooked vegetables and indifferent service.

"Don't worry about Lisbet. She'll do the review in good time. My interest in the Cock of the Walk has nothing to do with the food there. I think we have the opportunity to run a good story— and right a few wrongs along the way."

"How moral," I said. "How surprising."

"Yes, isn't it?" said Quentin. "It could ruin my reputation as a self-absorbed son of a bitch."

"That's not exactly what I meant," I protested.

Quentin laughed. "Certainly it is. Now, here's what we need to do to get you out of your wife-and-mommy funk. Shed that dreary little wraparound khaki skirt I know you have on." I looked down. It was denim, not khaki. "Put on something splendid, come to the city, and I'll take you to lunch and we'll talk about this piece."

"Can I wear a hat?"

Quentin was the only man of my acquaintance who actually liked women in hats. This, of course, irritated Michael, who found it further evidence that Quentin was "not his kind of guy." He wasn't, but for reasons Michael had yet to fathom.

"Certainly," said Quentin. "The little brown derby with the veil, I think. The one that makes you act like Myrna Loy."

"I'll run by the office just before noon?"

"No, come by my flat. I'm working at home this morning. We'll go somewhere in the neighborhood and eat decadent things."

ACROSS THE BAY

No one needs to issue lunch invitations twice to Maggie Fiori. Not to mention dangling a big, serious, and—okay—moral story.

By eleven thirty, with visions of a congratulatory letter from the Pulitzer Committee and a really good meal as motivation, I had knocked out a first draft of the lox piece, given instructions to Anya about starting dinner and retrieving the boys at school, and cleared up the worst of the kitchen clutter.

Quentin prompted a woman to rise to the occasion. The denim skirt was gone, replaced by a gabardine suit, silk shirt, pearls, and the little brown derby he liked so well. I surveyed myself in the mirror. "Maggie," I said, rearranging an undisciplined red curl under the derby, "you may feel like a suburban matron, but you put together a damn fine masquerade."

The feeling of fashion-forward well-being lasted until I opened the garage. The Fiori family owns matching turbocharged Volvo station wagons. So I had my choice of station wagon or station wagon, red or blue, but that was it. Today, Michael had left me the blue one, looking wholesome and cheerful underneath its battle scars of dents and grime.

Oh well, I thought, at least these things can move, and putting suede pump pedal to the metal, I whisked down MacArthur, onto the freeway, across the Bay Bridge, and into the city. Out Broadway, past the strip joints, past Chinatown, and then into the Broadway Tunnel and beyond, sweeping across Van Ness and up the hill into Pacific Heights. My favorite view in San Francisco comes at the corner of Broadway and Fillmore. Just past the block of exclusive private schools that educate the children of the privileged into a lifetime of noblesse oblige, the view waits. From the corner of Fillmore and Broadway you see: a precipitous descent into the Marina and the Bay, with boats snuggled close to the St. Francis Yacht Club, and the Bridge—the one and only, graceful and gleaming—the Golden Gate linking San Francisco with Marin County.

Quentin's no fool, I thought for the hundredth time, living here. For his flat, one of two in a meticulously restored Victorian, commanded that same view.

But the neighborhood has its drawbacks. Parking within three blocks of Quentin's flat could drive a person to desperation. Fully half my annual quota of parking tickets (a cost of living in the Greater Bay Area) came from throwing in the vehicular towel and, after countless circles around Quentin's block, parking in whatever illegal spot I could find. Driveways, fire hydrants, bus zones; you name it. I am pleased to report, however, that I always steer clear of disabled parking spaces. It's a bad example to set for the boys, and I didn't want it coming up in their "it's all my mother's fault" therapy fifteen years hence.

It was twelve-fifteen, and I was late. Quentin considered lateness in the same light he considered social diseases—an unforgivable lapse in manners. Still, I was getting my excuses in order. Quentin had promised on the phone to put his aged-but-perfect little Audi in his perfect little garage and leave me his driveway space. He must have forgotten, I thought. There sat his car in the driveway.

Live dangerously, I thought, as I trotted up the steps to the tiny porch in front of the doorways to the two flats. Life passes the conservative and cautious right on by. I'd acted on that philosophy. Since Quentin had so thoughtlessly co-opted his own driveway, I decided to go ahead and block him. Of course, the police had been known to put people away for eight to ten to punish lesser offenses, but I trusted Quentin, and I felt confident that I'd be in and out of his flat and on the way to lunch before any of San Francisco's finest discovered my transgression.

Two rings on the bell. No answer. Some raps on the door. No answer. "Quentin," I called. "It's Maggie." No answer.

He's gone, I thought. This is what happens when you're late to lunch with Quentin. "Quentin!" I tried again. "It's Maggie. Come on, I'm just fifteen minutes late and it's not even my fault," I could hear the whine in my voice, and stamped my foot in frustration. Very adult.

"He's not there, Maggie dear. Don't yell. It just wastes your instrument."

I whirled, embarrassed to be caught mid-tantrum. Quentin's downstairs neighbor was standing in her doorway.

"My instrument?" I asked the kimono-ed figure who confronted me.

"Your voice, darling, your voice," she explained patiently. "It's terrible to shriek. You mustn't, mustn't do it."

Madame DeBurgos (or DeBurger, as Michael likes to say in recognition of her generous proportions) was a retired operatic star. A minor diva, to be sure, but she had, in her time, sung roles in many of the major opera houses in Europe. We'd heard about "her time" each and every year at Quentin's Christmas party, which Madame DeBurgos always attended in one bejeweled extravaganza or another. She and Quentin and Claire had been neighbors for more than fifteen years.

"What do you mean, Quentin's gone? Did you see him go out? We had a lunch date."

"No, *cherie*, I didn't see him go out. But I heard him. My, my, I heard him." She broke off, looking smug and mysterious, patting the elaborate concoction into which she'd spun her improbably colored hair that morning.

I was getting impatient. "What do you mean? You heard him leave?"

"Well, I can't be certain," she hesitated.

"Oh, Madame, try." She looked as if she might waver. "If you know something, you should tell me. I'm really feeling cranky with Quentin right now."

"Well," she began with obvious relish. "You know, Quentin is such a considerate neighbor. I hardly hear a peep out of him. But this morning—such a noise. First, his stereo was turned up—my dear, I thought I might be deafened. Such a noise! And such music! It must have been—whatever is that strange young man's name?"

"Stuart Levesque," I supplied, beginning to feel nervous. I had an all-too-clear mental picture of Quentin popping out onto their shared porch any moment, finding me deep in speculation about his private life with Madame DeBurger.

"Yes, Stuart, that's it. Anyway, this dreadful noise was shaking the building. It stopped a little later, and I assumed Quentin had returned from walking Nuke and ordered Stuart to cease and desist that racket." She fluttered her hand in the air; half a papal wave, half an imperial order.

Nuke was Quentin's terrier mutt, a preternaturally ugly little creature he had named for what he assumed would happen to our species if a nuclear device were exploded at the corner of Broadway and Laguna. "We'd all end up looking like Nuke," he'd said. Despite Nuke's lack of visual appeal, Quentin was devoted to the dog and faithfully walked him each morning and evening.

"So you heard him go out after that?" I asked.

"Goodness, no," she said. "Then I heard—well, I heard the most awful quarrel. Such shouting and noises!"

"What was it about?"

"Maggie, dear!" She looked shocked. "Would I eavesdrop? However would I know what it was about?"

"I'm sorry. Of course not," I muttered.

"Then I heard the door slam, and that was that."

"Perhaps Stuart went out," I suggested.

"No, my dear. It must have been Quentin. Because shortly after the door slammed, that dreadful music began again. Now, you know Quentin wouldn't put that on."

"Well," I said, peering into the etched-glass panel on the door. "Then Stuart must be home."

"I should think so," said Madame. "I haven't heard music for a bit, but I haven't heard the door slam, either."

I rapped again. "Stuart," I called. "It's Maggie. Open up."

No answer. "I'll just leave Quentin a note," I said, rummaging in my bag. The only paper that came to hand was a book of deposit slips. I noted that Zach had already decorated them with rockets and monsters. "Madame, could I possibly borrow a piece of note paper?" I asked.

"Of course, my dear. I'll run and get you something." With that, Madame gathered her Cio Cio San–themed kimono around her and disappeared inside the door to her flat. I stood at Quentin's door. Damn Quentin! Damn lunch! And damn climbing into these clothes for nothing!

As I fumed, I reached out to give Quentin's doorknob an angry rattle.

It didn't rattle; it turned. Careless man. First, he forgets lunch dates, then he leaves the door unlocked. I pushed open the door and called, "Quentin? Stuart?"

The door opened onto a staircase that led into a tiled entryway. I climbed the stairs, expecting Quentin or Stuart to appear any moment. Not a sound. Just Quentin's pristine flat: all white walls, Berber carpets, netsuke, books, Japanese brush paintings. Michael always said, "If it gets any more serene in here, Quentin can sublet to Zen monks."

And that's the first thing I noticed that fall morning, with Madame DeBurgos caroling at me from the doorway. "Maggie, I've fetched you some note paper!"

What I noticed was this: Quentin's apartment wasn't so pristine any more. And, though I still couldn't hear a sound but Madame's labored breath as she puffed up Quentin's stairs, it wasn't so serene either.

A dead body in the living room cuts into your serenity something fierce.

BRIGHT MEETS JIP

Ms. Fiori?"

"Yes?" I turned, shivering in Madame's doorway, to see a tall, slender, Asian man with salt-and-pepper hair. He was dressed in a decidedly unrumpled trench coat and followed by two uniformed police officers. He held out his hand. I looked at it blankly, then remembered the social amenities. Introductions. Handshakes. Things like that. I extended my hand and wondered why he looked familiar.

"I'm sorry, I'm not very good at this. Yes, I'm Maggie Fiori. I'm the one who called you."

"John Moon. Homicide. Don't worry about not being good at—" He waved toward Quentin's doorway. "This. Most people aren't. It's a bad enough vocation. I don't recommend finding bodies for an *avocation*."

We shook hands. Mine was icy.

He gestured at Quentin's doorway. "In there?"

I nodded.

"Go ahead and get started," he said to the two uniformed officers, and they headed up the stairway into Quentin's flat.

"Do I know you?" I blurted. "I'm so addled, I just can't figure it out, but you look—"

He interrupted. "You're Michael Fiori's wife. I should have recognized the name. We met after one of the 'Geezrs on Ice' matches."

Some memory swam up to the surface. "Oh, of course. Senior hockey. I didn't recognize you without…." I gestured vaguely, up and down.

"Pads. Uniforms," he said.

"Right. And—you're a cop? I didn't know that. But then, I wouldn't need to…." I knew I was babbling and didn't know how to stop. "I'll shut up," I said. "What do you need to know?"

"Why don't you begin at the beginning?"

"I was supposed to have lunch with…" I gestured at the door again, "…Quentin, and he didn't answer the door. I wanted to leave him a note, but my checks had rocket ships on them. Zach, my son, draws all over them when we go out for pizza. So. Quentin's downstairs neighbor—the lady who lives here, Madame DeBurgos—went to get me some paper. But the door was open, which isn't like Quentin, so I came in—and there he was."

I couldn't bear to think about looking again. I closed my eyes. It didn't help. Open or shut, I could still see Quentin as I'd found him: seated at his writing table, face down, the back of his patrician head a mess of matted hair and blood. I'd forced myself to feel his throat for a pulse. Nothing. The nausea washed over me—and I had just enough time to get to the bathroom before losing my breakfast. When I'd rinsed my mouth and splashed my face with cold water, I dug my cell phone out of my purse and dialed 911. The dispatcher ordered me out of the house, in case the "perpetrator was still on the premises," as she said. I hadn't thought of that. I raced down the stairs and locked myself (and Madame) into her flat. Then, too restless to sit there among Madame's overstuffed furniture and memorabilia, I'd gone down to the tiny front porch to await the police.

I tried to concentrate. Moon was speaking again. "And Madame DeBurgos?"

"She's in her kitchen. Restoring herself, I think."

"Restoring herself?"

"With a little Pernod. She's not very good at this either." From the end of the hallway, I heard a throaty wail.

"Maggie, what's going on? Come tell me."

Moon put his hand on my arm and steered me into Madame's entryway. "Let's stand in here for a minute."

He pulled the door nearly closed and began, "Why don't you—" when footsteps sounded on the front steps that led up to Quentin and Madame's apartments.

"Quentin? Quent? Did you get picked up for bothering little boys? There's a bunch of fuzzmobiles out in your driveway."

Moon pulled Madame's door open and called, "We're in here. Come in, please."

A young man stopped between the two front doors, puzzled. "Who're you? Where's Quentin? What's going on?"

"Inspector Moon, homicide. Ms. Fiori, a friend of Mr. Hart."

"Homicide? Quentin doing a story? Where is he anyway? We're supposed to have lunch."

The porch grew very quiet for a moment. The young black man was beautiful. Early thirties, dressed in artfully, expensively casual clothes—leather boots, pleated pants, oversized sweater, plaid shirt and cashmere scarf.

Moon spoke. "He's in the living room in his apartment. And, I'm afraid lunch is… off."

"He's dead," I quavered. "Quentin's dead. Somebody killed him."

The young man looked from Moon to me and back again. "Quentin? Dead? Holy Christ."

Moon watched the young man a moment. "And you are?"

The young man shook his head, trying to understand. I sympathized; I still wasn't too clear myself. "I am? Oh, I'm Calvin Bright."

"I know you," I blurted.

He looked at me. "You do?"

"I know your work, I mean. Your photography. You shoot for *Small Town*. I've seen your fashion stuff in *Town & Country*. I'm Maggie Fiori."

Moon cleared his throat. "Well, you certainly seem to know all the players, Mrs. Fiori. And I'm sorry to interrupt the networking, but I have to get to my work now." He surveyed us. "I'll need to speak to you both. May I assume I can find you in…" he looked at his notes, "… Mrs. DeBurgos' apartment?" We nodded in unison, two chastened children, and watched Moon leave.

"Well," said Calvin, "Not quite what I expected in a homicide dick."

"Me either." I leaned against the wall. "What am I saying? What did I expect? I've never seen a homicide detective outside a whodunit or the tube. I just happen to know this one—a little bit."

Calvin looked puzzled. "You know this guy?"

I shrugged. "He plays hockey with my husband in a seniors' league. I mean, they're not senior citizens, they're just over forty."

"Ice hockey? In California? He can't windsurf or bungee jump or something normal?"

"That's almost precisely what Quentin used to say."

Calvin peered past me, into Madame's jungle-like hallway, lined with hanging ferns and dusty potted palms. He whispered, "Where are we? Who lives here?"

"Madam DeBurgos, Quentin's neighbor. Well, obviously she's his neighbor; but his friend, too. Could we go sit down? I'm feeling a little dizzy."

"Maggie, darling," called Madame.

"Coming," I said, and I gestured for Calvin to follow. In a few minutes, she had us settled at her kitchen table, littered with a week's worth of newspapers, back copies of *Opera News*, and several sticky jars of honey. She excused herself and returned from the sofa with a "just freshened-up" glass of Pernod.

Calvin cased the table. "She into bees?" he asked, looking at the honey.

"It's for her instrument," I whispered. "Her voice. She's a singer."

"Oh."

Silence fell. The sound of Madame's sniffles came from the living room.

"You found him?" asked Calvin.

I nodded.

"Jesus." Calvin shook his head. "What happened?"

"I don't know. But it looked as if—" I took a deep breath. "It looked as if somebody smacked him from behind with a walking stick."

"A walking stick?"

I nodded. "From the umbrella stand. Quentin always kept a couple of walking sticks in there. I think they were his father's."

"Hey," Calvin said. "I just got it. You're Maggie Fiori? You write all those wiseass food and literary pieces, right?"

"Right."

"I know your stuff. I like it."

"Thanks."

Silence. We looked at each other.

"Did you do it?" he asked.

"Kill Quentin? No! Jesus, what a question!" I bridled.

He managed a grin. "Just asking. Quentin didn't always see eye-to-eye with his writers."

"He was my pal." I felt myself losing control. "He was a great editor and the best person in the world to have lunch with. And, besides...." I stopped.

Calvin began patting his pockets. "Geez, my mom always told me to carry a handkerchief for moments like this."

I sniffled and dug in my purse. "It's okay. I'm a mom myself. I carry my own tissues."

"You know," said Calvin, "we were all supposed to have lunch together."

"We were?"

"Yep. Quentin called this morning, told me his favorite feature writer was shedding her suburban disguise and coming to town for lunch and that I should come on over. He said he had something we should work on together. He said it was a perfect job for me and 'the JIP'. You're the JIP, aren't you? The one Quentin calls the Jewish Italian Princess."

I sniffled some more. "Suburban disguise. That's not fair."

Calvin licked his thumb, reached over and rubbed at my cheek. "Your mascara's running."

"Thanks."

"Let's do it."

"What?"

"Let's get out of this…" he dropped his voice, "beehive mausoleum and have lunch. We'll drink to Quent."

It was an appalling thought. I was starved, though the thought of food made me feel nauseated all over again.

"I couldn't eat anything," I said.

"Fine," said Calvin. "You can watch me eat—and you look like you could use a drink."

"Or some hot tea," I said faintly.

Calvin gave me an exasperated look. "I've seen these movies before—the person who discovers the body is supposed to have a belt of something."

"This isn't a movie," I said.

His shoulders sagged. "I know. I'm just wising off 'cause this is all too weird for me. I'm sorry." He looked stricken.

"It's awful, but I mean, he wasn't exactly my friend or anything. Were you guys close?"

"Something like that," I said. And just like a bad movie montage, images of Quentin in a variety of settings flickered across my mind.

Calvin touched my cheek, "Hey, maybe you just need to be by yourself."

Time alone? Time to keep that Quentin movie playing along in my brain? Absolutely not.

"You know what?" I said, "I'd love a drink."

I stood up. "We have to talk to the cops before we go. Let's get it over with."

LIQUID LUNCH

It was almost three o'clock by the time Calvin and I walked into Pier 23 and claimed a minuscule table for our own.

We'd answered the inspector's questions while a battalion of people from the coroner's office swarmed over Quentin's flat. When I asked if I could go back into the flat, Inspector Moon hesitated for a moment. Then he nodded and put his hand on my elbow and walked me across a crinkly plastic runner the cops had put down in the living room. I had the unshakable feeling he was watching my every breath. I crept over to Quentin's body and stood there a minute. It was, after all, not the awful sight of his head that bothered me. It was his right hand, those perfect manicured fingers so still and so disengaged from everything they did well. I thought of that hand and all its past intimacies and felt cold in every part of me.

When I pulled myself together, I used my cell phone to make a brief condolence call to Claire, the "official" bereaved widow. Wasn't much of a condolence call. More of an announcement call, met with Claire's cool, "In the flat? He got himself murdered at home? Careless bastard," before I handed the phone over to the inspector. I also called *Small Town* and broke the news that Quentin wouldn't be back that afternoon—or ever. His assistant, Gertie Davies, became hysterical, so I asked for Glen Fox, Quent's managing editor and old friend. Glen swore into the phone and then said he'd handle things at the office. I couldn't figure out what to do about Stuart, Quentin's companion. There was no sign of him. Moon said he'd wait for his return, so I scribbled a note to him and left it on the kitchen counter.

Calvin and I looked in on Madame DeBurgos. She was nestled on the rose velvet loveseat in her front room—much, I imagine, as a destroyer might nestle into a slip at the Marina—her glass still cradled close to her bosom. She didn't sit up, but she opened an eye and presented Calvin with her hand to say goodbye. When we were halfway out the door, she summoned me back. "Maggie, come here, my dear, one tiny little second."

I stood at the foot of the loveseat. "Yes, Madame?"

She waved her Pernod at me. "What a luscious young man, darling. Does Michael know? Do you have one of those open, continental marriages?"

"Madame! I just met him. We were supposed to do an assignment together for Quentin. We're just going to get something to eat."

"Mm-hmm, how lovely. Just remember what the French say—a spot of *l'amour* is delectable for the instrument."

I snapped, "Which French proverb is that? I must have missed it." I was cranky, headachy, and, now that Calvin had introduced the idea, badly in need of a drink.

"It doesn't translate well, my dear. Just run off and have a lovely time. Think of me, though, in the throes of passion."

Instead, we thought of Madame in the throes of cracked Dungeness crab at Pier 23. Actually, that's how Calvin did his thinking. I did mine over a very handsome shot of Wild Turkey. It burned going down, but didn't come back up again, to my relief and surprise. And then, I did order a pot of English breakfast tea, strong and black, and proceeded to watch Calvin eat. I couldn't imagine how he had an appetite, but just watching him work his way through a cracked crab made me feel better. The sheer messiness of it was a kind of sensuous re-acquaintance with the business of being hungry—and being alive.

At night, Pier 23 jumps with jazz and jazz-lovers. But during the day, there's just food and drink and gossip, all delivered at ear-splitting decibel levels. If you go to make a phone call or use the restroom, there's a terrific view of the bay from the back porch. By the time Calvin had reduced his crustacean to rubble and I was on my second pot of tea, the place was almost deserted. I began breaking off pieces of sourdough bread, just to put something in my stomach.

To tell the truth, the events of the day—Quentin's body, finding out that Michael's hockey buddy was a homicide cop, a big dose of Madame, and bourbon on an empty stomach—were conspiring to make me the tiniest bit giddy. Suddenly, I sat straight up.

"The children!"

Calvin laughed. "I wasn't even sure we'd gotten beyond the first date. Are we already committed to reproducing ourselves?"

I glared at him. "No, I've already done it. Excuse me."

I picked my way through the tables and squeezed by the Rubenesque hostess to find a quiet nook to make a call. I needed more privacy than sitting at the table to talk on the phone.

Anya was home. She'd picked up the boys and was making a desultory tour through the refrigerator to start dinner.

"Anya, I'm still in the city." I re-described how to roast a chicken. What could go wrong with roast chicken?

"Maggie, Lily is visiting from next door and she wants the boys and the cats to come play Nintendo."

I got a life-size picture of my little ruffians following Lily's every command in front of the screen. Her two years of seniority over Josh, enormous vocabulary, and willingness to share her electronic paraphernalia gave her near-complete control over my boys. I didn't mind, though; she was a benevolent despot and a great civilizing influence. "Fine, but no snacks past five. I'll be home before seven."

I hung up and called Michael's office. His secretary said she hadn't seen him since before lunch. "He has a client back here at four-thirty. He should be here any minute," she said. I couldn't imagine leaving any of the day's events on his voice mail, so I simply left a message that dinner was at seven and I'd see him at home.

When I returned to the table, the waitress had cleared away the rubble and brought two china mugs of coffee. It smelled delicious. "I decided it was time for you to move on from that wimpy-ass tea," said Calvin.

I held my cup aloft. "We haven't done what we said we'd do. So here goes: To Quentin, wherever he may be—and whyever he's there."

Calvin clinked mugs with me.

"Get the kids straightened out?"

"Yes, fine. They're playing Nintendo with the little tyrant from next door."

"So Maggie, who did it?"

For a moment, the sight of Quentin's crumpled body—face down on his desk, blood Rorschach-like on the desk—came back to me. The table, the restaurant, even Calvin—everything seemed hostile and dangerous. I stood, a little unsteadily, and grabbed for the edge of the table.

"I've got to go." I put my hand out. "It's nice to meet you. Thanks for lunch."

Calvin ignored my hand. "Sit down. You're looking a little green around the gills."

I sat. "Yo' mama," I said glumly.

"What?"

"Yo' mama. It's an answer in the dozens. It's the black equivalent of 'so's your old man.' Only worse." I peered at Calvin and gestured. "You know—you keep exchanging and accelerating insults. Why am I explaining this to you? I'm the honky here."

"I know what the dozens are. I just don't know how to do them. How do you know how to do the dozens?"

"I grew up knowing how. I was a tough kid. The wrong side of L.A." I took a sip of coffee. Suddenly, I felt better. The image of Quentin's body began to recede. The world—or at least the restaurant and Calvin—seemed friendlier, familiar. No bodies would pop up here between the upright piano and the screen that hid the noisy, warmly fragrant kitchen.

"So if you didn't grow up with the dozens, how do you know what they are?"

Calvin grinned. "Black Lit. I took a course at Stanford. Learned how to be cool. Going to private schools and growing up in the Philadelphia suburbs doesn't teach you any of that stuff."

I laughed. "That's a great testimonial to your alma mater. Go to Stanford. Get in touch with your roots. I bet the Senator and Mrs. Stanford had just that thing in mind for privileged black students."

"Senator Stanford had never even heard of privileged black students. Now, Mrs. Jane, that might have been a different story. But I'm glad to hear you laugh. You looked a little panicked a few minutes ago."

I shivered. "I remembered Quentin. What he looked like lying there."

Calvin spoke, "So let's talk about it. What the hell happened?"

I shook my head. "I can't imagine. And that's just the beginning of the questions. Why did it happen? Why Quentin? And where's Stuart? And what about Madame? She's supposed to be an ex-paramour."

Calvin shuddered. "What a thought. Enough to put you off girls for life."

"I think that might be just what it did for Quentin," I said. "That, combined with marriage all those years to the lovely Mrs. Quentin."

"I don't think so. I'm not sure, but somehow I think there was still a woman in Quentin's life."

I rearranged the salt and pepper shakers. "Did you know?" I asked idly, "that the word 'salt' has origins in European, Icelandic, Greek, and Gothic roots?"

"Huh? Maggie, are you paying attention to me? I said I thought there might be some other woman in Quent's life."

I fixed my eyes on the salt and pepper, lining them up just so.

"Why do you think that? I didn't think you knew him that well," I asked.

"I don't. And it's certainly nothing he said. Just a feeling. One day I dropped some proofs off, and we walked out of *Small Town*'s offices up the street to lunch. Quent couldn't tear himself away from that antique jewelry store on Sutter. I don't think he was looking at earrings for himself, or that guy he lives with. You know anybody?"

I took a swallow of coffee. "Not really."

"There's something else," said Calvin. "Wasn't Quentin a little mysterious about this story he wanted us to do?"

"He was. I thought he was just trying to do me a favor with this piece. I'd been bitching that I was sick of the cooks-and-books circuit I was on."

"Cooks and books?"

"Oh, you know. Lisbet Traumer does the restaurant reviews for the magazine, but I do all the peripheral food stuff—101 places to buy capers and cornichons, and interviews with every precious little Eastern writer who comes to town."

"Oh, yeah. The Maggie Fiori Blue-Plate specials."

"Right. Well, I was having an attack of 'I want to be a real journalist when I grow up,' and Quentin told me he had just the thing for me."

"The Cock of the Walk story?"

"That's what we were supposed to work on together?"

"That's what Quentin told me."

A shadow fell across the table. The hostess, a generously proportioned walking advertisement for the excellence of the Pier 23 cuisine, was hovering.

"Excuse me. I'm sorry to interrupt such a pleasant tête-à-tête, but we need to close to get ready for dinner."

Out on the street, Calvin put his arm around me. "Tête-à-tête," he mused aloud. "That I did learn in the Philly suburbs."

"Yeah?" I said, ready to one-up him. "Here's a twist for you. Tête-à-tête is 'head-to-head', of course, but how about tête-àbêche?"

"Head to tail? Sounds like a French pornographic documentary."

"No, no. It's something in philately: two stamps reversed in relation to each other."

Calvin shook his head. "My, my, you are full of information."

I sighed. "I know. It's my hobby, or my obsession, or something. None of it's very useful, I'm afraid. It won't help find out what happened to Quent."

We lingered, not sure what to do next. It's tough to find a body, lose a friend, meet someone new, get mildly snockered, sober up, and say goodbye in the space of four hours.

"Give me your card, Maggie," said Calvin. "As a general rule, I know that's not what people do after a tête-à-tête, but I think we should keep in touch."

"Me, too." I dug in my purse for a card, checked it for shopping lists on the back, and handed it over.

Calvin looked at the card and looked back at me.

"Margaret? Your first name is Margaret?"

"That's generally what Maggie is short for, isn't it?"

"Well, yeah. But Margaret seems like a weird name for a Jewish chick."

"It is," I said. "But I was born in a Catholic hospital, before smoking became the eighth deadly sin. The nun who took care of my mom during labor kept a pack of Old Golds in the pocket of her habit. She'd light up and let my mom have a puff or two between contractions. My mom was so grateful she named me for her. I guess I'm just lucky she didn't name me Goldie, in honor of the smokes."

Calvin shook his head. "Named for a vice, Maggie. You ought to be up to your neck in sin by now."

"That explains everything," I muttered.

We hugged and headed our separate ways, me to my suburban-issue Volvo, Calvin to his MG convertible. I watched him push the top back to enjoy the last rays of fall sunshine. And sighed. Oh, to be young again. Or even innocent.

L'CHAIM

It's the ordinariness of daily life that comforts. Staves off the horrors, the headlines, the famines, the border skirmishes—even Quentin's death.

Our dining room looks onto the street through tall, floor-to-ceiling French doors. Makes for lousy privacy from outside, but great people-watching from inside. This time, I was on the outside looking in. Through the French doors, I could see and faintly hear the last moments of pre-prandial hullabaloo.

From the curb, when I saw all that normalcy—the flower beds, the front walk where Lily had chalked hopscotch, I instantly regretted every moment of longing for a day, never mind a year, of living dangerously. Josh was sitting at the table, engaged in his only significant domestic accomplishment, folding napkins into elaborate, decorative shapes. Zach was watching, napkin in hand, desperately trying to duplicate his older brother's maneuvers, which transferred the crinkliest Zee into graceful origami. I sympathized with Zach; I couldn't mimic Josh's skills either. I was just happy Josh had a place to put all that fretful energy.

Michael was carving a roast chicken, sneaking nibbles of skin. Anya was pouring milk for the boys. Watching them all, I felt like an intruder, bringing into a clean and ordered place all the wickedness and haphazard cruelty of a world where someone living and breathing could be reduced to a forensic set of facts in a split second. Well, okay, not so clean and ordered. I was, after all, the housekeeper-in-residence.

The front door was unlocked. I walked in, dropped keys and gloves on the hall table, sidestepped a fielder's mitt and three in-line skates, and hurried to the dining room. Zach hurled himself at my legs. Michael looked up and smiled. Raider threw himself on my feet and whimpered.

"Watch out, boys. Mom's been having an uptown afternoon in the city. She'll be full of books and gossip. Too rich for the likes of us." He stopped and caught sight of my face.

"What's wrong, *cara*?"

I shook my head, lifted Zach's solid little body and gave him a fierce hug. "Later."

Michael's face darkened.

"Really, truly, later," I said over Zach's sweet-smelling head.

He shrugged. "Okay. Why don't you wash up? We're ready to eat. I've got hungry hordes on my hands."

By the time I'd returned to the table, everyone was seated. The boys fidgeted for grace to be over and dinner to begin.

It was Zach's turn to ask the blessing, a custom we'd evolved in yet another attempt to integrate Michael's Italian Catholic upbringing with my laissez-faire secular Judaism.

"Thank you, God, for making it October and Halloween soon, and thanks for chicken because it has two legs and two of us like legs in this house. Amen."

Later, the kids bathed, cuddled, and in bed, Anya at her loom in the basement, Michael and I sat in front of the fire in the living room.

"Okay," he said. "You didn't eat. You spilled your wine twice. And cried when you tucked Josh in. Please tell me what the hell is wrong."

I told him. I told about finding Quentin and about Madame and Inspector Moon and Calvin. Michael listened without comment, except for a quick intake of breath when I described the sight of Quentin slumped over his desk. Throughout my story, he peeled a red pear carefully, so carefully that the peel came off in one long, burgundy-golden spiral.

When I finished, he went to the kitchen and came back with two glasses of cognac. He handed me one, pulled me up out of my chair and into his lap.

He touched his glass to mine. "You know what we say at weddings and bar mitzvahs," he said. "*L'chaim.*"

"*L'chaim,*" I whispered back. "I'm all for drinking to life tonight." I looked around the living room. We loved this room, both of us. It was the first room we finished when we'd moved in ten years ago. Somehow, in the intervening years, the decorators had caught up to us, and the deep gold walls were now fashionable. But family clutter saved it from serious trendiness—books, games, art projects, whistles, yo-yos, and neglected houseplants. Still, it was a comfort to sit in a room I knew with someone I loved and admire the cats as they watched a pear being peeled in front of the fire.

"What now?" asked Michael.

"I don't know. Now that the shock is wearing off, I'm feeling— bewildered. This happens in books, not in real life."

Michael sighed. "It's awful, Maggie, and terrible that you found him. It happens in real life every day. One of the joys of urban living."

"No," I said. "That's drugs and crime and domestic violence. That's what happens in the papers."

"So it's understandable in a book? In the papers? But not in your life? Maggie, listen to what you're saying. You think we live behind some invisible, magic shield?"

I remembered watching my family through the window. "I guess I do think that, or at least I did."

Michael sliced a piece of pear and offered it to me from the side of the knife.

"Guess again, *cara.*"

I waved the pear away. "Fine, there's no shield. It's a dangerous world. But that still doesn't answer a lot of questions."

"Like?"

"Who could possibly want Quentin dead? And just where the hell was Stuart when this awful thing was happening in the flat? And here's the really petty, unattractive, narcissistic part. Already, I'm wondering, what about *Small Town*? And what about my great breakthrough story?"

Michael grinned at me. "You do get yourself into a dither, don't you?"

"And another thing," I said. "How come you never told me you played hockey with a homicide cop?"

He shrugged. "We don't talk about work much," he said. "I mean, I know John's with the police, but most of the time we're either out on the ice or talking about the game."

"Just out of curiosity, what does he play?"

"Front line, left wing. He's very aggressive, very fast. Hard guy to check. You don't want to get in his way."

"He seemed so reserved, so gentlemanly," I said.

"Everybody changes on the ice," said Michael. "That's what you always say to me." I rearranged myself on his lap, draping my legs over the arm of the chair.

"I wonder," he said, stroking my hair, "what about right now? What do you feel like doing?"

I looked at him, at this kind, funny man who could peel a pear flawlessly. I managed a smile back.

"Are you suggesting that on the evening of Quentin's death I could be consoled by earthly pleasures?"

"Yep. And I'm just the man for consoling."

"Got anything special in mind?"

"Here's what Dr. Michael orders: Let's take these glasses up to bed, smoke a little of that exceptional Belize breeze Quentin gave us, and fuck our brains out."

A part of me felt sick and tired, wondering what had happened, and skirting one terrible speculation—that Quentin's death had something to do with me. In the face of that, and with the sight of Quentin's body still fresh whenever I closed my eyes, Michael's suggestion sounded blasphemous, trivial, and escapist to me.

But that's exactly what we did.

THE PEOPLE IN THE MIRROR

The phone rang early the next morning. Michael rolled over with a groan and handed it across to me.

It was Stuart. He sounded tight and controlled and very ragged around the edges.

"Maggie. The cops say you found Quent."

"I did, Stuart. God, I'm sorry."

"I'm sorry too—also pissed as hell and scared to death."

I could hear Stuart's breathing, uneven and hoarse, on the other end of the line.

"What can I do?"

"Nothing, I guess. I don't know—just come sit with me at the service."

By the time I'd finished with Stuart, Michael was up and rattling around the bathroom.

"Well," he said, "where was the lovely Stuart when Quentin was being done in?"

"Michael! I don't know. I didn't ask him."

"Yeah, well, I bet the cops asked him."

"I'm sure they did," I said. I remembered the exhausting conversation I'd had with one of Inspector Moon's investigators yesterday afternoon. Under her persistent questioning, I had explained and re-explained how I knew Quentin, what our lunch date was about, why I'd met him at the flat instead of the office, how *Small Town* wasn't exactly the kind of magazine to earn the editor serious enemies. "Unless it was for a really, really bad restaurant review," I'd joked nervously. "Only then, wouldn't you expect to find him with a vegetable parer to the heart?" The investigator looked up from her notes, jolted by my wisecrack, and then we stopped to watch Quentin's body, zipped into a bag stenciled "SF Coroner," carried out the door. It was my last joke of the afternoon.

Even though it was a tight fit in our bathroom, I wedged in behind Michael to survey him in the mirror.

I don't know how marriage survives modern housing. Two sinks in up market master bathrooms mean you don't have to duck and weave around each other in order to shave or put on eyeliner. During years of living in ancient houses, Michael and I had evolved a morning sink-time gavotte to cope with closet-size bathrooms. He shaved while I did non-mirror activities like tooth brushing. He combed his hair by feel while I put in my contacts. We have some of our liveliest talks over the sink.

"I'm going to wear a hat to the funeral, Michael," I said.

He stirred up shaving soap with his brush and didn't say anything.

"You know, I'll bet Quentin really was the last man who liked women in hats."

Michael was silent.

"Don't you think that's true?"

Michael clicked a new blade in his razor. "I think he was the last man who *loved* women in hats."

Michael's voice sounded cool and impersonal. I felt a little prickle on the back of my neck.

"What do you mean?"

Michael's eyes met mine in the mirror. He held his cheek taut and began to shave. "He loved you, Maggie. And you loved him."

"That's true, I did. He was a wonderful editor, and a wonderful friend."

Michael rinsed his razor. "Was he a wonderful lover, too?"

I could hear the boys downstairs, squabbling over whose turn it was to feed the pets. But they sounded miles away. I felt light-headed and leaned against the shower.

"What are you talking about?"

Michael splashed water on his face and turned to me, dripping. His eyes were contemptuous. "I knew, Maggie. I knew all about it."

He looked steadily at me.

"It's okay. I could have killed you for it—or Quentin, for that matter. But I didn't. I'm trying to get over it. I hope to hell you do, too."

I thought about his tireless lovemaking the night before. Just before I'd fallen asleep, he'd pulled me close and begun all over again. I thought he was trying to comfort me, to block out what I had seen. Suddenly, it seemed less loving, more territorial, as if he'd been trying to block out some tape in his head—or trying to brand me.

"Michael," I faltered.

"Don't," he said. "I don't want to talk about it. I never wanted to talk about it. I'm bringing it up now because I want you to do me the enormous favor of thinking twice about speaking so fucking well about the dead in the next few days. Can you do that?"

"Yes," I said. "I can do that."

"Thank you. I'll go help Anya with breakfast." The razor clattered into the mug. And he was gone.

I stared at my reflection in the mirror. Still me, still there, and still wondering who that woman was who betrayed her husband.

Couldn't have been me. I'm the good girl. "A real good girl," I said to the reflection. "Just swell." And turned on the shower—very hot.

Saturday morning meant "Vintage Sounds" on our local public radio station. While I scrubbed I listened to Fats Waller sing, "There'll be some changes made." I began to cry when I cut my leg with Michael's razor, and watched the blood mix with the shampoo and the soap. I thought about Quentin and I thought about Michael and I wished I were still a good girl.

With the hot water sluicing over me, I leaned against the shower and felt my insides go cold with memory. Actually, I had two versions of memory. One was hopelessly self-deluded and quite romantic: Dashing, enigmatic editor sweeps impressionable young writer off her feet.

The other, more truthful, more painful, was that I was not so young and not so swept—just a little restless, curious, and flattered that I'd stirred something in so cool a customer as Quentin.

If I were on the stand, I could testify to an eyelash how it happened, just eighteen months ago.

Quentin had invited me to cover the Junior League model tryouts at Saks. "Come watch with me," he said. "I promised Claire I'd send someone and you're my revenge. You'll write something vicious and she'll never ask me for coverage again."

So we went. And after two hours of watching what lots of time and attention can do to the affluent female form, I wasn't feeling vicious. I was depressed. I looked at the back of my un-pampered hands and imagined I could see liver spots forming in front of my very eyes. "Is this how it starts?" I asked Quentin. "One day you're a hot chick, the next day it's stretch marks and station wagons."

"Chick?" he said. "My, my, how un-feminist, how politically incorrect." Then he steered me downstairs to millinery. "Cheer up, Margaret," he said. "Let me spend some money on you. You'll feel better straightaway."

Under the amused eye of a millinery saleswoman, all in black from head to toe, I tried on hat after hat. Quentin sat on a stool, one leg elegantly crossed over the other, and shook his head. Finally, she brought out a fawn-colored cloche. It hugged the back of my head perfectly. I looked in the mirror and caught Quentin's eye. "That's it," he said. He slipped off the stool, came close and turned me around. "Let me fix the veil. Don't fidget." I stood as still as I could while he gently tugged the veil into place.

He put one hand on my cheek. "You are one beautiful chick, Margaret." I felt beautiful. Impulsively, I pulled his hand to my mouth and kissed it. A smile I'd never seen drifted across his mouth. Quentin handed the saleswoman his credit card. "Thank you," he said. "You can put this on my account."

Then Quentin took me by the arm and led me past the elevator into the stairwell. When the door closed, he took me by the other arm, pulled me to him and gave me the kind of kiss I thought detached, distant men of fiftysomething didn't have in them.

He stopped before I did. "Do you want lunch first, Margaret," he said, "Or shall we go directly to bed?"

"Are we going to talk about it over lunch?" I asked. My voice echoed in the hallway.

"No," he said.

"I think I want lunch, anyway," I said. "I have to show off my new hat." I was trying to buy some time to think, of course, but wouldn't say so. That was me, the Queen of Bravado.

So we had lunch and wine and very good coffee. I called Anya and asked her to preside over dinner and tell Michael I was having dinner with an out-of-town writer. The lies came easily. Years of coming up with creative leads on tight deadlines served me very well.

After lunch, we stood in the Sutter-Stockton Garage and Quentin watched me look for my keys.

"Aha!" I held them up. My hand was trembling.

Quentin took the keys, ushered me into the passenger side, settled up with the garage attendant, and headed my station wagon up the hill.

"Tell me," I quavered, "have you ever had a mistress who drove a station wagon before?"

Quentin smiled. "I don't have one now," he said, without taking his eyes off the road. "I have a very good friend who suddenly looks quite delicious to me. And do you know how I think I look to her?"

"How?"

"Dangerous and interesting. You look at me the way children look at boa constrictors in the snake house. You're fascinated and you're horrified."

He was right. So we didn't talk anymore.

I'd never really given much thought to adultery before. But when I had, I'd always assumed the appropriate setting was a cut-rate motel room. I had hazy fantasies about people ripping each other's clothes off, heaving and panting, sobbing in remorse, and driving home their separate ways—till the next week. Sort of a low-rent *Same Time, Next Year.*

Quentin's version of adultery was civilized. At his apartment, he took my coat and hung it up in the closet, taking time to button the top three buttons so it sat squarely on the hanger. He poured me a glass of Beaujolais, escorted me into the bedroom, and left the door wide open.

When you've been married for years and years, you begin to think there's only one way to make love. Michael makes love as he does everything else—easily, casually, playfully, cheerfully oblivious to phones ringing, dog or cats scratching to get in or out of the bedroom, books piled on the bed.

Over the next several months, I learned that Quentin knew other ways. He knew about complete, silent concentration on the task at hand. And he knew about context. He knew about eating smoked oysters on water biscuits and doing Double Crostics in bed, in ink. He knew about listening to scratchy recordings of Richard Burton reading John Donne's love poetry. He loved to brush my hair. Sometimes, he'd stand at the foot of the bed with his tenor saxophone and play. Naked. "Listen to this, Margaret," he'd say, and I'd hear almost anything; blues, jazz, and his own improvisations on Bach and Scarlatti.

Quentin was too cool for me by half. Though he liked Michael, it never seemed to occur to him to feel guilty. It was clear, however, that he took some pleasure in stirring things up. At a summer barbecue at the home of Glen Fox, *Small Town's* managing editor, Quentin followed me into the bathroom and unbuttoned my sundress.

"Quentin, what are you doing?" I whispered fiercely.

There, in the tiny bathroom hung with signs from Glen's beloved Irish pubs and crowded with kid paraphernalia, Quentin turned me so that we both faced the mirror. His hands reached in front of me and cupped my breasts. "Just checking. Couldn't imagine what you'd wear under that neckline." Then, he was gone. When I came out of the bathroom, he and Michael were sitting side by side on the couch watching the A's dispatch the Red Sox and puzzling about Jason Giambi's odd batting stance. Without taking his eyes from the screen, Michael patted the couch between them, "Come on, Maggie, your heartthrob Stairs is on deck."

Quentin raised his eyebrow as I settled between them.

"Stairs, hmm? Wouldn't have identified him as your type, Margaret."

Michael picked up his beer, "Oh, our Maggie is full of surprises. She still misses Bruce Bochte."

"I like a ballplayer who looks like an aging Marxist," I said defensively.

"Indeed," said Quentin.

Michael turned to me and frowned, smoothing the hair back from my forehead, "Feeling okay, *cara*? You're a little flushed." I felt like a dangerously triumphant felon, wicked but pleased because I was getting away with something.

Finally, a year almost to the day after Quentin bought me the hat, we stopped. I'd grown to love the afternoons in bed. But although I was exceedingly skilled at covering my tracks, I never got graceful at adultery. It was the slightly dangerous intrigue I liked, the feeling that I was different from all the other moms doing carpool.

And, when Stuart moved in with Quentin, I felt mindless, deep-as-a-well jealousy. That was enough.

Quentin and I saw each other almost as often as when we had been lovers. I wrote for him, did my very best work. We had lunch, traded books, kissed hello and goodbye. Occasionally, if we were alone—in his office, in my kitchen, he'd turn those social kisses into something else. But then he'd let me go. He never pressed for a return engagement. The Queen of Bravado thought she had escaped without a scratch.

But when I remembered the sight of Quentin's lifeless hand, the one I'd kissed so impulsively at the hat counter at Saks, the one that had edited my copy, and challenged my notion of myself as a smug and moral wife-and-mom, I felt ill all over again. In the steamy bathroom mirror my face was miserable and flushed. No "A" on my forehead, just guilt and regrets. I toweled off, swearing softly. "Dumb, careless, selfish bitch...." And then, through the post-shower mist and the remorse, one niggling little thought: How had Michael known? And why hadn't he confronted me? "Men," I said aloud, happy to be back on the path of self-righteousness. "All action, no talk."

There was a pounding at the door, "Mom!" Josh shouted, "I can't find my shinguards. Where are they?"

"Coming, honey," I said, refusing to wonder just what kind of action might have replaced Michael's talk.

OF WHOM SHALL WE SPEAK?

Quentin's memorial service made the front page of the *San Francisco Chronicle*. Everyone was there. Well, almost everyone.

The mayor was off in Central America, cementing yet another sister city relationship with an urban economy built on tourism and failing banks. So he had to miss the festivities. But he sent the chief of protocol. She made some fulsome remarks. Something to the effect that one of the city's literary lights had gone out. Quentin Hart, who grew up with the disaffected literati of the sixties, the experimentalists of the seventies and the brave young writers of the eighties and nineties, who had brought style and panache to a dying city magazine, and so forth and so on. You get the idea. Quentin would have hated every word of it. He once told me he had exorcised the word panache from his vocabulary when the French gave a sweet aperitif that name. Inspector Moon, sitting alone three pews back, caught my eye. He nodded pleasantly and raised his hand in a half wave to Michael.

"Should we see if he wants to sit with us?" I whispered to Michael. Michael shrugged, "Leave him alone. He's probably scanning for suspects."

Claire was there, swathed in politically incorrect fur. "Is that black mink," Michael whispered during the service, "or did a dozen skunks lay down half their hides for the grieving widow?"

I gave him a token rap on the arm with a rolled up program.

Fact was, I felt so grateful he was joking with me I could have thrown my arms around him. True to the tight-lipped statement he'd made in front of the mirror, he hadn't discussed my relationship with Quentin again. Instead, he treated me with the slightly distant formality you reserve for familiar, if fragile and rarely seen, maiden aunts. When I'd faltered an opening to the subject, his eyes had turned cold and distant. He had answered my single question— how had he known—with the kind of clinical distaste I'd only seen employed when he had to remove dead roof rats from our gutters. "The boys needed change for video games when they were going to the pizza parlor with Lily's family. I didn't have much. And your purse was on the kitchen counter, so I went looking for quarters." I knew what was coming. "I wondered why your diaphragm was in your purse. I didn't even think you had one anymore. I mean, we didn't need it." Michael, ever the dutiful husband, had responsibly had a vasectomy after Zach's birth. He shook his head. "I was going to ask you," he said, "but then I decided to wait."

"Michael—" I started. He held up his hand. "I may be a tax lawyer," he continued, "but once upon a time, I did very well in Evidence. I'm not a fool." He continued, "Events came together for me. I noticed that the diaphragm seemed to show up in your purse the night before you were going to *Small Town,* or you were meeting Quentin for lunch. Then it disappeared."

He looked at me in disgust and began unloading the dishwasher. "Where'd the diaphragm go, Maggie? Or did you and Quentin call it quits?"

I chose to answer the second question. "We called it quits. It was a stupid mistake and we stopped. Almost a year ago. But why...."

"Why what?"

"Why didn't you ask me about it?"

Silence. "I think you'd know me better than that by now, Maggie," he said. "I'm a man who can watch and wait when I need to."

"And that's what you're doing now?" I said.

"Maybe I am."

And that was the end of the conversation. The diaphragm hadn't disappeared; of course; it had simply taken up residence at Quentin's. I began to worry about retrieving it.

Josh, with his impeccably visceral sense of something amiss, had started every single day since Quentin's death with an upset stomach. I was beginning to think it was either back to the specialist or simply buy stock in Pepto-Bismol. Or perhaps, I observed to myself as we left the house for the service, Josh's mom could simply stick to the straight and narrow and not create tension and drama in the house. "Guilt, guilt, guilt," I muttered under my breath.

Alf Abbott, Claire's uncle and *Small Town*'s owner, escorted the widow to the service. As always, he had the well-oiled look of a man who spends too much time under the hands of a masseur. From the gently glazed look in his eye, my guess was that the inside of Uncle Alf was equally well-oiled.

The memorial service was held at the city's grandest Unitarian church. Of course, even grand Unitarian churches are pretty spare, which was, I felt sure, Quentin's exact taste in liturgical spaces. Against a backdrop of white French tulips on a gray stone altar, a parade of luminaries took turns behind the pulpit to tell affectionate stories about Quentin. I sat between Stuart and Michael, anchored to both. Stuart clutched my hand, and Michael kept his arm draped along the pew in back of me.

The proprietor of Hot Licks, a south of Market jazz club, talked about how Quentin used to drop in with his sax and sit in for a set. "He didn't sweat, he didn't smoke, he didn't even drink much. But that man could blow."

His tailor told an elaborate story about Quentin's proposal for smuggling Cuban cigars out of Hong Kong and into San Francisco by sewing into the lining of double-breasted suits. And he recounted, seemingly with admiration, Quentin's horror of fashion, how he'd changed neither his blazer size nor his style for twenty-five years.

Glen Fox, *Small Town*'s managing editor, tight-lipped and

dry-eyed, talked about Quentin's standards at the magazine. At the end of his witty, carefully prepared remarks, he folded his hands on the index cards and fought back tears. "Quentin and I were boys together," he said, "both of us strangers in a strange land. An American at Oxford, and a country Irish lad. We came together over Yeats and nearly came to blows over Thomas Wolfe." He stopped and bit his lip. "You're still wrong about Wolfe's puny talent, man, but I hope to God you *can* go home again. And that you're there."

Michael leaned over to me and whispered. "Does everyone sound better dead than alive?"

I looked at him. His face was impassive. "Just wondering," he mouthed silently.

A fresh-faced, crewcut young man in a blue denim shirt and khakis talked about Quentin's willingness to cover AIDS in a chic city magazine early on, before anyone wanted to talk about it.

Finally, the art director of *Small Town*, an elegant Vietnamese woman named Linda Quoc who was dressed in a silver-belted, turquoise silk jumpsuit, explained how Quentin taught her to play five card stud to fill the interminable hours during midnight press checks.

Madame sang Berlioz's "Sur les Lagunes." It was perhaps a trifle beyond her instrument's capabilities, but touching, nonetheless.

Then, Stuart let go of my hand and walked to the front of the church. He pulled a softcover copy of *The Complete Poems of Hart Crane* out of his jacket pocket. Crane was Quentin's favorite poet. I was never sure whether he was attracted to his controversial genius, his mysterious, tragic death, or just his eclectic romantic tastes. At any rate, I'd helped Stuart select "And Bees of Paradise." He steadied himself on the pulpit, looking very young and a little frightened. He'd played basketball as a kid, and despite his grown-up devotion to offbeat, slightly theatrical clothes, always looked as if he'd be more comfortable wrapping his long, rangy frame in the shorts and jersey he'd worn on the court. He ran a hand through his dark, stylishly cut hair, gripped the book, and began:

I had come all the way here from the sea,
Yet met the wave again between your arms
Where cliff and citadel—all verily
Dissolved within a sky of beacon forms—

Sea gardens lifted rainbow-wise through eyes
I found.

Yes, tall, inseparably our days
Pass sunward. We have walked the kindled skies
Inexorable and girded with your praise,

By the dove filled, and bees of Paradise.

Michael handed me his handkerchief. After the service, we ran into Glen, his wife Corinne, and their five children on the steps. "A very fine hat, Maggie," said Glen. "Quentin would have loved it."

"Thanks," I said, putting a hand to the cloche. I felt Michael stiffen next to me.

"Are your boys here?" asked Corinne.

"No, I'm afraid they're not as well regimented as your kids," I said. "They'd have wiggled."

Corinne smiled. "We had some wiggles, too. But Glen wanted the children to say goodbye to Quentin. He's been very kind to us, you know." She sighed. "Kept us out of the almshouse, in fact, when we came to America."

Glen put his arm around Corinne. "We need to be off, love."

"Soccer practice and choir rehearsals for the little ones," he explained over his shoulder. "I'll come by Quentin's after we get everyone delivered."

Calvin Bright trotted up the steps, camera bag slung over his left shoulder. I made the introductions. Michael shook hands with Calvin and said, "I hear you and my wife drowned your sorrows in some cracked crab the other day."

Calvin's mouth turned up in a dangerous grin.

"Actually, it was more voyeuristic than that. I ate, and she watched me. Too bad you couldn't join us. But I guess tax lawyers don't go in for long lazy lunches." Michael fixed him with a humorless smile. "No, but we do go in for mindless, vindictive behavior when anyone trespasses on our personal property."

Calvin looked bewildered by Michael's sharp tone. I tapped Calvin's camera bag. "Promise me you weren't shooting during the service?"

He shook his head. "No, too sleazy even for me. But it's good to be prepared in case someone really famous showed up. Plus, I wasn't so sure our pal Inspector Moon believed I was a real, live photographer at Quentin's place the other day. Thought I'd better show up with the tools of the trade."

"Are you serious?" I asked. "You really think Moon didn't believe you were a photographer?"

"Hey," said Calvin, "they always suspect the black guy first."

Michael snorted. "Not when he shows up with French cuffs and expensive cuff links, looking like an overpaid investment banker."

Calvin's eyes lit up. "That's just the look I was going for. Most photographers dress like bums. I love spending money on clothes. I've got one of those personal shoppers at Saks. She thinks I'm going to cave in and sleep with her some day, so she's always scouting the good sale stuff for me."

I didn't want to look at Michael. I knew he'd be wearing one of those looks that loosely translates into, "Sure, lawyers may be dull, but they're not certifiable lightweights like the people you hang out with."

"That is really shallow and disgusting," I said.

Calvin smiled, "Isn't it? But cool threads, huh?"

"Are you ever going to come across for Ms. Shopper?" asked Michael.

Calvin shrugged. "I don't know. Maybe. She's good looking, but she's got that fortysomething obsession about her body. She's always rubbing her throat because I know she's worried about her jawline. Of course, she'd probably put all that worry into one fine lay."

Michael chuckled. "Sounds great to me."

I looked at both of them. "Male bonding is so six weeks ago," I said.

They managed to look reprimanded, vaguely delighted, and very, very chummy all at once. It was a little nauseating, but far preferable to Michael acting sullen and jealous.

"Let's go get a drink and hear some more about Calvin's love life," said Michael.

"Later," I said. "We're invited back to Quentin's flat."

Calvin sighed, "Really? Do we have to go? That place creeps me out."

"We do," I said firmly. The two of them looked as if they were concocting excuses on the spot. "Besides," I added, "I want to corner Michael's pal, Inspector Moon. I'd like to know just what progress the cops are making."

And, of course, I was looking for an opportunity to retrieve my diaphragm from Quent's bedroom.

MOURNING AT QUENTIN'S

I t was Quentin's kind of party.

All traces of the violence that prompted the gathering had been tidied away. No yellow police tape. No uniformed officers. No vulgar arrangements from florists, just wildly expensive Peruvian lilies in tall black ceramic vases. Stuart had supervised the catering. There was sushi and sashimi and warm sake and cold Tsing-Tao beer. And lots of mourners, consoling themselves with good things to eat and drink. Claire was sitting in a corner, smoking, pouting, and leafing through a magazine. It wasn't *Small Town*.

Michael surveyed the scene in disgust. "This is no wake," he said. "This looks like a fund-raiser for the society to preserve leather interiors in upscale cars."

Calvin nudged me. "Is he always so hostile?"

"Just in the face of tasteful materialism," I said. "It's got something to do with Catholic guilt."

"You white people," said Calvin, "You're so confusing. I thought it was Jewish guilt and Catholic shame."

"Welcome to the magic of mixed marriages," I said. "You get the combo meal."

Michael had roamed away and returned with three bottles of beer. "Quick," he said, "take a swig out of the bottle before Stuart comes by and ruins it by pouring it into a glass."

We swigged. "Come on, Michael," I said. "Everyone grieves in his or her own way. Quentin would love all this—gossip, music, lots of well-dressed people."

He shook his head. "It's missing something."

"Like what?" asked Calvin.

"Casseroles. Chocolate cake. Little Italian ladies dressed in black with hairnets and faint mustaches on their upper lips." He sighed.

"Don't mind him," I said to Calvin. "Funerals make him nostalgic." I turned to Michael. "Besides, you love sushi."

"I know. I'm going off to drown my sorrows in some raw tuna." He wandered off again.

"I like that guy," said Calvin.

"Me, too," I said. I grinned. "He's not bad in the sack, even if he's not my fashion advisor."

"So judgmental, Maggie."

"Got it in one," I said.

"You women. You've really taken all the fun out of objectification of the opposite sex."

"Objectification?"

"Yeah. I used to have a shrink girlfriend and she took me to some of those conferences where the Berkeley lady therapists in Birkenstocks sit around and relive their girlhoods from a feminist perspective."

"You went?"

"Sure. One thing about those feminist conferences, they're great places to meet women. And they have to be nice to me, because I'm a..." He gestured quote marks in the air, "... man of color." He tilted his beer bottle and swigged, waggling his eyebrows in a bad imitation of W.C. Fields.

"You're reprehensible, Calvin."

"But lovable. You know, I like real women, too. Watch this. I'm going to hook up with the Empress of Ice over there." He gestured with his beer bottle. The object of his attention was *Small Town's* film critic, Andrea Storch. "Starchy Storch," the magazine staff called her. Boston-born, Wellesley-educated, she rarely appeared out of regulation uniform: tailored wool skirt and cashmere twinset. Usually gray. Pearls, of course, and a signet ring. I was willing to bet good money the ring had belonged to one of her very Episcopalian parents.

"Do your best, Calvin," I said. "I hope you two will be very happy."

As Calvin strolled over to assault the redoubtable Ms. Storch, I decided to search out the next of kin. Actually, I wasn't sure to whom I should tender my condolences. There was Claire, of course, but she was really the ex, even though I didn't think they'd ever actually filed for divorce. Or Stuart? But then, I'd never really understood that relationship either.

I'd been charming to Stuart, truly I had, including him in dinner invitations we extended to Quentin—all that Miss Manners stuff—but it had cost me.

I bumped into Stuart in the kitchen. He was at the counter, piling more tiny linen cocktail napkins on a tray. He had forsaken his usual Errol Flynn-style blousy silk shirt for a gray and white striped broadcloth shirt and tailored wool slacks. I touched his shoulder.

He turned. "Maggie." He pecked me on the cheek. "Thanks for sitting with me at the service."

"How are you holding up, Stuart?"

He shrugged. "Well, the widow and I are circling, trying to decide whose party this really is."

"You look wonderful. Very uptown; Quentin would approve."

He smiled. "He would, wouldn't he? He should, it's his shirt. This is as close as I come to Savile Row, I'm afraid."

"God, Stuart, I feel so awful for you. For me, too."

He adjusted his stack of napkins a millimeter this way and that. Without looking up, he said, "Tell me about finding him."

I suppressed a shudder. "There's not much to tell. We had a lunch date. Nobody answered the door. Madame went to get me some writing paper so I could leave a nasty note, and then I pushed the door open and walked up the stairs. He was," I swallowed hard, "just lying there, sort of crumpled, over the desk."

"I feel so guilty about all this."

My heart sank. "Why?"

"I should have been here when whoever it was came in."

"Why weren't you?"

"Quentin and I had a blowup. He'd gotten an invitation to a gallery opening up on Sutter Street. And I knew he wasn't going to take me."

"Why?"

"Oh, he hardly ever took me anywhere. I can't—couldn't—keep up with his ever-so-clever friends. I'd wear something wrong, a Hawaiian shirt or something." He stopped suddenly. "Listen to me, I sound like a whiny mistress. Besides, it's all past tense now, anyway." I considered Stuart. His face, which usually seemed boyish and even younger than his thirty-something years, looked tired and drawn.

"So you two had a fight and you stomped out and went where?"

Stuart shrugged. "Why are you asking me all these questions? Are you Inspector Moon's little helper?"

"I'm sorry," I said. "I just feel awful, and responsible, and impatient."

"Impatient?"

"Oh, you know. The sooner we—the cops figure this out, the sooner we can put it behind us and get life back to normal."

Stuart snorted. "Normal? What's that, Maggie? I don't have a little nest to run back to, remember? Quentin was it."

Keep going, Maggie, I said to myself. You can't make it much worse than this.

"Stuart, I'm just bumbling around. What I mean is, there's some nut out there who killed Quentin."

"Or," Stuart gestured toward the living room, "out there."

"Right," I said grimly. "Right out there in the living room. What's a little murder among friends? Isn't that a pleasant thought?"

Stuart picked up a napkin and carefully re-folded it. "Okay, so what did you want to know? Oh, where I went when I left here." He sighed. "I don't even know. I had on running clothes, so I put Nuke on the leash and I just ran. Somehow I ended up at the Golden Gate Bridge. I ran across and back, walked up the hill on Fillmore to cool off, and came home. When I got here, the place was crawling with cops. Moon told me that you and Calvin Bright had just left."

"I'm sorry we missed you," I said. I patted Stuart's shoulder ineffectually.

Stuart slammed his hand flat on the counter, so hard the silver tray jumped. "That's another thing that pissed me off," he said.

"What?" I was bewildered.

"That photographer. I think Quent had a little thing for him."

"That was his tough luck," I said wryly. "From my short acquaintance with Calvin, I'd say he's hopelessly straight."

"No, listen, Maggie. Quentin was on the phone all day the day before he died, asking everybody nosy questions about Calvin. Who were his friends? Did he do drugs? Why hadn't he left town yet? This guy is getting work from all the major consumer magazines. The agencies have him booked all the time. But he sticks around San Francisco. Why?"

"I don't know, Stuart. Maybe he's got a sweetie here? Maybe he likes the sourdough? Why do you stick around?"

He gave me a level look. "Because I loved Quentin."

I reached up and put my hand to Stuart's cheek. "Then he was probably a very lucky man."

He squeezed my hand. "Thanks, Maggie. Not many people understood our relationship. I didn't understand it very well, myself. I'm not smart or famous or good at very much. But I took care of Quentin. And Nuke. Who has, by the way, gone off to live with Glen Fox and all those kids of his."

"That should be a change for Nuke," I said. "You did take good care of them," I said. "But I'll tell you something, Stuart. You're really a lousy detective. Those questions Quentin was asking about Calvin? Those aren't the kinds of questions you ask when you're doing a background check on a prospective lover. He was looking for dirt on Calvin." I mused a moment. "I wonder if he found any."

"I don't think so," said Stuart. "At dinner he seemed very, very cheerful. You know what Quentin's like when he's hatching some plan. He just loved to stir things up. He said, 'Bright's my boy. He's smart, he's clean, he knows his way around.'" Stuart stopped.

"What else? What else did he say?"

"Well, that's what's odd. He said, 'And he and Margaret will get along famously.' At the time, I just thought he meant that you would approve of Calvin, more than you'd approve of me."

"Come on, Stuart, give me a break. What kind of an elitist snob do you think I am? I'm just a glorified housewife myself, you know."

Stuart smiled. "I've seen your kitchen, Maggie. For a housewife, you're a helluva writer. Though, Quentin always said that was your problem."

"What? My housekeeping?"

"No. That you thought of yourself as a dabbling housewife."

"Quentin was a little too perceptive for comfort," I said glumly. "But why do you think Quentin cared so much if Calvin and I got along? He wanted us to do a story together, according to Calvin. But it's not like we were going to spend the rest of our lives together. I've covered stories with photographers for years. You do some planning, do the research, do the job, have a few drinks, fight with the art director about which gets the most play—copy or photos—and then you say goodbye."

"I don't know, Maggie. Was it a big story?"

"A big story? What's the big story?" Uncle Alf Abbott leaned in the kitchen door.

I lied instinctively. "Capers," I said quickly. "I wanted to sell Quentin on a follow-up to my lox piece. I loved the idea of the headline, 'The Great Caper Caper.'" I smiled at Alf, feeling like an idiot.

Alf gave me a look I judged to be composed of equal parts

puzzlement and contempt. My smile faded. "I know this all seems silly right now. I really am very, very sorry for your loss, Mr. Abbott."

Alf stared back at me. "My loss?"

"Quentin," I reminded him.

"Oh, yes," he said bitterly. "It's two losses, actually. I've lost an ex-nephew-in-law and an editor."

"If there's anything I can do...." I began lamely.

Alf looked me up and down. "As a matter of fact, there is," he said briskly. Swell, I thought. Go ahead and volunteer. They probably want me to inventory Quentin's loafers and box them up for charity.

"Anything," I said. "Well, almost anything."

"I've called a staff meeting at *Small Town* for tomorrow morning at ten," said Alf. "Can you meet for breakfast first? The Clift at eight?"

"Sure," I said, mentally rearranging morning lunch making, school delivery schedules.

"Good." Alf gave me one more calculating look. "There will be three of us. I'll ask my niece to join us."

Alf turned on his heel and left the kitchen.

"Bye, Alf. So nice to see you again," said Stuart.

I slipped my arm around his waist. "Buck up," I said. "Remember what Groucho Marx used to say?"

"What?"

"'I wouldn't want to belong to any club that would take people like me as a member.' Just amend that. You wouldn't want to belong to any club that would take Alf, would you?"

He managed the kind of smile kids put on for daffy, well-meaning aunts. "What do you think we should call the club for Alf's kind, anyway?"

"Oh, I don't know. How about the Loyal Order of the Well-Pickled Snobs?" I looked around the kitchen. "Stuart, what are you going to do now?"

"You mean, now that I'm a kept man without a keeper?" he

said bitterly.

"Well, Quentin was your employer as well as your friend."

"Right you are," he said. "As a matter of fact, one of Quentin's friends has offered me the same kind of job."

"Oh?"

"Just the grown-up au pair stuff: shopping, running errands, cooking. But," and he placed both hands melodramatically over his heart, "no romance."

"I didn't ask."

"No, but you wondered."

"Okay, I did." I searched Stuart's face, looking for the signs all of us in San Francisco had come to dread—weight loss, tell-tale lesions. "And, Stuart, one other thing I was wondering.…"

"Wonder no more. I'm fine. I'm HIV-negative. I may be lonely, I may be a murder suspect, but I'm healthy. Quentin made me get tested before I moved in. He was pretty scrupulous for a guy who got around. If you know what I mean."

I did. I let my breath out. "Thank God. I mean, that's good, that's wonderful news about you."

He shrugged. "Yeah, well, thank whoever. Anyway, I'm not starting my new gig right away. Claire's asked me to stay on until she sells this place. She's Quent's beneficiary."

"For everything?"

"Well, for most of what there is. Which is surprisingly little. Quentin lived well, but Claire had most of the substantial assets. And they were in her name. According to Quent's attorney, he's left me a little bequest. Left you his books, by the way."

I tried to imagine Michael's reaction to Quentin's books taking up permanent residence in our house and couldn't quite manage. I looked at Stuart's tray. "Want me to run that around the room a little?"

"No, thanks. Gives me something to do. Thanks for the talk, though."

"Any time." Stuart picked up the tray and started out the kitchen door.

"Stuart, wait a minute."

He turned. "Something's been nagging at me, something Madame said when we found Quentin." He rested the tray on the counter.

"What?"

This was awkward. "Well, I'm afraid Madame DeBurgos heard the quarrel that you and Quentin had."

He smiled wryly. "I see the cops' little helper is back."

"Forget it," I said.

"No, I don't care. Go ahead and be nosy. I told the cops anyway. Madame DeBurgos spilled to them, too."

"Well, she said she heard the door slam. That must have been when you went out for a run. But here's the odd part. She said she heard loud music, rock music, after the door had already closed. That couldn't have been Quentin playing that music, could it?"

Stuart snorted, "Not likely. The fight started because I had the music on when he came out of the shower. He's—he was—really quite a tyrant about music. He liked a lot of different stuff, but not what I liked. Not ever. So I used to get my music fix while he was gone, or a quick hit while he was in the shower."

"That explains why it was on before the fight. But not after. You didn't come back until after Quentin was dead and Moon and his guys were here. So who put that music on?"

Stuart frowned, "I don't know. Quentin wasn't expecting anybody but you and Bright."

"Oh, well," I said lamely. "I just thought you might have a theory."

I followed Stuart out the kitchen door and bumped directly into a knot of people from the *Small Town* staff. Glen was with them, so he'd clearly returned from his kid-depositing errands around the city.

I touched Gertie, Quentin's assistant, on the arm. She turned. "Oh, Maggie, it's so strange to be here without Quentin. I keep thinking he'll walk in the door and, and…."

"Rearrange everythin'." A graying man in a pocketed khaki

shirt and trousers spoke up. I knew from Peter Wimsey novels—and from Quentin—that those dropped g's meant a British public school background. The group laughed. "You know Quentin," he said. "No matter how perfect things look, he could always improve them. Or try."

Gertie turned back to me, "Maggie Fiori, John Orlando." We shook hands.

"How do you know Quentin?" I asked.

"Here and there," he said. "Precisely like everybody else."

"Hey," Gertie said, "We can ask Maggie about the poem. Quentin always said she was an expert on useless information. Art. Music. Baseball stats."

"Don't forget how to get red wine out of linen tablecloths," I said.

"That's out of character, dear heart," said Glen. "It's useful info."

"So what's the question?" I said.

Orlando spoke up. "That bit Stuart read at the service. Seemed like an odd choice for a poem. Minor Crane and all that."

"Quentin loved Crane," I said, "major and minor stuff. Plus, I always thought that poem was Crane's premonition about his own death."

"Stung to death by 'bees of paradise?'" offered Glen.

"No," I said. "I had come all the way here from the sea." I sipped my drink.

"He drowned," said Orlando. "Under odd circumstances. Too young. A pity." The group fell silent.

I drew Gertie aside, "Who is that guy?"

She shrugged. "Illustrator friend of Quentin's and Glen's. Weird little guy. Sounds like a bad episode of *Upstairs, Downstairs* whenever he opens his mouth."

I sensed someone in back of me and turned around. It was John Moon. "Inspector Moon," I said, "Can we have a word?" He nodded and we sat together on Quentin's buttery, cream-colored leather sofa.

"I was surprised to see you at the service," I said. "Detecting, I guess?"

Moon gave me a non-committal smile. "Actually, I enjoyed hearing about Mr. Hart's life. It made me wish I'd known him. Although that seems an unlikely thing to have happened."

"Why do you say that?"

Moon gestured at the room, "Ms. Fiori, does this look like the kind of crowd that socializes with 'the boys in blue'?"

"I don't know," I said. "You're the only 'boy in blue' I've ever met."

He smiled. "My point exactly."

Great, I thought. A cop with angst about his place in the social order. Where's Columbo when you need him? "Actually...." I began.

"Yes?"

I looked him up and down, from his polished loafers to his gelled and slicked back hair.

I reached over to touch his sweater vest. He didn't move.

"Cashmere," I said, "very nice."

"Point taken," he said. "I have a weakness for good clothes."

"You ought to talk to Calvin Bright," I said. "Maybe the two of you can cook up a threesome with his personal shopper at Saks."

He smiled, "My wife is Hong Kong Chinese and says she has a culturally-based passion for bargain-hunting. She keeps me well-dressed."

"So," I said, "getting back to the case. What do we know so far?"

"We?" said Moon.

"Okay, you."

Moon cleared his throat. "Well, what have you read in the paper?"

"The police are following leads."

"That's about the size of it. The medical examiner puts the time of death at around 11 a.m. The weapon was the walking stick, and it's likely that the murderer was of medium height and right-handed. No evidence of forced entry, so our assumption is that the murderer was someone Mr. Hart knew. That's the bare bones we're releasing to the public, which includes you. Now, your turn to answer questions. Any new ideas since we talked?"

I reported my confusion over the heavy metal music theory. Who turned it on? And why?

"We don't know. That's the simple answer," said Moon. "Mrs. DeBurgos mentioned it to us, and I'd wondered the same thing. But who knows? Maybe Mr. Hart decided to give the music a fair hearing."

I shook my head. "That wasn't Quentin. There was music he liked and music he didn't. Heavy metal wouldn't merit a hearing, fair or otherwise. I think the music must mean something. It must be a clue."

"A clue? Perhaps. We'll have to see. Meanwhile, did you find any more information on that story Mr. Hart wanted you to do?"

"I never had anything," I said. "I told your colleague that the other day. Did you ask Gertie? There's not much she didn't know about what Quentin was up to."

"Mr. Hart's assistant? We did. And we've searched his office."

"The only other thing...."

"Yes?"

I replayed what Stuart had just told me, that Quentin had wanted to find out more information about Calvin before assigning him the Cock of the Walk story. "Stuart said it was as if Quentin needed to know that Calvin was really a straight arrow before he got him involved in this story."

"Straight arrow? In what way?"

"Oh, I don't know, as if he could be corrupted by the story— which is too weird for words, because we don't even know what it was about."

Inspector Moon shrugged. "I don't know. The story may be relevant, it may not. We'll continue to look into it."

"You're sure it wasn't a stranger? Some intruder?"

Moon shook his head. "Doesn't seem likely. Whoever it was, Mr. Hart let him, or her, in." He reached into a breast pocket and pulled out his card. "If you get an idea about anything—the music, the story—please call me." He looked at me closely. "Let me emphasize that. Call me. No amateur detecting."

"I wasn't...." I protested.

"No, but I can tell you're interested." He sighed. "Journalists always are. This isn't a game, and it isn't the movies. Someone out there, a specific someone, was very, very angry. Angry enough to commit murder. Now, if you'll excuse me."

I watched Moon make his way to the door. He stopped to shake hands with Michael on the way out. I watched them together. They seemed stiff and formal, not like two guys who skated together every week, joked over beers after games. At the same moment, they looked back into the room and caught me watching them. Inspector Moon put his hand on Michael's shoulder, and leaned in close to say something. Then he was gone, and Michael had wandered away.

Moon was right about my desire to meddle. I was curious and more than a little unsettled. Despite what Moon said, it seemed at least possible that my hot "breakthrough" story had something to do with Quentin's death. Serves you right, Maggie, I thought. You couldn't be happy with those fluffy little cooks-and-books stories, could you? You couldn't stay on the straight and narrow path with your perfectly lovable husband, oh no. Let's just see what trouble we can get into.

I looked around the room. Beautiful people, beautiful food, lots of flushed cheeks and laughter as the sake and Chinese beer washed out the more sombre feelings engendered at the Unitarian church.

This whole affair felt like a cross between Noel Coward and Hitchcock, and it didn't feel good. Was I, or was I not, sitting in my ex-lover's flat, wearing the hat he bought me, angling to retrieve my diaphragm from the bedroom, and wondering who, just who, among all these well dressed, well educated, well-spoken people had hated Quentin enough to kill him? And was there some perverse reason in the universe that the homicide cop investigating the murder had to be a hockey chum of my husband's?

I eyed the bedroom door, which opened off the living room. It was closed, and I couldn't see any conceivable way to get in there and retrieve my diaphragm without calling attention to myself. I stirred and set out in search of Michael, and promptly ran into Calvin and Andrea Storch. Both wore coats and were clearly on their way out together.

"Where are you two off to?" I asked innocently.

"Calvin picked a fight with me about New England cooking," said Andrea. "I'm taking him home for dinner to teach him a thing or two."

Calvin struggled without success to wipe a gloat off his face.

As I hugged Calvin goodbye, I whispered in his ear, "One small victory for you, one major setback for Ms. Saks Fifth Avenue."

He had the decency to look embarrassed.

DECISIONS IN THE FRENCH ROOM

If breakfast is served in heaven, it must be catered by the Clift Hotel.

I parked at the Union Square Garage, early enough to beat out all the professional shoppers, the ladies who lunch who would later prowl through Neiman Marcus, Saks, and Macy's. It was five after eight by the time I hurried up Geary to the Clift. Uncle Alf and Claire Hart were already sipping coffee at a white linen–covered table.

My single friends swear by the Redwood Room; all dark panels and discreet lights, just the place for a pre-assignation cocktail. But for the rest of us, there's the French Room, the hotel's main dining room, where breakfast has been advanced to a high art. Fresh, pulpy orange juice, coffee of a serious nature, and fluffy scrambled eggs on white china.

The waiter held the chair for me, whisked the napkin into my lap, and murmured about coffee. I murmured back affirmatively. I smiled brightly at Alf and Claire without a thought in my head about what to say.

"Well, isn't this nice?" I said. "It's fun for me to have breakfast with people who don't need help pouring syrup on their waffles."

Claire stared at me blankly. Alf managed a weak smile. "Oh, yes," he said. "Quentin often remarked that you had a delightful sense of humor."

Claire looked even stonier. "I'm afraid the joke eludes me," she said.

"God Almighty, Claire, the woman means she usually has breakfast with her children."

Claire shrugged.

"But you wouldn't know. You and Quentin never had any little vipers of your own."

I began longing for my bagel, my own little vipers, and breakfast at home. "Listen, I'm sorry," I began. "This is a terrible time to make wisecracks. Truly, I just don't know what to say. I miss Quentin already, so I can only begin to imagine how it must be for the two of you." Silence. "Being family and all." More silence.

Impulsively, I reached across the table and put my hand on Claire's. "I want you to know how much Quentin meant to me," I said. "I really loved him."

She withdrew her hand. Her perfectly lined and lipsticked mouth twitched. "Really? And were you sleeping with him, too?"

I felt my cheeks begin to burn and I stood up. "I'm sorry. I seem to be saying one wrong thing after another. I hope you'll accept my condolences."

Uncle Alf was on his feet, grabbing my hand. "Sit down, dear, sit down. Claire doesn't mean anything. She's just upset."

I sat. Uncle Alf still had hold of my hand. He smiled and reached out to hold Claire's hand as well. We looked as if we were having a séance. "Now, let's order some of that splendid French toast and have a nice chat together. If Claire can concentrate and remember not to be so poisonous, she'll recall we asked Mrs. Fiori here for a special reason."

We ordered. Contemplating the French toast distracted me for a moment from the "special reason." Whatever it was, I hoped it didn't have to be carried out in Claire's company. That kind of nastiness could only be contagious.

I took a sip of coffee to brace myself. "Mr. Abbott, when we were talking in the kitchen yesterday, you suggested that I could do something to help. I'd really like to."

Claire snapped her silver lighter open and looked at me. For a moment, I thought she was considering immolation. But Uncle Alf took it from her hand and lit her cigarette. Smoking was, of course, banned in all San Francisco restaurants, but who had the courage to confront Claire? She said, "Why? Why would you like to help?"

"Claire, please," said Alf.

"It's all right," I said. "I'm happy to tell you. I did love Quentin. I loved him because he was a tough, stylish editor. *Small Town* isn't exactly *The Paris Review.* But it's a good city magazine, because Quentin pushed all of us. I was terrified of sending him half-baked work. And he understood that. Maybe the rest of my life looks a little half-baked—I only write part time, and the rest of the time I run around doing a pretty mediocre job of behaving like Beaver Cleaver's mother. But I didn't write like the Beav's mother, and if I ever did, Quentin would never have given me another assignment."

It occurred to me that the Beav probably had not made it to syndication on the evil planet on which Claire was spawned. But I was warming to my task.

"I know there was a lot of fluff in the magazine, but Quentin did some of the earliest pieces on the ways AIDS was devastating the arts community, and he sponsored journalism internships at some decidedly unprivileged city high schools, and—"

Claire snorted. Alf looked uncomfortable. "I'm not an economic genius, either," I said. "But I also know a little about the history of *Small Town's* advertising revenue." I picked up my coffee cup and smiled sweetly. "As far as I can tell, the magazine came back from the brink of economic disaster under Quentin's guidance."

The waiter arrived with the French toast. He was a welcome diversion. I'd hoped to touch Claire and Uncle Alf with my little speech about Quentin. Instead, they both looked as if I'd put my elbows on the table and burped the theme to *The High and the Mighty.*

We busied ourselves with the butter and the syrup.

"Well, Mrs. Fiori, I'll tell you why I called this little meeting.

We're in a bit of a jam. You know that I own *Small Town*. And, though I'm publisher, I'm just not much of a magazine man. Got into the whole business by accident. Bad investment, didn't use the old noggin," he tapped his balding dome. "If you know what I mean."

I didn't really, but it seemed safest just to murmur an assent.

"So here we are with no editor in chief. Frankly, I'm going to take my time filling that spot. I might sell the magazine, I might bring someone in from New York or L.A. But in the meantime, we need a pinch hitter. I don't want to use someone from the permanent staff; I'm sure you understand."

"I don't, actually. What about Glen Fox? He's the managing editor already."

"Oh, Mr. Fox is still relatively new to the magazine, not to mention new to our shores. This is really his first assignment dealing with a, shall we say, for-profit publication. Which brings us to you."

I put my fork down. "Me?"

"You," he beamed. "You've edited before, even though it was for one of those dreadful trade magazines. As you point out, *Small Town* has a competent chief cook and bottle washer, that Irish fellow, Fox. So we just need someone to oversee the show, so to speak."

"Thank you, I think. But what makes you think I could… run the show?"

"You could. Quentin told me so."

My stomach turned over. "He picked his successor before he died?"

"Of course not. Good God, woman, how macabre! But we used to chat about who might succeed him in the job. I think he thought that when he and Claire finally divorced, we'd boot him out. Well, you've got the editorial credentials. According to Quentin, the staff likes you, and you haven't got a job already. So here's the bargain—fill in for a few issues until Claire and I decide what's what. We'll make it worth your while. Financially,

I mean." He named a figure that made me think longingly about deep-sixing one of the ancient Volvos, remodeling the kitchen, or even taking a vacation that didn't involve camping gear.

I turned to Claire. "What do you think of this idea?"

"I really couldn't care less," she said, removing a flake of tobacco from her tongue in a gesture I thought had disappeared with 1940s Bette Davis movies. "Alf wanted to see some jolly family unity, so I came along. It's a silly, shallow magazine, and I really don't see that the sun will rise or set on who runs the damn thing. I suppose you'd be as... serviceable as anyone."

I felt myself flush again, this time in anger. "You've got yourself a deal, Mr. Abbott," I said. We shook hands over the bud vase.

"Wonderful! Marvelous! Let's celebrate. Where is that waiter?" He waved and the waiter appeared. "Bloody Marys all around," he said. "Then we can drop by the office and you can rally the troops. I told 'em to be ready for a potential all-hands-on-deck sit-down this morning."

I started to protest, but Alf interrupted. "Just being optimistic, not presumptuous. But no time like the present. Magazine issues have to get out, don't they?"

I stole a look at my watch. It was ten minutes before nine. I'd just accepted a job I didn't think I wanted and probably couldn't do. I'd also broken a cardinal Fiori family household rule: consult your mate before making big decisions—or else. Should I worry first about the kids, Michael's reaction, or actually figuring out what to wear to work in the city again after all these years? My boss was a drunk. My predecessor's ex hated me. And the person who murdered the last editor in chief was still at large. Oh, go ahead, Maggie, just put a bulls-eye on your back and call it a day.

Clearly, a Bloody Mary was just what the doctor ordered. Perhaps two.

AT SMALL TOWN

The editorial offices of *Small Town* are just four blocks from the Clift.

A few minutes before ten, we parted company with Claire out in front of the hotel. I hoped my few sips of Bloody Mary would insulate me from the frostbite I seemed likely to contract from her parting handshake.

Alf, warmed by either his two Bloody Marys or my foolish, persistent good cheer, tucked my hand in his arm and we strolled down Geary, cut across the recently face-lifted Union Square, avoiding the early junkies, late drunks, stupefied pigeons, and shoppers.

At 270 Sutter, we turned into the door. The building and the elevator are faded San Francisco splendor—rococo, chipped gilt, and the lingering lobby smell of expensive perfume and less-expensive muscatel. But when the elevator doors opened directly onto the fourth floor it was clear that Quentin had very recently held court.

White walls, polished floors, a few good rugs. Even the coffee mugs were regulation dove gray, with tiny *Small Town* logotypes (Goudy Old Style) on them. Quentin was famous for his "bad taste purges," sweeping through the staff's offices and appropriating cups with cartoon characters or chirpy slogans, trimming plants of limp leaves, leaving yellow stickie messages that read "clean me" on grimy Rolodexes and "think again" on sixties-era oak picture frames.

The door to Quentin's office was closed. While Alf assembled the troops, I called Michael at his office.

"He's with a client, Mrs. Fiori. Shall I interrupt?"

This news needed a face-to-face delivery, I realized, slightly relieved he wasn't immediately available by phone. "No, no, I'll see him at home," I said hastily. "Don't bother him now."

We met in the conference room. The meeting was far easier than I'd imagined. Alf made a few pompous remarks, introduced me as interim editor, and settled himself unsteadily on the art director's high stool.

I looked around the room. The faces were friendly, but clearly puzzled. The full-time staff was quite small: Quentin as editor, his hand-picked assistant Gertie Davis, his managing editor Glen Fox, the art director Linda Quoc, and a staff editor who presided over a changing crew of proofreaders, factcheckers, interns, and production people.

As Quentin liked to point out, he and Gertie were the only permanent senior staff members without some kind of an off-shore accent. As for Gertie, who had applied for the job with Quentin the day she got off the plane from Chicago to start a new life away from Awful Husband Number One and grown but needy children, her loyalty was of the kind most often mythologized in golden retrievers.

The contributing editors, who were responsible for columns and occasional features, included Lisbet Traumer on restaurants, Andrea Storch on film, me on books, and a mustachioed ex-hockey player named Puck Morris on music. Musicians who received bad reviews were alerted ahead of time when Morris would send out one of his signature "Pucked by Morris" t-shirts.

Okay, Maggie, I cheered myself on. These folks know you as a fluffy feature writer who's always just a little bit late with assignments. Act like an editor! You used to do this for a living. I took a deep breath. "Mr. Abbott has asked me to fill in," I said, "until Kelly Girls turn up someone better." Everyone smiled but Alf.

I saw Gertie bite her lip and exchange a quick glance with Glen Fox.

"I'd like to huddle with Glen and Gertie right after this meeting, and then meet individually with the rest of you over the next few days. As for the contributing editors, since I'm the only one who's ever late, I'm going to assume we're on target with content and deadlines. Let's try and talk before the end of the week."

I took another breath. "I know this is tough and awkward for all of us. I'm not Quent, and no one else is either. I'm sure Mr. Abbott and Mrs. Hart will do everything they can to find someone who will do right by *Small Town*. In the meantime, all we can do is put out a magazine Quentin wouldn't have terribly minded finding on his nightstand."

That prompted a little round of applause. Then, we quickly set up a process for finishing the next issue and moving forward with the following few months. Like all monthly magazines except for create-on-the-screen 'zines, the upcoming issues of *Small Town* had schedules that overlapped. While one issue was in the last stages of production, the next was in design and editing, and the two or three after that were in planning and story assignment stages.

After the meeting, Alf disappeared. Glen went to get coffee for us. I took a deep breath, opened the door to Quentin's office, and went in. I couldn't face his desk, so I put pad and pencil on his small work table, pulled up chairs for Glen and Gertie, and waited. Quent's office looked not unlike his house—serene, perfectly ordered, the walls hung with framed covers from past issues of *Small Town*.

Glen backed in, thick file under one arm, two mugs of coffee in hand, a small bottle of Bushmill's under the other arm. Gertie followed, her face scrupulously clean of expression.

"This is just what we need, my girls," said Glen.

"Ordinarily, I'd agree with you," I said. "But breakfast with Alf, Claire, and a Bloody Mary have put me off a bit already."

Gertie shook her head. "Not for me, Glen. You know we wholesome Midwestern girls don't drink before noon."

"Okay," he said, "then this is just what I need." He unscrewed the lid, picked the bottle up, hovered it over the mug, then put it down again.

"Go ahead," I said.

"No, I think I won't," he said, screwing the lid back on. "I'm cutting back. Drives all those Irish stereotypers quite mad. Besides, we all have to take better care of ourselves these days. I'll face the music cold sober."

These two need to be my pals, and fast, I thought. "Before we jump into the issue, I want to tell both of you I didn't go after this job," I said.

Glen patted my hand. "I know you didn't, Maggie. I'm not hurt. I've only been here a year and, frankly, I know damn little about this city and this kind of magazine. I mean, if it's not rantin' and ravin' politics, I'm out of my home turf."

As Alf had pointed out, Glen was relatively new to the magazine, having landed in San Francisco when he'd been tossed off the radical Catholic weekly he'd edited back home in County Clare.

I laughed. "I always wondered if *Small Town* wasn't a little superficial for you."

"Actually, thanks to Quent, it's a world better than it has any right to be. Besides that, when I came to San Francisco with Corinne and the five mouths to feed, I was grateful to Quentin for the job. Gertie knows that. So I'll do anything I can to help you."

Gertie had been silent, her arms crossed, regarding me during Glen's little speech.

"So Gertie, how's about it?" I asked. "Are you with me?"

"I'm wondering if I still have a job," she said.

"If it's up to me, you do," I said.

"Thanks, I guess," she said. Her eyes welled with tears and she stood up.

"I've got to get out of here," she said.

I jumped up and put my arms around her. "I know."

She shook me off. "No, you don't, Maggie. You've got another life. I still don't know why Quent took a chance on an old reentry broad like me, but he gave me this job and a life I loved for the first time. He was an opinionated, arrogant, selfish son of a bitch, and I loved him to death." The room became very quiet. She dug in her pocket and blew her nose angrily. "Oh, you know what I mean. I'm so angry that he did something stupid enough to get somebody mad enough to kill him." She swiped at her nose again. "And the worst of it is, we don't even know why this happened."

I collected myself. "Gertie, you've lost Quentin and that's awful. It's awful for all of us. He rescued me, too, you know. I was about to go down for the count in carpools and play groups. But you haven't lost your job, and I can't possibly figure out this place without you. Now, are you in?"

"I'm in… for now," she said. "And of course, I'll try to help you, Maggie. I'm not angry at you. I'm furious at Quentin, but he's not here." She dabbed at her eyes with tissue. "Can you guys have this meeting without me? I'll be around later, but I just need some air."

"Fine, fine," I said, relieved she wasn't going to disappear forever. And then she was out the door.

Within fifteen minutes, Glen had the table covered with production schedules, story lineups, editorial and art budgets, and a messy stack of paper layouts printed out from the designers' screens.

"Here's the big picture," he said. "November issue goes to press next week. Linda Quoc and I will do the press check. She covers things from the design side, of course, and I handle the last-minute editorial stuff. So unless you're anxious to break in with an all-nighter…." I said I'd pass.

"Fine. Copy's in for December, except for your lox piece, and Linda and her fellows are designing the book. January is the trouble."

Glen pulled out the January story list. There was a line for each of the four major features with a working headline, the writer assigned, deadlines, and so on. At the bottom of the story list, the standing, or regular, features and columns were displayed.

"What's the problem?"

"Have a look."

There on the page, in Quentin's Spencerian hand, was the lineup for the January issue.

1. The Resolution Blues

Famous People talk about the art of not making New Year's resolutions.

Writer: Manfred Smith, deadline: 11/15.

2. Where the Sun Always Shines

Winter vacations for the indolent pale skins.

Writer: Liz Gruder, deadline: 11/15.

3. Looking for Daddy More-Bucks

An overview of funding for the city's major arts organizations.

Writer: Puck Morris, deadline: 11/15.

4. Trouble in Paradise: The Cock of the Walk

The writer and the deadline were blank, and there was no telegraphic description of the story.

"No problem, Glen," I said.

"Why?"

"I'm the writer. The day Quentin… died… we were supposed to have lunch and talk about the piece. Just give me the file and I'll do the piece myself."

Glen tapped his pencil on the list. "You haven't anything on the story? Anything at all?"

"No. But if you've got the file, then I'm sure we can put something together."

He picked up his coffee mug and swallowed. "That's the problem. There is no file. Well, there's a file, but there's nothing in it but a clipping from the *Chronicle*'s social notes about the opening. Big society bash. All the mink-and-fink set came out for that. It was a benefit for some AIDS group."

"Mink-and-fink?"

"You know, all those ladies with furs who come out and tittle-tattle about each other. Like our own beloved widow."

"Claire?"

"She's the one. Actually, she organized this little to-do."

"I don't get this. If the piece isn't a restaurant review, and it's not, or he'd have asked Lisbet to do it, then what is it? I can't believe Quentin just wanted to plug some place Claire hangs out."

"I don't know, Maggie. 'Trouble in Paradise' doesn't sound like a plug. But if you don't have any background, I think we've got to kill the story."

I sighed. "Damn. Quentin was tantalizing me with this story. I didn't even know what the piece was about and I was already writing my acceptance speech for some award."

"You don't know anything?"

I shook my head. "Nope. There may be something back at Quentin's apartment. I was meeting him there for lunch, so maybe he brought the contents of the file home with him. I'll ask that nice cop if I can have a look around. In the meantime, let's dig out the evergreen file and plan a backup."

In the magazine business, evergreen stories are an editor's life preserver. They're stories that aren't seasonal (hence, the name) and can be dropped in when a cowardly lawyer kills a piece or the interview subject dies or a writer botches a job.

Glen promised to pull some candidates from the evergreen file. As he stood up, the door swung open. Calvin Bright and Andrea "Starchy" Storch waited outside.

"I heard the news," said Calvin. "Came by to say congratulations, can I help, and are you sweet things free for lunch?"

"On principle," said Glen, "I never have lunch on a Friday with a fellow who calls me a sweet thing."

"I didn't mean you," grinned Calvin. "I mean these lovely ladies. But you're welcome."

"I'll take a raincheck, as you Yanks say."

"You're on," I said. "Come on, Andrea, we'll take you someplace sleazy and you can class the place up."

Half an hour later, we were all sitting in front of Anchor Steam beers at Hamburger Mary's. It's not that Hamburger Mary's is exactly sleazy; it's just not the kind of place you generally find Starchy Storch, the high brow film critic, bending her elbow. For openers, Mary is rumored to be a guy. After dark, it's hard to feel well-dressed without some heavy leather accessories (and I don't mean Coach handbags), but at any hour, the burgers are unbeatable.

"Let's toast Maggie's new job," said Calvin.

"Let's not," I said. "It's temporary. And it gives me the creeps. I've already made Gertie cry and driven Glen to drink. God, I wish the cops would figure out what happened."

Andrea shivered. "You know, until we came in to see if you wanted lunch, I'd not set foot in Quentin's office, since, you know...."

"Cheer up, girls," said Calvin. "I think Quentin would be one happy guy to see Maggie in that office. Besides, the SFPD will crack the case pretty soon. Maybe Mrs. Quent popped over and just nastied him to death."

Andrea put her beer down, regarded the napkins on the table with some distaste, and opened her purse. She came up with a linen handkerchief and patted her mouth. "Aren't you ever serious?" she asked.

"Only about love and work," said Calvin. He reached across the table, captured the hanky and helped Andrea pat some more.

"Speaking of work," I interrupted, "remember that piece we were supposed to do, Calvin?"

"Um-hmmm."

"Would you cut that out and listen to me? I'm going to report you to the Empress of Saks Fifth Avenue."

Calvin looked chagrined. "I don't think the personal shopper and I are going to find true happiness," he mumbled.

Andrea looked bewildered. Calvin hastily handed her the hanky. "I'll explain later."

"Okay, Mags, I'm listening. What story?"

"Our story. The Cock of the Walk piece. Did you have research or background on it?"

"Me? I'm just the shooter. Quentin wouldn't give me anything hard, like stuff to read or anything. Plus, the cops already asked me about it."

"They asked Gertie, too. And if she didn't know anything... well, unless the info is stashed in Quentin's flat, whatever research existed is gone. Glen didn't know anything about the file, didn't know Quent had talked to us, didn't even know what it's all about."

"I know where the background on that story is," volunteered Andrea.

We both looked at her.

She sipped her beer. "Whoever murdered Quentin took it."

We stared some more.

"Don't you two ever read mysteries?" she said. "If something disappears, and somebody gets offed at the same time—well, there's your clue."

"Offed?" I echoed, faintly. Andrea patted the knot of honey-colored hair she wore coiled at her neck. Clearly, she had dimensions I'd never explored.

"You may be right," I said, "but I'd sure like to paw through Quentin's desk at home. Maybe there's something there."

While Calvin and Andrea settled up the check, I rang Inspector Moon and explained my request.

"I'm pleased you called, Mrs. Fiori," he said. "If you don't mind my hanging around while you look for your file, I'll be delighted to let you in the apartment. I've been planning to call you soon, anyway."

"Really? Why?"

"Just a little chat. This and that," he said vaguely. "You know."

IN QUENTIN'S BEDROOM

As soon as Inspector Moon unlocked the door and gestured for me to precede him into the flat, I was glad I wasn't alone.

It was odd to be at Quentin's; not for lunch, not for love, not for grief, but in pursuit of a story. A story? A murder. "Nice work if you can get it," I said to myself.

Moon didn't hover. He stood in front of Quentin's floor-to-ceiling living room bookshelves, humming under his breath, acting for all the world like a man at leisure in the reading room of the public library.

It was clear that the flat was still Stuart's home. Moon had called to say we were coming over and Stuart had left a note on the kitchen counter.

"Coffee's made, ready in the thermos. Maggie knows where to find cream and sugar. Help yourselves."

I seated myself at Quentin's desk, marveling yet again at his organization. Check files, charity receipts, address books, even a Christmas shopping list. "Garnet earrings," it said next to my name, with a query, "Jane Austen bio?"

"He was very generous to his writers," said Moon, at my elbow. I jumped. "He was a friend, too," I said.

Moon wandered back to the bookshelves.

"We'd searched the place, of course," he said. "It seemed odd that Mr. Hart didn't have some kind of filing cabinet."

"Quentin hated clutter," I said. "It took a lot for him to hold onto something. I suppose he had personal papers, a will and things like that in a safe deposit box somewhere. But he wasn't much of a paper keeper. His assistant, Gertie, was always snatching things out of his hands at work before he tossed them."

There was nothing of particular interest in the desk. Some receipts, engraved note paper, a few letters tied together with the black ribbon that comes on stationery.

I held the letters up. "May I take these?" Moon shrugged. "I guess so. We've already been through them. I'm not sure who you'd ask. Stuart? Mrs. Hart?"

"I'm asking the police."

"Fine with me. You'll tell me if you find anything?" I looked at him.

"Probably."

He nodded. "Okay."

"I'd like to go in the bedroom now."

"I'll come with you."

On Quentin's nightstand: a tiny clock radio, the *New York Times* Book Review section, Eudora Welty's essays on writing, a tired-looking copy of Roger Angell's baseball classic *The Five Seasons*, a box of tissues. I opened the drawer. There, as I remembered, was a blue leather box, right where I left it nearly a year ago. "M.S.F." read the initials.

"What does the "S" stand for?" asked Moon from the doorway.

I held the box on my lap and looked up.

"Stern," I said, running my fingers over the raised gold letters.

"Your maiden name?" he asked politely.

"Yes."

"Open it," he said. "I apologize, but of course we've already searched it."

I didn't move, paralyzed by the inconsequential weight of the box on my lap.

"You created the combination, didn't you?" prodded Moon.

I did. Two, one, sixty five. My birthday.

Moon sat down beside me on the bed, carefully adjusting his gray flannel slacks to protect the crease, and watched me open the box.

Some notes from Quentin, tickets from a performance of *Un Ballo in Maschera* we'd seen together, a flat brown compact.

I picked it up. My diaphragm lay inside, right where I left it nearly a year ago.

"There's something I don't understand," he said. "Didn't you need this at home?"

"No. My husband had a vasectomy a few years ago." The room seemed very quiet.

"Ah, yes," said Moon. "He mentioned that in the locker room, after a game. One of the referees was discussing the possibility, and he was nervous. Michael reassured him."

The room was silent. Moon cleared his throat.

"You know," he said, almost to himself, "before I joined the police, I used to be a high school counselor. I learned something from those kids. If you just shut up, people will eventually tell you their story."

I breathed in and out, lovely Lamaze skills that transferred nicely from hard labor to moments just like this.

"Listen, I know this looks awful. But my relationship with Quentin had nothing to do with my husband. Or," I faltered, thinking of Michael's white rage at me and his refusal to talk about it, "maybe it does. But Quentin and I hadn't been lovers for almost a year."

"I see," he said. "Then why, may I ask, is the box still here? That seems out of character for a man who liked to clear out unnecessary clutter."

"Because the box was mine," I said fiercely, "not his. And maybe he hoped I'd need it again one day. Which I didn't, but I hadn't claimed it either. I don't know why."

Suddenly I felt ill. I stood up, clutching the box.

"You think I killed Quentin?"

Moon patted the bed. "Sit down, sit down." I sat.

"It had occurred to me as a possibility," he said. "But the evidence suggests it was very unlikely. "You're close to the right height, but you're left-handed. However, once we discovered you and Hart were… intimate, that opened a world of suspects."

"It did?" I asked faintly.

"Oh, yes, indeed. There's jealousy, of course, so that leads us to think about Mrs. Hart, Stuart, other lovers. And," he hesitated. "Of course, there's your husband."

I stared at him. "Michael?" He nodded.

"That's ridiculous." The room felt very warm.

"I take it he's not a jealous man?" asked Moon. "Or perhaps he didn't know?"

"How did you find out?"

"Ah, Mrs. Fiori, this is a terrible city for secrets. What is it you call your magazine? *Small Town*?" He shook his head. "Very small, very small indeed."

"You're enjoying this," I said, looking at him with distaste, wondering if the entire world would soon know how stupidly I'd strayed.

"That's not correct," he said. "I am doing my job. That often means finding out about things people would prefer I don't know. But I don't enter people's lives, or," he gestured, "their bedrooms, without a reason."

"It's a job," I muttered.

"Yes, it is. And I'm good at it."

"If you're so good at it," I retorted, "who killed Quentin? You still don't know, do you?"

He shook his head. "No, we don't. But we will. We are very certain Mr. Hart was not killed by a stranger. He was killed by someone who knew him. Slowly and surely, we are examining every possibility."

"Good luck," I said bitterly. "Quentin knew a lot of people."

He sighed, "Yes, he did."

Something struck me. "If Michael is really a suspect, you wouldn't be investigating this, would you? You know him. Isn't that a conflict of interest or something?"

"Or something," he said. "The forensics are all wrong for Michael. He's too tall, for one thing. And you're correct, if your husband hadn't been ruled out fairly quickly, I would have been taken off the team. Right now, it's somewhat helpful to know the players."

"Because...."

Moon smiled, "Don't you and Michael ever say 'just because' to your kids?"

"Because," I persisted, "even if Michael and I aren't real suspects, you can pump us for information."

He sighed again, "The British have a nicer way of describing this. They say 'someone is helping the police with inquiries.'"

"Too bad we're here and not there," I snapped, quickly placing the contents of the blue box back inside.

He nodded.

Half an hour later I was in my car, heading home, still feeling as if I'd been measured and found wanting after the conversation with Inspector Moon.

"Smart-ass detective," I muttered. "Thinks he's got the whole picture. I'm sure he's got a perfect, unsullied marriage, unlike the rest of us weak-willed lowlifes."

I smacked the steering wheel hard and gunned the motor, waiting for the light to turn on Broadway.

I thought of the inspector's face as he opened my diaphragm case and I felt my own cheeks turn hot. "Dammit, Maggie, you *are* a weak-willed lowlife, you deserve this," I grumbled.

But what? What did I deserve? And, even if I did deserve this—this shock, suspicion, Michael's anger—and, okay, I did, did Quentin deserve what happened to him?

And what did happen? It now seemed very important to find out who had spilled the beans about Quentin and me to Moon. I pulled over at the next corner and called Moon on the cell phone. I didn't want to be changing lanes for this conversation.

Moon answered on the second ring.

"Inspector Moon? It's Maggie Fiori."

"Yes, Mrs. Fiori?"

"I need to know. Who told you about my relationship with Quentin?"

He was silent.

"Please."

"Actually, I believe it was Mr. Morris, your magazine's music critic. And, he didn't exactly tell. I made an educated guess."

"How?"

"During questioning, he made it clear how very upsetting it must have been for you, in particular, to find Mr. Hart. I said, why, yes, for anyone it's a shock. Then, Mr. Morris—well, he blushed. And suddenly, it seemed quite obvious."

"I see," I said grimly, watching the traffic slow on Broadway.

"Well, thanks for your candor."

"A pleasure," he said. "Please call me if you find anything in those letters."

I agreed immediately. Then, after I hung up, I remembered how foolish I felt in Quentin's bedroom under Moon's neutral gaze.

"Maybe I will," I said petulantly. "And maybe I won't." And drove home.

THE HEART OF A JEALOUS MAN

I t was Friday night at Ratto's.

Ratto's is an Oakland institution, an Italian grocery that carried a dozen kinds of olive oil before the yups ever discovered the difference between virgin and extra virgin.

Adjoining the grocery, there's a cavernous room where the fortunate eat dinner on Friday nights. Serve-it-yourself salad, pasta, dessert, wine and coffee. Then, when everyone's full and the children begin to get sleepy, the entertainment starts. There's usually a slightly manic accompanist and three or four singers. Opera, glorious, glorious opera. Old favorites, so the singers clink wine glasses with the patrons and bellow the drinking song from *La Traviata,* and some surprises, especially with young singers trying an ambitious aria out in front of a friendly crowd.

When the singing started at eight o'clock, Zach was in my lap, drowsing. Josh seemed wonderfully relaxed, leaning against Michael, mesmerized by the soprano's bosom, heaving up and down to *Musetta's Waltz.*

"Dad," he whispered, "what do you call that line on her chest?"

"Cleavage," Michael whispered back.

The mezzo, dressed in black with a scarlet chiffon scarf wound 'round her throat, announced Dalila's passionate aria from *Samson et Dalila,* "*Mon coeur s'ouvre a ta voix.*" It is Dalila's most wicked moment. "My heart opens at thy sweet voice," she sings to Samson, luring him to his ruin.

Josh tugged at Michael's sleeve, "What's it about, Dad?"

Michael caught my eye. "It's about the perfidy of women." Josh was puzzled. "Mom's the writer. Ask her what perfidy means."

The children were both asleep by the time we got home. Michael carried them from the car, one at a time. I tucked them in their cocoons of stuffed creatures and blankets. Then I poured two brandies and brought them into the living room. Michael sat in the dark. I turned on a lamp and handed him a glass.

"Perfidy's a pretty big word," I said. Silence.

"Michael, I hate it that you'd use Josh like that." More silence.

"Michael, why won't you talk to me about this?"

"I don't need to talk to you," he said bitterly. "John Moon's already invited me down to headquarters. I had a chance to talk to him. Imagine how interested he was to know when I'd figured out you and that pretentious asshole were having an affair."

"Oh my God."

Michael stared at me. "I didn't do it, Maggie. I didn't kill him. I could have, but I didn't."

"I know you didn't, Michael." When I closed my eyes to keep the tears back, I could see Michael sitting at Ratto's, pulling Josh close and whispering the lyrics in his ear so he could shout "Libiamo, *libiamo*" with the singers. "Does Moon think you killed him?"

"I don't know. He was very polite, told me they might have more questions for me later. I was on the road at the time Quent was killed, so I don't have much of an alibi. And, I'm right-handed."

"Where were you going? Can't somebody vouch for when you arrived?"

"That would be awkward."

Michael put his glass down. "Want to know where I was going?"

"Yes."

"I went to the city—for a blood test."

"Why? What's wrong with you?"

"Nothing. Absolutely nothing."

I waited.

"However, since I'm married to a woman stupid enough to have an affair with somebody who sleeps with boys and girls, lots and lots of boys and girls—after stewing about it for several months, I thought I should have the AIDS test."

The brandy turned to acid in my mouth. I had done the exact same thing, after Quentin began his affair with Stuart, and after I realized what a dangerous game I had been playing. Gone to the public health office in the Castro, sat in the waiting room with a half dozen terrified looking young men, and browsed through the safe sex propaganda. The week-long wait had been excruciating. Just for good measure, I prayed to every Catholic saint I'd ever heard Michael's mother mention. I paid particular attention to St. Rita da Cascia, the patron saint of incurable diseases and impossible causes. Rita had been listening. I was HIV-negative.

I looked at Michael, stricken.

He made a gesture of impatience. "I'm fine." Michael sprang up, came and knelt at my side. "God, Maggie! What were you thinking of? It's not bad enough you fucked around. You had to go fuck around with someone who could've killed you, or me? Jesus, you're supposed to be so smart. What the hell's wrong with you?"

Then I cried. I hadn't cried since that day in the shower. Not at the funeral, not at Quent's office, not while the mezzo sang her wicked love song.

Michael watched me as if I were a not particularly pleasant specimen under a microscope.

"I can't explain what was wrong with me. It's as if there are two different versions of my life. There's the version with you and the boys—I love you, I love them, I love our life. But sometimes I feel like such an amateur. I don't do anything very, very well any more. I can't even keep house without Anya."

Michael snorted. "You're not supposed to keep house. That's why Anya's here. You're supposed to write. This is not Ozzie and Harriet—I don't earn all the money and you don't wait for me in the goddamn window."

"I know. But…."

"But what? What's the other version?"

"I don't know. Fast cars and passports and calling stories in from weird places. I know I sound like a spoiled brat, but I hear some young reporter on National Public Radio reporting from Beirut and I want to be there."

"I knew it." Michael shook his head in disgust. "You want to be in the middle of a drama, don't you?"

"I don't know," I said helplessly. "I just feel like such a dilettante."

"A dilettante? Maggie, we cooked up this life we have together. You never said you wanted to work full time, nevermind calling in stories from places where people get blown up every day."

"I know," I said feebly.

"And then you go and take this job at *Small Town* without so much as a discussion with me. You'd have killed me if I took a new job without talking to you."

"I screwed up," I started.

"Yeah, well… and there may be some nut out there ready to get another notch in his gun by knocking off the new editor."

"Walking stick," I faltered, "not a gun."

Michael shook my shoulders. "Look at me!"

He got up, picked up our glasses and walked into the kitchen. I heard a cupboard open, and then slam shut. He came back into the living room, refilled glasses in hand.

"Thank you," I sniffled.

"We're going to talk about this now," said Michael. "And then I don't want to talk about it again. Ever. And I want you to know how furious I am at you. I feel like this is the worst in a long line of feminist propaganda crap—and what makes me really angry is that I bought into all of it. I did! Goddamnit, I've tried to out-Alan Alda all of them. I married you because you were the smartest, funniest woman I knew. I'm not trying to get in your way, but we agreed together to all this—this house, these kids, the dog, the cats, everything! Now it's not dangerous enough for you. Now it bores you. Maybe I bore you."

"Michael, you can't bore me! You don't bore me. I meant it—I do love our life together. But this isn't feminist propaganda. People ask you what you do—you tell them you're a lawyer. It's a real job, you've got a title and an office."

"I can't believe you're saying this. Is that what you want? A title and an office?"

"I don't know. Maybe I do. Maybe I need all the trappings so I know how to structure my time. As it is, I'm always scrambling for my deadlines, daydreaming half the morning, and then making excuses."

"That's bullshit. You always make your deadlines."

"Just barely."

Michael looked exasperated. "I can't believe we're fighting over your deadlines. You'd just barely make deadlines if you had a suite of offices, six titles and a battery of secretaries. You like that rush of brinkmanship—which is, I think, why I'm so pissed at you. I don't think you fell in love with Quentin. I think you liked the goddamn adventure of juggling him and your work and still being little Miss Semi-Perfect Homemaker."

I shivered. Something told me Michael had come perilously close to the truth.

"You're right," I said. "I mean, you may be right. I mean, I do care about Quentin, I did. And I did feel something sexual for him."

Michael looked grim. "If you did, you can kindly shut the fuck up about it."

"But you were right about the main thing. It felt like an adventure."

Michael moved over to the hassock at my feet. He took my hand and put it on his chest. "Let me tell you about adventures, about danger, *cara*. You feel this?" I felt his heart, a little fast, pounding in his chest. "That's the heart of a jealous, possessive man. If there's another adventure, it will be your last."

I looked in his eyes. "Are you threatening me, Michael?"

He nodded. "I won't hurt you. I don't think I could. But I will want to—so I will leave." He let go of my hand. "Do you understand?"

"I understand."

"Good."

"But I want to keep the job, at least for now."

"Title and an office?"

"No. Well, maybe a little. At least," I touched his face, "it'll keep me out of worse trouble."

Late that night, after we'd made fierce and not particularly affectionate love, I wrapped up in my robe and came downstairs. I felt as if I'd been underwater for too long, had struggled to the surface, and wondered if I could still breathe on my own. Had my wicked ways turned my wife-and-mother self into another person? Had I really strayed for reasons that sounded so self-centered and frivolous in the telling? I made a cup of chamomile tea and carried it into the living room. With just one lamp lit, the light fell soft and golden in a pool around my chair and the side table where my tea rested. Next to the tea lay the bundle of Quentin's letters.

I picked up the letters. They sat in my lap for a moment while I half heartedly wrestled with my conscience. Curiosity won out over a reluctance to invade Quentin's privacy. Rationalizations leaked into my mind. I would figure this out! I would restore order! I'd gone back to the straight and narrow, and I would stay there. No more mysteries, no more lies, no more fantasy alternative lives—and solving Quentin's murder would be a terrific start. For one guilty moment, it occurred to me that this could be yet another adventure, one other way to rebel against my sweet suburban life.

I sipped the tea and thought about Inspector Moon, how cranky this would make him, but how, somehow, I would feel less embarrassed about my straying if the murder were wrapped up and we could put it all behind us. I sighed. Somehow, Nancy Drew's motivations seemed purer than mine. But then, with Hannah the housekeeper watching her like a hawk, poor Nancy never had time for inappropriate love affairs.

I slipped the ribbon off the letters and shuffled through, looking at return addresses. Quentin's acquaintance was wide and international. And old-fashioned—paper instead of electronics.

Fortified with another sip of tea, I began reading. Letters from writers, from friends in Nice, Barcelona, and Greenwich, Connecticut. Many were from women, and the unfamiliar handwriting and distant intimacy they suggested gave me a little frisson of jealousy again.

"Oh, Maggie," I said aloud, "Cut it out." With that, the Riddler, the youngest and wildest of the cats, stirred from his drowse on the couch. He stretched, spied company, and made the trip to my lap in two leaps.

"One more letter, Riddler," I said. "And then it's off to bed for us."

The last letter was postmarked London and dated two weeks ago.

Dear Quent,

How odd to hear from you after so many years. I'm a bit of a grudge holder, so it had never occurred to me to "bury the hatchet" as you Yanks say. But I'm glad you and Giovanni have hooked up, and that life is good to you. He's a talented fellow, and the misfortunes that came his way never seemed quite deserved to me. Times have changed, I daresay, and all that bloody fuss might not have happened if we were young today—instead of thirty years ago.

In fact, I find myself quite cheery thinking of you paying us a call next spring. Do let us know when you'll be here and we'll have you round to the flat. Leslie's health is a little fragile these days. So we stay quiet and try to cram our fun in the good days. It actually suits me to live quietly—that may surprise you! But I treasure my students—even the misguided ones who read all those faddish American writers—and the life Leslie and I have together.

Stay well, dear fellow. Now that I've put pen to paper, I find myself thinking of you with great affection.

Best,
Douglas

PS Thanks for your kind words about the new biography. Until it was out at the booksellers, I wasn't, as the old lady said to Gully himself, "fit for the gypsies."

The Riddler snuggled close and swished his tail under my nose. I sneezed and felt in my robe pocket for tissues. No luck.

With a sigh, I tucked Riddler under my arm and headed for the stairs. Who was Giovanni? Who was Douglas? And what hatchet did they have to bury? Surely, just a little investigation wouldn't hurt. "It's the kind of adventure to have without a diaphragm," I said to Riddler. But he was already busy with his own adventures in feline dreamdom.

TRANSATLANTIC DETECTION

Things seemed better at breakfast than they'd been since Quentin was killed.

Michael read the funnies aloud to all of us, teased Anya about her newest beau, and cajoled Josh into finishing his orange juice.

"Come on, boys," he said.

"Hustle those plates into the kitchen and I'll drop you off at school. Mom's got a title now and she's got to get to her office."

"It's temporary," I muttered.

"Cheer up," he said, helping Zach with his jacket. "Maybe you'll take to organizational life. You can have your people get back to my people about what's for dinner. Very post-feminist."

The boys raced out the door. I caught Michael by the arm. "Do you hate me?" I asked and held my breath waiting for the answer.

He kissed me lightly on the lips. "No. I don't hold grudges."

I whispered, "Thank you."

"And I don't forget."

I stiffened. "That sounds like a life sentence, Michael."

He shrugged my arm off. "Good. That's how it's supposed to sound."

"Michael," I started to protest.

He held up his hand. "Of course, maybe our friend John Moon will decide I really did kill Quentin. Life sentence for me, and lifetime freedom for you to screw around."

I was speechless.

He grinned. "Just kidding, *cara*. Lighten up. Besides, the hockey team would have to go out and find a new center."

Then they were gone.

Michael wasn't really a suspect. At least, it didn't seem that way from my conversation with Moon. Of course, I could call Moon and just ask him. Well, not just ask right out, but maybe... inquire.

I poured another cup of coffee and pulled Douglas's letter from last night out of my pocket. Then I reached for the phone, thinking about calling Inspector Moon. It seemed as if I might have useful information, which perhaps he'd be willing to trade me for the reassurance that Michael wasn't remotely a suspect.

I glanced at the clock. Just after eight, too early to call Moon. But on the other hand, my scalp prickled, the perfect time to call London.

"Bad idea," I said aloud, antidote to the "adventure without a diaphragm" revelation of last night.

"You shouldn't play detective, Maggie. Bad, bad idea." Then I thought about Michael's dark joke at the kitchen door. It was my fault; I had gotten us into this mess. I should—I could—get us out. The police were busy; certainly they could use the help of a concerned citizen like me. I took a sip of coffee. For a moment, I dutifully considered my motives. Was I interested in helping the cops because it would help Michael, or because I knew I was just as smart as Moon, or just because? "This is a terrible idea," I said aloud. Then, I dialed. It was just after four in the afternoon in London, and Sara Jenkins would be getting the children's tea. What harm could it do to ask for her help?

"Sara? It's Maggie."

"Maggie! I can't believe you called. Colin's having the worst time practicing. I wish you were here to help."

"What's the piece?"

"It's not a piece. It's one of those fill-in-as-you-go notebooks on music theory."

"Uh huh, what's he studying?" I glanced at the clock again, getting impatient. Colin's transatlantic musical coaching was ticking away at many cents a minute.

"Intervals. He says he can't hear the difference between a fourth and a fifth. Is that right? Aren't they things to drink?"

I laughed. "Tell him to go sit at the piano and play fourths and fifths with a little trick in mind: the fourths always sound like 'here comes the bride' and the fifths always sound like 'twinkle, twinkle, little star.' It works anywhere on the piano."

"Oh, Maggie, thanks."

"Wait, wait, don't hang up! I called you. Listen, Sara, are you still tutoring university students?"

"Yes."

"Well, I have a little academic detecting for you to do. I'm looking for a professor."

"What's the name?"

"That's what I don't know, exactly. His first name's Douglas, he's married to someone named Leslie, and I think he's written a biography rather recently."

"About?"

"Isn't Gully the name of one of Joyce Cary's characters?"

"*The Horse's Mouth*, Gully Jimson."

"That's what I thought. Okay, my guess is it's a bio about Cary."

"So you want me to ask 'round about this guy? Then what?"

"Just get me his name and a number where I can reach him. And the sooner the better. I'll explain later. I'm late for work."

Sara chuckled. "You must be on deadline again."

"Deadline nothing. I've got a real job!" And with that, I hung up.

Half an hour later I was in *Small Town's* offices. I picked up a stack of pink message slips at the front desk, poured coffee, and settled in behind Quentin's desk. Uncle Alf, Inspector Moon, Manfred Smith, the writer on the January resolution piece had all called.

Linda Quoc, the art director, pushed the door open, her arms full of layouts. As usual, she was in requisite designer black, head to toe, except for her hot pink eyeglass frames.

"Maggie, you've got to look at these spreads for January. Glen's seen them all and wants your approval before we commission art. And I've got portfolios of illustrators we want to use for this issue, so please take a look so I can call these people and get them going."

"Show me," I said. "I don't want to return any of these phone calls anyway."

I approved layouts, shifted some stories around, trying to recapture Quentin's unerring eye for leading with substance yet leavening with enough sexy fluff to keep people reading. Then I looked at illustrator portfolios. The last one bothered me.

"Who is this guy?" I asked Linda.

"John Orlando," she said. "You met him at Quentin's funeral. Stocky dude in Banana Republic regalia." She perched her glasses atop her elegantly spiked haircut and looked at me. "Do you like his work?"

I leafed through the portfolio again. He worked in pen and ink, dense fine-lined drawings that looked like the op-ed pages of *The New York Times*. All had elaborate, tiny signatures, with the last "O" of Orlando filled in with heavy ornamentation.

"It's okay."

"But?"

I closed the portfolio.

"But I think it's awfully heavy-handed for *Small Town*."

She sighed. "If you like him, Linda," I said hastily, "I'm okay with it. I gather he does a lot of work for the magazine."

"I don't like him," she said crossly. "I never did like him. But Quentin was his... his advocate, and then when Glen came, he seemed to agree. Twice I put my foot down, because the assignments he turned in were so grim and depressing I couldn't stand to use them."

"What happened?"

"Quent supported me, so we didn't use the drawings. We paid a very handsome kill fee, but Glen was cranky for a week."

Kill fees, the money you pay an artist or writer for commissioning a piece and then not using it, can deplete a magazine budget and throw a schedule off track.

She tapped her pencil on the drawing. "I don't even know what he was cranky about. Quent or Glen, I don't remember which one, managed to persuade the people over at the Sunday magazine supplement to buy that drawing. I offered to think about it for another issue, but Glen and Quent said that Orlando's drawings are—what did they say?—*perishable*. You've got to use them when they've been commissioned or they go bad."

"They go bad? Since when has illustration become spoil-able? That's nuts. It's not like they're topical or political cartoons or anything."

Linda smiled. "I couldn't agree more."

"I hate to be a new broom," I said. "But I think he's wrong for this resolutions story. It's supposed to be lighthearted and fun."

Linda smiled. "Fine," she said. "You break the news to Glen."

She got up to leave. "Chicken!" I called after her.

"Hey, Maggie," she said. "You may actually work out as a boss."

"I may, huh?" I asked. "Okay, boss's privilege. I've got a question for you."

She leaned against the doorjamb. "Go ahead."

"How come I've never seen you in anything except black—ever except at Quentin's funeral?"

"Oh, Maggie, that's a personal question. Don't you ever read that multicultural, diversity sensitivity stuff? You know Asians don't like to answer personal questions."

I grinned. "Uh huh, I know," I said. "But seeing as how you left Vietnam when you were five, and you already told me you grew up on Count Chocula cereal and Barbie dolls, I figure you're just obnoxiously American enough to blab about yourself like the rest of us. So tell me, is it true they make you take the all-black pledge in design school?"

She laughed. "Sort of. I do think color is way too intense to use casually. So it keeps me calm if there's no color on me. Plus, now that I have kids, it's all I can do to get out of the house in the morning. And they wear all those crayon colors that make my eyes hurt. When I look in my own closet and the choices are black, black, and black, it makes it quick and easy to get dressed."

"Okay, that's everyday," I said, "but what about the turquoise?"

She looked away, seeming to consider, then back at me. "Some friend of Quentin's brought a bolt of turquoise silk back from Hong Kong and Claire didn't want it. So he brought it here and one day when I was sitting at the table in his office, he jumped up and held the fabric next to my face. He made me stand in front of a mirror with him and look at myself with all that silk wrapped around my shoulders."

Her eyes filled with tears. "It was as if I was seeing myself in some different way. I looked, I don't know, exotic or glamorous or something." She thought for a minute, "I looked like a more intriguing version of me."

I thought about Quentin in the millinery department at Saks, buying me just the right hat.

I handed Linda a tissue. "I know what you mean," I said.

"So anyway," she continued, "I took the silk and my mother made me that jumpsuit you saw at the funeral. Pretty peculiar, wasn't it? Everyone else puts on black for a funeral, and I put on turquoise. But I thought Quentin would like it." She swiped at her eyes with the tissue. "I'm getting back to work. See you later."

I turned to the message slips. One of the feature writers, predictably, wanted a teeny-weeny extension. Uncle Alf was just "checking in," and wanted me to know he'd be reviewing the books very carefully each month. And could Michael and I have dinner with him and Claire later in the week? Just to chat?

"Of course," I said cheerfully, and hung up, ruminating about what horrible reparations I would have to make to Michael in return for a dinner with Alf and Claire.

"Dentists," I muttered to myself. "I'll have to take the kids to every single dental appointment for the next five years."

Glen stood in the doorway. "You're not doing well, dear heart," he said. "You're talking to yourself about dentists."

I motioned for him to come sit down.

"What do you and Corinne do about dentists, Glen?"

"I pay their infernal bills," he said.

"No, I mean about who takes the kids when," I said. "We're always negotiating."

"Ah, you Americans with modern marriages," he said. "We don't negotiate. Since Corinne's a schoolteacher, it's hard for her to get away. So I always take the little ones."

I patted his hand. "You're a good dad, Glen."

"It's all I ever wanted, Maggie. It was a pleasure too long deferred. When I left the priesthood, I wasn't dreaming about women or riches or fancy houses. I was dreaming about being a real father."

The intercom buzzed and Gertie's voice squawked. "Maggie? It's that Inspector Moon. Again."

I looked apologetically at Glen. "I better take this." He gestured towards the door. "Want a bit of privacy?"

I shook my head and picked up the phone.

Moon's voice came over receiver, cool and mannerly. "Mrs. Fiori? Remember the file you were looking for at Mr. Hart's flat?"

"Yes?"

"I believe we have it," he said. "If you'd like to drop by my office, we can go through it together."

I glanced at my watch and calculated. "Good, I wanted to talk to you anyway. I'll be by around two. Is that okay?"

"Fine. By the way, my colleagues met with your husband the other day."

"So I heard," I said frostily.

"Relax," he said, "we have to talk to everyone. I told you Michael's not really a suspect. My team said he just seems like a good guy." I tasted bile.

"A good guy?" I said. "Is that how cops talk? He's my husband.

He's a helluva lot more than a good guy."

Moon was quiet for a moment. "I'm not the one who needs convincing, Mrs. Fiori. I skate next to him every week. You can tell a lot about a man by the way he behaves on the ice."

I thought about watching Michael play hockey. To a spectator like me, he looked fierce, bloodthirsty, and unstoppable. I'm not sure I wanted to hear Moon's opinion.

He continued, "I'll look forward to seeing you this afternoon."

I looked miserably at Glen.

"Not wise to piss off the constabulary, Maggie," he said.

"I know. Can you believe this? They had Michael in for questioning."

Glen shrugged. "They're questioning everybody. Did Michael know something?"

I swallowed. "Well, nothing helpful. Quentin was really *my* friend, after all."

Glen caught my eye and then looked away. "Yes, indeed. He was."

"Well, anyway," I muttered, "Inspector Moon thinks he found the file on that story Quent wanted us to do."

Glen raised his eyebrows. "Really? Where'd Quentin have it tucked away?"

"I don't know. I'll find out this afternoon."

The intercom buzzed again. "Maggie, it's Calvin Bright. He says he needs you for just one minute."

I punched the hands-free button and Calvin's voice filled the room.

"Be quick," I said, "I'm in the middle of a meeting."

"Maggie? Just starting the job and you're already pretentious. A speakerphone, yet!"

"Calvin," I began.

"Listen, gotta run. But I've made a reservation for lunch at Cock of the Walk. I want to see if we can figure out what Quent's story was about."

I considered. I was getting pretty interested in the subject myself. "What time? I've got to meet Inspector Moon at two."

"11:45. Be there or be square," and Calvin was gone.

"Want to come, Glen?" I asked.

He thought for a moment. "Thank you, no. I'm not much at playing Sherlock Holmes." He stood. "I'll catch up with you later."

"Oh, Glen, wait," I said as he started for the door. "I wanted to talk to you about Orlando doing the illustration for the resolutions story."

He paused. "Yes?"

I forged ahead. "Can we take a pass? I really think he's wrong for the piece."

"Quentin suggested him. For this story. For this issue."

"Yeah, I know. But I think he's wrong. We'll use him for something else."

Glen was quiet. "Come on, Glen," I coaxed. "I don't think this was Quentin's dying wish or anything, that we use Orlando for this story."

Glen's face went blank. "You're the chief." And he was gone.

The phone buzzed, "Maggie, it's Michael."

Michael's voice sounded matter-of-fact and friendly. "*Cara*, I'm going to be in the city for a conference this afternoon. Want to grab a sandwich together?"

"Oh, I can't. I'm meeting Calvin at that place Quentin wanted us to cover—you know, Cock of the Walk?"

"Oh."

"Why don't you join us?"

"No, thanks. Not my cup of tea."

"The restaurant? Me? Calvin?" I pushed.

"Who knows?" said Michael vaguely. "Well, how's your morning in executive life?"

"Swell," I said grimly. "I've asked Linda Quoc personal questions, irritated Glen, thrown my weight around, and I have to go see Moon after lunch. He's got a file he wants me to see."

"Have fun, Maggie," said Michael. "I'll see you tonight, assuming you can squeeze us in." He hung up.

I listened to the dial tone. "S.O.B.," I pronounced to no one in particular. "Smug, smart-mouth, vengeful prick." Mmm, that felt better. Surely there was some way I could feel self-righteous about this.

On the way out the door to lunch, I knocked on Puck Morris's door. His was the only corner of the office that showed clear defiance of Quentin's prejudices about clean lines and white and gray as background colors of choice. The walls were hung with posters that looked like moments stolen from MTV, Puck's black leather jacket was flung on a chair that leaked stuffing from every seam, and I could hear faint bass and drum sounds from the iPod that held him in thrall. I touched him on the shoulder. He looked up, pulled the earbuds out, and grinned.

"Hey, Maggie, how they hangin'?"

"Hanging? Just ducky, Mr. Morris."

He started to put the earbuds back in, and I stopped him.

"Wait a sec, Puck," I said. "I want to talk."

He gestured at the chair, and I sat.

"Shoot, boss," he said. "But make it snappy. I've got a lunch date with the manager over at the Warfield. She's got a half a dozen new high-concept metal groups she wants me to hear."

"High-concept?"

"You know," he said. "Kind of like this generation's version of The Ramones. They know about three chords, can't carry a tune, but they dress great and have lots of attitude."

I laughed. "I smell a raft of 'Pucked by Morris' t-shirts coming their way."

"You bet." Puck leaned back in his chair, smoothed his thinning sandy hair with both hands, and gave me a level gaze.

"So how *are* you doing, Maggie?"

I shrugged. "Up and down."

"Must be tough."

I took a deep breath. "Puck, I know you didn't mean to do it, but your little revelations to Inspector Moon put me in a tight spot."

He picked up a paper clip and began straightening it out. "Hey, I didn't mean to leak anything."

"Yeah, well, what is it the road to hell is paved with?"

"Well, Holy Christ, Maggie, it was kind of dumb. I mean Quentin is—was—a pretty interesting guy, but I sure as hell don't see what you were doing mixed up with him. I mean, Michael's, well, he's…."

"He's great," I said brusquely. "This wasn't about Michael and I didn't really want to discuss my personal life."

He tossed the paperclip up in the air and caught it with the same hand. "Yeah? So what did you want to discuss?" He was clearly perturbed.

I felt my face go hot. "I'm sorry, Puck, I don't mean to be rude. I'm just feeling so confused and upset—and as if I've screwed up in a pretty big way."

"Not my business, lady," he said, "but I've got to agree."

"Well, thanks," I said. "We all make mistakes."

He grinned. "Not me." He held up his left hand and wiggled the fingers at me. "No ring, see? No commitments, I fool around with, what's the word?"

"Impunity," I said dryly.

"You got it," he said. "But seriously, I'm sorry I spilled to Moon. I didn't mean to."

"How'd you know?" I asked.

"I dunno. I just did. Quentin wasn't as discreet as he might have been."

"You mean he said something?"

"No, just the way he talked about you. And Quentin always had a little something on the side, as long as I've known him. And the way he kinda championed you. Quentin wasn't all that nice to people unless he had a reason. I just figured it had to be you."

"There must have been something else. Something concrete."

Puck considered. "Mmm, not really. Well, I saw you guys dance at the Art Directors's Christmas party last year. Looked like lust-in-the-foxtrot to me."

I remembered that night. Michael had been at a seminar, so I'd been alone. Except for Quentin. I squirmed, thinking about how we looked on the dance floor, me with just enough champagne inside to act silly.

"So Quentin always had a sweetie," I said. "I guess I knew that all along. I didn't kill him, but maybe one of those other side interests did." I surveyed Puck. "Tell me about my many predecessors."

"Come on, Maggie, you don't really want to hear that stuff, do you? The cops pried it all out of me already."

"Try me," I said grimly.

"Let's see. There was Monica Swanson, the lady who owned the photography gallery on Sutter. And maybe her son. Quentin went through his younger man phase for a while, even before Stuart."

"Maybe Mom got pissed at both of them."

"I'm sure she did," said Puck. "But they moved to Chicago last year."

"Go on. Who else?"

"The hostess at Hot Licks, Esther or Aster or something like that; they call her 'Stare'. Geez, I didn't blame him. She is one unbelievable babe. And Andrea."

"Andrea? Are you kidding?"

"Before she started contributing to the magazine. I don't think it was a big deal."

"Jesus H. Christ."

"No," said Puck, "not him."

"Puck!"

"Hey, you asked. I told you he always had something going on the side."

"For what it's worth," I said, "I wasn't exactly on the side. Quentin and Claire had already separated."

Puck shook his head. "That, I would have to say, is what you call your 'distinction without a difference.' If you know what I mean."

"So," I said, "enough about all these sordid personal lives. I wanted to ask you about music."

"Puck's all ears, honey."

"You hadn't talked Quentin into listening to new music, had you?"

"New music? You mean that New Age soulful harp and flute crap?"

"No, rock. Metal."

"Are you kidding? Quentin? Get real."

"That's what I thought. Okay, think about this: Who among Quentin's friends likes that kind of music?"

"Stuart?"

"Who else? Quentin ever ask you for tickets to a concert for a friend?"

He frowned. "Not that I remember. Is it important?"

"I don't know. Maybe, but think about it, okay?"

I launched myself out of the easy chair. "This office is quite a sight, Puck."

"I know," he grinned. "Isn't it great? Quentin just hated it. Come on, I'll walk you out."

CHASING THE WILD GOOSE

I was running late, so Calvin was already at the bar by the time I hurried into Cock of the Walk.

He raised his glass and waved me over. I hopped on the bar stool next to him and ordered a tonic water and lime. I definitely needed my wits about me.

"Calvin," I said, "your drink."

He looked at it. "What about it?

"It has a little umbrella in it."

"It does, doesn't it?" He looked over my shoulder and waved. "We're over here," he said, and I turned in time to see Andrea walk in.

"Well, well," she said, "it's the boss. Drinking at noon, I see."

I lifted my glass in a toast. "It's research, Ms. Storch."

"I invited Andrea to join us," said Calvin. "I didn't think you'd mind. *Small Town* is buying, right?"

I looked around the restaurant. Somehow, it didn't seem like Quentin's kind of place, a little too "done," with giant roosters everywhere; on the cocktail napkins, patterned on the carpet, and worst of all, a giant rooster mural. Each rooster had a San Francisco celebrity's face painted under the comb. Though my biology was shaky, I could have sworn roosters were males of the species. Yet, here were socialites, dowagers, cabaret singers, even a past mayor herself, masquerading as cocks of the walk. Ah, San Francisco.

Calvin touched my arm. "Join the party, Mags, we can sit

down now." A short, stocky man holding menus was gesturing us to follow him. He looked familiar from the back and then he turned around. It was John Orlando, the illustrator I'd just axed from *Small Town*'s next issue.

"Mr. Orlando?" I said, "I'm Maggie Fiori. We met at Quentin's service." He regarded me carefully and held out his hand. "Oh, yes, I remember. Filling in at *Small Town,* are you?"

"Yes," I indicated Calvin and Andrea. "You've all met?"

Round of introductions, though everyone insisted they'd crossed paths before. San Francisco is like that. Two hundred people in the entire city, a friend once insisted to me, and everything else is done with mirrors.

After he left the table, Andrea closed her menu and sniffed.

"I know that sniff by now," said Calvin. "It means our own Ice Queen has something negative to say and wild horses wouldn't drag it out of her."

"Come on, Andrea," I said. "Give. Pretend the wild horses have come and gone."

She folded her hands in front of her. "Well, I was just thinking that Orlando is a man of many hats."

"I know what you mean," I said.

"I don't," said Calvin. "Enlighten me a little, ladies."

"He's an illustrator," I said. "In fact, he does work for *Small Town* besides passing out menus here. And," I sipped my drink, "as an illustrator, he's a terrific maître d'."

"Maggie," said Andrea, "how unkind. Besides, he's more than a menu-passer-outer. I think he's part-owner of this place. At least that's what Quentin told me."

"So talk, Andrea," I pushed. "Is that what you meant about wearing a lot of hats?"

"I guess," she said. "He always seems like a fellow with a lot of irons in a lot of fires." She sighed. "Hats, fires. I seem to be mixing oodles of metaphors."

"See," interrupted Calvin, "this is why you're so appealing, Starchy. Real people don't say 'fellow,' they say 'guy.' And oodles, wow! I love that whole boarding school sound you've got going on."

Andrea looked exasperated.

"Calvin," I said, "would you like to let up on the sociolinguistics commentary for a minute so we can concentrate?"

"Sure," he answered. "I just thought you'd be interested to know how sexy it is."

Andrea ignored him. "Anyway, he's been showing up at the magazine rather frequently over the past few years with his big black portfolio."

"Oh, baby," said Calvin. "I love it when you talk dirty to me."

"Quiet. Anyway, he'd just moved here from England, and I guess Quentin was being nice to him. But it's as if he was launching a new career just for the fun of it. Illustrator, restaurant owner, and with no visible means of support."

"Maybe he was one of the day-trading zillionaires," I said. "They must have had them in the boom times in England, too."

"Maybe," she said doubtfully. "I know it's not polite, but I asked Quentin once."

"You asked a nosy question?" I was shocked.

"Well, not directly. I just wondered what Orlando had done before to be so flush with resources."

"What'd Quentin say?"

"He said that Orlando was a very entrepreneurial..." she glanced at Calvin, "entrepreneurial guy."

Orlando was greeting a crowd of new arrivals. Lots of air-kissing and hugs. We all surveyed him.

"Well, maybe he used to teach art," I speculated. "Lots of illustrators supplement their income doing that."

"Maggie," said Andrea, "be serious. Art teachers don't get rich."

"Wait," said Calvin, "maybe there was some huge sexual harassment scandal back home in England, and he had to leave town with his little black portfolio and come to San Francisco. Maybe he put the moves on some little cupcake from Devon or Dorset and her daddy paid him off to get out of town."

Andrea and I exchanged glances. "Calvin," I said, "Orlando's gay. If there was a sex scandal it had to be with some guy cupcake from Devon or Dorset."

"That's cool," said Calvin. "I say take those school romances anyway you can get them. Hey girls, want to hear my authentically African-American Sam Cooke rendition of "Teach Me Tonight?" Andrea and I ignored him.

Lunch was unremarkable. The usual assortment of Chinese chicken salad, grilled veggies, thresher shark, ahi, and lots of kiwi-raspberry embroidery on the desserts.

Orlando stopped by the table twice, checking to see if we were happy.

"He did it," said Calvin flatly.

"Did what?"

"Killed Quentin."

"Uh huh. And where does this theory come from?" I asked.

"Simple. The guy's clearly hiding something. He's had multiple lives, he's an artist, he runs a restaurant, he corrupted sweet young boys in some godforsaken English village, he's on the lam."

"Calvin," Andrea interrupted, "control yourself. We're making all this stuff up. That's how dreadful rumors get started."

"Well, I contend he's at least a suspect," said Calvin.

"Fine," I said, glancing at my watch, "he's an official suspect, along with just about everybody else Quentin ever knew. And since you brought the subject up, let's talk about it. Isn't that why we're here?"

"Why are we here?" asked Andrea. "I thought this was an eccentric choice for lunch. But then, you two keep coming up with unusual places to dine."

Calvin grinned. "Come on, baby, you said the burgers at Hamburger Mary's were great."

"Well, culinary adventures aside," I said, "Calvin and I were here to talk about Quentin's story."

"The question," said Calvin, "is what the story was, and if it had anything to do with Quentin's death."

Andrea reached inside her blazer and pulled a fountain pen out of her pocket. "Goodie. I'll take notes. I love a little organization mixed in with all this chaos." She looked doubtful for a moment.

"Actually, aren't the police supposed to do these things?"

"They do. They are. But...." I hesitated. I didn't want to tell Calvin and Andrea that my interest in finding Quentin's killer derived from a growing conviction that if we could just sort out the murder, all the other messes in my life would magically straighten themselves out as well. I felt responsible, especially for the way Michael had been dragged into this. Plus, every time I thought about Michael having to discuss my infidelity with some guy on his hockey team, my skin crawled with shame.

Calvin and Andrea were watching me, puzzled.

"Look, the cops said it wasn't a stranger who did this, plus Quentin was our friend," I said, catching Andrea's eye. Couldn't hurt to let her wonder what I knew about how "friendly" she'd been with Quentin. "So shouldn't we help figure this out?" I sounded lame, even to me. "If nothing else, we'll sell a lot of issues when we solve the case."

Andrea looked horrified.

I touched her hand. "Andrea," I said gently. "I'm just making a bad joke."

She smiled wanly. "I know." She tapped her pen on the napkin. "Okay, what do we know about the Cock of the Walk story?"

"We know the story couldn't have been a restaurant review," I said. "Lisbet would do that. What else?"

"An exposé of some kind? Some health department thing?"

"Doesn't sound like *Small Town*," said Calvin.

"What can restaurants front for?" I mused. "Drugs? Gambling?" I looked around the room. As was usually the case in San Francisco restaurants, the waiters and bus staff comprised a mini-UN of ethnic and national origins. "Immigration?"

Andrea noted each possibility on the napkin.

"Maybe Quent was just doing Orlando a favor, promoting the restaurant," I offered.

"I don't know," said Andrea doubtfully. "PR fluff for a restaurant doesn't sound like Quentin's kind of story. Plus, why would he make such a big deal out of it to you?"

"Well, let's ask him," I said, catching sight of Orlando and waving him over.

"John, sit down with us a minute."

He glanced over his shoulder and looked uncomfortable. "Lunch is really a busy time," he protested.

"I know, I know, just for a second." He sat. We all looked at each other. I cleared my throat. "Terrible about Quentin, wasn't it?"

"Yes," he said. "Ghastly."

Calvin caught my eye and did a poor imitation of William F. Buckley, mouthing 'ghastly' in silence. I gave him the kind of look I give my boys when they're acting up at the table.

"You two were old friends?"

Orlando looked around the table. Calvin's face was carefully bland.

"We'd known each other for many years. After I moved here, I sent my portfolio over to *Small Town* and Quentin set up an appointment with your art director, Linda Quoc."

"Many years?" I persisted. "You grew up together?"

Orlando laughed shortly. "Not quite that many years. Although we did know each other in college."

"Really? In England?"

"Yes. In fact, I met Quentin in a workshop opera production. He played in the orchestra, and I sang—a very mediocre tenor, I must confess. Of course, since then, my musical tastes have broadened. Quentin's, I'm afraid, hadn't strayed much. He really didn't want to hear things that had been written in the last hundred years. Except for straight-ahead jazz, of course."

"And you do?" I asked politely.

"Oh, yes," he beamed, looking around the table. "We host a new music series here on Saturday afternoon. Lots of young talent. Even the odd rock sound now and again." He patted my hand.

"You have youngsters, don't you, Ms. Fiori? You should bring them by one afternoon."

I smiled noncommittally. "And Quentin's ex-wife, Claire? You know her?" I prodded.

He looked distracted and lifted the corners of his mouth in a token smile. "Claire? Yes, certainly. We share a few… causes."

"Oh, that's right," I felt myself babbling. "You hosted a benefit here for Claire? As part of your opening?"

Orlando seemed to relax. "Yes, Claire's on the board of Skunkworks. It's an AIDS group, perhaps you've heard of it?"

None of us had. We said so. "What's the name about?"

"Tom Peters wrote about the Skunkworks idea in his first business book."

"*In Search of Excellence*?" I asked.

"Right, right. It's the idea of speeding up innovation. You keep a small, flexible group, no bureaucracy, and you get really creative. So Skunkworks funds creative independent efforts in research and distribution. New drugs, things like that."

"No bureaucracy?" I asked. "So no FDA?"

"Exactly." He corrected himself hastily. "I mean, eventually, the FDA has to be involved, of course, but our group helps jump-start the process."

Silence fell. Andrea cleared her throat. "You know, Mr. Orlando," she said idly, "this really is a small world."

"Oh?" he said, getting to his feet.

"Yes," she said. "Quentin had assigned Maggie and Calvin to do a story about your restaurant."

He sat back down. "That so? Wasn't that lovely of him?"

"Well," I hedged, "we don't know that it was lovely of him, exactly. We didn't know what the story was all about."

"Really?" he said, looking around the restaurant.

"Did you?"

"No, so sorry, afraid I can't help you," he said. He stood.

"Of course, what do they say? Doesn't matter what they write about you as long as they spell your name right."

LINDA LEE PETERSON 117

"Well, we're at a loss to pursue the story now," I said.

"Ah, well, dies with Quentin, I guess. Pity, but that was another country."

"And now the wench is dead," I said under my breath. Calvin and Andrea looked puzzled.

"Duchess of Malfi," I explained.

"Sorry, you were saying?"

He gave a little wave. "Nothing, nothing of importance. Perhaps another time. Now I've really got to run."

As he disappeared into the crush around the bar, our waitress arrived with coffee and a folded piece of paper.

"Are you Maggie Fiori?" she asked. I nodded.

"A phone call came in for you. They said your cell phone wasn't picking up." She handed me the note. It read: "Please come to Josh's school as soon as you can. He's not feeling well."

"I'll be right back," I said, lunch turning to stone in my stomach. "I've got to call my son's school." The answering machine was on. "You have reached The Webster School. All of the teachers are busy and cannot come to the phone. Please leave a message at the tone." I did, and returned to the table. "It's lunch time, the damn answering machine is on at school. I've got to run, gang," I said. "Josh is sick."

"Isn't Michael closer to school?" asked Andrea.

"He is, but he's in the city today. Besides, when kids are sick they always want Mom." Calvin caught my arm. "Maggie, how about Inspector Moon?"

I paused. "Why don't you two meet him? Andrea's from the magazine, I'm sure Moon will release the file to her. I'll give him a quick call on my way out."

On the drive across the Bay Bridge, every mother anxiety in the world came up. "This is what I get for taking a real job," I muttered. "God's not a feminist. This is His way of saying I'm supposed to be home."

Half an hour later, I was standing in the director's office. "Mrs. Schwab? I came as soon as I could. Where's Josh? Is he resting?"

She looked up from her desk. "Mrs. Fiori? Is something wrong?"

"I got a message that you called, that Josh was ill." She looked puzzled. "I didn't call. Josh is fine. At least, I think he's fine."

Fine he was. Out on the playground after lunch, practicing baskets with fierce concentration. He barely looked over at me. "Hi, Mom. What's up?"

I felt disoriented. "Nothing, sweetie. Come over here a minute."

"Aw, Mom." He shot, recaptured the ball, and dribbled it over to me.

"Honey, you feel fine?" I smoothed the hair off his forehead. He brushed me away.

"Fine, fine."

"You didn't tell one of the teachers you felt lousy? You didn't feel like you were getting one of your upset stomachs?"

He regarded me with suspicion. "Why? Did somebody say I did?"

I hugged him to me. "Never mind, baby. Go shoot some more. I'll watch for a while."

There he went, all brown arms and legs, struggling to ape the graceful run, jump, shoot sequences he watched on television. While I watched, I thought.

"Hey," I called. "I'm going to talk to Mrs. Schwab. I'll catch you later."

Mrs. Schwab was waiting for me, looking ruffled. "I've checked around. No one called you."

I nodded. "Can I use your phone?" I rang The Cock of the Walk and asked to speak to the waitress. While I waited for her to come on the line, I ran over the possibilities. It had to be a stupid mix-up. But how? And just suppose it wasn't?

"Oh, hi, Mrs. Fiori," she said. "How's your son?"

"He's fine," I said shortly. "I was just wondering, did you take the call from his school?"

"No," she said. "It was the hostess, I think."

"May I speak with her?"

"Sure." She paused. "Is anything wrong?"

"No, no, just some confusion, I think." I pray, I said to myself.

The hostess answered promptly. She was sure about the message, she'd just relayed what the caller said.

"She asked for me?"

"Not she, he. The guy even described what you had on. He said it wasn't really an emergency, but he knew you'd want to get to school as soon as you could and he was sure you didn't mind your lunch being interrupted."

"Thanks." I put the receiver down and turned to Mrs. Schwab. "It was a man who called."

She shook her head. "Well, that narrows things down a bit. Joe Connolly, the art teacher, is the only possible suspect. He knows Josh and I sometimes ask him to track parents down in an emergency."

"Can I talk with him?"

"As it happens, I already did."

"He didn't call?"

"He says he didn't."

She touched my hand. "Can I get you a cup of coffee? You look a little shaky."

"Thanks." With a cup of coffee steaming in front of me, I pulled the phone over to check in on Zach. He was fine, the school director assured me. "Sorry to bother you," I said, as I felt my heart slow. "We had a little confusion at Josh's school and I'm just being neurotic." I hung up and called the office.

Gertie answered. "Maggie? How's Josh? Andrea called to tell us what happened."

"He's fine," I said. "It was just a mix-up. But I'm a little too creeped-out to leave him and head back to the city. Listen, is Glen there?"

"No, he's not. Oh, wait, I hear him coming down the hall."

Glen came on the line. "Hi, Maggie. Are you fine, now? Josh, too?"

I sighed. "Josh is fine. It was a false alarm. I think someone was playing a trick on me—and I don't much like it."

"Are you worried?"

"No, not really." I thought for a minute. "Well, I guess I am. I mean, I've been sitting here stewing about it and the only thing I can figure out is somebody didn't want me to keep my date with Moon."

"You were seeing the Inspector?"

"Yes," I said impatiently. "Remember he called? He's got Quent's file on that mystery story."

"Want me to send a messenger for the file?"

"No, I sent Andrea and Calvin."

"Ah," he said. "Clever idea."

"When Andrea comes back to the office, ask her to call me," I said.

"I'll do better than that," said Glen. "I'll bring the file by your house tonight."

"Oh, Glen, I can wait."

"No, no. I want you to look at the illustrator Linda's considering as a substitute for Orlando anyway. She wants to place a call to his agent tomorrow. He works in some remote farmhouse in eastern Montana. No phone."

"Couldn't she find someone more difficult? Speaking of artistic types, I had a little chat with your friend John Orlando today."

"Maggie, he's not exactly my friend. I believe he and Quent were friends. Went to school together, or something."

Mrs. Schwab tapped on the door. I waved her in. "Well, then," I said impatiently, "wouldn't he have gone to school with you, as well?"

"In a way," he said. "Different years, you know."

"I've got to run, Glen. I'll see you tonight, if you're sure it's convenient to come."

"It's fine, Maggie. I'll stop by about eight-thirty. I'd like to read my little ones a story first."

By now, it really was too late to go back into the city, so I assuaged my guilty feelings by stopping at the market and planning a better-than-usual weekday dinner. When Michael walked in the door, he let out a cheer and headed directly for the kitchen. I was at the stove stirring risotto.

"I think I like you having a regular job, *'cara*. I knew as soon as I opened the front door this wasn't Anya cooking. What is it?"

"Risotto with artichoke hearts and mushrooms."

Michael slipped his hand under the hair on my neck and massaged.

"What a little homemaker. Why is it that Scandinavian cooking can't smell like this?"

"I don't think reindeer fat compares very favorably with olive oil," I said.

Michael moved to the refrigerator. "You can't leave the pot, right? Have to keep stirring?

"Right."

"Well, then, here's a glass of wine for you." He handed it over with a flourish, "and one for me."

He sat at the scrubbed and scarred pine kitchen table, cleared Zach's crayoned airplane fantasies out of the way, and loosened his tie. "So tell me. Now that you're a fulfilled and gainfully employed woman, tough day at the office?"

I frowned.

"That good, huh?"

"No, it was fine. But something weird happened."

As I explained, Michael's grin faded.

"I don't like it, Maggie," he said.

"I don't either. I mean, maybe it's some silly misunderstanding— but maybe it isn't."

I turned the heat down on the risotto. "I keep thinking there must be something in that file. Glen's bringing it by after dinner."

"Maggie, whoever didn't want you to see the file knew exactly how to stop you. That's what I don't like."

"What do you mean?"

He gestured impatiently. "One, he knew Josh's name. Two, he knew you'd jump like a rabbit, that you worry about Josh's sensitive digestive system. Three, he knew where you were having lunch."

A little buzz went off in my head. "And four," I said turning from the stove. "He knew what I was wearing today!"

"He did?"

"Yes. The hostess who took the call said he described what I had on."

"That's a lot of people. Everyone at your office, Anya, the kids," he paused. "Me."

"It wasn't you, Michael."

"How do you know?"

"You'd never use the kids to keep me from doing something. You're too superstitious. You'd think that was tempting fate." I gestured in the air, like his mother, "*Mal'occhio*! Evil eye."

He laughed. "You're right." He sobered. "Really, Maggie, who else knew what you had on?"

"I don't know. That's what I keep asking myself."

"Unless," said Michael, "someone at your office—who saw you all morning—let someone at the school know."

"That's pretty conspiratorial," I said. The idea of a *Small Town* plus Webster School cabal seemed both sinister and ridiculous. When in doubt, eat. I tasted the risotto.

"Let's gather the mob. This is done. Just get the salad out of the fridge, would you?"

I spooned the risotto into my Aunt Sadye's rose-rimmed casserole. For her, it had held brisket and noodles, good *shabbas* food. For me, it was just as likely to hold what Michael called EC (ethnic cooking) or takeout.

Michael caught my arm as I kneed the swinging door open from the kitchen into the dining-room. "I'm not kidding. I don't like this one damn bit. Let's talk after dinner."

But after dinner, there was cleanup, baths, a story for Zach, and Josh begged for a game of checkers. When Glen rang the doorbell and was established in the living room with coffee, Michael summoned me into the kitchen.

"I'm going to let Anya put the kids to bed, Maggie," he said.

"I want to sit in on this conversation." He sounded proprietary, lawyerly and cranky. I raised my eyebrow at him. "Loosen up, Michael. I'm not a client."

"Good thing," he muttered under his breath.

While Michael cleared the last of the dinner clutter, I looked through the substitute portfolio Glen brought. "Looks fine," I said. "Go ahead and have Linda give the agent a ring."

"Good. I still think Orlando would have been a grand choice, but it's up to you."

"I'm sorry, I just don't agree, Glen," I said.

"Well, then," he said brusquely, "let's get on with it."

Glen glanced up as Michael came in. "Sorry to intrude," said Michael. "But I'm feeling just a little freaky about the mix-up this afternoon. It seems as if somebody didn't want Maggie to get her hands on this file."

Glen fished a manila file out of his briefcase. "Here it is. I can't imagine what's so dangerous in there."

"Hey," I asked, "did Moon say where they found it?"

"In Quentin's briefcase. They'd searched his flat, but they hadn't rummaged round the car yet. I guess he'd packed up his briefcase with what he needed to take to work."

I patted the couch. "Michael, come sit here and we'll look together."

The file was slender, labeled, "Cock of the Walk," and had the usual story summary sheet stapled to the inside front cover and a few other pages. All were in Quentin's hand, blue ink on yellow lined paper.

We turned to the story summary sheet first. Whenever work was begun on a new piece, Gertie began a data sheet. It carried the working title, lists of contacts, the name of the writer assigned, a photographer or illustrator if one had been identified, and the name of the computer file where the notes and drafts could be found.

"Did you check the hard drive?" I asked Glen.

He nodded. "There's a file with that name, but nothing in it."

"Someone could have erased it," I said. "We could check the zip drive. Everything's supposed to be backed up there once a week, anyway."

"And do you back everything up, Mags?" asked Glen.

"Well, no," I confessed. "But we should check." Glen volunteered to do it.

We scanned Quentin's notes in silence, a list of dates and events at Cock of the Walk; the opening, a fashion show, the new music series.

"Did Inspector Moon make anything of it?"

"Not according to Andrea. He'd just glanced at the file, and wanted to have your thoughts. She told him what had happened, and that you would check in with him tomorrow."

Glen reached for the file. "I'll win that home for you, Maggie?"

"What?"

He laughed. "In County Clare, that's what you call getting the turf home after it's dry so you can burn it in the fireplace." He gestured at the fireplace. "Looking at your fire made me think of it."

I sipped my coffee. "Do you miss home, Glen?"

"Some, but not the life we led there. Too many people still poor who will never be otherwise, too many rules about what you can and can't do and think. But losing Quentin put me in mind of other things I've lost."

Just then the fire crackled, and a piece of log sizzled, sparked, and fell off the andirons.

"I'm not sure that oak was completely dried out," said Michael.

"Ash, fresh and green, makes a fire fit for a queen," said Glen.

"Ahh," said Michael, "maybe that's what I should burn for Maggie, now that she's Chief and Queen at *Small Town*."

"Michael, please," I said, hearing something brittle creep in his voice.

Glen stood. "Well, I'll leave you friends in peace," he said.

I stood as well, slipping my arms around Glen for a hug.

After a moment, Glen pulled away from the hug, a look of

concern in his eyes. "It's scary, what they've done so far," he said, and, turning to Michael, "If she were my wife, I'd...."

"Dissuade her from this little amateur investigation of hers?" Michael finished. "I'm doing my best. Maggie, think a little bit. They know something about you. About Josh. About us."

I looked at the two of them, a little smug, a little paternal, more than a little male.

"I don't like that part at all. But I think I might be on to something. At least, I want to talk to Moon about it."

"Something? Like what?" asked Glen.

"I don't know. Just something odd I found in some letters at Quentin's."

"Go on," urged Glen.

So I explained about the letter from Douglas, and about my inquiries.

"You're a woman of resources, Maggie, I'll hand you that," said Glen. "But it's hard to see what the letter has to do with Quentin's death."

"So when you and Quentin were in school together, did you remember anyone named Douglas? Or Giovanni?"

"Not Giovanni. Douglas, I knew one or two."

"Someone close to Quentin?"

Glen shook his head. "Long ago and far away, Maggie."

He reached for the file. Michael folded it up. "I'd still like to have a closer look. I'll send it along with Maggie tomorrow."

Glen hesitated, then reached over to peck me on the cheek. "Fine. I'd better be running along. But Maggie, I'd still think twice about playing detective. If someone—even indirectly—threatened me through one of my children, well, I'd drop it, I can tell you that."

I patted his shoulder and began walking him toward the door. "You may be right. Thanks for coming over." I stood on the front porch, idly deadheading the mums in the planter boxes while I watched Glen drive off. If only tidying up the rest of my life were so easy.

When I came back into the living room, Michael was looking sober. "Glen's right," he said. "Leave it alone."

"I will, I will. I just need to talk to John Moon tomorrow. Then, I'll forget it."

Michael scrutinized me. "I don't believe you."

"Michael—"I began to protest.

He held up a hand. "We don't need to discuss it, Maggie. We've got a seven a.m. practice tomorrow at the Oakland rink, and I just called John Moon to come a little early. He'll meet you in the grandstands at six-thirty."

I prickled. "I can make my own arrangements to talk to Moon, Michael. You're treating me like one of the kids."

He shrugged. "Not really. At this point, I think the boys have a far more secure grasp on the concept of telling the truth and keeping commitments than you do. Besides," he added, "I'll be right down there on the ice. I want to watch you tell Moon every last thing you're thinking about."

We went to bed in silence.

ON THIN ICE

When I arrived at Skate Oakland, the pink streaks of morning were just showing up in the night sky. It had been a polite-but-businesslike start to the day at home. Michael and I had exchanged information, but not affection. Schedules, rearrangements so Anya could drop the kids off at school, negotiations over the dental appointments and soccer practice later in the week. The kind of parental juggling dialogue that takes the place of conversation in modern, middle-class households. Especially when the wife is an adulteress and the husband is pouting. Michael and I left in separate cars for Skate Oakland since we were both going on to work, and neither of us leaned toward the other in the driveway, even for our routine goodbye kiss. I fretted about the omission all the way to downtown Oakland, vaguely remembering that I'd read that husbands who got a goodbye kiss every morning were at lower risk for heart attacks. Great, now I could feel guilt about damaging every facet of Michael's heart.

The ice rink had seen more bourgeois days. Once it had been home to indulged kids' birthday parties—the kind where the birthday girl would show up in a little sequined pink skating skirt, her hair pulled back in a ballet-style bun. Now it was distinctly seedy and existed primarily for the pleasure of hard-core skating enthusiasts, homesick Canadians who would come after work or early in the morning, lace up and take to the ice, and head into the center to execute half-forgotten turns, camels, and spins. It was also home to the Oakland Ice Devils, one of the East Bay's official entrants in the Northern California senior ice hockey league. They referred to themselves as "Geezrs on Ice," a self-deprecating name that belied how seriously they took their sport. The Ice Devils were a motley group, tied together by nothing more than age (all forty-plus) and the fact they couldn't remember a day when they hadn't skated—or wanted to—since they had learned to walk.

A couple Canadians, of course, half a dozen guys from Midwestern places where *pierogi* or *lutefisk* had been on their mother's tables, a Norwegian who'd left Trondheim behind for the right engineering opportunity in Silicon Valley, Michael, who grew up worshipping the two Bobbies (Orr and Hull), and one Korean-American cop—John Moon.

Moon and I sat in the grandstands and watched the pre-dawn skaters glide off the ice as the Ice Devils filed out of the locker room and started warming up. Moon, his skates next to him, was sipping from a commuter mug. He held up his thermos. "Want some herb tea?"

I shook my head. "Thanks, I'm all-caffeine in the morning."

"Okay," he said, "let's hear it. Michael says you've got some more theories."

"Not theories, really, just some loose ends."

"Such as?"

I told him about the mix-up at Josh's school, and our worry that it was a deliberate way to keep me from looking at the file.

"But you did eventually see the story file?"

"Yes, Glen Fox brought it over last night." I shook my head.

"And there didn't seem to be anything substantive in it. Either all the good stuff had been removed, or Quentin hadn't put much in it to begin with."

Moon took a notebook out of his duffel bag, flipped to a page and handed it to me. "Look at this inventory of what was in the file. See anything missing?"

I scanned it. "No."

"Tell me everything about the call you got at the restaurant about your son," he said. "Don't leave anything out."

I talked him through the whole incident, including what Michael and I had sorted out the night before—someone who knew our family, who knew where I was having lunch, who knew what I had on, even knew the school would have the answering machine on at lunchtime.

"And the call came from a man," I said. "And there's only one male teacher at the school." Moon listened carefully.

"I don't think that means much. The caller only said he was calling from the school. That doesn't mean he was actually there, or even on staff. Anything else? An accent? Sound old or young?"

I shook my head. "I didn't ask about that," I said. Of course, it's pretty noisy in the restaurant, so it's likely the hostess didn't hear all that clearly."

"I'll have one of my guys talk to the hostess at Cock of the Walk again," said Moon.

I handed back his notebook. "So what should I do?" I asked. "Do you think there's any chance Josh is in danger?"

He shook his head. "Probably not. It sounds to me like an expedient way to delay your look at the file. But since there's nothing missing, that doesn't make much sense. What does concern me, however, is that whoever dreamed up this scheme knows a good deal about you. More confirmation of what we already suspected—whoever murdered Mr. Hart is someone you know."

Stated so baldly, this information twisted knots in my stomach.

"Great," I muttered. "So what else can I do to help?"

"Keep thinking. If you get more ideas or information, call me. Other than that, I'd concentrate on your life, if I were you." He poured a little more tea into the thermos cup. "You should be pretty busy, between the kids and your new job."

I looked back at the ice. Michael was doing warm-up sprints. Watching him move, so assured and intense, so physically present, I felt that familiar little flutter inside. I remembered the day

Michael and I met, at an ice rink. My do-good college sorority had taken a group of street-tough kids on an outing. When the lights went down for one of those corny "couples only" sessions, Michael had skated over to our little giggling group, gave a mock bow to all the girls, and asked me to waltz. He was such a wonder on the ice, it didn't matter how mediocre I was. "Just relax and trust me," he said, and I'd found myself skating backward, swooping across the ice with a grace I didn't know I had. My sorority sisters and our little charges burst into applause when the tinny recording *of The Skater's Waltz* drew to a close. Boy, did that seem like a long time ago.

"And what with my marriage on thin ice, and all," I said bleakly, "since we're here at the rink." I paused. "You know, we met at an ice skating rink."

"Michael told me," said Moon. "I know he takes your sons skating. But you don't join them?"

I shook my head. "No, it's a chance for them to have guy-time, without me hanging around." I shrugged. "They don't usually invite me, anyway."

Moon cleared his throat. "People's marriages are always mysteries to outsiders, aren't they? They're like those puzzle boxes. You can't figure out how they open unless you know the right combination of moves. And usually, only the two people inside the relationship know those moves."

"How about yours?" I said, "A puzzle box, too?"

Moon smiled noncommittally. "Does your shamelessness about prying come from being a journalist? You have license to ask anyone anything you want?"

I sighed. "And my mother raised me to have such lovely manners," I said. "I used to ask people questions for a living, but now I'm just trying to understand what kind of a mess I'm in— and what part of it is my own making."

"Which mess are we discussing?" asked Moon. "Quentin's murder, or your marriage?"

"Both, I guess," I said.

"Only you can know what you've done to the relationship with Michael," said Moon. "You and Michael have to sort that out. And that's private. But murder is a public business, and that's why it's in the hands of public servants like me and my colleagues. Your job is to keep thinking and keep me informed." He screwed the top back onto his thermos. "And to stay out of harm's way." He packed the thermos into his gym bag. "And now I'll answer the question you asked me a few minutes ago. My wife and I have been married for twenty-six years, so after all this time, I'm sure our marriage is a puzzle box to the outside world. Most days, it's a puzzle to us, as well."

"In what way?"

"Who knows why any marriage works? In both my jobs—as a high school counselor and now as a cop—I see domestic lives that look like broken-down wrecks at the junkyard. Parents who can't talk to their sons or daughters. Daughters and sons who keep secrets. Husbands and wives who let things get to such a terrible place that a marriage is irreparably broken, or worse, becomes violent." He stood up and slung the strap of the bag over his shoulder. "And then I go home, determined not to succumb to the pressures that drive people apart." He looked at me. "Police officers often have very tumultuous—and frequently, not very successful home lives, you know."

"I thought that was just in the movies."

"Occasionally movies tell the truth."

"But you've been married for a long time," I persisted. "Beating the odds?"

He smiled. "I hope so. I have a few rules for myself. I try to leave the job on the job. And I try to pay attention to what the AA people say—one day at a time."

"What do you mean?"

"I try not to worry what trouble my son may get into when he becomes a teenager. I just try to teach him every silly card game I know. I try not to worry that my daughter won't get into the music conservatory she's got her heart set on. Instead, I just show up at all her concerts and recitals and applaud until she gives me the 'Okay, Dad, now you're embarrassing me' look."

"And your wife?"

"Ah, my wife," he smiled, "Well, you already know I let her shop for my clothes."

"And?"

"And, same thing as with our kids: one day at a time. I try to concentrate on what will make this evening pleasant, instead of worrying about all the chores we have to do on the weekend, or feeling hurt that her mother doesn't approve of my profession, or that my mother thinks she isn't much of a cook because she's not Korean and can't make *kimchi*."

I thought about my early-morning parting with Michael, and the goodbye kiss that didn't happen. If we were being measured on the one-day-at-a-time standard, we'd failed the test before it was even light outside.

"But you must know these things," said Moon. "You and Michael have been married a long time as well."

"Twelve years," I said. "And we seem to have hit a bump in the road."

"Over, under, or through," said Moon. "I tried to sleepwalk through my military service, but that's the one infantry lesson I remember." He looked down at the rink. "I'm older enough to give you some advice, Maggie. Get past the bump." He gestured at the rink. "I've got to get out on the ice."

I looked up at him. "Thanks for meeting me this morning."

He smiled. "I don't think Michael gave either one of us much of a choice, did he?" He maneuvered down the steep stairs, stopping to exchange shoes for skates, opened the gate, and glided onto the ice. I took a deep breath, picked up my handbag, and went out into the full light of day.

GELATO AND CONVERSATION

Calvin was waiting in my office when I arrived at work. Waiting? More like ensconced. Feet up on my desk, telephone receiver tucked under his chin, he gestured me in with a mug of coffee. My mug.

I sat down in the visitor's chair. "My, my, we look comfortable."

"Okay, okay, I got it," he said into the receiver. "Hold on a sec." He put his hand over the receiver. "Be with you in a minute, Maggie."

"Take your time," I said.

"Good, good," he said, "Catch you later."

He beamed at me. "So the plot thickens."

"I beg your pardon?"

"I heard about the screw-up with your kid yesterday."

I grimaced. "I don't like it. And you should have heard Michael on the subject."

"Maggie, it's a warning. We're onto something."

"We?"

"Yes, we. We're in this together. Quentin wanted it that way. The two of us were..." he paused dramatically, "the last date on his Palm before he died."

I snorted, "Quentin had a little leather datebook. He thought Palm Pilots were pretentious and inconvenient, and besides, they ruined the line of a man's jacket. Furthermore," I added, "I've just come from listening to lectures from Michael and Moon. They don't want me running around being a detective, and I can't say I blame them. That's what the cops are supposed to do, blah, blah, blah. Besides, if somebody's going to go after one of my kids...."

"Hey, get serious. If somebody knows you're snooping around, and they know about your kids, nobody's safe until we figure this thing out."

"Get thee behind me, Satan," I said. On the one hand, there they were, the voices of reason—Michael, Glen, Inspector Moon. On the other, Calvin and his youthful arrogance that we could figure this out. Plus, my own need to "tidy things up," and not to do what I was told. And some bastard thought he could get at me through my kid. I felt a flush of anger wash right over what I knew I should do—throw Calvin out and get to work.

"Over, under or through," I muttered, conveniently forgetting the context but latching onto the idea. I glanced at my watch. "Okay, maybe we can nose around a little bit more, just to see if we can feed information to Inspector Moon."

"I knew you'd see it my way," he said, patting his pockets. "Now, last night I reviewed what we know and what we don't." He pulled a notepad out of his breast pocket, much like the one Moon carried. He flipped open the cover and re-established his feet on the desk.

"Here's what we know: average size killer, could be tallish woman or a medium-height man. Someone Quentin knew, probably, since he let them in. Someone who either knows you—"

"Don't remind me." I shuddered.

Calvin looked up briefly. "Buck up, Mags. Or knows *about* you and the kids."

"Okay, that narrows it down to fifty of our dearest, most intimate friends."

"Come on, Maggie, it does not. There actually can't be that many people who knew Quentin, know about you and the kids—and have a motive."

"You're right," I said. "But I think we're on the wrong track here."

"Such as?"

"Remember what Andrea said about mystery stories? About if something disappears and someone gets 'offed', I believe, was the term she used, then there's your murderer."

"And so?"

"Well, Andrea got me reading mysteries again. I haven't done it for years. Last night when I couldn't sleep, I started reading one of the Maigret mysteries—you know, Georges Simenon. And Inspector Maigret says, 'I shall know the murderer when I know the victim well.'"

"The victim? Quentin?"

"Right. There's something about Quentin we need to know, and when we do, we'll know who killed him."

"Like something from his past?"

"Maybe. I've got a friend sleuthing in London for me."

Calvin cocked one eyebrow and tapped his pencil on his teeth. "London?"

"Yes. Quentin went to school there. Some old friend of his wrote him recently, and there was peculiar stuff in the letter."

"Hey," said Calvin. "For someone who doesn't want to detect, you certainly seem to have an international network of investigators at work for you."

I grinned. "Just a resourceful little housewife."

"Housewife-editor," said a voice from the door. Gertie was leaning in the doorway, clutching a batch of pink message slips. "Just a housewife-editor who needs to get an issue out."

Guiltily, I said, "Gertie, I'm sorry. I'm here! I'm working. Throw this guy out."

Calvin stood. "No need to throw me out. I've got an assignment out at the Broadway Test Kitchens."

"What are you shooting?"

"Not shooting. Just meeting. There's a convention of food editors in town and they want to talk with me about doing a coast-to-coast photo essay on harvesting greens."

"Greens."

"Greens. Mustard. Arugula. Radicchio. That stuff."

"Actually, radicchio is red," I pointed out.

"Whatever happened to poor old iceberg lettuce? Didn't it have a renaissance a while ago?" mused Gertie.

"Don't ask," said Calvin. "It's back in salad purgatory, covered with Thousand Island dressing, waiting to be recalled to service."

"Go," I said.

"I'll call you later," he said. "We're onto something; I know we are."

After Calvin disappeared, Gertie sat down opposite me, clearing a space on her side of the desk.

"Don't tell me," I said. "I know it never looked like this when Quentin was here."

"Okay," she said, "I won't tell you. You already know. Now here we go, Madame Editor," she said.

In half an hour, we covered correspondence, reviewed the editorial, design, and production budget for the next quarter, and scheduled the next staff meeting. Gertie gathered her notes and started to stand. She stopped.

"Maggie?"

"What have I forgotten?"

"It's not that." She picked up Quentin's Rolodex and riffled the pages. "I know you really loved Quentin."

"You did, too."

"I did, I did. But I didn't idealize him." She put the Rolodex down and looked at me. "You know how they say no man is a gentleman to his valet? Well, no man is perfect to his secretary or whatever highfalutin title they've given me. Quentin wasn't an exception."

"I knew that."

She shook her head. "I'm not sure you did." She hesitated. "I knew about the two of you."

"You," I said, "and the rest of the city, apparently."

"Don't flatter yourself," she said dryly. "But I kept pretty close track of Quentin's schedule. I knew where he was and when—and with whom."

"Listen, Gertie—"

She held up her hand. "You don't need to explain anything to me. It was your business and Quentin's. But you should know, there was a certain ruthlessness about Quent. He knew what he wanted and he went after it. You may think what took place between you two was an accident or something that just happened. But I'm willing to wager Quentin had it in some master plan. I know how he talked about you and what he thought of you. And I think he decided, for better or worse, that some day he'd make his move. Or let you make yours."

I remembered Saks. Whose move was it?

"I think," said Gertie, "that's why Claire hated him so much. I think she felt as if she'd fallen into, and then out of, some grand scheme Quentin had."

"Why are you telling me this, Gertie?"

"I just want you to know I think you are on to something."

"What do you mean?"

"When I came in, you and Calvin were talking about knowing the victim. That's right, I somehow feel it. Pay attention to who Quentin really was. And you'll find out who killed him."

"I think that, too," I began.

She interrupted, "Of course, a plainspoken midwestern girl like myself can't help but wonder why you're so involved in all this."

I struggled to explain. "It's the same question I keep asking myself. I think it's a whole collection of bad reasons. Maybe because I found his body, and that makes me feel responsible in some weird way. Or because he was waiting for Calvin and me to arrive when it happened. Maybe because I feel so awful about—"

"Cheating on Michael?"

"That's part of it. I feel as if I contributed to some enormous mess in the world, and sooner or later, somebody has to pay for messes."

"If that's so," observed Gertie, "I'd say that Quentin's the one who paid the price. And you're making a big assumption that it had anything to do with you."

"I'm not," I insisted. "I just feel responsible for something."

Gertie sighed. "You are. You're responsible for fixing things up with Michael, but that's not my business. But who am I to talk? I couldn't make my marriage work." She stood up. "Of course, he was a jerk, and I just had to wait 'til the kids were out of the house so I could get on a plane and get out of town. But then, Michael doesn't seem like a jerk to me."

"He's not," I began. "But Gertie—"

She held up her hand. "Uh-uh. You're my boss now; go confide in a girlfriend about your marriage. But this magazine is my business, so…" she gestured at the message slips, "get to work. You're in a business with deadlines." She stopped at the doorway, and I could feel one parting shot coming. "You know, Maggie, you're the girl who thinks she's smarter than anybody else. If you ask me, that's the real reason I think you keep poking your nose into the cops' business."

I looked at her. "Is that a respectful way to talk to your boss?"

"Quentin trained me to be insubordinate," she said, and disappeared down the hallway.

Gertie was right about way too many things. Though I couldn't imagine confiding in any of my friends about my screw-up with Quentin. They all thought Michael was near-perfect. "You're so lucky," they were always cooing. "Michael's a nice guy, and he cooks, and he's great with the kids, yada-yada-yada." Damn, it's a pain being married to Signor Perfect, when you're the one who's not, who's restless, who went looking for excitement in inappropriate places.

So work I did. Reviewed page proofs, harangued a tardy writer or two, looked at comps (full-size color comprehensive mock-ups) of the next issue, confirmed press time at the printer, and reassured the advertising sales manager that *Small Town* was good for the next quarter. Gertie brought me a salad for lunch—iceberg lettuce, yet—and I ate it with the phone tucked beneath my chin. I looked up to see Andrea crooking a finger at me from the doorway.

"Come on, get up," she said. "Fresh air, sunshine, a little exercise."

"I can't," I said.

"Indeed you can," she said. "I've been working at real jobs a lot longer than you have. You need to be up, up and about. Let's go. Twenty-minute walk up to Chinatown and back. Do you a world of good."

"Okay, okay. One call first."

And I picked up the phone to check in at the Webster School. The night before, Michael and I had agreed to a twice daily check-in at the school, just to make sure nothing was amiss. Plus, we had wheedled permission from the school to let Josh carry a cell phone, just for a week or so.

"Everything fine?" Andrea asked as we rode down the elevator.

"I guess so," I said.

"Good. I've been thinking about our detecting careers. Shall I tell you what I'm wondering?"

"Tell away."

"I'm wondering about the benefit that Claire was running at the Cock of the Walk. Who was it benefiting again?"

"Skunkworks." I groaned as Claire's face floated into my memory.

"What's wrong?" asked Andrea.

"I'm just remembering I'll get a chance to ask the horrible Mrs. Hart about it myself. Live and in person. We're having dinner with her and Uncle Alf tomorrow night."

"Lucky you," said Andrea. "But anyway, you can get some information out of her about Cock of the Walk."

"You've been talking to Calvin," I said as we came to Portsmouth Square in the heart of Chinatown. "He thinks that story is the key to all this."

"What do you think?"

"I think he may be right. There's something Quentin wanted us to go after in that story, and we just can't figure out what it is."

"How have you gone after it?"

"I haven't done anything since our field trip there yesterday."

"Calvin's done some digging, though."

"I know, he started to fill me in this morning until Gertie threw him out."

Andrea smiled. "I wish I'd seen that. Well, he didn't find out much. Orlando owns Cock of the Walk with some silent partners. He's listed as managing partner of the Catalog Club in the city records. That's the name of the partnership. Apparently, this group came up with a lot of cash, because Calvin talked to the restaurant designer who did the place over when they bought it. It may not be our taste, but they spent a lot of money. That, plus that big benefit opening they did for Claire, means someone had to come up with serious money."

"Maybe illustration is a more lucrative line of work than I'd thought," I said.

Andrea wrinkled her nose. "I'd say not. I checked with Linda Quoc, and she claims Orlando seems pretty cavalier about his fees. He's more interested in placement and illustration credit."

"Wealthy family?"

Andrea shrugged. "Maybe. I know we talked about it yesterday, and I'm even more convinced he must have some other source of income."

She tugged at my arm. "Detour, right through here."

"Andrea, I've got to get back."

"Me too. But we need some gelato first."

And she was right again. The curbside gelateria on Sacramento was doing a brisk business. Equipped with samplers of pistachio and mandarin orange, we nibbled our way back to the office.

"So Andrea," I ventured. "Do I sense a little something cooking between you and Calvin?"

She smiled. "In my family, you never, ever ask questions like that."

"Good thing I'm a friend, and not family," I countered. "Plus, I know you're a few years older than Calvin, and I'm thinking that's a trend—older woman, younger man—so we should probably do a story on it in the magazine. What do you think?"

"And," she continued, ignoring my question, "in my family, people keep company for something in excess of fifteen years before it can be said there's anything 'cooking', as you so delicately put it."

"Mm-hmm."

"What does that mean?"

"That means I don't see Calvin waiting around for fifteen minutes, never mind fifteen years."

"Well, we shall see, what we shall see," said Andrea, pushing the double doors open into the lobby of our building. As you so tactfully pointed out, I've got a good five years on Calvin. Perhaps I can teach him a little patience."

"Is that family code for something?"

"Why, yes, I believe it is."

We both jabbed at the elevator button at the same time. "Andrea, I was also wondering…."

She looked amused. "You're certainly doing a lot of that."

I gulped. "About you and Quentin."

Her face went blank. "What about us?"

"Why'd it start? Why'd it end?"

"Well, it's not really any of your business," she began.

"I know, I know, but murder changes the rules about being nosy."

The elevator creaked to the lobby and opened its doors. We stepped in. The doors closed. Neither one of us reached to press 4.

"I'm not sure it does change the rules, unless you've been appointed to the police force while I wasn't looking," she said tartly. "But here's what I'm willing to tell you. I met Quentin before I started writing for *Small Town*. He was very charming, and we became go-to-film-opening friends. Claire said movies gave her headaches, so Quentin and I used to go see films a lot. I don't remember why it happened, but it did. We still went to movies but then, there was, you might say, a post-film agenda." She reached out and punched 4, hard. She looked me dead in the eye. "He was a great lay, as I believe you were aware. With virtually no messy emotional strings attached."

The elevator creaked upwards. "Why'd it end?"

She shrugged. "It just did. There was someone else. Or a couple of someone elses. I'm not good at being an ensemble player."

The door opened.

Andrea swung her coat off her shoulders and turned away. I caught her wrist.

"Thanks for talking to me," I said.

She looked down at my hand on her wrist, as if wondering how it got there. I let go.

"It's okay," she said. "I'm sorry I was so short. But it's not something I'm proud about. Claire's not anybody I care for particularly, and Quentin never seemed to give fidelity two pins' worth of thought, but still...."

"I know," I said grimly. "Boy, do I know."

When I got to my desk, the message slip I'd been waiting for was there.

Sara Jenkins had called.

Miracles of direct dialing, I had her on the phone in under a minute.

"Maggie, what a detective I am! And with so little to go on."

"Stop congratulating yourself," I said. "Spill the goods."

"Okay, here goes. Douglas is Douglas Thurston. He's a don at Oxford, and yes indeed, he does have a new biography out on Joyce Cary."

"That's great! How'd you figure it out?"

Sara snorted. "Not terribly difficult. Just because I can't make hollandaise doesn't mean I'm a ninny. I marched over to the corner academic bookstore and asked."

"Oh," I said. "Good work."

"So anyway. Douglas isn't married, exactly. He's gay. Not like most public school Englishmen—not temporarily boffing little boys because there's nothing else around. He's permanently gay.

And he lives with an architect."

"Named Leslie?"

"Exactly. Leslie Dover-Couch. They've been together for years, since school I gather."

"The plot thickens."

"Yes, indeed. And they were all chums of Quentin's at Oxford."

"How'd you find out?"

"Called him up and asked. He'd just heard the news about Quentin and was quite anxious to get details. I told him you might ring up."

"I just might. Give me the number."

Sara repeated it twice. "So tell me about the job. Is this it? You're a private eye?"

"Part-time," I said. "Don't worry, I'm not packing a pistol yet."

Sara laughed. "What does Michael think about all this?"

I felt the lightness drain out of me.

"Maggie? Anything wrong?"

"Oh, it's too long a story to tell over the phone," I said, "but I wish you were here, because I could use somebody to talk to." I sighed. "The short answer is, I've actually sort of promised Michael I wouldn't be running around detecting."

"But now you are?"

"Well, I'm worried about... some problems I created. And it seems to me that figuring out what happened to Quentin will help clear things up. So I'm really not doing much, just asking around."

"And putting me to work as your operative," Sara observed. "Be careful. I love Michael, but he's got a temper. I wouldn't be telling him any tales if I were you."

"Yeah, I wish I'd taken that advice a while ago," I said ruefully.

"But now you're in it, aren't you?" asked Sara. "I can tell you're in that steamroller mode of yours we all find so—"

"Charming," I finished for her. Then I realized something was bothering me. "Sara, wait, how'd Douglas hear about Quentin?"

"From someone named Glen Fox. He says they all went to school together."

Glen Fox. Quentin. Douglas. Something needed to jiggle into place.

Sara was talking "Come on, tell me about this job, if you're not being paid to be a private eye, that is."

"I'm Glen Fox's boss," I said. "I took Quentin's place at the magazine."

"Well, be careful, love. It sounds like a dangerous spot. Being editor, I mean." We chatted a few minutes more, I walked Sara through how to make a stand-up paper collar for her soufflé dish, and she gave me her new e-mail address.

"It's good to have this, Maggie," she concluded. "If I'm going to be your across-the-pond detecting assistant and marriage counselor, we can't waste all our capital on trunk calls."

"Trunk calls? Isn't that something people talk about in old Greer Garson movies?"

Sara laughed. "Probably. It's what my penny-pinching mother-in-law calls them whenever Richard complains I've been on the phone to you again."

After we hung up, I sat staring at the receiver. Then I picked it up and dialed Douglas Thurston's number. A deep voice rumbled in my ear, "Yes? Thurston here."

"Margaret Fiori, here." Two can play that game.

"Ah, yes, Mrs. Fiori. You're Sara Jenkins's friend?"

I said indeed I was. He wanted more information about Quentin's death. I told him as much as I knew and then I got down to cases.

"This is awkward," I began, "but I read the last letter you sent to Quentin."

"Yes?" said Thurston coolly. "What interesting manners you Americans have, reading other people's mail."

"We were very close," I improvised, "and the police, well, they invited me to take a look at this correspondence." Some truth in that statement, wasn't there?

"Anyway," I continued, "I wondered about some things in that letter." I took a deep breath. "Specifically, I wondered about

Giovanni. Who was he? Who is he?"

"He's an old friend of Quentin's and mine. Someone we went to school with. I can't really see what this has to do with you."

"It doesn't. Except, now that Quentin's dead—murdered—anything we know feels like it ought to be my business."

"Surely the police have matters in hand."

I temporized. "Surely they do. But I have some personal reasons for wanting to help." A familiar phrase from public television floated into my consciousness. "I'm helping the police with their inquiries," I said briskly. "Now, please tell me, who's Giovanni?"

"Just who I said. An old friend. His name isn't really Giovanni. It's Jack Rowland. But he loved Italian opera. He's a tenor. Never pursued it as a career, but he'd memorized whole chunks of the Italian repertoire. And he was rather promiscuous in the old days, so we called him 'Don Giovanni'."

"Where is he now?"

"Well, he's in San Francisco. That's what Quentin wrote to tell me."

"And this falling-out they had?"

"Oh, it was silly. Jack got himself in a few scrapes. He always claimed Quentin was his co-conspirator, but somehow Quentin never got caught. Anyway, last scrape out at Oxford was fairly serious. Jack got sent down."

"Sent down? You mean bounced? Expelled?"

"Yes. Something like that."

"What was the scrape?"

Thurston was quiet, clearly thinking things through.

"You don't know Jack Rowland, I take it? Paths haven't crossed?"

"No. Never heard of him before today."

"Yes, well, can't think there's any harm in talking about it after all these years."

I waited.

"Jack was picking up pocket money by tutoring some local town boys. Latin, I believe. Anyway, it turned out that promiscuous itch got the better of his judgment. He'd been buggering one or two of them."

"Little boys?" I asked, horrified.

"No, no. Not quite. Teenagers, seventeen or so, but still, their parents didn't take kindly to it. Especially one of the dads. Probably not a good idea to practice the love that dare not speak its name on the vicar's son."

"Probably not. But what did Quentin have to do with it?"

"Well, this wasn't the seventies, you have to remember, my dear. It was, let's see, mid-1960s, and I'm afraid young Quentin and Jack had also introduced these young men to the joys of marijuana. Quentin had a little cadre of musician friends, black and Moroccan fellows he'd 'jam with', as you Americans say. They kept Quentin and Jack well supplied."

"So Quentin wasn't carrying on with the boys, I take it?"

"I think not. Quentin was rather intensely a ladies' man at that stage in his life."

"So Jack was out, and Quentin was in."

"That's right. Jack went back to America and bummed around a bit. He returned to graduate school in the late sixties. Somewhere on one of your coasts, east, west, something like that. Can't say I know which. Then he came back here for a while. We've kept in touch very sporadically."

"Did he go to graduate school in music?"

"Oh, no. That was just a hobby. But then his parents died, and Jack inherited some money, so I'm not quite sure what he pursued as a livelihood."

"So if I understand Quentin's letter correctly, Jack's in San Francisco now, and they'd kissed and made up."

"Quite so."

I mused on all this. "You wouldn't happen to know where I could reach him?"

"No, I'm afraid I wouldn't. I was counting on Quentin to put us in touch with each other. You might ask Glen Fox, though. You must know him."

"Yes, we work together at *Small Town*."

"Well, interrogate him, then. If Quentin's been in touch with Jack, surely Glen might know where he's hanging about."

As we talked, I fingered through the "R's" in Quentin's Rolodex. No luck, no Rowland. And nobody in "G" for Giovanni, either.

I thanked Douglas Thurston for his help, and we agreed we'd plan a drink or dinner to toast Quentin's memory when he came to San Francisco. I hung up and sat, thinking.

Then I buzzed Glen. He was just on the way out the door.

"Soccer practice for the boys, Maggie. But you said it was quick?"

It was. I asked him if he knew how I could reach Jack Rowland.

"Jack Rowland? Rowland from Oxford?"

"Yes."

The answer was no. Glen hadn't heard from him or seen him in many, many years.

It wasn't the answer I wanted. But it was the one I expected. I put on my hat and coat and went home.

BUT NOT FOR LOVE

When I walked in the front door, the unmistakable soy-ginger-garlic scents of stir-fry were emanating from the kitchen. I threw keys and handbag on the entry table and headed for the kitchen to investigate. Zach was kneeling on a kitchen stool, wielding a wooden spoon and agitating slices of chicken breast in a wok; Josh was at the cutting board, slicing peppers; Michael was leaning against a counter, wineglass in hand, supervising. Louis Armstrong was blasting out of the kitchen speakers. The whole atmosphere in the room felt significantly better than it had that morning. "*Cara*," Michael said, waving his glass to include the boys in the gesture, "just another dull night of domestic bliss." I nestled under his arm for a squeeze and whispered sweetly in his ear, "Screw you."

He patted my shoulder and grinned down at me. "A capital idea. Perhaps later."

"I'm so sorry," I said, "I didn't kiss you goodbye this morning."

"We'd come kiss you, Mom," said Josh, "but we're busy."

"That's okay," I said, "I'll come kiss you—I love coming home to a house full of cooks. Where's Anya?"

Michael rolled his eyes. "Upstairs, brooding. I believe there's romantic trouble again. I came home early and I coaxed her to come with me to take the boys out for a bike ride around Lake Merritt, but her heart wasn't in it."

Anya fell in and out of love with considerable regularity.

Since summertime, we'd been treated to high melodrama over a fellow art student, a young associate in Michael's office, the gutter repair guy we summoned after the first fall rain, and one or two others. Personally, I was pulling for Harrison, the young man from Grateful Gutters. I figured we might get a discount. But he, like all others, ran afoul of Anya's cinema-inspired standards.

I sighed. "I guess we'll hear about it at dinner."

At least, I thought, once we'd gathered around the table, affairs of the heart didn't inhibit Anya's appetite. Between sniffles, she complimented Michael and the boys on their stir-fry, and polished off three servings, rice, and salad. The boys, on the other hand, picked at dinner. It emerged that the entire household—minus me, of course—had gone on a post-bike riding outing for ice cream. I was winding up for a lecture on ruining the boys' dinner, but Anya was still completing her tale of romantic woe.

"You know, Maggie," she concluded, "it was just like the end of *Casablanca*."

"How, Anya? You said goodbye out on the tarmac?"

"No, no," she said dreamily. "He was giving me up for a higher cause. He's been offered a job in Dayton, Ohio, working on a very important project at the Air Force Museum there."

I had a hard time picturing Humphrey Bogart, trenchcoat and all, disappearing into the mist to go to Dayton and catalog antique propellers in a museum, but it seemed best to leave Anya with her tragic ending intact.

"Well, buck up, Anya," said Michael. "You know, 'Men have died from time to time and worms have eaten them, but not for love.'"

"Yuck," exclaimed Josh. Zach, I could see, was about to wind up for a rendition of a classic he'd been forbidden to sing at the table, featuring the lyrics, "the worms crawl in/the worms crawl out/the worms play pinochle on your snout."

Anya simply looked puzzled. "Shakespeare," I explained. "Rosalind offers Orlando that comforting thought in *As You Like It*."

"Another tender-hearted, compassionate woman," observed Michael.

"Well, she's just trying to be realistic." I was warming to the topic, glad to have a little Shakespeare at the dinner table. Improving young minds and all that.

Michael sighed, "Here we go." He looked at his wristwatch. "Try and do the plot summary in under a half hour, *cara*."

I reached for my wineglass and stopped, frozen. "Michael, that's it."

"What?" he said, distracted. "Joshie, send me down just a little more of that delectable rice we steamed up. Ask Mom why hers is never this fluffy, why don't you?"

"Excuse me a moment," I said, dashing for the stairs. "Where's my Shakespeare?"

I found it in the den. Three volumes, A.L. Rowse, trying to retain its dignity sandwiched between the *Sunset Western Garden Book* and a dozen tattered Tintin comics.

"Yes! Yes!" I shouted. There it was, staring me in the face. Michael, napkin in hand, stuck his head in. "Are you nuts?"

"Look at this! It's been right in front of me the entire time." I turned the book so he could see, open to the dramatis personae of *As You Like It.*

"Okay, I'll bite. I don't see."

"See? Oliver, Jaques and Orlando—they're all sons of Sir Rowland de Boys. I always thought of them as Sir Rowland and the boys, which is why Zach and Josh reminded me of his name."

"And?"

"And if you were named Jack Rowland and you wanted to change your name, why not John Orlando?"

"Who is?"

"This weird guy you met at the memorial for Quentin. He's the one I had a fight with Glen about. He's an illustrator, and he owns the restaurant Quentin wanted me to do the story on—the Cock of the Walk."

"So why'd he change his name?"

"Exactly. Why? And another thing: why did Glen lie to me about knowing him? According to Douglas Thurston—I'll explain who he is later—Glen, Quent, and Rowland were all at Oxford together. But when I asked Glen if he'd seen or heard from Rowland, he said no, not for years." I banged the book shut and stood up. "But all the time, he was right here! With a different name, working for Quentin." I grabbed Michael's arm. "I'm on to something. God! This is what it's like being a detective."

Michael's face darkened. He took hold of my shoulders and turned me to him. "Maggie, this is exactly what I asked you not to do. You're not a detective. And if you're not careful, someone's going to get hurt. Try to remember that phone call about Josh for a few minutes, would you? How effective do you think our little jerry-rigged check-in system is going to be if someone really wanted to threaten the kids?"

His face swam before me. I tried to concentrate and breathe easily, regularly. "Okay, okay. You're right. I'll call Moon, right after dinner."

"Promise?"

"Honest. I swear."

And I did. But I called Glen, too. Which may have been a mistake.

OKAY BY ME IN AMERICA

Glen and Corinne's Mission District Victorian wasn't exactly on the way to Hot Licks, but both were south of Market, and in a city only seven miles across, how far out of the way could anything be?

The Mission is the oldest, most diverse (in the new, politically correct parlance for integrated), and one of the most happening areas in San Francisco. Spreading out from the historic Mission Dolores, it's an eclectic mix of family neighborhoods, parks, taquerias, yuppified coffee bars, alternative theatre, and art spaces. It's home to churches, feminist bookstores, a proper soda fountain (the St. Francis Fountain and Candy Store), and Good Vibrations, a disarmingly wholesome purveyor of erotic goodies. Glen and Corinne lived on Liberty, a sunny, leafy street that showcased a fine collection of San Francisco's "painted ladies," Victorian buildings so beautiful that their residents almost forget that the high ceilings gobble heat and the plumbing has to be coaxed to work.

I whipped the Volvo into their driveway, grabbed the folder of invoices, and trotted up the front steps. The sign on the glossy green front door said, "Bell is unreliable. Please give the door a thump." I did. No answer. I thumped again and heard Glen's voice. "Coming, coming."

The door opened. Glen was in jeans and a denim shirt, eyes bloodshot, unshaven.

"Ah, Maggie. How are you?"

"I'm fine. How are you?"

"Oh, well," he rubbed his cheek. "A little worn round the edges. Some flu thing the kids probably brought home."

The wind was brisk on the front porch. I thrust the folder at Glen.

"What's this, love?" he asked.

I explained about the invoices and asked him to call his okays in to Gertie. He said fine and looked expectant, clearly waiting for me to be on my way.

"Glen, can't I come in for a minute? I want to ask you about something else. That's why I called you last night."

"Ah, Mags," he said, "where are my manners? Sure, sure. Come in and have a drop to warm yourself."

In Glen's white tiled kitchen, I sat down at a round, golden oak table stacked with children's drawings, supermarket coupons, and what looked like the disassembled body parts of many Power Rangers. I'm sure there are families with kids without cluttered kitchens, but if I ever found one, I'd be hostile beyond belief.

While he filled the teakettle, he called over his shoulder, "Shove that trash to the side, Maggie, and make room for a cuppa."

When we were settled in front of two mugs of fragrant black tea, I felt brave enough to broach the subject.

"Glen, here's what I'm wondering. You've told me a whole string of lies about—well, about who you know and who you don't. And I guess I'm wondering why?"

Glen's face got stony. He sipped his tea.

"Lies? For example?"

"For example. You did know Douglas Thurston, because you're the one who told him about Quent's death."

"Who told you that?"

"He did. Douglas. I talked to him on the telephone. And another thing, you did know that Jack Rowland and John Orlando are the same person—and you didn't tell me that either." I leaned back, relieved I'd gotten it all out. "Okay, so tell me what's going on?"

Glen sipped his tea again. "Why?"

"Why what?"

"Why should I tell you?"

I felt flustered. "Because… because, for heaven's sake, Glen, we're all in this together." I was warming to my subject now. "Quentin was our friend; he's been killed. Don't you want to know what happened, and why? And why would you lie to me? Aren't we friends?"

Glen smiled thinly.

"You know, Maggie. Here's what you're like. You're like the girl who's always encouraging people to try things, to play a game of charades, or try ice-skating or something. And you know why you do it? Because you believe that everyone in the world is just like you. And you know that if you're coaxed to do something, you'll do it. And you'll probably be okay at it. And there will be another sweet Jesus happy ending."

"Glen," I started to protest.

"No, Maggie. Now, it's time to listen to me." He got up and began pacing the kitchen, strides from refrigerator to table and back.

"You've got a problem. I'm not one of those American husbands who's been sensitized into thinking that communication is a grand thing. For an inky wretch, for a words man, I'm not much of a talker. What's private is private." He stopped and fixed me. "And I might add, for all your communication all the day long, you're not above keeping some private business to yourself, too."

I felt my face burn. "Agreed."

"Yes, well, this isn't a debatin' society, now. This is me telling you what's what. So the real story is that I didn't own up to knowing Douglas and Jack Rowland because I had my reasons. And they're mine, not yours. I had a whole life before I came here, Maggie. And, I have answered every single question the police have put to me, so I believe I've done my good citizen duty."

"Glen," I began.

"No, let me finish. I'm going to tell you my version of this story. And it's going to be what I'm willing to tell you. And the rest, you'll pardon my bad manners, is my business." Glen stopped pacing and sat down across from me again. I felt as if I'd come in the middle of a Byzantine foreign movie. I'd only left for a few minutes, just to get popcorn or something, and the plot had galloped ahead of me. Where were the subtitles? Why was Glen so angry?

He took a gulp of his tea and folded his hands. "Once upon a time—isn't that how all stories begin?"

I nodded.

"Well then, once upon a time, there were a number of very bright, very confused, little adventurous boys who had gone up to Oxford. Quentin. Jack. Douglas. And me." He tapped his chest.

"So there we were, all of us young, all of us trying to prove we were something more than the lives we'd left behind. It was, in many ways, a grand time. We read everything. We argued. We drank. We ran around with the locals. We listened to music."

He stopped, looked around the kitchen, as if puzzled by how that intense and fun-loving young man had been transported, as if by magic, into a city flat, crammed with the artifacts of husband-and-daddy-dom.

"We got in trouble from time to time. I think you probably know about the scrape Jack Rowland got in. Douglas told you?"

I nodded. "He had a relationship with a minister's son."

Glen sighed. "Yes, not the best judgment, that. But it was more. He'd been pissing away his study time, and so when the troubles came about, his tutor was too annoyed to stand up for him. Plus, it wasn't so much the sex. The rumor was that all of us had been steadily leading a group of local boys astray. Lots of Algerian weed, and harder stuff, too."

"All of you?"

"Well, none of us was blameless. Except Douglas; he was a little bit of a goody-goody. And I was rather intensely into my heir-of-Thomas-Merton period, thinking I had a religious vocation. Quentin and Jack offered to take the fall—Jack, after all, had been the one who'd led the rosy-cheeked boy down love's forbidden path. And Quentin, well, everyone assumed he'd sleep with anyone or anything."

"Comforting thought," I said.

"Yes, well, we all have lapses, my girl. That's why the confessional can be such a busy, busy place." He smiled, looking amused for the first time since we'd sat down.

"Perhaps we can discuss my transgressions another time," I said. "Go on."

"So the long and short of it was that all of us misbehaved to one degree or another. If I were ranking the villains, I guess I'd have to say that Jack, Quentin, and I were most to blame."

"Were you?"

"Having it off with the vicar's boy?" He smiled bitterly. "Not him, but others. I was… confused. But I was close to Jack and I could have kept him in tighter rein."

"So then what happened?"

"Well, that's another story. Jack got sent down and finished up at some redbrick college, then came to the States, made some money, then moved back to London. Quentin and Douglas finished up. I came close, but then decided I had a vocation and returned to Ireland to the seminary."

"And Douglas stayed on in Oxford and Quentin came to the States. And none of you met again?"

"Oh, no. Quentin and Douglas have seen each other from time to time over the years, although things were always a bit frosty because Douglas thought Quentin hadn't stood up for Jack. I'd see Quent occasionally when he came to Ireland. As I think you know, he helped me and Corinne and the kids immensely when we came here."

We both fell silent, the sounds of the Mission faint outside the kitchen windows—city buses, kids shouting. I remembered Glen's remarks at Quentin's funeral. Okay, I thought, it's now or never. Get the rest of the story and get out.

"But then Jack Rowland, a.k.a. John Orlando, surfaced in the

States again? In San Francisco?"

"Well, he'd been here before, as I said. Knocking around. Doing this and that."

"Such as?"

Glen reached across the table and captured my hands in his.

"Listen to me, Maggie. I'll finish this story—or what I choose to tell you of it. And then I want you to be done with it."

I nodded. I knew I had virtually no intention of honoring what Glen was asking, and somehow, my old kid's-eye view of following the letter—not the spirit—of the law, meant that if I didn't speak, if I didn't say "I promise" aloud, I could do what I wanted. I nodded again and thought to myself; geez, Maggie, first adultery, then promises I had no intention of keeping. No ethics, no ethics whatsoever.

"All right, then. I landed here a few years ago, as you know. Jack Rowland came to town shortly after that. He'd always been an arty fellow, and now, he had this portfolio under his arm. He'd turned himself into a Bohemian. He'd taken up illustration. Quentin and I saw him, liked his work."

I wrinkled my nose.

"Yes, well, Maggie, now you're in charge, you're free not to like his stuff. But Quent and I did. And I suppose we both felt a little guilt over the old days. We'd gotten away with most of our hijinks—and Jack had paid."

"So he blackmailed you into hiring him?"

"No, no, not at all. We liked his stuff. We've been using him. Besides," Glen picked up my tea mug and his and carried them to the sink and began rinsing them. "I hardly think Jack was depending on us to keep body and soul together. He's got that fancy new restaurant of his."

"Exactly! And where did he get the money for that?"

Glen shrugged. "Who knows? Those ritzy Hong Kong friends of his, I guess. And what business is it of yours, miss, I'd like to know?"

"Well, I think when there's been a murder, it's everybody's

business."

Glen raised his hand. "Stop. That's where you're wrong. It's Quentin's business—and he's dead. So now it's police business."

I regarded Glen. None of this seemed so terrible. Why hadn't he told me before? He looked back at me, his face impassive. It reminded me of a playground stand-off.

"Maggie, you know who Charles Parnell was?"

"Irish hero, right?"

"In a way. There are some who think his strategies, his indiscreet love affair with the wife of an MP, well, they led to his ruination. And you, my girl, you remind me of Charles Stewart Parnell. You've got a good head. You've got prospects. But you can't leave well enough alone. Do it. That's my advice to you."

"How did he end up?"

"Parnell? He died a very young man, fiftyish or so. Worn out, rejected by his party."

"But in love."

"Ah, yes. In love, he finally married his 'Queenie'. Not many years of happiness they had, I'm afraid."

"Glen," I said impatiently. "This is a little cryptic for me. Maybe I'm not Joycean enough to figure out what your story is about. So why don't you say what's on your mind?"

He laughed. "That's not very Irish. All right then, I'll be direct, just like you Americans. Think about this: you've got a good life, you've got a good job—at least for the moment—don't be overstirring the pot. The coppers have it in hand."

I considered my options. "Oh, Glen, you're right, I suppose. I'm just so unsettled. I'm sure I feel a little guilty—well, a lot guilty about some of the choices I made. And I worry that my relationship with Quentin had something to do with this. Then, you know, the police were questioning Michael, and I felt so terrible."

"Yes, indeed, I understand," Glen said. "And if I might suggest something to you. You felt terrible because you'd done something you shouldn't. You're not Catholic, so there's no confessional for you, my friend. I'd simply recommend that you leave off doing things you oughtn't."

"The voice of experience?" I asked.

He laughed again, shortly. "Yes, the voice of experience. We pay, one way or another, for all our sins, I assure you."

"Quentin certainly did," I said. "Whatever those sins were. Knowing Quentin, I assume they were legion."

"Safe assumption," said Glen. "I always worried Quentin would turn up HIV-positive. He was so free with his favors."

We both let that statement sit there for a bit.

"And you're certain he wasn't?" I ventured.

Glen looked at me for a moment. "No, he wasn't. He was quite careful, even with all his adventures. And he got himself tested regularly. He was a lucky man."

"Until the end," I said.

Glen looked up at the kitchen clock.

"Well, now, where does the time fly? Let's have a look at those invoices and I'll send you on your way." I pushed the envelope in his direction and let Glen riffle through. He scanned the pages, one by one, muttering under his breath, circling a few items, initialing other pages.

"Sorry," he said, "just be a moment."

"Take your time," I said as I stood and wandered over to the Fox family bulletin board. School pictures of the Fox brood, a soccer phone tree, Mass schedule from St. Peter and Paul's, a chore chart, adorned with many check marks and the occasional stick-on gold star, and a patchwork of other family photos.

"St. Peter and Paul's?" I called. "Isn't that far to troop everyone for Mass?"

Glen looked up. "Oh, yes, a little. Corinne and the kids go here in the neighborhood, but I like the North Beach scene, so I ramble over there from time to time. You know, have an espresso afterward with friends."

"Mm-hmm." I leaned against the refrigerator and surveyed the kitchen.

How settled Glen and Corinne seemed here, how American. I

wondered if they felt that way. It was hard to know what was okay to ask. I'd just pried into Glen's past, and had been made to feel even nosier than I already considered myself, but, oh well, might as well be hung for a sheep as a goat.

"Glen," I ventured, "do you feel like you're raising an American family?"

He looked up. "American, Maggie? As opposed to what? Bosnian?"

"No, Irish."

He snorted. "Hardly. Do you have the slightest idea how pervasive you Yanks are? You wander through Trinity College in Dublin and you'd swear you were at UC Berkeley. The kids wear the same T-shirts, pierce the same body parts, listen to the same music, tell the same jokes. Even Irish culture gets co-opted. You know who's on the cover of Rolling Stone this month?"

I shook my head. Only Puck could tell me. "The Cranberries. There's that sweet-faced Dolores O'Riordan, looking like an American girl and singin' her heart out. I mean, you know she's Irish, but I'll tell you, we're all of us, everywhere in the world these days, just a little bit American." He gestured around the kitchen.

"I'm raisin' American kids, and I say that's just fine. There's not many other places in the world a man can start over."

"Like the song in *West Side Story*?"

Glen looked up, puzzled.

"*I want to be in America. Okay by me in America,*" I sang.

"Don't quit your day job, Maggie," he said and went back to the invoices.

"Wait," I protested. "You started over. In the seminary in Ireland, after Oxford."

"Oh, well," said Glen, "that's another matter now. The Catholic Church is a world unto itself—just like America, but without the rock and roll."

Silence hung in the kitchen again, and I was reminded of what private lives we all lead, more of Inspector Moon's puzzle boxes. Opened occasionally, in some flash, some moment, and then shuttered again, away from even those we think we trust. And I began to think that my stupid, stubborn reluctance to let go of Quentin's murder must have something to do with proving my own trustworthiness to Michael again. Bring him the solution, the way the cats bring something they've conquered and leave it on the mat. See what I've done for you! The memory of those poor ravaged creatures—half-eaten mice and chipmunks—brought me perilously close to remembering Quentin's body the morning I found him.

"Okay, that's about it," I said hastily. "I'll leave you in peace, and Gertie will be pleased to get your approvals on these."

Glen stood and we walked together through the dark hallway to the front door. Impulsively, I moved to give Glen a hug. He hesitated and then wrapped his arms around me and hugged back. "Ah, Maggie," he said, "so California. Fix anything with a hug."

I released him. "Just being friendly," I said. "Besides, maybe I'll catch your flu. I wouldn't mind a day or two in bed with a stack of trashy novels."

"Yes, well, what do they say about being careful what you wish for?"

I waved from the station wagon, keeping one eye on the rearview mirror to see what suicidal driver had decided to make Liberty Street personal territory. Glen stood in the doorway, slight, rumpled, the light catching his gingery hair.

His face was still tired and drawn.

"It's nothing," I said to myself, maneuvering the Volvo out onto the street. "You wouldn't look so perky yourself if you were coping with city life, five kids, and the flu."

And with that almost comforting thought, I headed toward Mission to angle across the great divide, Market Street.

IF MUSIC BE
THE FOOD OF LOVE

There are those who treasure the pleasures of rural life: muddy tramps on country roads, speaking to your neighbors and home to your own wood stove.

There are those who treasure the suburbs, with their organized sports, PTAs and community task forces, and oversized sport utility vehicles lined up after school.

And then there are those who like the drama of urban life, the theaters and cafes and after-hours places, and dark, dimly lit bars that serve real martinis. San Francisco, bless her diverse, beloved heart, is the country-cum-suburb-cum-city that cheerfully, even elegantly, integrates them all. And nowhere demonstrates that more clearly than the south of Market, or SoMa, scene, an updated Greenwich Village moved way out west. Just minutes away from parent-obsessed neighborhoods like Potrero Hill, a few short miles away from the great country-scene-within-a-city that is Golden Gate Park, there is SoMa. Bright lights, neon, shops that offer piercing in anatomical locations never before imagined, clubs with mosh pits where Gen Xers and slackers fling themselves onto dance floors seemingly designed by the architect of Dante's Inferno, hip multimedia ghettos where gearheads create cyberworlds of reality beyond the virtual, gay bars that offer everything from down-home Texas two-step dancing lessons to biker hangouts, converted live-work lofts where childless couples live in art-directed gray and white, clean-lined, Bauhaus-approved splendor.

Hot Licks, despite its sexy name, is actually something of a tame player in the neighborhood. It's a traditional jazz club, though after hours the club's open-mike policy welcomes the more avant-garde—musicians, comedians, and the kind of people who cover themselves in glue and birdseed and apply for NEA grants as performance artists. The drinks are generous, the bar food is good but not chichi, and famous visitors love to drop by and sit in for a set with the house band. It's owned by a Chicago-transplanted couple and it shows, with an honest Midwest-joint feel in a neighborhood that has more attitude than anything else.

As I pulled up to the door on Eighth Street, I noticed that yet another auto body shop had given way to SoMa-ization and been replaced by a billiards parlor and champagne bar. Another place for the overpaid and overanxious younger set to wile away time and money, I groused to myself, sounding ever more like a bourgeois housewife. I resolved then and there to persuade Puck to take me along on one of his famous late-night SoMa crawls, so that I could feel marginally less stuffy.

In the meantime, Hot Licks's notorious hostess, she of the flame-colored hair and lingerie modeling career, awaited. She would be disappointed when she heard I was hopeless with a saxophone.

I pulled open the door and stepped inside, transported from dim fall sunshine into that eerie nobody-home darkness nightclubs have in the middle of the afternoon.

"Hello?" I called. "Anybody here?"

"We're not open! Go away," I heard someone shout back. I peered into the darkness and made out a t-shirted young man, putting bottles away in back of the bar.

I marched over and hoisted myself onto the bar. I grinned at the young man and admired the line of turquoise studs marching up his right ear. I counted five.

"Hi." I stuck out my hand. "I'm Maggie Fiori."

He shook. "And I'm Casper. But we're still not open, lady—uh, Maggie."

I turned on what I remembered as a beguiling smile. "Oh, I know. I'm a friend of Quentin's. He used to play sax in your Sunday jam sessions?"

He shook his head. "I remember. Cool guy. Shame he got… done in."

"I know. Anyway, someone called from here and wanted to know if I'd sit in for him." Casper regarded me suspiciously. I don't think the suburban matron getup led him to believe I was capable of delivering licks, hot or otherwise. I disabused him of that notion quickly. "Don't worry, I'm not here to play. I'm just talking to people who knew Quentin. Since I'm temporarily filling in for him at *Small Town*, I'm gathering material for a memorial piece."

He looked interested. "Oh, yeah? Well, you shouldn't talk to me. I hardly knew the guy. You ought to talk to our hostess, Stare."

"Stare?"

"Yeah. I think it's like Esther or something. But she's kinda cool for one of those Biblical names. So we call her Stare, 'cause, well—when you see her, you'll understand."

I got the drift. "You mean she's great looking and men stare at her, huh?"

He laughed. "Men. Women. Children. Small animals."

"So is she here?"

"Yeah, she's in the office. Want me to get her?"

"Please."

Casper disappeared through a swinging door behind the bar, leaving me to contemplate myself dispiritedly in the mirror behind the bottles. Stare, huh? Wonder what you have to look like to get called that? After Puck had mentioned her to me, I'd heard more about her from other people—little nuggets here and there. Heard about the modeling jobs for the Victoria's Secret catalog. Featured heavily in the teddy, brassiere, and bustier sections. Hmmph, I snorted inwardly, all that upper body emphasis must mean she's got less than gorgeous thighs. And was she conversant with the pluperfect tense? And did she know all the verses to John Jacob Jingelheimer-Schmidt? Get a hold of yourself, Maggie. This is envy so low, so degraded, so—and then, I stopped, because Stare was walking through the door and any envy I could have imagined was inadequate to the challenge.

Right off, the goddamn thighs were fine. I could see that because she had on a miniskirt—or not. It was so short, it was sort of a Zen skirt; you just had to imagine it was there. And there was that obnoxious cleavage. "Wonderbra," I thought to myself. "I could look like that."

And then there was that red hair, lots of it, redder than mine, in one of those dated, curly, cascading to the shoulders looks that men claim to love. It's what they mean when they sigh and say, "Why can't you wear your hair like...." Creamy skin, green eyes (contact-enhanced, I felt sure), and twenty-minute lips.

The pieces were terrific, but it was the sum of the parts that knocked a person out. Most of all, I realized, it was the way she moved all that gorgeousness across the floor. Something like warm caramel dripping off a spoon liquid, languorous, and melting everything in its path.

"Maggie? Gee, it's really great to meet you. Quentin talked about you a lot."

Yeah, I thought to myself bitterly, pillow talk, when he was contrasting your glamorous self to his frumpy, hausfrau stationwagon-driving suburban squeeze.

She hoisted her perfect little butt onto the barstool adjoining mine and reached awkwardly over to give me a hug. "I feel as if we know each other." I didn't. But it seemed rude to say so.

"Thanks for seeing me," I said. "Did Casper tell you I was doing a piece on Quentin?"

I couldn't take my eyes off all that perfection. Those billiard-table felt green eyes welled with tears. She nodded. "He told me. I'd love to help. What can I do?"

I felt the knot of envy dissolve. I'd like to think it was some grand feminist principle that made me feel petty to envy someone so beautiful. But probably not.

Maybe it was being past thirty and knowing that even in my

prime, I'd been the farm team to Stare's major league. Or maybe it was just that she was so perfect, so pleasurable to contemplate. I felt a little like an art student, struck happily dumb before a canvas of some pre-Raphaelite beauty. Stare was well-named.

So I simply launched into what I have to consider as a very fine piece of amateur detection. How she met Quentin? At the club. What their relationship was? More tears, but, well, just magical, Quent was so brainy and stuff. Who else Quent hung out with at the club? You know, just everyone. Any enemies? No, everyone liked him. Kinda quiet for this crowd, but very funny, good musician, very generous.

"Generous?" I asked, thinking about Quentin's real-life assets, separate from Claire.

Stare dabbed her eyes with a Hot Licks napkin. "Uh huh. You know, treating people to… well, treats."

"Standing drinks?" I asked.

"Oh, well, no. I mean, if you play here, the bartenders really take care of you."

"Okay, then, what do you mean? Making loans to people?" I couldn't quite conjure up an image of Quentin as a loan shark, but then, you never know.

"No, no," said Stare, and shifted uneasily on the barstool. "I just meant…."

Tiny bells went off in the back of my head. "Dope? He treated the guys to drugs."

A look of both relief and discomfort flitted over those art-directed features.

"Oh, you know. Nothing hard. But he'd bring hash in now or then, or good grass, and he was generous with it."

I guiltily remembered our small, suburban stash of Belize Breeze, also courtesy of Quentin, and began to wonder.

"He didn't sell, did he?"

Stare looked horrified. "Sell? Oh, no. He wasn't a dealer. He just seemed, every now and then, to have access to quite a bit of very high-quality stuff. And we'd all share the goodies."

I could see the headlines now. "Preppy Magazine Editor Doles Dope Largesse, in Places High and Low." Michael and I would probably be busted along with the musicians at Hot Licks. Oh well, at least there'd be more than Muzak in jail.

"So, Stare," I pressed on. "Any idea where this stuff came from? A friend of Quentin's? Somebody he worked with?"

She shrugged. "Who knows? We didn't ask. Quentin's—was—a kinda private guy. I mean, he had that bitchy Pacific Heights wife of his, and then...." she gestured toward herself.

"You?" I filled in politely.

"Yeah," she said. "Me. And hey I wasn't kidding myself. A whole lot of others. Boys and girls. That Quentin, he got around. You know...."

I knew. How nice to be part of a large extended family. "So as long as we're discussing Quentin's love life," I continued, "any past sweeties who were really pissed at him?"

Stare blew her nose, furrowed her brow, and appeared to give the matter some thought. "I don't think so. You know, with Quentin, no one ever took things very seriously. And he was so polite. I mean, he didn't really dump anybody. He just moved on. And it was okay; you just felt like you were part of a club or something."

"An alumni association," I commented, wondering if we should plan a reunion.

"Yes, that's it," she said brightly. "It was never love. It was fun with Quent. You felt as if you were his project for a while, and then the next project came up. But he didn't forget you or anything."

I nodded and made a mental note to call Inspector Moon.

"So, is what I said going to be part of the article?" asked Stare. "Seems kinda weird."

For a moment I was bewildered, and then I remembered my ruse for speaking with Stare. What a lousy detective. Got to keep those stories straight. "It's all background," I said. "But everything you said has been helpful." I had a sudden, queasy thought.

"Stare, did you tell the cops any of the stuff about drugs you told me?"

She shook her head. "No, they just asked us about enemies he might have had at the bar. I think they thought it was a different kind of place, that people get in fights here. You know."

Back at my office, Gertie was happy to get the signed invoices and relieved to hear that Glen was on the mend and would probably be in the next day. I dealt with the usual collection of pink message slips and then wandered down the hall to Puck's office.

He was in full writing mode. Gone was the laid-back, leather-jacketed, cooler-than-cool look. Jacket discarded on the floor, he was hunched over the word processor, three half-empty coffee mugs scattered over his desk, index cards taped to his walls. He looked undistractable, so I began to creep away. Without looking up, he barked at me. "Stop. Don't sneak out. Don't leave. Save me, save me!"

I wavered in the doorway. "You look like you're in the middle of it."

"I am, I am, and that bitch Fiori has me on deadline."

"Ooh, I love it when you call me names," I cooed to him.

Puck swiveled his chair around, away from the screen, and pointed at his disreputable armchair. "Sit, sit. I need a break. The bitch will have to wait."

"Well, thanks," I said. "Speaking schizophrenically, I'm sure she will."

He brightened. "You will?"

"Yeah, for about twenty four hours. So we'll make this a quick break."

Puck sighed. "Okay, what's up?"

"I want to know about drugs," I said. "I think Quentin had access to stuff, and I'd like to know where and when and why."

Puck looked annoyed. "Oh, you would, would you? Who issued you a badge, little lady?"

"Come on, Puck. I think you know something."

Puck carefully examined the toes of his black, reptile-skin boots. He held his foot up for me to check out. "Think these heels seem like I'm trying too hard to look tall?"

"Yeah, I do," I said briskly. "I think they point out once again how insecure all you boys under six feet are, and I don't think you're fooling anyone, and I know you're…" I looked him up and down, "no more than five feet ten, and if you can't fool a middle-aged, out-of-circulation old bat like me, you're sure not gonna fool those little girls with uncorrected twenty-twenty vision at the clubs."

Puck looked genuinely wounded. "Holy shit, you don't have to be so brutal."

"Hey, I've just spent a delightful hour with the curvaceous and, as I believe you boys say, 'eminently fuckable' Stare from Hot Licks, so I'm not in the mood to coddle anybody's ego. Mine's pretty much headed out of town for the winter."

Puck's expression brightened. "God, Stare. Mmmm. Isn't she a piece of work? Plus, she studied at the Sorbonne or something. In all my fantasies, she's talking dirty to me in French."

"In the pluperfect tense," I muttered.

Puck wasn't listening. He continued, "Man, I couldn't believe old Quent actually reeled her in. She needed somebody much, much younger."

"Yeah, well, I think she goes for tall ones," I said. "Save your energy."

Puck launched himself out of the office chair and began straightening up the piles of paper. "Okay, Maggie, make it quick. Now that you've dropped by to ruin my ego and my day, I do have to get back to my story."

"Well," I began, "before we were distracted by this delightful interlude dismantling each other's self-esteem, I believe I asked you about drugs."

He continued straightening, and muttered over his shoulder. "And I believe I asked you what business it was of yours?"

"Come on, I'm not just being nosy. Look at me." He turned around. I held up my right hand in Brownie pledge position. "I'm going to call Inspector Moon right away, I promise, but I think Quentin was into something peculiar, and maybe if we—if the cops—figure it out, they can wrap up this murder investigation. And we'll all be a lot happier."

Puck regarded me and then sank back into his desk chair, a wad of files leaking papers on his lap. "You mean *you'll* be a lot happier."

"Oh, you really want to have some murderer wandering around San Francisco? Maybe whoever it is will systematically knock off the entire staff of *Small Town*."

Puck snorted. "Bullshit, Maggie. This is turning into your little obsession. What's the matter? The cops coming after you—or old Mikey, the wronged husband?"

I winced.

"Gotcha," he said.

"Humor me," I said.

"Okay, but I don't know much, and I'm not all that hot to talk to the cops."

"That's fine," I said eagerly, "you can be my source. I don't think I have to reveal you."

Puck looked disgusted. "What you know about first amendment law could fit into the brain cells of—I don't know—a roadie."

"Okay, okay. This isn't my kind of journalism, as we all know. But you might as well tell me, and I can summarize for the cops."

"Summarize? What are you, the recording secretary of the PT-fuckin-A around here?" Puck shook his head. "Maggie, you drive me just a little bit nuts, even if you are my boss."

I didn't say anything. I was making it worse, and I figured Puck was still young enough to fall for the same psychology I used on Zach and Josh—and Inspector Moon had used on me. Shut up and wait, and eventually they'll tell you what's on their minds.

It worked. Puck felt around in back of him for a mug, picked it up, sipped, shuddered, and said, "So here goes. You just can't hang around at the clubs without running into drugs of some kind. I assume you know that?"

I nodded, trying to look non-judgmental.

"I mean, in the eighties, all those gay clubs had lots of drugs, amyl nitrate poppers and everything else."

"And alcohol," I offered brightly.

"Yeah, yeah, alcohol, the social drug of choice," agreed Puck. "Now, it's much different. There's a whole lot of health obsession going on, especially among us aging boomers."

I looked at him. "Okay, maybe not this aging boomer. But the kids," he shook his head. "Jesus, they're dumb. They're still willing to do anything, try anything, eat anything."

A picture of Josh and Zach swam into my head, their undiscriminating little palates constantly starved for gummy worms, Big Macs, and every other forbidden treasure.

"I know what you mean," I said.

Puck grimaced. "You think you do," he said. "Just wait 'til the little monsters are teenagers."

"I can wait," I said grimly. "Go on."

"Yeah, so, well, it's a lot pickier out there now, except for the kids. But, you know, I think musicians always feel like they're some kind of God Almighty privileged princes. They can blow what they want, some of 'em even think they can shoot what they want." Needles, I thought. Just put AIDS on an express train.

Puck made a face at me. "Don't give me one of those prissy Mom looks. I know you and old Mikey smoke a little yourselves now and then."

I sighed. "We do. Courtesy of Quentin and left over from our youth. But no more."

"Oh, yeah?"

"Yeah. We've been talking about it anyway. I want to be able to tell the 'little monsters,' as you so charmingly call them, that we don't do drugs."

"You don't lie to the little buggers?"

"Sure, we do. Regularly. About Santa Claus, and about what happens if you don't get enough vitamin C, and about how toys deactivate if you don't write thank-you notes to Gramma right away. But I'd just as soon not lie about this."

Inwardly, I felt a pang of regret saying goodbye to those sweet, nostalgic evenings, making love on just a little dope. But hey, what's a mom to do? Just another parental sacrifice. You start by giving up your vices, and first thing you know, you're really dull and respectable.

"Okay, enough about my child-rearing practices. So, what's the real story on Quentin and drugs?"

He laced his fingers behind his neck, leaned back, and regarded me warily.

"Well, I don't know much. But here it is: Quentin always had access to pretty good stuff. He never did coke, not even when people were walking around with those silly spoons around their necks fifteen years ago. But he always had pretty good grass and hash."

"And he didn't sell?"

Puck looked horrified. "Geez. No, absolutely not. Just, you know, late at night, if we were out at clubs, or at a friend's, as long as Claire-the-Witch-Woman wasn't along, he'd haul stuff out, and he was always very free with it. Like there was plenty more where that came from."

"And you don't know where it did come from?"

He shook his head. "No, not really. Quentin had a, how you say, wide acquaintance. And for an old guy, you know, he was pretty hip. So I guess those random young friends of his kept him supplied."

"That's it?"

"That's it, sister. Not much to tell. Now, what are you going to do with this paltry little sum of info?"

I didn't know. I said so. The intercom buzzed on Puck's desk and we both jumped. Gertie's voice said, "Puck? Is Maggie in there with you?"

Puck grinned at me. "She is, but she's just leaving."

I shot a rubber band at him. "We're just talking about drugs we've known and loved, Gertie. Do you need me?"

The intercom rasped again. "Aren't you two just adorable?

Well, Maggie, that nice police officer is here again. He's standing right next to my desk."

I felt my cheeks turn hot. Swell, caught being a wise-mouth again with Inspector Moon. I couldn't begin to imagine what he thought about my moral fibre. Well, actually, I could begin to imagine, and it wasn't very pleasant.

Puck was trying to control his delight, and without much success. "Hey, Mags," he called after me, as I headed for the hall, "wasn't it much less embarrassing when you were just a cute little housewife?"

"Back to work, big guy. You're on deadline," I said over my shoulder. I turned back. "On second thought, wait right here!"

In a few minutes, I was back, Moon in tow. "Sit down, sit down," I said. "Don't mind that clutter. We've got news."

I perched myself on Puck's least disgusting chair and said, "We've been asking around a little bit and we have some information."

"What do you mean 'we', white woman?" Puck asked innocently. "Not me, Inspector. It's all Nancy Drew here." He shot me a vile look. "In fact, I believe I distinctly said I didn't want to chat with the cops."

Inspector Moon crossed his legs. "Oh, I'm quite sure of that. And I'll have a little talk with Miss Drew. But why don't you two tell me what you've come up with before I begin my daily formal lecture about not meddling in police affairs."

I scowled at Puck, and then, between the two of us, we brought Moon up to date on what we'd found out. He listened carefully, made a few notes in his book, and said nothing until we'd finished.

"That's it?" he asked.

"That's it? I think it's a lot. Look," I said, warming to my task, "here's the deal. Why and how could Quentin afford to be so generous with dope?"

Moon looked doubtful. "Well, I don't know. I saw his home; he certainly appeared to be prosperous."

I waved impatiently. "Nuh-uh. This place pays dirt. He had

some money from Claire, but not enough to be Mr. Big with musicians. We think—" out of the corner of my eye, I saw Puck raise a warning hand.

"Correction, *I* think Quentin was getting dope, maybe as a gift from someone."

"Any ideas about who that someone might be?" asked Moon.

And here my grand theory began fraying at its imaginative little edges.

"I don't know," I confessed. "I mean, it could be anyone over at the club, but that doesn't make sense, because that's where he was handing it out."

"Anyone here at the magazine?" asked Moon.

I looked at Puck. "I don't think so. We may look hip, but most of the people here are too old to be doing much of the drug thing. I mean, there's the clerical staff, and God knows those bike messengers who charge in here have got to be involved with drugs, or they couldn't stand their jobs—or ride their bikes the way they do."

"You could ask Gertie," I offered helpfully. "She's been here the longest. She knows everybody and everything."

Moon stood. "Good idea. Now Maggie, I'd really like a word with you. In private."

"In private?" protested Puck. "Aren't you going to give her one of those 'stay out of police business' lectures? I'd love to listen."

"I'm sure you would," I said frostily, pointedly looking at my watch. "Well, I have a very few minutes right now, Inspector. If you'd care to join me in my office."

He followed me down the hall, while I mentally rehearsed all the reasons it was dangerous, blah blah blah, inappropriate, blah blah blah, and unwelcome, blah blah blah for me to be "investigating."

Boy, was I on the money. He went right into the mini-lecture, while I listened with a polite, good-girl-getting-lectured-by-the-headmaster look on my face. There was a big finish.

"Maggie, I know you're not taking me seriously. And I want

you to. I don't mind—wait, let me correct that, I welcome your ideas, your suggestions, your information. Frankly, we're run through all the obvious possibilities and we haven't come up with much."

"Like no fingerprints on the walking stick?" I asked eagerly.

"Like no fingerprints on the walking stick," he said. "But let me assure you, we've gone beyond the obvious."

"Wiped clean," I said.

Moon looked exasperated. "May I continue? I do appreciate your ideas and your help. But I cannot emphasize strongly enough that you cannot, you must not, run around the city acting like a detective."

I nodded. "I know, I know."

He stood to go and gave me a hard look. "I know your type. I used to run into girls just like you when I was a high school counselor. Too smart for your own good, and quick to confuse obstinacy with strength of character."

I smiled sweetly. "Here's a deal: I'll stop detecting if you stop asking dumb questions about Michael and his temper."

He put his hand on the door knob. "No deal. If you ask a lot of dumb questions in a murder investigation, smart ones sneak in there after awhile. And since you're so busy worrying about your family, let me remind you that you're a mother. I don't want to have to explain to your children that something happened to you because you didn't listen to me."

"That," I said, "is a low, low blow."

For the first moment that afternoon, he smiled. "I know. Isn't it? I love mothers; they're so easy to manipulate."

THE SOT AND THE
WITCH WOMAN

As planned (and negotiated with Michael), we met Alf and Claire for dinner at one of those well-reviewed new restaurants that manage to combine deafening noise, outrageous prices, and a patronizing staff under one roof. It was, as usual, packed.

We entered the front door and walked down the kind of badly canted, difficult-to-navigate ramp that made a girl grateful to be wearing flats. Michael surveyed the room and snorted. There was not a warm or welcoming surface in the place. High ceilings, triple-washed in glazed colors, hard aluminum chairs, metallic tables with edges just right for impaling unwary diners. There was an open kitchen, and within it was a heavily sweating staff, all visible, all wearing the kind of microphone headgear Beyoncé wears in concert.

Michael put his mouth close to my ear,

"Do you think they're involved in hostage negotiations, simultaneous translations at the UN, or just opening for Metallica?"

I gave him the "you promised you'd behave" spousal look. He gave me a smile of complete non-commitment.

"Remember, I'm a murder suspect; I have very little motivation to behave."

"You are not," I hissed.

"Okay, I'm a wife-beater."

"Not that either. And stop joking."

I had confided Inspector Moon's queries to Michael. Instead of getting angry, he seemed to find it amusing, when he wasn't using that information to make me feel even more awful than I already did.

Across the room, I saw Uncle Alf settled in one of the booths at the perimeter. He waved, I waved back, and, avoiding the "I'm cool and you're so, so not" host, we began winding our way to their table.

Uncle Alf had a little lineup of glasses in front of his plate, Claire was toying with a martini and snapping her lighter open and closed. Uncle Alf's greeting was hearty; Claire flicked her eyes up and down me, suppressed a sigh, and turned to Michael.

"Oh, yes, Mr. Fiori," she said, "I know we've met. You're the do-good tax lawyer." Michael took her outstretched hand and leaned close. "I am, Mrs. Hart," he said, "it pays so much better than doing evil. But then," he paused and grinned, "perhaps you know that."

"Michael," I whimpered, "please...."

We slid into the booth. Unlike the chairs at the tables in the center of the room, the booths actually had upholstery. But it was woven from metallic thread and was both itchy to touch and inadequately padded to offer any protection against the brutal stainless steel seat.

Michael smiled and gestured at the room. "Well, isn't this uncomfortable?"

"Beg pardon?" Uncle Alf said, gesturing at the waiter.

"He said, 'isn't this cozy?'" I interpreted, and gave Michael a gentle nudge under the table.

Painful small talk, a review of the almost incomprehensible menu, and our first course followed.

Uncle Alf, with a few Scotch rocks in him, had reached that happy glazed state he found so reassuring. He lifted his glass and said, "I propose a toast."

The table fell silent. Michael and I warily lifted our glasses. Claire looked bored and raised her martini a centimeter off the table's surface.

"To Maggie," said Uncle Alf. "She's doing a helluva job over at the magazine. Keeping the place running, keeping the natives un-restless. Good show, Maggie."

I mumbled my thanks, we all sipped, and returned to our highly decorated plates. Michael began unrolling a piece of endive that had been coaxed into an unnatural shape. Information, I thought to myself, that's all I can possibly salvage from this evening.

"So tell me, Claire," I said, "all about Skunkworks. I hear you're on the board. And, of course," I smiled at her, "Quentin mentioned to me that the Cock of the Walk opening was a benefit for your group."

Claire regarded me with a flicker of interest. "I didn't know you kept up with such things."

"Such things?" I asked. "You mean, AIDS groups? Actually, I do try to keep up."

Claire speared a white asparagus and nibbled the end. She said, "Oh, I meant boards and things like that. I didn't think that kind of news actually drifted across the Bay to Oakland."

"Yes, we've got our little crystal set tuned to High Society-Free America," said Michael.

"Well," I persisted, "the Skunkworks isn't exactly the Symphony or the Opera, is it?"

"No, it's not," Claire said tartly. "But I'm very proud of what we do."

"Wonderful work, wonderful work," mumbled Alf, draining his third or fourth drink.

"So tell me about it, Claire," I said. "I'm really interested. You know, Quentin had talked to me about doing a story on that benefit."

"Did he?" asked Claire, narrowing her eyes. "Wasn't that lovely of him?"

"It was," I responded.

Silence fell again. This was not going well. "Okay," I prompted, "I know you all help fund research for drugs that aren't far enough along in the FDA pipeline. Isn't that right?"

"Yes," she said. "We all know the FDA is much, much too slow in moving drugs along."

"Point of fact," interrupted Michael, "I believe they're doing a little better these days, especially for AIDS drugs. That's part of what ACT UP helped push. They've got several drugs on fast tracks, and they're making them available on a limited basis to AIDS patients who meet certain criteria. After clinical trials, before final approval."

Claire looked nonplussed. "You sound quite knowledgeable."

Michael sipped his wine. "Two of my clients are the nonprofit foundations of pharmaceutical companies. I try to keep up. With a wife in those fast-moving media circles, I've got to be more than a pretty face, you know." He patted my hand.

"So then, Claire," I continued. "The money you raise goes to what? Research grants?"

"Absolutely," she said, snapping her lighter open and closed again. "Well, some of it. The rest goes to individuals."

"Individuals?" Michael inquired.

"Yes, yes," she said blithely. "People who can't get into trials."

"How interesting," Michael said. "And how does it get distributed?"

Claire looked impatient. "There's a committee. John Orlando, the fellow who owns Cock of the Walk, is on the committee. Along with some others. You're both very welcome to review our bylaws."

"I wasn't questioning your motives," I said "I was just wondering, just curious."

Uncle Alf came to for a minute. "And that's what killed the cat, isn't it?"

He laughed.

Silence fell again.

"Well," Claire said briskly, "I imagine that story is moot, isn't it? The benefit's long gone, as is Quentin, of course, so you'll just have to find some other little social do to cover, won't you?"

"Well," Michael protested, "I don't think Maggie was planning to cover this as a social notes story."

I gave Michael another gentle kick.

"Really?" asked Claire. "What did you have in mind, then?"

"I don't know," I said. "That's why I was going to meet Quentin the day he died. We were going to talk about a story angle. I thought you could help me out on that?"

Claire sighed. "Sorry. No idea; I simply thought Quentin was doing the right thing and giving us a little publicity."

"*Do the Right Thing*," said Alf, drifting into the conversation again. "Isn't that the movie by that colored fella, Lee Spike, Spike Jones, something like that? All the rage a few years back?"

Michael gave me his most innocent look. "Don't think you've got that quite right, Alf. But you might want to put that question to Maggie's friend Calvin next time you see him."

"Oh, actual filmmaker, is he?" asked Alf.

"No," said Michael. "Actual colored person."

The dessert cart came and went. It was actually a highly anodized wheelbarrow with pedestals spiraling from its bed, each holding an intricately engineered concoction, heavy on cloudberries and light on chocolate. We all passed.

"Looks just like the one I use to haul chicken manure around the backyard," observed Michael.

"Funny people, Claire," said Alf. She ignored him. "Damn fine senses of humor. Keeps things moving merrily along, I s'pose."

"Very merry," said Michael. "The fun never stops at our house."

Over coffee, Alf got down to business. He and the Witch-Woman were pleased with what I was doing at the magazine. Would I be willing to stay on for another six months?

I took a deep breath and said precisely the right thing. "Oh, thank you so much. Michael and I will need to discuss that first."

"In a merry, merry way, of course," said Michael, very solemnly.

Claire rolled her eyes.

"May I get back to you?" I asked sweetly.

"Of course, of course," said Alf. "Don't wait too long, though."

He waved for the check. Meanwhile, Claire was scanning the room looking for someone, anyone more interesting than the present company. Bingo! Her eyes lit up, and she waggled her fingers in the air. Across the room, John Orlando waved back and headed over to the table.

He and Claire air-kissed, both cheeks, very European, he shook hands with Alf and Michael, then turned to me.

"Mrs. Fiori, out celebrating an anniversary on the new job?" he asked dryly.

I smiled, "Something like that. I'm surprised to see you here. Who's running the show over at your place?"

"Busman's holiday," he said, "got to see what the competition is up to. Research, you know."

"Must get expensive," I said, "all this dining out. Guess the restaurant business must be very lucrative."

"Maggie," chided Michael, turning to Orlando. "You'll have to forgive my wife. Once a journalist, always a journalist, ask anybody anything."

Orlando smiled. "Quite all right. Quite. Yes, well, this is a restaurant town, isn't it?" He gestured around the room. "Fortunately, there seems to be more than enough business to go around." He bent and air-kissed Claire again. "Must run, must get back to my own little lunchroom." He looked pointedly at me. "'Fraid the new regime isn't tip-top market for my artwork, so I've got to grind out my living at the restaurant trough."

"I'm sure we'll find a way to work together in the future," I said stiffly.

"Yes, well, mustn't put all the eggs in one hopeful little basket," he said. Gestured at the table. "Lovely to see you all."

"Didn't follow all that, did you?" asked Alf, after he'd gone.

It seemed best not to explain. We thanked Alf and Claire for dinner and headed out to redeem our beat-up stationwagon from the contemptuous young valet.

On the way home, Michael suggested I say yes to Alf and Claire's offer to extend my employment.

"Really?" I asked. "You think it's okay?"

"I think it's great," he said. "Keeps you too busy to play amateur detective, cuts down on the time you have to ask people nosy questions. Plus, there doesn't seem to be anyone else on that staff for you to have an affair with."

I started to protest.

"Just joking," he said. "But, you know, I actually think it's making the boys a tiny bit more independent, and Anya a little more competent. Takes her mind off that perpetually broken heart. And if it's making you happy...."

And I realized it was. I liked the routine, I liked the people, I liked the sense of accomplishment of moving from one issue to the next. "It is," I said. "It surprises me, but it is."

"And very little time to play detective?"

I was silent.

"Maggie, why can't you leave this alone?"

"Because I keep thinking that I can put this together and make it all go away."

"Oh, that's not arrogant, is it?"

"Well, yes, it is. On the other hand, I was there! And the truth of the matter is, the cops haven't figured it out, so I don't think they have much to feel arrogant about either."

"I can't forbid you."

I snorted, "You certainly can't."

"But I can ask you in the strongest possible terms to think about what you're doing. Think about the kids and think about me. And then it's up to you."

"Thank you," I said meekly. "I'm being very careful, I'm really just passing along anything I figure out to John Moon."

"Well, here's the good news in all this," said Michael. "With your new job, I think you'll continue to feel conflicted and guilty, and you're just Jewish enough to make that up to us by cooking better dinners, and keeping Anya out of the kitchen. So I say we may all come out ahead." He turned back to the road, humming a little under his breath.

"Michael, is something up with you?" I asked.

"Why?"

"You're way too easy about this."

He shook his head. "For a smart girl, you can be so, so dumb. I don't care if you want to work at the magazine. I never cared if you wanted to go out and be a captain of industry. I just wish you'd talked to me before."

"Before Quentin," I said.

"Yeah. Before him. But what's done is done. And the son of a bitch is dead and gone. I want to trust you; it's now abundantly clear to me that I can't unless you're happy. And if working at *Small Town*, in Quentin's old job, makes you happy—and too busy to get into trouble—then I'm happy. QED."

"How lawyerly," I said.

"Yes, well, that can't be a big surprise to you, can it? Frankly, I'd prefer for Quentin and anything that had anything to do with him to vanish off the face of the earth."

"I'm really sorry—" I began.

"Enough, Maggie. I know you are. And I'm almost getting used to the cops showing up at my office to ask questions from time to time," he said bitterly. "My poor protective secretary keeps telling everyone that all these guys are potential new squash partners. Oh, one thing I should mention...."

"What?"

"It's not a big deal, at least not to me."

"Michael, what is it?"

"The senior partners have asked me to step down from the management committee. At least until the murder investigation is over."

How much more wretched could I feel? "I'm so sorry," I began.

"Maggie, don't bother. I don't care. It's one less thing to worry about."

Silence fell in the car. Then Michael spoke. "So I'm very motivated to keep you busy and out of mischief. I'd prefer not to put any of us through this again. Ever."

Maybe I can make it all go away, I thought to myself.

"Are you listening to me, Maggie?" Michael said.

"Oh, yes," I said. "I heard every word you said."

O IS FOR ORNAMENTATION

The weeks sped by. The sycamores and birches in our front yard were completely denuded, the kids had celebrated Halloween and were recovered from their sugar rush. The home magazines were featuring photographs of brown and glistening turkeys, exhorting us drop-out Martha Stewarts that our lives would be richer, more complete, if we grew, harvested, shelled, and roasted our own chestnuts for the stuffing.

At work, as Michael had observed, I was genuinely enjoying the rhythm of getting out the magazine. Glen and Gertie knew everything there was to know about the production side, but that left me presiding over the unruly group of writers who gave *Small Town* its voice. Thinking about story angles, chasing deadlines, and showing up for periodic reviews with the alcohol-addled Uncle Alf pretty much drove detecting out of my everyday consciousness. Quentin, on the other hand, was still omnipresent. I felt him in the room with me, watching me at his desk. Would he be glad I was there, or tsk-tsk over some lame decision I made?

Inspector Moon and I had struck up something resembling a friendship. Since the Neruda conversation, I knew he was interested in poetry, so I had invited him and his wife to use two of *Small Town's* comp tickets and join us for a benefit reading at San Francisco's flossy new main library. Mostly, I'd wanted to see if he'd come out on a social outing, assuming that would mean Michael was really, truly in the clear.

"Don't you pay any attention in the movies?" Michael asked me. "Cops *like* to socialize with suspects; they catch them off-guard that way." I felt my face freeze in dismay until Michael assured me he was joking.

When Moon was in the neighborhood, he'd drop by my office occasionally, and let me pester him with questions about the investigation. But mostly I was too preoccupied with the magazine to get into much mischief.

Only Calvin kept after me. I'd come back from lunch and find a message slip with a terse, "How about the INS?" or "CIA involvement." For Calvin it was a lark, an adventure—he had come close to something dangerous and he couldn't give up worrying it, like our dog Raider with an old pot roast bone. Of course, every time I heard from him, my own unfinished business with Quentin would pop up again. I'd conjure Michael's voice floating to me in the dark car after dinner with Alf and Claire, wishing Quentin out of our lives.

At home, the household seemed to have re-settled itself around my work schedule. I had worried that Josh would suffer the most, since any disruption in routine could lead to upheavals in his delicate digestive system. But, aside from the usual Friday morning pre-spelling test jitters, things actually seemed a little easier for him. Since Michael's office was just a few minutes from our house, he was often home before me, and early enough to sweep the boys out for pre-dinner fun playing catch at the park, riding bikes around Lake Merritt, or drinking hot chocolate at the ice cream parlor. Sometimes Anya would go with them and I'd come home to a kitchen full of laughter, all four of them with their cheeks rouged by the fall wind. I'd feel a little like an intruder until I got caught up in the flurry of dinner, stories, bath, and bedtime. Maybe, I groused to myself, I should take my wicked, straying self out of the picture, and let Michael and Anya raise the children. Then I'd remember what a dreadful cook Anya was and how much my husband valued good food. Saved by the Italian passion for pleasures of the *cucina,* I thought.

In the back of my mind was one guilt-stricken reality: Michael had all this extra time on his hands because his partners had asked him to step down from the management committee of the firm.

Michael insisted he didn't care.

"One less committee meeting, *cara*," he said; "maybe you did me a favor."

I felt awful, especially when we went to social outings with other people in the firm and I could see people exchange glances when we walked in.

"Gives me big points with the secretaries," said Michael. "They love the idea that some stuffy tax lawyer might be capable of a crime of passion."

Michael was so cool, so removed during these conversations that I knew he wouldn't talk to me about it in any serious way.

"Swell, Maggie," I muttered to myself in the ladies' room after one particularly self-conscious exchange with the senior partner's wife. "Go ahead and ruin Michael's career along with your marriage." But Michael refused to discuss any of these repercussions.

In keeping with our marital malaise, the gray, discouraging November skies began leaking rain. One gloomy morning I struggled in to the office, books and files under one arm, juggling an umbrella and a caffe latte on the other side. Calvin was at my desk leafing through old issues of *Small Town* and sipping out of a commuter mug. I was not charmed to see him.

I flung my coat over the coat rack and shook my umbrella over his head. A mini-shower of rain cascaded on to him.

"Calvin. Get up this instant, I've got tons of stuff to do this morning and I've got to get out of here by three today to see Josh's soccer game or it's off to the Bad Mommy Farm for me."

"Haven't we become the little overachiever?" He gestured at the visitor chair. "Sit down, Maggie. Relax. Suck up that caffeine and let's talk."

The day's schedule rolled through my head, scrolling at top speed like a computer screen out of control. I sighed. "Come on. I really don't have time."

"Yeah, yeah, I know. Things to do. People to see. Just chill one little minute. I want to show you something."

"Okay, five minutes. I mean it. Show me, and then you're history 'cause I've got to get to it."

Calvin swept my desktop debris into a corner. "Wait, wait a second," I protested.

"You know, Maggie," he said, "it never looked like this when Quentin had this office."

"Thanks," I said grimly. "I'll add tidiness to my 'improving my character' list."

He grinned. "Good idea. What else have you got on that list?"

I glared at him. "Upgrading the company I keep, thank you very much. "

Calvin ignored me. He was busy lining up past issues of *Small Town* in front of me. Each was open to a spread, and each featured a black and white pen and ink illustration.

"Uh huh," I said. "Orlando's stuff. I don't like it much, but I know Quentin and Glen used him a lot. So?"

Calvin rearranged the spreads carefully, aligning them just so. "Take a good look."

I was getting exasperated. "I have. I know his stuff."

Now Calvin was getting excited. "Okay, look at these. See how they're all different subject matter?"

"Yes, they are. They're all illustrations for very different stories." As I glanced, I could see one on a boxing program at the Y, a piece on erotic bookstores, one on classic Viennese bakeries, a profile on a city supervisor.

Calvin leaned forward, pushing up the sleeves of his sweater impatiently.

"Now, what's the same on every illustration?"

I looked. Hard. They were all in the same style, intricate, almost scratchboard-like, a little William Blake-ish.

"I don't see anything, Calvin. Unless you mean that they all have the same look—and the same signature."

He exploded out of his chair. "Exactly! They all have the same signature—or almost the same. Look closely."

I did. Each was signed with the illustrator's last name—Orlando. And the first O was heavily ornamented. Calvin sat back down at my desk, yanked open the center drawer, and began pawing around.

"Calvin! Do you mind? What are you looking for?"

"Where's your loupe? Aha! Got it." He held up the small magnifying glass used to look at photographic contact sheets. He came around in back of me and placed the loupe on one of Orlando's signatures. "Okay, take a close look."

I bent over and put my eye right on the loupe. I could feel Calvin leaning over me, quick intakes of breath.

"Hey," I mumbled. "Could you back up a little? I can't see anything with you hovering over me."

Under the loupe, the O's ornaments came into focus. Ivy leaves, with what appeared to be "2/3/345876" inside the leaves. What were they? The dates the illustration was complete? A file number? Did the guy inventory his work? What?

I looked up at Calvin, bewildered. He gestured to the next spread. "Look at a few more, go ahead."

I did. I moved the loupe from drawing to drawing, Orlando to Orlando, O to O. And in each initial O, upon close inspection, there it was—some sort of leaf-bedecked set of numbers, 1/6/231572—none of these could be dates.

I looked up at Calvin. The morning's work seemed like an annoyance, a mosquito buzzing around. I slipped my shoes off, put my feet on the heat vent under the desk, and felt the soggy nylons start to steam.

"What is this? Do you know what these numbers are?"

Calvin shook his head. "No idea. But don't you think it's exciting they're there?"

I did. And I felt—no, I knew—we were about to get in over our heads. "How'd you find them?"

"I'm a genius," he said. "Well, maybe not. I was just looking at his stuff, I spread it around. You know—we visual thinkers—we need to look at things."

"Nice work," I said. "If it means anything." I mused, "It's like Hirschfeld."

"Pardon?" said Calvin.

"So, Mr. Visual Thinker, you know the illustrator who did all those sketches of theater people? Anyway, he sometimes draws his daughter's name right into the sketch. If you squint at a necktie someone's wearing in one of his illustrations, you'll see the lines of the design form her name."

"How do you know all this weird, miscellaneous stuff, Maggie?"

I shrugged. "I don't really understand the infield fly rule or the names of all the big-time Catholic saints. Leaves plenty of room in my brain to fill up with trivia. But here's the thing about those Hirschfeld drawings—you wouldn't find Nina's name unless you knew to look for it. Kinda like this situation."

"Good point," said Calvin. "Now, very quietly, very calmly, we're going to figure out what the options are. And then," he gestured theatrically, "we're going to crack this case."

"This case? Calvin, we don't know that these numbers have meaning, sinister or otherwise. And we don't know they have anything to do with Quentin's death. I mean, they may just be some weird numbering system this guy has. Who knows?"

I wiggled my toes, grateful for the warmth creeping in. I retrieved my coffee cup, pried the lid off, and took a sip. "Besides, old John's got some ironclad alibi. He was at the restaurant, and zillions of people saw him." Calvin leaned against the window sill and closed his eyes. "Are you ill?" I inquired politely. "Because I'd just as soon you not throw up in my office. I'm only cheerful about cleaning up if it's one of my kids."

"Jesus, Maggie," he said without opening his eyes, "I thought you mother types were supposed to be compassionate. And I'm not sick. I'm just thinking."

He held up a finger. "Theory one, there's some weird code in these O's—and all those zillions of people who saw Orlando at the restaurant are lying."

"Trust me, Calvin," I said. "I know group behavior. I've done time as chair of the PTA World Culture Day. You can't get more than three people to agree on a time for a meeting, how could you get them all to agree to tell the same lie?"

I continued, "Still, I kinda like your theory. It could be a code of some kind, you know, like 'one if by land and two if by sea.'"

"Very patriotic, Mags," said Calvin.

"Okay, a code for what?"

He shook his head. "Smuggling something? Industrial espionage? Maybe when they all add up, it's a series of addresses on the Internet. Maybe it's insider stock trading or something?"

We looked at each other. "Inspector Moon," I said.

"I know. We've got to call him. But I just wish, I mean, there's something there, I know there is."

"Wait a minute, wait a minute," I muttered. "Something's nagging at me."

Calvin regarded me eagerly. "Go with the flow, babe. Let it happen."

"Calvin, cut the New Age crap."

"You know what I mean. If you stop struggling over something, if you just relax and let it happen, it's like it's out there waiting for you."

And the bell went *ping*! "Calvin, that's it. This is tied to time in some way. Remember how particular Quentin and Glen were about when these things ran?" Calvin looked puzzled.

"Of course, you don't," I said. "Somebody here at *Small Town* told me that, and they told me because I wanted to hold up on a drawing. They said something about… the drawing had to be fresh."

"That's nuts," said Calvin, "unless they're political editorial cartoons, which they're not as far as I can tell, these things don't have shelf lives."

"I know, I know. Of course they don't. But somebody told

me they did, and then—who was it? Maybe Andrea said that when they couldn't use an illustration, it ran right away, that same month, in the Sunday supplement. So it must have something to do with timing!"

Gertie chose that moment to enter, with Glen hard on her heels. "Maggie—" they both began.

Calvin leaned over my desk and in one swift move, began folding the magazines up, stacking them neatly. Gertie looked puzzled. "What is this? A review of past glories?"

"Yes," I said, at, of course, the same moment Calvin said, "No."

Glen looked from one to the other of us. "Well now, and which is it? I've only seen guiltier faces goin' into the confessional."

Instinctively, I knew I didn't want to talk about Calvin's discovery.

"Calvin's going to squeeze us into his ever-so-busy schedule," I said. "We were looking at editorial photographs in past issues so that he could be darn sure he out-did everyone else."

"I see," Glen said dryly. "That certainly explains everything."

Well, it was damn lame, but it got us through the moment. Calvin disappeared, magazines under his arm. Gertie called after him, "Just a minute, young man. Are those archival copies?"

"I'll take very good care of them," Calvin called over his shoulder.

Within minutes, Gertie, Glen, and I were plunged back into the day-to-day business of the magazine. Negotiating squabbles between the copy editor and a writer who went in for totally original, and excessive, uses of punctuation. Repaginating the magazine—deciding what went where and in which order to accommodate a last minute burst of energy from the ad sales staff, who had overpromised "right hand page, far forward" to all and sundry. Looking at portfolios. Bitching about Uncle Alf's tight hold on the purse strings, and complaining—yet again—about what a lousy magazine town San Francisco is.

"The weather's too nice here," said Glen. "You can't produce a walloping lot of stuff to read in a place like San Francisco. The sun shines, the cafés are full, there are races to run and kites to fly on the Marina Green. No one wants to sit inside and read."

"It's raining today," I pointed out.

"And if more days were like this, we'd have a more literary city."

"You think so?" Gertie asked skeptically.

"Absolutely," said Glen. "Who produces the most literature in the Western world? The English. And you know why? Because it's cold and gray and foggy 360 days of the year. There's nothing to do but sit inside and read."

"How about the Irish?" I teased.

"Ah, we're prolific for different reasons," he said. "There's all that misery you've got to work out. And Ireland is full of the kind of things that spur writers on—too little money, too many pubs, and no guilt-free sex."

"Very perceptive analysis," I said. "I'm sure those things could be worked into the curriculum in all the creative writing programs in America."

Gertie stood. "Enough of this meaningless literary chit-chat," she said, looking at her watch. "I'm starved. Anyone for middle eastern food?"

Glen and I brightened. The best hummus and baba ghanouj were just around the corner at the teeny-tiny Cafe Krivaar. The whole place smelled of garlic and roasting lamb, although, in the spirit of international understanding, the Krivaar also offered Middle Eastern versions of pizza. It was presided over by Grandpa Vic and his squadron of family members, gifted poets who penned such signs as, "Don't be a weinie/Try our iced cappucini," or, "Don't be a poop/Try our soup." Gertie volunteered to make the run to Krivaar for takeout and Glen went back to his office.

I picked up the phone and, like an obedient little Girl Scout, called Inspector Moon, spilled Calvin's findings, and offered to courier a set of the magazines over to his office so he could check out what we found. Soon Michael would be back on that awful committee and I'd stop breathing guilt in and out with every puff of air. I sat back, feeling like I'd finally done the right thing, looking forward to wolfing my pita stuffed with hummus with a completely clean conscience. For a change.

NUMEROLOGY AT THE DINNER TABLE

It was Thursday evening, my favorite of the week. Nothing but downhill ahead of us—one more set of lunches to make, one more set of homework assignments to nag through, sweet Friday and the weekend stretching ahead. I was watching Michael grate mozzarella, parmesan, and reggiano for a heart-stopping, cholesterol-filled batch of his grandmother's baked ziti. Stuart and Anya were playing Parcheesi with the boys. Stuart's loneliness, thinly disguised under a nonstop stream of gossip about his new employer and a free-from-Quentin unending series of bad Hawaiian shirts, wrenched my heart. He'd become a regular dinner guest, teaching Josh the fine points of the hook shot and playing video games with Zach.

"I feel as if we have another kid around when Stuart's here," observed Michael.

"Yeah, and he's got the kids' unclear concept of fair play," I said. "None of them has yet explained the rules of Parcheesi to poor Anya."

"So how's the detective biz?" asked Michael. "Since I know good and well you're still on the case despite—" and here he raised the grater and shook it at me threateningly, "my explicit orders to leave it alone."

I surveyed the floor, where little wisps of grated cheese had drifted downwards with each shake. "Raider," I called, "cheese on the floor." Raider padded in and began a serviceable cleanup.

"As if you'd even look at a woman who followed explicit orders," I said. "Besides," I ventured, taking a sip of Chianti, "shows what you know. Calvin and I did turn up a very fine clue, and I very virtuously, and very correctly, called Inspector Moon up straightaway."

"Uh huh," said Michael, "And then what?"

"Well, unlike what happens in detective novels where the amateur sleuth outwits the cops, it turned out that Moon snatched our clue and ran with it. Energetically."

Michael continued to grate. "So what was the clue and what did he find out?"

I explained about the weird numbers in the O, and that Moon had listened very intently, examined the magazines, and cranked up the computers.

"But they haven't figured anything out yet. He's got one of those hackers-turned-good guys trying to feed the numbers in all sorts of ways."

"How about just asking Orlando?" said Michael. "Maybe there's some innocent explanation for the numbers."

"Well, that's what I thought. But whatever answer Moon got, he didn't tell me, and it must not have satisfied him, because he's got those gearheads working on solutions. Although," I sipped my wine, "he explained the 24/72 rule to me."

"And that would be...."

"How come you're not a criminal lawyer? You'd know these things."

"Because one significant shortcoming of being a criminal lawyer is that most of the time you hang out with criminals. And may I remind you that even being associated with a felony hasn't precisely enhanced my career."

"Of course, you get to hang out with people looking for tax loopholes," I countered. "A much classier group of folks."

"Maggie."

"Okay, okay. Anyway, most homicides are solved within twenty-four hours, according to Moon. Because the usual suspects are easy to figure out—the boyfriend, the wife, the pissed off coworker, etc."

"The cruelly wronged husband," added Michael.

I tried to ignore him. "Then, if you don't make that deadline, you start looking real hard while the evidence is fresh, and that takes you to seventy-two hours."

"And then?" he asked.

"Well, if you haven't figured it out in seventy-two hours, the likelihood that you ever will drops dramatically. I think they're keeping this case live just because Quentin was a high profile guy."

Michael sighed.

"What?"

"I know why the police are keeping the case alive," he said. "It's you I worry about. Why can't you leave it alone?"

"I don't know," I confessed. "I've wondered that myself. I guess I feel as if Quentin was pretty dangerous to me—to us."

"You have no idea," muttered Michael, giving the parmesan a particularly vigorous swipe down the grater.

"So now he's dead. And as long as we don't know the why or the who, something still feels dangerous to me. Unfinished."

Michael looked at me. "It's not your job to finish."

"I know," I said. "And frankly, the magazine has kept me so busy, I haven't had much time to get into trouble. And believe it or not, I do think the cops know what they're doing."

"But?"

"But I feel as if I endangered everything that matters to me."

"You did," he said.

Michael folded the last of the cheese into in a giant casserole dish.

"In some weird, terrible way the murder brought good things to me," I said.

"Your job?"

"Yes, my job. But also, it meant that there wasn't this awful secret between us any more. So if the murderer isn't thrown in jail—"

"Forgetting due process," interrupted Michael.

"Oh, you know what I mean. If the murderer isn't brought to justice, then it's as if this tragic thing happened and I benefited from it, and nobody's paying in any serious way."

"Well," said Michael, "it's another happy ending for you, isn't it?"

"For us," I corrected.

Silence.

"I do like my life, Michael," I faltered. "And I can't tell you how awful I feel about you being dragged into all of this."

"I'm glad to hear that," he said. "And I'm looking forward to you remembering it. Now how about getting the oven door for me?"

I watched Michael put the casserole in the oven. When he was done talking about something, there was not a lot of room for revisiting the topic.

"Salad?" I inquired.

"I'm taking that as an offer to make one," he said. "I'll take that chair and that Chianti and just watch. I figure as long as you're occupied here in the kitchen, you can't be out chasing down murderers like Hercule Poirot."

"I believe," I said, compliantly rummaging through the crispers, looking for green things that hadn't yet wilted, "that Poirot was a guy. Don't you know any chick detectives?"

I held up a cucumber. Michael grinned. "Too large to be Poirot's instrument. Must be mine."

"Very funny. I was just wondering if you knew the current status of Zach's feelings about cucumbers in the salad. In or out?"

"In. But he likes the side fluted in that artsy-fartsy way you girls do them," he groused.

"Oh, forgive me. I didn't realize I was compromising your precious son's masculinity by art-decorating the vegetables."

I liked the feeling in the kitchen: a little serious talk, a little chat, a little bicker, a little teasing. It felt the way it was supposed to feel to me, before I'd strayed off the moral straight and narrow.

I thought about Hot Licks and about Stare, about the attractions of the unknown, the hip and the cool. Tempting, but still, my own gem, little kitchen and life could feel awfully good. Besides, unless I dyed my hair and rearranged what passed for curves on my body, I couldn't keep up in that world. As I thought, I trimmed radishes, sliced peppers, and broke off chunks of lettuce.

"You know," I observed, "no one eats iceberg lettuce any more."

"No one?" asked Michael. "That seems to be untrue, *prima facie.* I believe we ourselves are about to eat iceberg this very evening. Or, wait, is that the point? We're nobodies *because* we eat iceberg?"

"Plus," I continued, "there's virtually nothing of food value in iceberg. We need to eat dark, leafy greens—spinach, kale, that stuff."

Michael sipped his wine. "Uh huh. Well, why don't you pick an evening when I'm working late to introduce that 'stuff' to the boys. I'd just as soon not be here to hear their response."

And with that, the kitchen door flew open and the little gourmands in question swept in, shouting about their victory over Anya and Stuart.

"Josh," I suggested, "you know, if you were nice guys you'd explain the rules to Anya. I still don't think she gets the intricacies of Parcheesi. That's why she keeps losing."

Josh flopped in a kitchen chair and shook his head. "Huh-uh, Mom. We've explained. She just doesn't pay attention."

I poured Stuart a glass of wine and handed it to him.

"And how about you, Stuart? What's your excuse?"

He sat at the table. "For losing or for not explaining the rules to Anya?"

Zach was struggling with the refrigerator door.

"Honey," I called. "Stay out of there, we're two minutes away from dinner."

When we sat down, I decided to unleash the not inconsiderable brainpower of the boys on my problem. "Okay you guys," I said. "Listen up. I want you to tell me all the things in the world you think have numbers attached to them."

"Huh?" Zach, baffled, swigged his milk and then swiped the remaining mustache on his sleeve.

"Zach, is that a napkin on your lap?" I reminded him. "Numbers. You know, like football players and combination locks and telephones and, well, anything you can think of." I waved my fork at Michael, Anya, and Stuart.

"You guys can play, too." I shot Michael an "Is this okay?" look. He shrugged.

"I give up," he said. "Go, fight, win."

"What do we win, Mom?" asked Josh, ever the negotiator.

"I don't know. Something nifty. Come on, just say what comes into your head."

"Peach ice cream for breakfast!" said Zach.

"That's no number," I protested.

He giggled. "I know. That's the prize I want, Mommy."

"You got it," I said. "Anything you want for breakfast on Saturday for a whole month—if I get a right answer out of this."

And with that, the dinner table was electric. Athletes, shoes, calculators, telephones, ATM cards, fax machines.

"Basketball stats," offered Stuart.

"I know," shouted Josh. "Girls!"

"Girls?" Michael inquired.

Josh laughed and carved an hourglass in front of him. "You know, like in *Playboy*—36, 24, 36."

I fixed Michael with a look. "I can't imagine where, when, or how he's seen a *Playboy*," I said sternly.

"Hetero indoctrination," said Stuart. "You've got to start very early."

Anya sighed and contributed, "Piers."

"Piers?"

"Yes," she said, sighing again. "You know, where the ships come in. And where that restaurant is—you know, Pier 23? My friend, Harrison, from Good 'n' Gutters, took me there to hear music."

The boys continued their suggestions, getting sillier and giddier by the moment, thoughts of contraband ice cream for breakfast egging them on.

Michael sipped his wine and looked thoughtful.

"Maggie, wait a minute," he said.

"Pipe down, you two. What about piers? Suppose there's something coming in, or going out? Isn't what's-his-toes in partnership with import-export big shots?"

"Orlando," I said, "John Orlando. Jack Rowland, whoever the hell he is."

"Mom!" protested Josh.

"Sorry, sweetie. Okay, let me think." I closed my eyes and pictured the string of piers, a long necklace of hangar-looking buildings along the Embarcadero. Something was nagging at me, some little tumblers in the lock, rolling and rolling and not yet clicking.

I sighed. "I don't know, Michael. The numbers looked more like numbered art prints. You know, 16/231572, like that."

Michael shook his head. "You're the detective, *cara*, despite all my excellent counsel to the contrary. You and the gang here," he gestured at the boys.

"If you please," protested Anya, "I came up with the pier idea."

"There you go," said Michael. "And Anya was motivated by romantic memories. That's got to be good luck."

"Not always," said Stuart. "Maggie, pass me that wine bottle."

"Only if you're spending the night," I said. "Otherwise, it's some lovely black coffee for you."

After dinner, Stuart and I companionably cleaned up in the kitchen.

"Here we are again," he said, loading the dishwasher, "two little hausfrauen doing the dishes."

"Speak for yourself," I said, swiping the counters. I took a deep breath. This was my chance to find out about Quentin's mysterious access to drugs and money."

"Hey, Stuart," I began, "I was just wondering...."

"Maggie Fiori, girl detective, is back," he said.

I forged ahead.

"About drugs."

He looked perplexed. "Drugs?"

"Drugs and Quentin. Did it seem to you that Quentin had a lot of drugs around?"

"What kind of drugs?"

"Oh, recreational stuff."

Stuart laughed, "Well, old-fashioned stuff. A little hash, lots of dope—marijuana, I mean."

"Where'd he get it?"

He shrugged. "I don't know. He just always had a stash around. He never introduced me to his dealer, if that's what you mean."

"You think he had a dealer?"

Stuart shrugged. "Meaning somebody who actually sold stuff for a living? Not that I know of. It's just that he always seemed pretty well supplied." He closed the dishwasher. "He didn't do drugs all that much," he said, "but he was pretty generous with his stuff."

Almost exactly the same language Stare had used at Hot Licks. "So what about money? Did Quentin seem worried about it?"

Stuart thought for a moment. "Not really. He wasn't cavalier about money, and he certainly thought that Claire was a tightwad and that the magazine didn't pay him nearly enough. But he seemed to have enough to live the way he wanted to. Although...."

"What?"

"Well, it's funny, you asking about money. Shortly before he died, Quentin told me we might have to tighten our belts a little in the future."

"Did he say why?"

"Nope. But he was pretty close mouthed about money." Stuart leaned against the counter and shook his head. "I'm sure he thought I was too much of a dim bulb to follow any complex financial arrangements."

"Or," I said, "he was protecting you."

Stuart shrugged. "Who knows? Too late to speculate." He leaned over and kissed my cheek.

"Thanks for dinner, Maggie. It's nice to hang out with you guys." And he was gone.

Anya's pier idea seemed worth passing along to Inspector Moon. After Stuart had disappeared, I called and left Moon a message. I was tempted to leave it in Spanish to see how his Neruda study was coming along, but my street Spanish just didn't seem up to the task. Plus I didn't know the word for smuggling.

HIGH-TECH DETECTIVE

When I hit the office the next morning, Calvin was once again occupying my chair. Drinking coffee from my cup. Leafing through my magazines on my desk.

I pointed this out to him.

"My, my," he said, not looking up, "aren't we proprietary about a—what'd you call this, a 'temp' job?"

"Yeah, well, the mug's not temp," I pointed out. "It's got my name on it."

Calvin examined the mug and grinned at me. "Well, whaddya know? Hey, aren't I a secure guy? Drinking from a mug with a girl's name on it?"

"Oh, you're secure, all right," I observed. "That's why you've got to keep half a dozen women on the string."

Calvin's face lit up with a wicked smile. "Why, Mags? Are you jealous? Would you like to apply? Actually, I think I'm down to no more than two or three at the moment. There may be openings. You know, we men of color have to live up to our mythologies."

Before I could squash him like the inconsequential, ego-driven, testosterone-ridden fool that he was, Andrea appeared at the door. "Openings?" she asked. "Who's applying for what?"

I smiled sweetly at Calvin. "Oh, Calvin will explain."

He leapt to his feet and gestured I should come take my chair back.

"Another time," he said. "Now look, girls, as long as all of us are here, let's have a little detective catch-up. What say?"

Andrea sat, straight-backed and composed, and regarded Calvin as if he were a lab specimen. "What say?" she repeated incredulously. "Is there some reason you have to sound so, so—"

"Episcopalian? "I chimed in.

"Ladies, ladies," Calvin said. "Let go of those outworn ethnic clichés. This is San Francisco, this is the millennium, this is multi-culti heaven."

"You're right, it is," I said. "We've got detectives who read Neruda, and a dead editor who slept with people of every persuasion, and his ex-lover who, according to my kids, has an awesome hook shot, so, why shouldn't we have a black—excuse me, African-American, photographer who sounds like a highly privileged, over-educated, spoiled little snot?"

"Because," Calvin beamed, "that's exactly what I am. That's how my Mama raised me."

"Children, children," said Andrea, "let's not have any unpleasantness."

She raised her hand. "Now, let's do what Calvin—the aforementioned spoiled brat—suggested. Let's review what we do and do not know."

They both looked at me. Expectantly. I began to protest, thinking about deadlines, the magazine, the temp job I was beginning to feel a little too passionately attached to, and the presence of Gertie, the Editor's Conscience, probably lurking just outside the door. But, well, the hell with it. I already knew Moon's passion and priority about this case had cooled. We were way past seventy-two hours. Michael already knew I had reneged on my promise to let the police handle things. He'd even said, "go, fight, win," hadn't he? And if we didn't figure it out....

"Okay," I said. "Here goes. First, we can assume that Quentin was murdered by someone who knew him. No sign of struggle or forced entry. Correct?"

They nodded.

"Next. We know that he was murdered by a tallish woman, or

an average sized man. Right-handed. And we know that shortly before or after the murder, Madame DeBurgos heard the sounds of very un-Quentin-like music coming out of the apartment."

"Excuse me, Miss Marple," said Calvin, "but I have a little theory about that."

"And that would be...."

"Suppose whoever did the big guy in just punched the stereo system to create some noise, any noise. He—or she—wasn't interested in the music. He or she just wanted to cover up noise in the apartment. So Madame heard the kind of music she did just because that's the CD that happened to be in the player. It's not that Quentin chose that music, it just happened to be on because Stuart had been listening to it last."

Puzzle lines appeared on Andrea's Grecian brow. "What kind of noise?"

Calvin shrugged. "I don't know. Maybe, maybe—"

"Wait!" I yelled. "Wait, suppose the murderer was searching for something, turning drawers out, rummaging through closets, you know?"

Calvin looked doubtful. "I don't know, Maggie. How much noise could that cause? And besides, wouldn't the cops have found evidence of a search that was so messy?"

"Yeah, okay."

We sat glum, silent. "Okay, let's keep going," Andrea said. "What else do we know?"

"Lots of weird, probably unconnected stuff," said Calvin.

"On the day he was murdered, Quentin wanted to sic Maggie and me on a story at the Cock of the Walk."

We all began talking at once. "Hey, hey," protested Calvin. "I've got the floor. All right, lots of loose ends there." He held up his hand and began ticking things off on his fingers. "One, Mr. Banana Republic, man-of-a-thousand-identities John Orlando owns the joint. Two, he owns it with a bunch of other folks, also somewhat suspicious."

"Buyers from Macy's are suspicious?" Andrea inquired politely.

"Whatever. They are when they've been shuttling back and forth from the Far East, land of sin, opiates and Suzy Wong."

I laughed. "Boy, are you behind the times, Calvin," I said. "I think it's officially the land of electronic components, capital, and action movies these days."

"Whatever. May I continue?"

Andrea and I exchanged a glance and nodded at him. "Okay, so there's John Orlando, but he's got his ass covered with some convenient alibi for the time of the murder. On the other hand, he does have this squirrelly thing going on with these anal little illustrations, and clearly he had Quentin over some barrel about running them."

"And they had to be run at a certain time."

"Huh?" Calvin and Andrea were staring at me.

"That's what was nagging at me last night when the kids were coming up with theories about these numbers. Remember?"

They both looked blank.

I was getting that edgy, something's-about-to-happen feeling I get when I'm on a roll with a story. "See, here's what I mean. Suppose those little numbers in the bottom of John's illustrations were coded signals for something that had to happen at a certain time?"

"Like what?" Andrea asked.

"Like, like," Calvin was on his feet, pacing, "something getting delivered? Or someone important arriving?"

"Deliveries?" came a voice from the door. It was Glen. Andrea waved him in and patted the couch next to her.

"Hi, it's the a.m. session of the Happy Detectives Club. Come on in."

He leaned against the doorjamb. "No, thanks, not my kind of thing. And besides, I thought Maggie had been persuaded to give all that up." He waved a sheaf of page proofs at me. "So will you have time to look at these later this morning?"

"I will. I do, right this minute," I said. "Scram, you guys; I am supposed to be working for a living. Actually, we all are. We'll leave this to the cops."

Andrea and Calvin exchanged glances. "But, Maggie—" began Calvin. I held up my hand. "Enough, guys. Really, truly, I've got to get through a pile of stuff today." Calvin sighed and reached a hand out to Andrea.

"Come on, Andrea, let's go back to your office and I'll see if I can't have my way with you on that tidy desk of yours."

Andrea shot Calvin a serene, pitying look, ignored his hand and sailed out the door.

Glen perched on the edge of my desk, shaking his head. "Formidable conquest, that Andrea. Calvin's a brave man."

"He's a nitwit," I said. "He doesn't know any better. You should see the kind of girl he's used to."

"I have," said Glen. He began sorting through the proofs, circling corrections in the margins for me to see. "Maggie," he said, "I thought you were retired from the detective enterprise."

"I am, I am," I lied. "But the cops keep showing up at Michael's office to ask him questions."

Glen frowned, "Surely they can't think Michael was involved."

"Surely they can," I said, "but at this point, I just think they're trying to make him nervous."

"Are they?" asked Glen.

I bridled. "He doesn't have anything to be nervous about. But...."

"But what?"

"Oh, they've bumped him off the management committee at the firm. Until things clear up. But if things never do...."

"He should get a good lawyer, and you should stay out of it, Maggie," muttered Glen.

"I know. Honestly, I haven't even been thinking all that much about the whole thing. But last night, I don't know, I started brainstorming with the kids about something weird on John Orlando's illustrations."

"Something weird?"

"Yeah. Haven't you ever noticed? If you look at the bottom of his illustrations, where his signature appears, there's some peculiar number thing going on inside the O. You know how he always does those highly ornamented Os?"

Glen nodded. "I'm familiar with his signature. But did you ask him about the numbers? Perhaps it's his inventory system."

I sighed. "I know. It probably is, but I think that's probably what he told Inspector Moon."

"You presented this theory to Moon?"

"Yes, yes. You know, I promised Michael—and you, too, I guess—that I'd run our little ideas by him, instead of detecting on my own. And I've kept my word." More or less, I thought to myself.

"Well, then," said Glen, "that's about that, I guess. Now help me cut some of the extraneous matter out of this frivolous lox piece of yours."

"Frivolous?" I protested. "This is important investigative journalism." I waved the galleys at him. "Without it, no bagel is safe from inferior Nova Scotia anywhere in the Bay Area."

Glen's face lit up. "Ah, Maggie, it's nice to have you around. It's nice to hear you be silly. It's even," he regarded me solemnly, "nice to have you as a Mother Superior."

"Perish the thought!"

We spent a collegial half hour bickering back and forth about what to cut, pulling quotes, reviewing the factchecker's notes on the story. As a typically lazy and somewhat haphazard writer, I had grown dependent on the factchecker's due diligence on my pieces. Now, as an editor, I had to be willing to stand behind what we said. For *Small Town*, that usually involved nothing riskier than the price of smoked salmon in delis from Mill Valley to Milpitas, but the idea of the responsibility was sharpening my respect for the truth.

The truth. That's exactly what was preoccupying me after Glen left. In some ways, the surface of life had smoothed right out after Quentin's death. It was if the shock of his murder had been a rock, crashing into the surface of my peaceful little lake of a life. Now, with him gone, only the tiniest of ripples remained. In many ways, the surface was smoother than ever. My "temp" job had solved my who-am-I woes, Michael and I seemed miraculously undamaged by my indiscretion, Josh's stomach troubles had improved, probably without mom hovering over him so much, and I'd grown to feel ever more attached to the gang at *Small Town*. That's what I'd been trying to tell Michael in the kitchen—some days I felt as if I was the one who got away with murder.

But still, I wanted to know. Who had killed Quentin, and why? If the cops didn't figure it out, or couldn't figure it out, would it hang forever over Michael? Worse yet, over Michael and me? What about Stuart? He had to want to know. Of course, in some ways, finding the truth could be more frightening than not knowing at all. If it was someone close to me.... And with that, the urge to get up, find more caffeine, bother somebody in another office became overwhelming. Because that kind of truth seemed just too unthinkable.

"Geez, Maggie, what a chicken," I said aloud. I punched in Moon's number.

He answered on the second ring. "Anything new on the number on Orlando's drawings?" I asked.

"Maggie, how very nice to hear from you," he said.

"Uh huh. Very nice, I'm sure. I bet you're sitting there rolling your eyes and wondering when I'll go away."

"Not rolling my eyes," he said. "Not yet. Oddly enough, other people keep inconveniently getting killed in our fair city, so I do have one or two other things to attend to. What's on your mind?"

"Well, I was wondering if you got my message last night."

"I did."

"And?"

"And nothing yet. I did pass the idea along to the information services people who are looking at those numbers. I also—just so you don't think I ignore every fine lead you send my way—did talk to some gallery owners about how artists number their work."

"What'd you find out?"

"Well, I faxed Orlando's drawings to several people. None of them recognized his signature as a numbering system they knew for prints or serigraphs or anything."

"But that's how he explained it, right?"

"Right. And just because gallery owners don't understand his system, that doesn't make him guilty of something."

"I know. Well, keep me posted."

There was an audible sigh on the other end of the line. "And to be perfectly clear, Maggie, I should keep you posted because...."

"Because," I said in my wannabe mover-and-shaker voice, "A. You are a public servant, right? I do pay your salary."

Moon chuckled. "Yes, that's entirely correct. We never forget who we work for. And was there a B?"

"Well, B is, after all, I am editor of a major city magazine. I am a member of the Fourth Estate."

"Acting editor, I believe," said Moon tartly. "And unless I'm mistaken, *Small Town*'s mission in life seems to be covering important retail and culinary trends, not current events."

I thought about the lox piece. He had me there. "Hey," I said, "press is press. And C is, well, aren't we friends?"

"We are friendly acquaintances," he said. "And I don't ask you to share confidential information from your job, and you shouldn't ask me to share confidential information from mine. I've already raised eyebrows going out socially with you and your husband."

"Okay, let's go back to reason B," I said.

"Mm-hmm," he said. "Well, as I mentioned to you, I'm most grateful for any ideas, and I assure you we'll be following up on the results of the important investigative session you carried out at your dinner table last night. Say hello to Michael for me."

All very cordial. All very polite. All very patronizing. But I was convinced nothing was happening with our hot idea. I wandered down the hall to the coffee machine and ran into Jorge, one of the factcheckers. The copy chief tended to hire college students as factcheckers, interns whom we can cheerfully exploit. They need the work experience, we need their labor. Mutual abuse. Jorge was a case in point. Senior at Berkeley in journalism, dressed in kid-couture du jour—multiple ear piercings, one eyebrow piercing, Courtney Love T-shirt, jeans worn well below the waist. Despite his grunge looks, he was sweet, responsible, and exceptionally hard working.

"Hey, good work on my lox piece," I said.

He blushed. "Your stuff is pretty clean," he said. "You get people's names right."

"I know," I said, rooting in the mini-fridge for half and half that had an expiration date in this calendar quarter. "But I get careless about the other stuff—numbers, times, addresses."

He blushed even deeper. "Thanks, Maggie. I'm glad you like my work."

I regarded him carefully, feeling my hipness slip away as I mourned over all those holes in that gorgeous young face. Oh, well, preview of times to come at my house, I guessed.

"Hey, Maggie, I've been fooling around with a new home page for *Small Town*. Can I show you later?"

Under Quentin's nineteenth-century sensibility, *Small Town* had been dawdling on the journey into cyberspace. But, led by Jorge and a few of the other young info junkies, the magazine had been playing catch-up with increasing speed. "Sure," I said vaguely. "Maybe this afternoon." And then those little tumblers, rattling around, trying to find their home, started up in my head.

"Hey, Jorge," I called. "Wait up a sec."

I followed him to his desk and computer terminal, and in a few minutes had learned what I needed to know. The old *Daily Commercial News,* San Francisco's longstanding chronicle of shipping news, a publication that had flourished in the days when the city was an important port, was no more. But the information the paper had carried—what ships moved in and out of which piers, carrying what cargo—was still available. Online.

Jorge logged on, accessed an online service, and began scrolling through pages and pages of shipping news.

"So what are we looking for, Maggie?" he asked.

"I'm not sure exactly. But I want you to check out any time these sets of numbers come together," and I scribbled a series of numbers from Orlando's signature.

"Come together?"

"Yeah, like if on the third day of the fifth month, there's a container ship arriving at Pier 31, I want to know the particulars. What ship, what's it carrying, like that."

Jorge grinned and flashed me a thumbs up. "Got it. And what do I win if I figure it out?"

"Geez, that's exactly what my kids asked me last night," I protested. "Doesn't anybody do anything for the fun of it anymore?"

"Oh, yeah," Jorge laughed. "I do plenty of random stuff for the fun of it. But you don't want to hear about it."

"Probably not."

"Okay, here's the deal." He swiveled his chair to look at me. "I find something, and you give me a real writing assignment."

"What do you want to write about?"

"Hey, I don't care. I just want to see a byline sometime before I'm—"

"Ancient?" I asked.

He blushed. "Well, not ancient, but you know, over-the-hill."

I patted his hand. "Jorge, you're making it worse. We got a deal. Find me some juicy numbers and I'll find you an assignment."

We shook on it and I left him to his screen.

NOSY SLUT

The Fiori Volvos were so aged and battered, veterans of so many urban and suburban wars, that it was, at first glance, hard to tell what was different about my car. Same color, same dents, same slightly askew right-side mirror.

But as I drew closer in the parking lot, I saw there was an added attraction. *Guercino's Girl Is a Nosy Slut,* the side panel read. I circled the car. Correction, *Guercino's Girl Is a Nosy Slut* decorated both side panels. The hood and rear window had been abbreviated to *Nosy Slut.* "Thorough," I thought to myself, and then a wave of nausea hit me. I leaned against a cold, concrete pillar in the parking lot and willed my lunch not to come up. Someone nasty knew I hadn't given up detecting, and that someone was pissed enough to embarrass me.

I called Inspector Moon and he was there within twenty minutes.

"I don't get it," he said. "Who's Guercino? Some other guy you're seeing on the side?"

"Watch it," I said. "Not that it's your business, but I'm not seeing anyone."

"Okay, so who's this guy, Guercino?"

"A painter," I said, "Italian, 1600s, I think."

"So are you supposed to be Guercino's Girl?"

"I don't know," I said. "I'll figure it out."

A sweet-faced uniformed cop had accompanied Moon and

asked me more practical questions. Who knew where I parked my car? Did I keep a regular schedule, etc. After she left, Moon suggested we sit in the car.

"Once again, just to pry into things that may not be my business," he said, "have you called Michael yet?"

I felt sick again. Michael. Oops. He'd probably agree with the judgment of the auto graffiti expert and be pissed as hell all over again. I kept these thoughts to myself.

"No, I haven't called him," I snapped. "But actually, he'll be thrilled. It's time to paint the old wreck anyway." The Queen of Bravado was back and lying through her teeth.

Moon permitted himself a small, smug, superior smile. "Forgive me for saying so, but I believe you are full of horseshit."

I leaned my head on the steering wheel. "I know I am. And Michael's going to be furious. He doesn't care about the car—what's to care about—but we'd sort of made peace about this detective stuff. I told him I was telling him everything I knew, and he believed me.

"Hmm," said Moon. "I'd be surprised if he were that accomplished at self-deception." He reached in his pocket and pulled out his little reporter's notebook. "So as long as you are foolishly, and against my direct orders, putting yourself and your family in harm's way with this Nancy Drew stuff, why don't you tell me what you know that's new and different since our conversation this morning?"

Surrender seemed in order. I quickly ran down a summary of the conversation Andrea, Calvin and I had had. Moon interrupted with a question or two, took a few notes, and let me finish.

"That's it?" he inquired. "You're sure?"

I nodded. "Oh, of course, there's Jorge."

"Why am I not surprised?" said Moon. "And who is Jorge, and what's he doing?"

I explained. He smiled. "I see our information systems people were too slow for you," he said.

I felt myself blush. "Well, not too slow," I said, "but I'm sure they're busy tracking down all those offshore stashes of funds some local Catholic church keeps embezzling."

Moon raised an eyebrow. "Don't you ever worry about what you say, Maggie? I could be Catholic. You could be offending me, you know?"

"Hey, I'm married to a Catholic myself. I just read the papers. Aren't all those local priests turning into the Michael Milkens of the new millennium? Besides, I'm hoping they're socking some extra away to help put my little half-Catholic waifs through expensive private colleges. And besides," I finished with a flourish, "shouldn't you be Buddhist?"

"I believe that's what's called none of your business," he said, closing his notebook. "And now, since you informed me this morning that we're friends, I'm going to talk to you like a friend. Maggie, you've got to cut it out."

I began to protest, "I didn't really do anything—"

"Well, someone thinks you did. Asking questions and exploiting your magazine help to do your legwork for you looks like a lot of something to somebody. Just cut it out or something more permanent than mysterious name-calling graffiti is going to happen." He shook his head. "You know, that's what bothers me about this prank."

"Bothers *you*? It's my car."

He ignored me. "Remember, I worked for years in high schools. This is the kind of thing teenagers do. It's like tepee-ing a neighbor's house. It's meant to scare and humiliate you, I guess, but it doesn't seem very threatening. And it's meant to puzzle you. So it's somebody who knows you well enough to assume you'll figure it out."

"You mean, like Glenn Close boiling the kid's bunny?"

He smiled. "Your kids have a bunny?"

"No, thank heavens."

"Well, you see what I mean, don't you? This isn't life threatening. It's meant to look scary, but it isn't really."

"So you think I'm being stalked by a teenager?"

He gave a short laugh. "Maybe. It's more like you're being warned off by someone who actually cares about you—and just can't bring himself or herself to really scare you in a serious way."

We were silent for a moment.

"Michael?" ventured Moon.

"Michael what?" I asked crossly.

"Michael wouldn't do something like this?"

I snorted. "Just because he's Italian doesn't mean he knows anything about sixteenth century painters," I said. "And besides, he just wouldn't."

Moon shook his head. "I'm remembering our conversation at Skate Oakland. Husbands and wives. Do we ever really know each other?"

"Uh huh," I said noncommittally, distracted by the distressing series of phone calls I had still in front of me—to Michael, to our cranky insurance agent who never seemed happy to hear from me.

Moon asked me a few more questions, trying to pin down exactly who did and didn't know about my contraband sleuthing, then unfolded himself out of the defaced Volvo and sent me on my way.

I couldn't stand the thought of parking the newly enhanced Fiori-mobile in front of our house, so I dropped it at one of those discount paint places my insurance agent kinda, sorta pre-approved and called Anya to come fetch me.

The kids were in the back seat of her equally disreputable aged VW bug, singing "Take Me Out to the Ball Game," and favoring the back of the seat with those high-force kid kicks that convince you terminal kidney disease is just around the corner.

I blew kisses at everybody, discouraged the kicks, and closed my eyes.

"Shhh, kids," Anya cautioned, "your mom's not feeling good."

I sighed. "I'm okay, Anya, I feel fine. It's just been a complicated day." And then I sat bolt upright in Anya's grimy passenger seat.

"Anya's an art student, you idiot!"

Anya looked miffed. "Who are you talking to, Maggie? I'm

right here. Of course I'm an art student."

"Good. So you know who Guercino was, right?"

"Italian painter, Bolognese school, inspired by Titian."

"Okay, what else do you know about him?"

"He took over the supervision of the Bolognese school from Guido Reni."

"Guido, Uh huh. What else?"

"I don't know that much more," Anya said. "He really had just one famous painting."

"And that was?"

"The picture of Jesus and Mary Magdalene. I think it's called *Christ with the Woman Taken in Adultery.*"

"That's it," I said grimly. "So if somebody was called Guercino's girl, what would she be?"

"Oh," Anya said, "a bad woman, an adulteress."

I fell silent. The graffiti artist clearly knew about my wicked ways. Of course, as time went by, I was becoming convinced that could include most of the population of the greater Bay Area.

"I have something to cheer you up, Maggie," said Anya. "Two somethings."

"Good," I said, "I can use some cheering up."

"Michael's bringing home ribs from Everett & Jones." A cheer went up from the backseat. Everett & Jones was a hole-in-the-wall paradise for lovers of authentic down-to-the-last-spoonful-of-spicy-coleslaw barbecue. I felt a little like cheering myself.

"So," Anya wagged a finger at the kids in the rear-view mirror, "no reindeer souffle!"

Fortunately, she was good-natured about her lack of cooking skills, and about the incrementally preposterous dishes Michael was always promising the kids she would make.

"Okay, I agree, great news number one," I said. "What's next?"

"Oh, someone must be—do you say, 'sweet on you'?" asked Anya.

"We do say that," I said, "under certain circumstances. Why?"

"Well, someone left a big bouquet on the front steps," she said.

"And it must be from their garden, because there's no florist note, just a little envelope with your name on it."

By the time we reached home, the pinching/scuffling activities in the backseat had escalated. We turned the kids out in the driveway, Anya disappeared into the basement to work on her senior project—which consisted of many large, metal, rusty objects scavenged from trips to the "pick 'n pull" wrecking yard destined for eventual soldering into one large, increasingly hideous, and, I feared, unmovable, sculpture.

Anya had put my bouquet on the dining table, arranged in a large crystal vase. And before I even saw the note, I felt my heart sink. I leaned on the table and called, "Anya? Can you come a minute?"

Anya came in, caught sight of my face, and said, "Maggie? What's wrong? What's wrong? Sit down."

"Do you see anything odd about this bouquet?" I asked.

Anya regarded it. "No, I mean, I don't know much about flowers, but these are… unusual. I don't think I've seen many of them in a bouquet before."

"And there's a reason," I said. "They're all poisonous."

"Poisonous?" Anya recoiled.

"Yes," I said, gesturing at each different kind, ticking them off. "Oleanders, solanum, foxglove, even the foliage—it's poison oak. Did you touch these leaves?" I asked.

Anya's eyes grew wide. "Maybe."

"Well, go have a good, soapy shower just to be sure. I'm going to dump these things. And where's the note?"

"In with the mail on the hall table," Anya sprang to her feet.

The envelope looked innocuous enough, although my name was in typeface, clearly cut from something in print—*Small Town's* masthead, I would have guessed. I had the envelope slit and open and the note halfway out before I remembered to worry about letter bombs. Nothing exploded, except the message.

"Sweets to the sweets," it read, "and poison *fiori* to the Nosy Fiori Slut."

"How charming," I said. My graffiti-artist worked in mixed media. Fiori is Italian for "flowers."

I pulled on rubber gloves to protect against the poison oak, unfolded newspaper on the dining room table, swept the offending bouquet into it, and marched to the trash can. Then I considered my options. I could call Inspector Moon—who would deliver yet another lecture; I could tell Michael, who would probably try to put me under house arrest; or I could let it ride. I made the dumb, expedient decision and let it ride. It must have been Moon's past life as an authority figure in high school, but against all reason, I resisted being a well behaved little citizen. I had reported dutifully: with Orlando's signature, with my kids' theories, with my car, and where was it getting us? Michael's career was in a holding pattern. This was our life some nut was intruding on, and it seemed as if the cops weren't making progress on much of anything. When Anya emerged from the bathroom, her hair still dripping from the shower, I suggested to her that the bouquet could be our little secret.

That night I dreamed about the Garden of Eden. I wasn't sure if I was Eve or just a visitor. And it was a beautiful garden, no black spot on the roses, no leaf curl on the fruit trees—that's how I knew it wasn't my garden. But everywhere I looked, when I leaned in to smell a lilac bush, reached to pick a peach, there was a *hisssss*—and a serpent appeared. And not just one wicked, tempting snake in the garden. Soon the air was filled with the sound that Emily Dickinson says makes us go "zero at the bone," and I awoke, drenched in sweat. I lay there panting for a moment, then swung my feet over the bed. I had a momentary panic about what narrow, slithering surprise I might find when I nudged my feet into my bedroom slippers, but nothing happened."

Downstairs, I hung on the refrigerator door and stared inside. Beer sounded good, cold and wet, but I had sudden visions of turning into a three a.m. drinker and settled for orange juice.

I pulled the "nosy Fiori slut" note from my robe. Of course, I'd handled it and probably obliterated all fingerprints. But geez, what kind of idiot harasser didn't know to wear gloves, I consoled myself. I was sure there was nothing to see. I heard Inspector Moon in my head: "But then, of course, we won't know, will we?"

"No, we won't," I said aloud, surprising Raider from his slumber under the kitchen table. He came over to the sink expectantly. Humans up? At this hour? Could a walk happen? A treat? He regarded me with more than moderate interest.

"Sorry, big fella," I said.

And then, as long as I was up, I decided to get some work done. So Raider and I settled ourselves, me at the table, he back underneath, and with my feet resting on the warm comfort of his fur, I worked my way through several piles of proofs. At four thirty, with just a little light showing in the kitchen window, I put my head down on the table and drifted into a mercifully dreamless, snake-less sleep.

SHIPSHAPE

Gertie was enormously impressed with my overnight productivity when I dragged into the office the next morning. That was the good news. Plus, as a midwesterner with farm roots, she approved of getting up at dawn. "Wait 'til menopause starts," she advised me, "you'll have permanent insomnia and hot flashes so you'll be up anyway in the middle of the night."

"Can't wait," I said.

I felt haggard, hollow-eyed and, after seeing the bill for the repainting of the Volvo and remembering the king-sized deductible we had, newly impoverished.

I grouched through morning meetings and snapped at Puck about a late piece. I had just begun rooting in Quentin's cabinet for some aspirin when I looked up to see poor, blameless Jorge standing there, grinning triumphantly.

He settled into a chair, folded his arms, and said, "Okay, Mrs. Fiori, I am ready for my writing assignment."

"Look, Jorge," I began, "this isn't exactly a good day… wait, wait, does this mean?" I felt my headache begin to loosen.

His grin widened. "It does. I am one superhot, incredibly brilliant, persistent cyber-dick."

I laughed and reached for the folder. "Uh huh—and I'm sure your mom would be thrilled to hear you describe her precious baby boy in just those terms. Come on, give me what you've got."

Jorge leaped to his feet and came around to my side of the

desk. "It's easiest if I show you on the screen. Get up, Maggie, let me sit there."

"Is this any way to address your boss?" I said, giving him the chair and watching as he punched in, in double time, a series of numbers.

"Okay, we're connecting to the Internet, finding our site. Here we go, shipping schedules."

A maze of names, numbers, dates, and symbols came up on the screen.

"You understand this stuff?" I asked Jorge.

"Yeah, it's pretty easy to figure out the abbreviations, and the stuff I didn't know, I called my cousin who works at the container yard over at Oakland. He knows what all this stuff means." Quickly he explained some key acronyms and shorthand—"reefers" weren't marijuana joints, they were refrigerated containers, LTL was "less than loaded."

"Okay, let's chill with the coaching," Jorge said. "You're not going into the shipping business anyway, right?"

"Right," I said.

"Now, check this out," and a new screen appeared. Even with the mini-lesson from Jorge, it looked like a bewildering set of tables and charts.

"Let me guess," I said, "it's the Periodic Table of the Elements in Armenian?"

Jorge didn't even look away from the screen. "What's it gonna be? Jokes or answers?" he asked.

"Answers," I said, humbled in the presence of my cyber-superior.

Jorge moved the cursor to darken a few numbers. "Here's what we've got. These numbers look familiar?"

"Maybe."

"They should, 1/6/231572. They're the numbers you gave me and here's what's interesting: I thought your thing about ship and piers and stuff was a little whacked-out, but you might have been on the right track. You can identify a specific ship with a specific container, arriving on a specific date at a specific pier, only they call them berths, and they come into Oakland, not San Francisco. Oakland's got virtually all the container ship business these days."

I looked at the screen. "I don't get it."

"Look, look," said Jorge impatiently. "The first day of the sixth month, you've got container 231572 coming in. And when you cross check that container, you see...." He highlighted the number, and a full name opened up: Galaxy Star, Unit 231572. "That's the name of the shipper, the vessel, and the container number."

"And can you make that combination happen with all the numbers?"

"Yep," he said triumphantly, scrolling to the next screen.

"So that means—"

"Well, I don't know what it means, exactly," said Jorge. "I was just trying to make the numbers make sense."

"But it must mean something," I said. "It can't be an accident you can get all these numbers to come together. There must be...." I felt a flutter in my stomach.

"What?" asked Jorge.

"It must be some signal about that container. We need to find out what's inside those containers."

Jorge shrugged. "How hard can that be?"

"Well, we could call your cousin," I said hopefully. Jorge looked doubtful.

"Maybe. Can't you just call that Inspector who keeps hanging around here?" asked Jorge.

I hate it when the right idea comes to people so much younger and less experienced than I am. I thought about all the snakes in my dream last night. I thought about the opportunity to get back in Inspector Moon's good graces, and about the fact that he already knew what Jorge was up to.

"What a swell idea," I said to Jorge. "You're... the bomb."

Jorge snickered, "That is so six weeks ago, Maggie. But hey, if you think I'm a genius now, wait'll you see how good my article will be."

"A deal's a deal," I said. "What do you want to write about?"

We batted some ideas around for a while. Jorge wanted to write about the Mexican Day of the Dead, but the magazine had done a story on that a few years ago. So we started talking about the importance of costumes in lots of holidays—Halloween, Day of the Dead, Carnevale, Mardi Gras—and we both got excited. What would psychologists say? What neighborhoods have the best costume shops? We agreed he'd do a little research, organize an intro and an outline, and pitch it to me.

"After all," I explained, "I've got to give you an assignment because that's our agreement. But you want to be ready to pitch some other, not so charming and friendly, editor somewhere down the line."

Jorge let a grin sneak onto his face. "You're charming and friendly?" he inquired.

"Darn right," I said, heading back to my office to call Moon. "And don't you forget it when you're out there in the wide wicked world selling stories to heartless editors."

Within a few minutes, I had Moon on the phone. "What's wrong?" he said before I had more than my name out.

"Relax," I said, "it's just your favorite Detective Assistant, Junior Grade."

"Junior Grade is correct," he said evenly.

But he listened carefully when I laid out Jorge's findings and, in fact, admitted he could easily find out what cargo the ships were carrying.

"How?" I asked. "Just wondering. I promise I won't try to do it myself."

"And," he inquired dryly, "hasn't your word proven to be as good as gold?"

"Hey," I protested, "I called you with this info, didn't I?"

"You did," he said. "And I promise to call you as soon as we know anything. I think it's probably a wild goose chase—remember Orlando's the guy with the rock-solid, unbreakable alibi—but it can't hurt to find out."

Two minutes after we hung up, he was back on the phone.

"Maggie, I want to talk to that kid who figured this out."

"No recruiting," I said. "He's a great factchecker and he may be a good writer."

"I don't want to recruit him. I want to find out who else knows he's been doing your detective work for you." I passed him on to Jorge, who told me later that not even his cousin the shipping giant knew why he was looking at all this information.

"Come to think of it," said Jorge, "I didn't even know what I was doing. I was just following orders so I could get a writing assignment. Am I in some kind of trouble?"

I reassured him he wasn't and spent the rest of the day doing Gertie and Glen's bidding: reviewing story lists for the next quarter's issues, looking over a direct mail letter to pitch fallen-away subscribers, answering e-mail. Just as I was about to log off, my mailbox beeped to let me know I had one more recently arrived piece of mail. I clicked and saw a new return address. When I saw the greeting, "Darling Maggie-Know-It-All," I knew it was from Sara. "Well, well," I said to the screen, "Sara joins the electronic universe." Her message read:

"Mags… isn't this way cool? Much less dear than ringing you up… Jaysus, Mary & Joseph, do I sound pseudo-Brit or what? Okay, dollink, here's the story—I had tea with your 'source' the other day. Douglas Thurston? What a dish. A little sepulchral, but handsome in that tweedy, pasty, never-sees-the-light-of-day way these dons go in for. If you know what I mean. Anyway, he had a zillion questions about you, and—not to put it too nicely—why you were nosing around about some guy named Jack Rowland. So e-mail me back, my love, and tell all. Best to you, the barrister and the Little Men. Xxoo Sara J."

God, I love e-mail! Sara and I had once been great letter writers, but the demands of modern life, time, and pressing priorities around home and hearth had eroded our correspondence. Clearly, e-mail was resurrecting the writerly aspects of our relationship. I didn't quite see Virginia Woolf and the Bloomsbury gang e-mailing each other, but surely they would have loved the principle of the thing.

I tapped in a summary of events, sordid and otherwise, and zapped the "reply now" key, delighted to know there was no waiting for ship or plane to wend its way across the Atlantic. Sara would have my thoughts that instant.

On the way home, it did occur to me to worry about Sara detecting on my behalf across the Atlantic. But I shrugged it off— it seemed hard to imagine that some miscreant could vandalize matron-mobiles in such widely dispersed time zones.

A HANDLE ON CRIME

Pots and pans," said Inspector Moon, when I picked up the phone the next morning.

In my kitchen, there was enough early morning pots-and-pans variety racket happening in the background that I couldn't be sure what he said. Zach was dipping his finger in the milk and apparently writing his initials on the table while rhythmically kicking his chair. Michael was drilling Josh on his spelling words; Anya had the radio tuned to something that sounded like Abba meets Snoop Doggy Dog. "Hey, guys," I waved at the table, "could you keep it down a minute?" They ignored me.

"Hang on, John," I said, and pushed the swinging door out of the kitchen into the dining room. The din was at some remove.

"Now," I said, "I thought I heard you say 'pots and pans.'"

"I did," he said. "That's what was in those mysterious shipments on the days in question."

"Pots and pans? As in housewares?" I asked.

"Correct."

"Swell."

"Not very exciting, I'm afraid," Moon continued. "But worth looking into."

"Looking into?"

"Sure. Pots and pans are empty, you know. Could be something inside them." This seemed unlikely to me in the extreme. Who's dumb enough to smuggle something inside a pot or pan?

"I guess. What do you have to do to look inside the shipment?"

"Get a warrant. It's in the works. I'll let you know."

"Mom!" yelled Zach from the other room. "Come see what I did."

I covered the receiver with my hand. "Coming, honey, just a second."

"And Maggie, one more time," said Moon, "remember, you're the editor, I'm the detective."

"Uh huh," I mumbled, "I remember," punching the off button, and heading into the kitchen to see what wonders Zach had wrought.

Zach, my precociously literary child, had in fact written M O M—in milk on the kitchen table. It was a mess, but who could criticize his accomplishment or his choice of people to immortalize in low-fat, homogenized splendor?

"Wonderful, honey," I said, ruffling his hair.

Michael was on his feet, brushing crumbs, gulping coffee, looking for his briefcase. "Okay, guys," he called, "the Dad-mobile is leaving the station. Let's get all hands on deck." The next five minutes were consumed with the chaos of search for jackets, lunches, kisses goodbye to me and Raider and Anya—not particularly in that order—and then, silence, blissful silence, as Anya disappeared upstairs to collect her portfolio and Guatemalan handbag, and climb into her incredibly hideous lace-up boots. When I heard the clomp-clomp on the stairs, I knew she was on her way.

"Bye, Maggie," she called. "Leave me a note about dinner."

"That's okay," I hollered hastily, "I've got tonight covered." Cooking continued to be Anya's weak spot. Which put me in mind, of course, of pots and pans. And set me to wondering about the possibilities that lay therein.

I meditated on those all the way into the city. It was a relief to be in the Volvo, assuming that no one could vandalize the poor thing while I was in it. "Great assumption," I said under my breath. "I bet the taggers have cellular spray paint systems or something.

Maybe they'll get me as I cross the Bay Bridge."

The thought made me grumpy, jumpy, and apprehensive, and when some poor soul in a battered pea green Futura moved into the lane without signaling, I shot the driver my most baleful look.

Pots and pans could hold what? Microchips? Heroin? Industrial espionage information? Tiny works of art? "Oh, sure," I muttered, "let's just break up the Elgin marbles and ship them into the States inside double boilers. Cool concept." Perhaps, I thought, I don't have a grand-scale criminal mind.

Juggling briefcase, cappuccino-to-go, and a bag holding two pairs of Michael's shoes that needed new soles, I sailed through *Small Town*'s minuscule lobby, down the hall, into my office, and collapsed at my desk. Gertie stuck her head in, with a look I'd come to know as, "good thing you're here, I have something that needs your immediate personal attention."

"Good morning, Gertie," I said. "What'd I forget? Who should I call? It's not my fault, whatever it is."

She smiled serenely. "Aren't we defensive this morning? Another sleepless night? Perhaps I just wanted to say good morning."

"Uh huh," I said. "And perhaps pigs have wings and chickens have lips." I pried the lid off my coffee, licked the foam from the top of the lid, and took a sip.

"Come on, Gertie, just tell me."

"Okay. Notice those guys in the waiting room you walked right by?"

"What guys? I didn't notice anything."

"Really, Maggie," she remonstrated, "for a journalist, you're certainly not very observant."

I sipped some more. "I used to be a journalist, Gertie," I corrected. "Now I'm a captain of industry. A media mogul."

She raised an eyebrow. "My, my, we have delusions of grandeur, don't we?"

"Yes," I said cheerfully, "I've got a job and a title and I'm not afraid to use 'em. Now come on, cut to the chase. Who are those guys and what have I screwed up now?"

"Nothing yet," she conceded. "The cute young guy is one of Claire's friends from Skunkworks. I think he's on the staff. The other one's a priest, Father somebody or other from somewhere."

"Gee, that's helpful," I said. "And they want what?"

She smiled sweetly. "To see you. As soon as possible, that's a quote. Shall I show them in?"

I sighed, "Sure, sure. Probably soliciting for the Pope's personal bingo game." I remembered my anti-Catholic remarks addressed to Inspector Moon and began to worry he'd sent a delegation to show me the error of my ways.

Gertie disappeared down the hall and then reappeared a few minutes later with two men. The younger, an every-mother's dream of a wholesome youth, extended his hand. "Mrs. Fiori? I'm Gregory Bender. We met at Quentin's memorial service." I remembered him and his crew cut. He had spoken passionately about Quentin's willingness to cover HIV in the elitist and worldly pages of *Small Town*.

Young Bender turned to the priest. "And this is Father Timothy Grogan. He's on our board." Father Timothy extended his hand and we shook. I gestured to them to sit down, and we all sat surveying each other. Bender looked about two minutes out of prep school, from his pressed oxford cloth shirt to his Bass loafers. He had that overly pink countenance children get when their mothers scrub them down with a rough cloth and cold water, and when he smiled, he had the straight white teeth that suggested many years of expensive orthodontia.

Father Timothy, on the other hand, looked, as my mother used to say, as if "he'd been rode hard and put away wet." His faced was lined, his shave uneven, his graying hair in need of a brush and comb.

"I'm sorry," I began, "Father Timothy is on your board, and that would be...?"

"Skunkworks," they volunteered in unison.

I grinned and wiggled my little finger. "Link up," I said. Father Timothy looked mystified. Bender broke into a wide grin, exposing still more of those picture-perfect teeth, and explained, "You know, for luck. When you say the same thing at the same time, you're supposed to link little fingers and make a wish."

Father Timothy looked as if he'd like to be sitting in a nice cool, dark bar, with a short brown drink, and absolutely no one around to chirp about linked little fingers. "Well," said Father Timothy, "can't say that I remember such a custom."

"Okay, then," I said briskly, hoping to move things along. "So much for those quaint childhood games. Now, what can I do for you?" I sneaked a glance at my watch and wondered when I could start being pretentious enough to insist that I only saw people with appointments. Probably right around the next millennium, and only then if Gertie could enforce the rule.

The priest and the prepster (as I realized I thought of them) exchanged glances. They both started at once, and then the priest nodded at the young man. "Go on, Gregory."

Gregory leaned forward and gave me the kind of smile that would enable him to go very far in life. "It's like this, Mrs. Fiori," he began. "We know that you were working on a story about Skunkworks when Mr. Hart died."

"Well," I protested, "I wasn't really working on it. I didn't even know what it was about. My editor had just given me the assignment." I smiled beatifically at them. "So you see, I really knew very little about your organization." Bender and the good Father exchanged glances.

"We were just wondering," continued Bender, "if you were still planning a story. And if so, could we do anything to help you out?"

They both settled back in their chairs and looked expectant.

"Well, I don't know," I began. "I mean, the magazine's story list is pretty much booked for the next several issues." The priest managed a smile at this, and the look that crept over Bender's face looked a lot like relief to me. What was this all about? Nonprofits were usually starved for publicity.

"But then," I equivocated, "you just don't know what's going to fall in or out. Why don't you bring me up to date?"

"It's a pretty simple story," began Bender. "As you know, a number of organizations have been putting pressure on the FDA to speed up the approval timetable of drugs for use against HIV. Now that everyone's starting to worry about the long-term effectiveness of combination therapies, it's becoming even more important to have multiple options."

"And the FDA's responded," I pointed out, remembering Michael's observations to Claire during our ever-so-pleasant evening together.

"Yes and no," said Father Timothy abruptly. "Look, it's like this. ACT UP got us part of the way there; the FDA has certainly thinned out the molasses in the system. But when you've got people dying, when the conventional therapies don't work, they don't want to hear about twenty-four-month timetables instead of thirty-six-month ones. They want something to try now."

"And that's where Skunkworks comes in," added Bender. "We identify high-potential drugs, match patients who are in the most need, and arrange to get the drugs to them."

"How?" I asked. "Through the pharmaceutical company that's doing the trial? Through the FDA?"

"That's a little complex," Father Timothy said. "Suffice it to say, it happens. And we work with volunteer physicians who track how patients are doing."

"So you're an all-volunteer organization?" I pressed.

"Mostly," said Bender. "I'm the executive director, and we have a part-time bookkeeper, but everyone else is a volunteer." Silence fell in the room. We looked at each other some more. I sipped my cappuccino and started longing for something I felt clear about, selling candy bars for the T-ball league, say, even making small talk at Michael's partner meetings. I took a breath.

"Well," I said, smiling at both of them in my very finest "class dismissed" mode. "It's been so interesting hearing about Skunkworks. I can't say when, or if, we'll pursue a story." I stood. They looked at each other and stood as well. I held out my hand.

"I'm so grateful you took the time to come in, and if we do decide to do a piece on Skunkworks, you'll certainly be the first folks I'll call."

Young Bender beamed at me. "Oh, thank you, Mrs. Fiori. We really appreciate your interest." Father Timothy looked distinctly relieved. "Nice to have met you," he said. He edged Bender to the door, they both smiled one last time, and disappeared. I sipped and contemplated a minute more, and then wandered down the hall to Puck's office. The door was closed and covered with yellow stickie notes that read, variously, "Do not disturb, Brilliant Music Critic at Work," "Enter upon pain of death," and most warmly, "Just Fuck Off." I tapped on the door and pushed it open. The office was in its usual disarray, Billie Holiday was crooning *God Bless the Child* over the stereo, and Puck was accompanying the music with a series of gentle groans interspersed with snores. He was lying flat on the floor, fully clothed, with the exception of his boots, which sat atop his desk. He was all in black, except for some hot pink socks decorated with a lovely overall pattern of Mick Jagger-esque out-thrust tongues. "Nice socks, Morris," I observed.

Silence. "Puck," I called. "Puck, darling, wake up."

More silence. "Puck," I said, a little more firmly, "I really, truly need to talk to you."

He hauled himself to a sitting position and half-opened his eyes. "I am way, way too old for this."

"For what? Gainful employment?"

"No. Partying all night." He squinted up at me. "And it's your fault. It was some record release party." He creaked to a standing position and flopped into his chair. "Is that sissy swill you're drinking caffeinated?"

"Sure is. Want some?"

"Yeah, thanks," he reached for the cup, drank it down, and ricocheted the empty container into the trash can.

"Okay, I'm here, I'm among you, I'm so, so happy to be alive," he grimaced.

"You don't look happy," I noted. "You look terrible."

Puck regarded me sourly. "Is there any chance at all Quentin will come back from the dead and take this job away from you, Miss Priss?" he asked. "He knew enough to leave me alone after a big opening night."

"No chance at all," I responded. "I believe you're stuck with me, and if you want to go get yourself some more coffee and a couple of aspirin, I'll wait right here. I have a little assignment for you."

Puck looked as if he were considering an argument, thought better of it, then rambled down the hall. While he was gone, I used his phone to call Stuart and ask if Puck and I could stop by later that morning.

An hour later, with Puck somewhat revived, but bitterly complaining about out-of-office assignments that didn't involve alcohol, drugs, or rock and roll, we pulled into Quentin's drive. Stuart met us at the door. "You want to go through the kitchen, Maggie? You think we've got one of your Dutch ovens?"

"Uh huh," I said vaguely, heading to the kitchen. "I know you've got errands to run, Stuart. Go on; I promise to put everything away when I'm done."

Stuart looked puzzled, but collected his keys and headed down the stairs.

"Don't forget to lock up when you guys go," he called over his shoulder.

Within twenty minutes, Puck and I had every pot and pan out of Quentin's cupboard. And with miniature screwdrivers in hand, we began removing every handle from every pot. Inside the handle of a lovely copper-bottomed sauté pan I found what I was looking for: An elongated, foil-wrapped cylinder. We looked at each other. I weighed the cylinder in my hand, then peeled the heavy foil off. Inside lay a plastic-wrapped vial filled with clear, amber liquid.

"Holy shit," said Puck. "How'd you know there'd be something in these handles, Maggie?"

"A hunch. I thought I smelled a skunk at work," I said, feeling smug. "It's that nonlinear, sissy-swill-drinking brain of mine."

"Well, that's that," said Puck. "Let's call your big buddy over at the SFPD."

"Not so fast," I said. "I invited you along because you're my drug expert."

"Gee, imagine how flattered I am," said Puck.

I was busy attempting to pry the stopper off.

"So does this look like anything you know?" I asked.

"You mean, like something recreational," asked Puck. "Gimme a sniff of it." I passed the vial over. While he examined it, I took a closer look at the aluminum foil. "What does this wrapping stuff look like to you?" I asked, tossing it to him.

"Heavy, isn't it?" he said, puzzled. Then his face cleared. "You know what this stuff is? It's like the seal they used to put on wine bottles, the one that's lined with lead, the one they're replacing so all us winos don't die of lead poisoning."

I looked at Puck. "Even when you're hungover you're pretty good," I said. "Of course it's lead-lined. That's so you can't see inside the handles if you X-ray them."

Puck sat back on his heels.

"Well, Maggie, you're one smart broad, but I don't know what you're going to do with this information. I have no idea what this stuff is—it doesn't look like anything I've seen sold on the street to be smoked or sniffed or shot up. But then, I'm not as up to date as I used to be."

"That seems like a step in the right direction," I said.

"Yeah, well, don't sound so self-righteous. Let's remember who came to whom for an expert opinion." We sat in silence for a few minutes.

"Puck, start putting this stuff away, would you?" I asked, and headed into the living room.

"And do it quickly, would you?"

"Hey," he called, "thanks for the help. Whatever happened to 'if you make a mess, you've got to help pick it up?'"

But I wasn't listening to Puck talking, I was listening to the very particular kind of racket it makes to move a lot of pots and pans very quickly. And I was thinking that the perfect thing to cover that noise up was some heavy metal rock.

We left Stuart a note, claiming we couldn't find the allegedly missing Dutch oven, and surveyed the kitchen for any telltale signs. Then I tucked the vial in my purse and we headed out the door.

Puck dozed off in the front seat, exhausted by the heavy lifting, I guess. He woke up as we pulled into the garage. We set out up Sutter Street back to the offices, with Puck alternating complaints about all the work I'd dragged him away from and pressing me for assurances I'd call Inspector Moon.

"I'm calling, I'm calling," I said. "I just need to think some things through."

"Yeah, well, while you're thinking things through, there could be some nut out there who gets wind of the fact you're interfering with his hot scheme to ship essence-of-sheep-pituitary into the good old US of A," said Puck. "And, not to be a coward, lady, but when they come after you, I'd just as soon not be around."

"My, how gallant," I said, as we stopped at the door to Puck's office.

He caught my hand. "Come on, Maggie, I'm serious. Get some help with this stuff. You're getting in way over your head."

"Oh, I'm getting some help," I said. "I'm definitely going to some higher authorities."

Puck let his breath out and examined my face, clearly looking for signs of truthfulness and good character. I obediently put on my good Girl Scout face.

"Cool," he said. "I knew you'd wise up."

"Very soon," I said, disengaging my hand. "First, I think I need to pray about it."

OF MASS AND MAH-JONGG

J ust before we turned out the light on Saturday night, I flung my book on the floor, snuggled up to Michael, and said, "I've got a great idea about tomorrow morning."

Michael didn't stir. He was engrossed in *Sports Illustrated*.

"Michael?" I slipped my hand under his t-shirt and rubbed his stomach.

"Hmm?"

"What are you reading?"

"A story about basketball salaries." He turned a page. "You didn't marry the right Michael," he observed. "If you'd married one of these others—Jordan, say we wouldn't have to worry about putting the kids through college. We could just buy their way in. Actually, if you'd married somebody named Shaquille, we'd simply buy them a college outright."

"Don't you want to hear my cool idea about tomorrow morning?"

He let *Sports Illustrated* fall to his chest and regarded me with suspicion.

"Does it involve trowels or chicken manure in any way?"

"Not at all. I was thinking church."

He regarded me with disbelief. "Church? What kind?"

"Mass," I said briskly. "St. Peter's and Paul's, ten a.m. And then we can take the kids to some funky Italian North Beach place for brunch. And we can hang out at City Lights bookstore for a while. And then," I concluded, warming to my topic, "when your mother calls Sunday night you can tell her what we did with the little heathens. It will make up for them telling her latkes are their favorite food." Michael's sainted mother lived in terror the boys would turn into little Hasidic Jews while she wasn't looking. She kept asking me how Jesus fit into my worldview. I always told her I thought anybody who could turn water into wine was my idea of the perfect house guest. Michael turned out the light and pulled me to him.

"That's a great idea, honey. I love that church, I love that neighborhood, and it won't kill any of us to spend Sunday morning that way."

"We can pray for the resurrection of your career," I said.

Michael looked at me. "Always a wisecrack, huh?"

"I'm sorry," I said. "I feel so miserable about this cloud hanging over you."

He pulled me closer. "Someday the cops will figure out who killed your elderly, slimeball lover, and I'll be back to going to boring, contentious executive committee meetings."

"Aside from the elderly and slimeball comments, this is more evidence that you're a generous guy," I said.

"Remember," he said, "even my generosity has its limits." With that, he kissed my nose, turned over, and fell asleep.

As I drowsed away, more pangs of guilt drifted into my consciousness. I was accumulating vast numbers of spousal points for simply suggesting Mass, and of course, my motives were far, far from pure. But then, I thought vaguely as I drifted off, doesn't the end justify the means, or the Mass, or some m-word....

Sunday morning found the Fiori clan scrubbed and wholesome, scrambling up the steps to St. Peter's and Paul's as the bells rang. It was a perfect, wintry San Francisco morning. Blue skies, chilly air, the last of the scarlet and gold leaves clinging to the trees in the square, and dozens of ancient Italian ladies, dressed in black from their headscarves to their sensible shoes, making their way to choice seats in the church. It was a Mass that hovered somewhere between New Age and Classic Vatican II—a few references to social justice, a cherubic boys' choir, a few pleas for help in the weekly soup kitchen, and bingo announcements. I gave Michael a superior smile and he leaned over to whisper in my ear, "Someone who comes from a culture that elevates mah-jongg to a holy ritual has no cause to look so uppity about a few bingo cards."

I was prepared to deliver my mah-jongg is an ancient Chinese game requiring great skill and cunning, not to mention its prominence in *The Joy Luck Club,* not to mention the fact that my Great Aunt Floss, a player of brilliance and acumen, also made *kugel* for which Michael was willing to perform unnatural acts, when Josh leaned over, waved a remonstrative finger, and said, "Mommy, we zip our lips in church."

Damn children. They absorb your lectures and feed them right back to you.

Later, as we were gathering coats and scarves to head out into the weak, wintry sunshine, I caught sight of a familiar face. Several, in fact. "Michael, make sure the boys don't forget anything. I want to say hi to somebody."

I began weaving through the crowd, trying not to knock any elderly worshipers to the ground, and came out to the front steps. Standing at the bottom of the steps were John Orlando (a.k.a. Jack Rowland), Glen, Father Timothy from Skunkworks, and another young man, very pale, dressed in khakis, a collarless shirt, and a leather jacket. None of them looked particularly happy, or sanctified, for that matter, but they were so engrossed in their conversation, they didn't see me 'til I arrived, somewhat breathless, at Glen's side, and slipped my arm through his.

"Glen, what a nice surprise," I said.

Glen looked like the surprise was anything but nice. His arm stiffened, then relaxed. "Maggie. The surprise is mine. Didn't know you went in for Mass on a Sunday morning."

I smiled at the entire circle, "Oh, you know, trying to give our boys an ecumenical upbringing. Michael's Catholic, you know."

"I know," said Glen, "and there's that lovely St. Luke's just two blocks from your house."

"Lousy cookies and coffee," I said. "I hear they serve biscotti here. And besides," I added, "there's that lovely Mission Dolores two blocks from your house."

"I take your point," said Glen. He gestured to his companions. "You all know each other, I believe."

Father Timothy nodded, "Mrs. Fiori, so pleasant to see you again."

The other young man smiled at me and gave a little wave. He looked very familiar, so I assumed I'd seen him around *Small Town's* offices.

John Orlando looked anything but friendly. He fidgeted and glanced at his watch. "You turn up everywhere, Mrs. Fiori, fancy that. But we've got to be running along, chaps, don't we?"

"Group outing?" I asked sweetly.

The circle fell silent. "Espresso," Glen said. "We meet a group of fellows afterwards. Corinne gives me Sunday morning off, away from the little ones."

"Well, I won't keep you," I said. "We're taking our little ones out for brunch and over to City Lights." I relinquished Glen's arm. He reached over and pecked me on the cheek. His lips were cold, and when he moved away, he seemed to give a little shiver.

"Bundle up, Glen," I called as they headed across the square of urban park in front of the church. "It's windy out; you'll catch cold."

"Ever the mother," said Michael, coming up with Josh and Zach in tow, just as the group disappeared from view.

"Hey, was that Glen? Who are those guys with him?"

"Bunch of people I know from work."

He hugged me to him. "It's chilly out here. Let's go find some hot coffee and lots of pancakes!" Josh and Zach began chanting, "We want pancakes, we want pancakes," and we set out across the park into the heart of North Beach, while I wondered what it meant that exactly what I'd expected to find turned up at St. Peter's and Paul's.

We had a great morning rambling around North Beach, steering the boys away from the barkers on Broadway, those luring the tourists into the topless, bottomless, and otherwise clothes-unencumbered, shows, and buying coffee, salami, a chunk of reggiano, and pastries to take home. Michael chatted in Italian with the ladies behind the bakery counter, and charmed, they tucked extra *cannoli* into the bag. "*Per gli ragazzi,*" they said, beaming at the boys. "*Mille grazie,*" they replied in chorus, thereby unleashing more sighs of admiration from the adoring ladies. I beamed at all three of my charming Mediterranean boys and made a note to let Michael's mother know that not only had Josh and Zach set foot inside a bona fide Catholic church, but that the Italian lessons she was conducting long distance were serving them very well, indeed.

We ended up browsing used books at City Lights, that holy mecca of the Literary Beat movement. Josh and Zach installed themselves in the kids section, Zach sitting on the dusty floor leafing through picture books while Josh cruised the shelves for virtually anything that featured armies, navies, and guns. We had no idea how a little military nut could come out of our peace-loving family, but a book is a book, as far as I was concerned. I touched Josh on the shoulder. "Keep an eye on Zach, honey," I said. "Dad and I are going downstairs for a few minutes."

Michael headed for the history shelves. I began picking my way through vintage cookbooks, separating them into gotta-haves and nice-to-haves. I explained my cataloging system to Michael. He sighed. "You and books, Maggie. How come there aren't any out-and-out rejects?"

"Reject a book outright? I'm worried I'd hurt its feelings."

When we wandered back upstairs, both of us were carrying a few treasures. Zach was exactly where we left him. No sign of Josh. "Where's your brother?" I asked.

Zach looked up and looked around. "I don't know."

I glanced around the store. No sign of Josh.

Michael frowned. "It's not like Josh to wander off. He didn't say anything?" he asked Zach.

Zach looked puzzled, then brightened. "I think he had a tummy ache."

"That's it," I said, relieved, though not happy Josh left Zach on his own. "Michael, check the restroom," I called. Michael disappeared and was back in a minute. "Nobody there," he said grimly.

I felt my heart begin to pound. How could we have left the boys alone even for a minute? What was I thinking? Michael touched my shoulder. "Okay, we're not panicking, Maggie. You stay here with Zach." Within a few minutes, Michael had the entire bookstore mobilized, from the grizzled guys behind the counter to every customer in sight. No one had seen anything. Many remembered seeing the boys at the bookshelves, but no one had seen Josh walk out the door.

"Mommy," Zach pulled at my sleeve. "I remembered something."

I knelt down in the dust next to him, breathing in his warm, little boy essence. "What? What did you remember, honey?"

"When Josh said his stomach hurt, a man said he'd take him to the bathroom."

I took a deep breath. "And what did he look like?"

"I don't know. I was looking at a book, but he was a grown-up."

"Michael," I called.

"I'm going up the street to check out some of the other stores," he said.

"No. Come here a minute. Zach remembered something."

And just at that moment, just as the nightmares about child molesters and kidnapping and every other terror in the world were about to overwhelm me, Josh walked in the door. He waved, caught sight of his father's face, and turned pale. "Dad, I'm sorry I left Zach, but I had to, had to, had to go to the bathroom."

Michael's face, with relief and rage fighting for dominance, darkened. I held my arms out for Josh. "Come here, honey. It's fine. Just tell us what happened."

And he did. He'd been seized with one of his upset stomachs and was clutching his middle, looking around for the bathroom, when a man—kinda young, he wasn't sure—stepped up and called him by name.

"By name?" I asked. "Did you know him?"

He shook his head. "No, but he acted like he knew me. He knew my name. And I thought he might have been somebody Dad worked with or you or something and I'd just forgotten him or something. And he told me that the bathroom was out of order here, and he'd take me to his place, that he had a bathroom there."

Michael and I exchanged glances. "And you don't know his name?"

Josh shrugged. "No, I was embarrassed to ask. I thought he knew me, and all I cared about was finding a bathroom." He looked up at me. "I'm really sorry I left Zach, but I thought I'd just be gone a minute."

"Where did he take you?" asked Michael. "Can you find the place again?"

Josh said he'd try, and we spent the next half hour wandering up and down the streets. Unfortunately, the North Beach-Chinatown intersection is a maze of narrow streets, alleyways, and tiny plazas. We stopped when it was clear Josh was simply confused, tired, and upset. Michael, trying hard not to interrogate him, kept probing.

"And what did he say when he sent you back to the store, this guy?" asked Michael.

"He said goodbye."

"Nothing else?" pressed Michael, as we headed for the parking lot.

"Oh, yeah," said Josh, "I almost forgot. He told me to give Mom a message."

"Mom! you're crushing my hand," objected Zach, shaking me loose.

"I'm sorry, honey," I said, distracted. "What message?"

"He told me he hoped you remembered the seventh."

Michael stopped, dead in his tracks. Our eyes met.

"The seventh?"

I looked at Michael and mouthed, "Commandment."

Michael gave me an icy look and put his hand around Josh's shoulder. "Well, don't worry about it, pal. I'm sure whoever this guy was, he was just kidding around. Maybe he was talking about baseball."

"Baseball?" asked Josh. "Oh, the seventh-inning stretch."

Right, I thought to myself, Thou shalt not commit the seventh-inning stretch.

The entire Volvo smelled wonderful on the way back across the bridge, and once again, nearly faint with relief at having Josh back, I remembered how seductive a mistress San Francisco can be. I breathed in that heady combination of strong coffee and even stronger salami and closed my eyes. A little nap, just a little nap, before I had to endure Michael's lecture—and my own self-recriminations—and then, just before I drifted off, the young man who had looked vaguely familiar to me outside the church snapped into focus.

"Sweetie," I said to Josh, "what's the art teacher's name at school?"

The boys were dozing, too, stuffed with brunch and fresh air and the aftermath of an adventure. "Mr. Connolly," he mumbled.

"It wasn't Mr. Connolly who took you to his place, was it?" I asked.

He opened his eyes. "Mom! What kind of a dummy do you think I am? I know Mr. Connolly."

"Of course you do," I said. "That was a silly question. It's just that I saw someone who looked just like him today."

THE USUAL SUSPECTS

Sunday night was something other than restful. After I heard, in considerable detail, what Michael thought about putting our son in danger, even inadvertently, we decided to call Inspector Moon. His office paged him, and he sent an officer out to interview Josh. Michael called it quits when it was clear Josh had reported as accurately as he could and we weren't going to turn up anything new. Moon called back late that night.

"It's more of the same, Maggie. I know it was awful for you guys, but he didn't even have Josh gone long enough to be serious. Think about who cares enough to scare you just a little."

"What about the seventh commandment warning?" I asked.

"That doesn't tell us much new," he said. "It's just like the graffiti on the car. It's somebody who knows about your indiscretion and thinks you're probably suffering over it."

"Well, doesn't it rule out Michael?" I asked.

"Who knows?" said Moon.

"Get some rest. We can talk tomorrow."

When we finally went to bed, I was too hot, then too cold, then too panicked to sleep. Every time I started to drift off, I'd jerk awake, frozen in that moment when we didn't know where Josh had gone.

On Monday morning, Michael and I squabbled about whether or not to send him to school. In the end, I called Mrs. Schwab, explained what happened, and persuaded her to let Josh carry my cell phone again.

When I turned my computer on at my office, my e-mail was blinking a greeting. E-mail over the weekend could only mean some whiny, procrastinating writer asking for an extension.

"No better than I was," I muttered under my breath as I typed in my password. I was wrong. The e-mail was from Sara.

Hullo from the Sloan Ranger. Am busy detecting on your behalf. Here's a weird thing. Your dead guy must have had some lovely little pile of American capital. Douglas and I had tea the other day and he told me that Quent had offered to loan him money when his sweetie (Leslie) first become ill and had to resign his teaching post. Guess this new job of yours must be pretty swank. Does that mean you and your best beloved and the kidlets can pop over for a holiday visit? Let me know. We'd deck the halls and all that.

I replied immediately, thanking Sara for the info and disabusing her of the notion that the Fiori family finances were lush enough to support a transatlantic visit.

Money, money, money. Money was somehow at the root of all this. If I could connect the money with whatever that stuff was in the pot handle, I'd figure it out. I unlocked my bottom drawer and took out the box of tampons I kept for emergencies. I slipped my hand inside the box, and there, just as I'd left it, nestled among the crinkly paper-wrapped tubes, was the vial I'd "liberated" from Quentin's pan handle.

The door flew open and in walked Calvin. "Hey, Maggie," he began, then broke off when he caught sight of the box. "Put that stuff away, would you?"

I grinned at him, lifted the box and gave it a rattle. "What's the matter, Calvin? Don't you celebrate all those important little lunar cycles with your harem?"

"Thanks, but no thanks," he shuddered. He flung himself on the couch and groaned. "Puffy ankles, moodiness, uncontrollable impulses to eat chocolate and kill old boyfriends. Forget that noise. In fact," he began unbuttoning his cuffs and rolling up his sleeves, "want to hear my new idea for the harem?"

"I can't wait," I said grimly.

"Older women," he beamed. "Past the change. No birth control worries, no cyclical murderous impulses. Often quite wealthy. Just think, Maggie, in a few years you'd even make it onto my short list."

"Calvin," I said, "I'm going to give you a very big benefit of the doubt and assume you're joking." I held up one finger. "Number one, I'm at least ten years away from 'the change,' as you so charmingly call it. Number two, when I go for younger men, they're going to be much, much, much younger. You're not even on the radar screen. I'm talking the seventeen-year-old box-boys at the Safeway. And number three," I said, flourishing a third finger at him, "I have no idea what you're rolling up your sleeves for, since I'm unconvinced you've done anything more physical than snap a shutter in your entire life, and what's more—"

"That's number four," he interjected.

"Number four," I said, getting to my feet, "I only tolerate your presence to do my dirty detective work, so unless you're here to take instructions, you'd better skedaddle."

Calvin let a slow, sleepy smile spread across his face. "Skedaddle? Well, aren't we the wholesome country girl?"

"No, we're not," I said briskly. "And you'd better be darn glad of it, because if I were I wouldn't hang out with the likes of you."

Calvin put his feet on Quentin's freeform marble-top coffee table and regarded me with interest. "I'm here, I'm ready to do your scut work." He indicated his rolled-up sleeves with a grand gesture. "And as you can see, I'm ready for action."

"Okay, here's the deal," I said, fishing in the tampon box and pulling out the vial. I handed it over to him. And proceeded to bring him up to date. About Puck and about our panic in North Beach.

The grin faded from his face. "Wow. You guys must have been scared to death." I nodded, my eyes welling with tears.

"Plus Michael's ready to kill me," I said.

"So I guess that's finally the end of Maggie Fiori, girl detective," he said.

I dabbed at my eyes. "Probably."

He held up the vial. "So what about this weird thing? You say Puck found this with you?" he asked.

I nodded. "Is that a good idea?" he asked. "I mean, Puck could be a suspect. All those clubs he goes to are just dens of drugs and iniquity."

"Well, Puck's not exactly pure as the driven snow," I said, "but he's off my list."

"Your list?"

I pulled a reporter's notebook, slim, spiral-bound, from the same drawer that was home to the feminine hygiene emergency stash. "Well, here's what I did. I went through everyone here at the magazine and some other people close to Quentin, and I've figured out who was around—and who wasn't—during the time of Quentin's murder."

"Girl detective back at work?" he asked.

"It's my swan song," I said.

Calvin crooked a finger. "Hand it over. Let me see what you've got."

I handed it across. He paged through.

"Pretty good work, Maggie," he said. "So if I understand what you've been digging into, everyone at the magazine except Glen and Andrea is accounted for."

"Right."

"So have you asked them where they were?"

I shook my head. "The cops questioned everyone. I assume they must be satisfied with what they said. And I don't exactly know how to bring it up casually in conversation without seeming like I'm nosing around."

"Oh, and that would be a big surprise to everyone, wouldn't it?" observed Calvin, turning back to the notebook.

"Well, forget them for a minute. Outside *Small Town,* Orlando's got this watertight alibi from all those people at his cock-a-doodle-doo restaurant, and the delectable Mrs. Quent was seen having her talons sharpened and painted at Nails by Neta on Union Street."

He looked up "How'd you turn up that little piece of info?"

I smiled sweetly. "We have our methods."

"And those would be…?"

"Well, Gertie gets her nails done at the same place, and even though Quentin and Claire are divorced, she still makes Mrs. Quent's important appointments. You know, dentist, hairdresser—"

"Plastic surgeon, blood bank, Poison Control center for withdrawals," interrupted Calvin.

I laughed. "Right."

"So how about Orlando's partners? How about the people at Skunkworks? There's lots of other people. There's even Stuart." He hesitated. "There's even Michael." He held up his hand. "Don't get pissed at me for saying it. You already said that Moon's theory was that it was someone 'friendly' warning you off."

I sighed and flipped the notebook shut. "It's not Michael." My watch alarmed pinged.

"Hang on a minute, Calvin," I said. I dialed Josh's school, got the hourly reassurance from Mrs. Schwab, and called Michael.

Calvin watched me. "So Maggie, Moon knows everything you know?"

"Mostly," I said.

"What's mostly?"

"I didn't talk to him about the vial."

"Why not? That seems like a big find."

"Oh, I will, but I have another place I'd like to check this vial out myself."

He tossed it back to me. "Hey, much as I'd like a big scoop and lots of credit for breaking the case, you really do need to talk to the cops about this stuff. You know, I was a big fan of this detective shit, but I think we may be getting in way too deep. Somebody's gonna get hurt. And I'd sure hate for it to be somebody I really care about, like myself, for example. Or even your kid. Just in case

Moon's suspect stops being so harmless and friendly."

"Calvin, you're a pal," I said.

He continued, "Wait a minute. Incoming bad thought! Suppose the murderer really is Andrea? I'm getting kinda tight with that WASPy princess."

I chuckled. "Remember that movie *So I Married an Axe Murderer*?"

"That's not so funny. Besides, Andrea's only a suspect on your little list because she wasn't accounted for during the murder."

"And," I added, "she was one of Quentin's paramours."

"Yeah, well, she's gotta take a number to be part of that crowd, from what I understand," said Calvin, giving me an arch look.

"Oh, please," I said, "I believe I've taken enough grief for that. The next time I stray, well, there won't be a next time."

"Not married to old Mikey there won't be," observed Calvin. "Italian guy like that, he's probably got sixteen uncles in the Mob."

"I believe the Italian Anti-Defamation League breaks your legs if you make jokes in that vein," I said. "However, as I was saying, not that I'd ever make this mistake again, but I assure you if I did, I'd pick somebody who isn't quite so visible or so catholic in his tastes."

"Right," said Calvin, "we already know you have your eye on teenage box-boys. That's going to be a juicy little scandal right there."

I flipped through the pages of my notebook. "There's something else," I said.

"Cough it up," said Calvin.

"Well, there's this art teacher at Josh's school, Joe Connolly."

"Uh huh, and?"

"And, I think he's the guy who called that day we were having lunch at Cock of the Walk and made up the story about Josh being sick."

"I'm not following."

"Well," I said impatiently, "look, someone wanted to get to me before I got to the file that Moon was holding for me. And that someone knew the quickest, most foolproof thing to do was to distract me with one of the kids."

"And why do you think it was Connolly?"

"It's all too much of a coincidence. He knows Glen and that Skunkworks gang, he knows Josh, and he knew how to find me. And he probably knew what I had on that day, because he could have seen me when I dropped Josh off at school." I put my hand on the receiver.

Calvin glanced at his watch, unfolded his elegant legs and got to his feet. "Look, Maggie, I hope you're twitching over that receiver because you're going to call Inspector Moon."

"I'm thinking about it," I said.

Calvin reached across the desk and patted me on the head. "Good girl."

And with that, he disappeared out the door. I picked up the phone and dialed The Webster School again. The student who answered the phone reassured me that she'd just seen Josh and, in answer to my request, said she'd have Joe Connolly give me a call. I thanked her and was about to hang up when she said, "But Mrs. Fiori, it might be a while before he calls you back."

"Is he on vacation?" I asked.

"No," she said. "He's really, really sick again. His doctor put him in the hospital late last night."

"I'm so sorry to hear that," I said, and then, on an impulse, "Is Mrs. Schwab around?" In a minute, the principal was on the line.

"Mrs. Fiori? Is something wrong?" she asked.

"Oh, no, Mrs. Schwab," I said. "I'm sorry to bother you again. I was trying to reach Joe Connolly, but the student who answered the phone said that he's in the hospital. I didn't even know he was sick."

"We're all pretty upset about it," said Mrs. Schwab. She sounded as if she wanted to say something more, and then stopped.

"I just saw him yesterday," I said. "Outside St. Peter's and Paul's, in the city."

"Oh, dear," said Mrs. Schwab.

"Well," I pried gently, "I hope it isn't serious. He's been a real favorite of my son's, ever since he let him do his papier-mâché sculpture on the Warriors."

"Yes," mused Mrs. Schwab, "Joe is very creative with the kids."

"So," I said briskly, "I'd really like to go see him, bring him a plant or something. Where is he? Is he up to visitors?"

"I don't know," Mrs. Schwab replied doubtfully. "I don't know about company. But you could call Alta Bates and see what the nurse says."

"I'll do that," I said.

TREASURE IN THE TRASH

Alta Bates is one of those something old, something new hospitals, squatting on a particularly unlovely corner in Berkeley. That is, you can feel the presence of the dehumanized and dehumanizing HMO mentality: fewer RNs, physicians who frown a lot and look at their watches as they calculate if it's worth the hassle to order expensive tests, and chirpy patient-quality slogans that propagandize about the benefits of managed care.

Named for a nurse, part of Berkeley's culture for generations, still populated by sweet-faced blue hairs and slightly-less-sullen-than-usual teenagers as volunteers, Alta Bates carries the weight of new age, bureaucratic medicine relatively lightly. Best of all, the Bay Area obsession with coffee has led to an espresso vendor in the cafeteria, so there's always a way to get a cappuccino fix on the way in or out of the hospital.

I inquired about Joe Connolly at the front desk and was directed upstairs to the east wing nursing station. Vintage Motown was pouring out of a tabletop portable stereo behind the waist-high counter, and two middle-aged women, one white and one black, with pink stethoscopes draped around their necks. were gently rocking out. Both dressed in white leggings and flowered overblouses, both a little overweight, they looked like slightly updated versions of plump flowers from *Fantasia*.

A young volunteer clutching a stack of newspapers was leaning against the counter, giggling. "Kick it, you guys," she said and then caught sight of me. She rolled her eyes a little, gave me a "grown-ups, who can understand them?" look, and took off down the corridor.

Aretha wound down in her quest for respect on the radio, and one of the women, a blonde with dark roots and stylish spikes, turned the sound down and smiled at me. "Can I help you?"

"Nice moves," I said. "I'm looking for Joe Connolly."

The two women exchanged glances.

"Are you a family member?" the other woman asked.

"No." I said, "My son is one of his students."

"Well," the blonde said doubtfully, "he's pretty out of it right now. He's already got a friend in there visiting with him. We don't want to tire him out."

She smiled at my potted azalea, wrapped in tissue paper. "You're shedding a little," she said, gesturing at the floor. I looked down. There was a small, steady flood of glitter falling from the tissue onto the floor.

"I'm so sorry," I said, attempting to hold the pot closer. That seemed to compound the problem, and another multicolored, sparkly shower fell to the floor.

"My kids decorated the paper," I apologized. "I know there's lots of glue on here, but I'm not sure it's actually coming in contact with all the glitter."

The blonde smiled good-naturedly. "That's okay, maybe it will perk him up. After all, he is an art teacher."

Her rock 'n' roll colleague chuckled. "I've got kids," she said. "No matter how bad our floor looks, I bet yours looks worse. More glitter, I mean."

I laughed. "No doubt. So can I see Joe? Just for a minute?"

"Sure," the blonde said. "Make it a short visit, though."

I headed down the hall to Joe's room. The door was partly closed, so I tapped on it. "Joe?" I called softly, and stepped into the room.

Though it was late afternoon, the winter sunshine had still

been shining bravely outside. But Joe's room was in dusk. His bed was cranked to a half-sitting position, and he lay against the white pillows, his dark hair a smudge of contrast. Another man sat in the visitor's chair in the corner, silent, vigilant, his face obscured in shadow. I approached the bed, glitter drifting behind me. "Hey, Joe."

He wiggled to a more upright position and raised his hand in a wave. "Mrs. Fiori."

I put the plant on the nightstand. He reached to his chest and gestured a brushing motion. He grinned at me. "You're wearing a little glitter."

I smiled at him. "I know. The boys wanted to add a little do-it-yourself art to the plant when I said I was coming to see you. See what an influence you've had."

He nodded. "Thanks, I guess."

I regarded him closely. He was wan and fragile looking, but he certainly didn't seem out of it to me. "Gee, Joe, you seem a little better than your nurses think," I blurted.

He smiled. "Yeah, you know I'm just faking it here." A cough crept up on him, he turned away till it passed. "Really, I'm lots better," he said. "Gregory's a great tonic."

And then the man in the chair spoke. "Hello, Mrs. Fiori."

I turned and saw Gregory Bender, Skunkworks executive director, sitting in the chair. His wholesome young face looked strained, tired.

"Mr. Bender," I said, "how nice to see you again."

I pulled the second visitor chair up to the side of Joe's bed and settled down.

"Okay, guys," I said. "For starters, why don't you tell me what's wrong with our friend here?"

Silence.

"Okay, why don't I tell you?" I said. "I think Joe's HIV-positive, and some nasty opportunistic infection has gotten hold of him."

More silence.

"Further," I said, "I don't think this is the first time. And

I think when Joe said that Gregory was a good tonic for him, he meant that quite literally."

"Mrs. Fiori," Gregory began, a little warning creeping into his voice. "Why don't you stop before you go prowling any further where you're not invited."

"Why don't I?" I said. "Because there's something ugly going on, and I'm absolutely, positively convinced it had something to do with Quentin's murder."

"Which," Gregory interrupted," the cops are hard at work solving."

"And further," I said, "I think somebody you guys know snatched my kid yesterday."

Joe looked alarmed. "What?"

"Relax," I said. "I think it was just a scare tactic. It was such a civilized and brief kidnapping, it had to be done by very nice people." I looked directly at Bender. "It was you, I bet, using my kid to tell me to watch out. Kinda chickenshit, if you ask me."

He flushed.

"And watch out for what exactly? Dangerous books in City Lights? Kidnappers in North Beach? Or investigating Quentin's murder?"

"I don't know what you're talking about," said Gregory, "but I repeat, aren't the cops working on Quentin's murder?"

"Well, I think they'd be moving along a darn sight faster if everybody who knew something was just a little more forthcoming," I pointed out.

The door edged open again, and one of the nurses from the front desk poked her head in. "Hey, how we doing?" she asked, and then she stopped and double-timed over to the bed.

She picked up Joe's wrist, consulted her watch for a moment, and then popped one of those new wave thermometers in his mouth. We all fell silent. I felt Bender's distinctly unfriendly gaze on me, as we waited together for the telltale beep.

"Mmm," the nurse said, "your fever's way down."

She turned to Bender and me and smiled. "Well, you guys are

clearly good for what ails him," she said.

"I'm going to have Dr. Mazur take a look at you when he comes in for rounds. Maybe we can spring you from this joint tomorrow morning."

"That would be great," Joe responded.

The nurse checked the IV bag holding medication and shook her head. "Boy, you haven't even had enough of these antibiotics to work this fast," she said. She smoothed the hair back from his forehead "You're a resilient guy, Joe Connolly, I've gotta hand it to you."

After the nurse left, I dug in my pocket for a tissue. "Where's the trash can in this place, guys?" I asked, looking around, gesturing I needed to toss something out.

Gregory caught Joe's eye and gave a tiny shake of the head. "I think you need to throw it out in the bathroom," Joe said hastily. "They keep this one sterile or something."

"Uh huh," I said, catching sight of the can near the sink. On the wall was a dispenser of latex gloves. I plucked one from the dispenser and tugged it on.

"What are you doing, Mrs. Fiori?" asked Joe.

I stirred in the trash with my gloved hand. "Even though I'm a mom, and I've certainly been up to my elbows in yucky stuff on a regular basis," I said, "I don't care to rummage around the garbage without some protection." And then I spotted it, under some paper towels. I fished out a little plastic cylinder, just like the one I'd liberated from the handle of Quentin's sauté pan. I held it up. "Found it."

Joe and Gregory looked at each other in dismay and then back at me. I wrapped the cylinder in a clean paper towel, and tucked it into my purse.

"Okay, here's my suggestion," I said. "Talk to me or talk to the cops. I don't much care which happens first." The two men looked at each other once again. After a pause, Gregory nodded as if in assent.

"You're right, Mrs. Fiori," began Joe. "I'm beyond being HIV-positive. I've had a whole bunch of opportunistic infections, so I've got AIDS. But my doctor's been keeping me fairly healthy—until recently. I'm just getting too exhausted to fight much more."

"I'm sorry," I said.

"Yeah, well, everybody's sorry," said Joe. "Mrs. Schwab's been great, fixing my schedule so I can work when I feel up to it. But I've been missing a lot of time, and I'm really getting worried. I mean, if I can't work, can't go to school and see the kids, I might as well flick it in."

"Prayer isn't enough, I take it?"

"Prayer?" he looked puzzled.

"I saw you at Mass yesterday," I reminded him.

"Oh, yeah, well, that's more a chance to get together with friends. But sure, I've been praying. And it must have helped, because, along comes Skunkworks with this… stuff."

"Stuff?" I asked.

"BZT," said Gregory.

"You mean AZT?" I asked, naming one of the most commonly used AIDS drugs.

"No, this is new. It's one of the drugs we're very excited about."

"Uh huh," I said, "I can see why. The nurses kept telling me how sick Joe was, and here you are, looking pretty darn good. So your doctor is one of the people who's tracking drugs for Skunkworks."

Joe looked puzzled. "My doctor? He doesn't know anything about this."

Gregory hastily interjected, "I'd explained to Mrs. Fiori about the docs who work with us." Joe's puzzled look vanished.

"Oh, yes. That's true."

I looked at Joe and then back at Gregory. "Okay, this is truly a whole lot of horse manure," I said. "You're not working with any doc with this drug, or you wouldn't be hiding the container in the trash."

They both looked miserable. "Come on," I said. "My kids lie better than this."

The bedside phone rang, startling all of us.

Joe looked at it uneasily. "Go ahead and get it," I said. "I'll wait."

"Hello?" he said, and looked beseechingly over at Gregory.

"Oh, hi. Can I call you back? I have company."

He paused. "A surprise visit," he said. "One of my students' moms dropped by." He listened. "Right. Okay, I'll call you back in a while."

Silence. We all looked at each other. The nurse rapped gently on the door again and came in. "I'm shooing you guys out of here," she said. "Let's let Joe get a little rest, and maybe he can go home tomorrow."

Gregory practically fell over his feet disappearing. I lingered for a minute.

"Joe," I said, "I don't know what's going on. But I'm sorry as hell you're sick, and whatever's helping to make you better, I'm all for it."

He smiled and gestured at the tissue-wrapped azalea. "Thank Josh for the plant for me," he said.

"Thank him yourself," I retorted. "Looks to me like you'll be back to work very soon."

The nursing station was deserted when I came out. I leaned on the counter and waited, and in a few minutes the African American rock 'n' roller came out of a room with a tray of medications. She put the tray on a cart behind the counter and smiled at me. "I hear your friend's a lot better," she said.

"He is," I replied. "Can I ask you some questions about medications?"

She looked doubtful. "Well, unless you're a family member, I can't really talk to you about Joe's meds."

"I know," I said. "I just meant AIDS drugs in general. It seems pretty confusing."

"It is confusing," she said. "That's because we're kind of making it up as we go along."

"Okay, can you tell me the basics?" I asked.

She sighed. "Just the basics? Well, here's how it works. There's a whole group of drugs that we use to treat people before they get sick, or before they're very sick—AZT and drugs like that. Plus, there are the relatively new protease inhibitors; maybe you've heard about those?" I nodded. She continued. "They're all used as part of what we call combination therapies or cocktails—you combine different drugs in hopes that you'll make the viral load count go down."

"Viral load?"

She nodded. "That's the measure that tells us how much of the virus you've got making trouble in your body."

"And how about T-cells?"

"That's a whole different count. We're looking to keep that number up, because the T-cells indicate how much fight you've got left in the body."

"And then once somebody gets sick?"

She sighed. "Well, there's a whole other family of drugs—some conventional antibiotics for infections, and an aerosol drug called pentamidine we use to ward off a special kind of pneumonia."

"I'm not asking you about Joe, specifically," I said. "But how about somebody like him? Is it too late for all the combination therapies?"

"People in Joe's situation are in a tough spot. Once you start getting really sick really often, you get into a cycle that's hard to reverse. And, of course, some of these drugs have pretty crummy side effects, so if you're already weakened, they can be tough to take."

"So," I said, growing increasingly conscious of the cylinder in my purse, "is there some new special thing that you can give to perk up somebody really sick, so they'll get strong enough to benefit from the combination therapies?"

She gave a short, humorless laugh. "You mean something that's the equivalent of jacking a car up and running new tires underneath?"

I smiled, "Yeah, kinda like that."

She shook her head. "Not that I know of. But you have to remember that AIDS drug research is going on in so many places, so many trials, that it's hard for us folks in the trenches just to keep up."

"Ever heard of something called BZT?" I asked.

She shook her head again. "New to me, but like I said, there's something different every day."

I thanked her and headed for the elevator. All the way down to the ground floor, walking to the garage, my head felt absolutely fugal—different voices asking related and unrelated questions, overlapping, tumbling over each other faster than I could consider an answer. What was going on? Was this some illegal drug? Were there pot-handle pharmacies all over the city dispensing this stuff? If the stuff was in the pot handles, it was clearly coming in from Asia, if Jorge's analysis of the shipping codes were accurate. And why the secrecy? If the drug worked, why wasn't some American pharmaceutical house cranking it out, pushing it through trials? And somebody, somebody, had to be making money on all this— and had it been Quentin? Was he dealing in AIDS drugs, and that's where his unexplained cash flow came from? I shuddered at such an ugly thought. Quentin had been no saint, that was clear, but the idea of my friend—okay, my lover—trafficking in human misery was a little more than I wanted to contemplate.

And was Bender really the guy who grabbed Josh yesterday? He didn't seem very scary, but then… somebody had murdered Quentin. The question was, who? And would they commit murder again?

REVELATIONS BY THE BAY

y the time I'd edged my car out of the Alta Bates parking lot, I was working up a good head of anger. I was going to call John Moon, spill every single thing I knew or thought, and find the bastard who had scared my kid. And cook a good dinner. And tell Michael the thousand and one reasons I'd never, ever, ever stray again.

Though it was only a little after six, it was already dark on the streets. As I carried on the eternal internal rush hour debate—surface streets versus freeway home—I dug in the bottom of my purse for Inspector Moon's card, with his home phone number scribbled on the back. "I need to get my cell phone back from Josh," I said to myself.

"I could be calling John, getting things sorted out, getting lectured on off-limits detecting, all while I'm sitting in traffic."

Only the radio answered back, squawking traffic reports that told me what I already knew. Late rush hour, early winter darkness, an incoming fog bank and who knows what else were combining to create gridlock on Ashby, the main thoroughfare to anywhere from Alta Bates. I inched down Ashby towards the freeway and then slipped onto the frontage road, a little-used two-laner that edged the Bay. Even with the windows rolled up, the faint salty, sour smells of low tide drifted inside the car. Through the darkness, I could see the silhouettes of the driftwood sculptures that punctuated the coastline. Grotesque, oversized, exuberantly creative, cobbled together from trash and driftwood by renegade uncredited artists, they stood like winter sentries to the dark and murky bay.

The frontage road was clear, and I headed south, looking with satisfaction at the headlight-to-taillight jam on the freeway on my left. A shadow slinked across the road ahead of me, some furtive creature trying out for roadkill, and I tapped the brake to slow down.

And nothing happened.

No slowing, no change at all. I squeezed the brakes again. Nothing. Pushed the brake pedal flat to the floor. Nothing.

"Stay calm, Maggie," I said, "you're a professional driver," remembering the all-too-short Road Atlanta course Quentin had put me through on my first assignment for *Small Town*.

I lifted my foot off the brake and pumped gently again. Nothing. The road was taking a gentle dip, and the station wagon picked up speed down the hill and then, mercifully, slowed a little on the uphill.

"Okay, Maggie," I chatted comfortingly to myself. "Remember, that's why they call those gizmos 'emergency' brakes." I steered the car over to the side of the road and pulled up on the emergency brake.

Nothing. The brake came up loosely in my hand, making a soft, sickening, not-engaging-anything ratcheting noise. I steered the car back into the middle of the road and began praying very earnestly for a lovely, sustained uphill. Instead, the road dipped down, and just ahead of me was the intersection where the main drag of Emeryville poured across the frontage road. The frontage road, of course, had a stop sign. The intersection approached, and I began honking, honking, honking, hoping I'd scare off anyone who was in the intersection. "Oh my God," I said, and on four wheels, a prayer, and a string of swear words, I sailed through the intersection safely, with the frantic honks of enraged drivers following me. Ahead, the frontage road took another dip. I knew I had less than half a mile to the next intersection, and with that,

I steered the car into the soft, muddy shoulder and turned the ignition off. The car shuddered, lurched, and came to a stop directly in front of a Don Quixote–like driftwood sculpture.

"I really, really need my cell phone," I said again, just to hear the sound of my voice. The cold, black waters of the bay lapped outside. Okay, flares were clearly in order. I took a deep breath, unlatched the seat belt, opened the door, and stepped straight down into a foot of mud. A deep voice said, "Car trouble?"

Through the dim, foggy air, I saw someone approaching me. "Need some help?"

Great, I thought, serial killer offs dumb station wagon–driving mom.

"Oh, I'm okay," I began to babble, peering at the figure. And then he came closer, and I saw it was someone I knew.

John Orlando extended his hand to me. "Come step out of that muck, Mrs. Fiori."

I grabbed his hand and hoisted myself out of the mud, back onto the frontage road. I realized I was shaking, and began to babble, "I can't believe you're here. I mean, that someone I know is here—or that anyone is here." I had to shout over the roar of the distant freeway.

"What happened?" he said, gently guiding me away from the car. I could see a blue van parked a few hundred yards away.

"I don't know. My brakes stopped working, and then I couldn't get the emergency brake to engage, so I just kind of used the mud to stop the car."

I stopped dead in my tracks. "What are you doing here?" I asked suspiciously.

"You must be freezing," he said, ignoring my question. "Come get in my car. I've got an old sweater in the backseat and a cell phone; we can call Triple A."

"Oh, thank you," I said, wondering how wise it was to get into his car. But I was shivering, and he had hold of my arm. It seemed churlish not to accept the help.

"Are you always a Good Samaritan," I asked as we picked our

way to his van. "Or did you know it was me? I mean, someone you knew."

Orlando didn't answer. We'd arrived at his van, and he wrenched the side panel open. "Hop in," he said. "The sweater's in the back."

"My shoes are all muddy," I protested. "I'll wreck your car."

He put his hands on both sides of my waist and unceremoniously half-lifted me up. "Get in," he said roughly. And I did, landing on the seat with a thump. The door swung shut, clicked locked, and I found myself side by side with Glen Fox. He didn't greet me, however. He was bound, hand and foot, and had a gag in his mouth. I regarded him with more curiosity than fear. And then the confusion fell from me like a warm cloak, and I began to shiver for real.

I heard Orlando climb into the front seat and snap his seat belt into place. Oh, great, I thought. Got to keep those good safety practices in mind, even when you're in the middle of kidnapping innocent people. I looked around. I couldn't actually see the front seat because there was a scratched metal divider between the front seat and the back. Suddenly, it clanged open, and I saw two things—the muzzle of a gun and Orlando's eyes.

"Okay, Miss Nosy," he said, "here we are together. Now, we're going to go for a little ride. You're going to sit very still and make not one single sound or—"

"Or what?" I said. "You're going to shoot me? You're supposed to be an artist." I felt a thump at ankle level. Glen had edged his bound feet in my direction and was giving me a premonitory kick.

"Yes, shooting you seems like a fine idea," said Orlando. And with that, he slammed the divider shut, turned over the engine, and we took off.

I looked at Glen miserably. "I feel really bad about suspecting you," I said.

He blinked rapidly, and I saw tears well in his eyes. "Don't start," I said. "I know I'm married to an emotional Italian, but I don't do well with guys who cry."

I looked around the back seat. Why had Orlando left me unbound? Well, for openers, there didn't appear to be much damage I could do. The window and door handles were missing on the inside, and the windows were tinted so that no one could see in. I scrambled over Glen to get to the window side. Maybe if I pressed my face against the window, some passerby would spot me. I tried it, but for all I could see there were no passersby. We lurched and bumped along a road that was absolutely deserted. Between the darkness of night and Orlando's lightless travel, it was hard to make anything out, but it looked as if he had managed to find the only absolutely non-trafficked road in the entire Bay Area. Since we were clearly off the frontage road, I assumed he'd taken one of the fire access trails leading down to the water.

I turned my attention to my fellow prisoner. His hands and feet were actually shackled, and short of finding a key, I couldn't imagine getting him loose. Glen watched me rattle the chain links and shook his head. The gag, though, might be an entirely different matter. I knelt on the seat and reached in back of him. Taking the gag off completely seemed as if it might provoke our charmless warden to retaliation. But if I simply loosened it, it could be slipped back into place. I got a few fingers between the back of Glen's head and the terrycloth gag and edged it down just over his mouth.

"Probably not a good idea, Maggie," he whispered.

"I'll put it back in a minute," I said. "What in the hell is going on?"

Glen grimaced. "Long story. But don't apologize for suspecting me." He licked his lips. "I did it."

"You did what?" I whispered back.

"I killed Quentin."

With that, the van lurched to a stop. I frantically slipped Glen's gag back in place and composed myself on the seat. Staying calm seemed like the only possible option. Surely he wouldn't just gun us down. Surely.

The door slid open.

Orlando, gun in hand, gestured impatiently. "Come on out, both of you."

"Let me come first," I said, crawling over Glen, "and I'll help him out."

"Ever the Helpful Hannah," muttered Orlando. "Hurry it up."

Glen scooted across the seat to the edge. I helped him duck, and half-caught him as he propelled himself out the door. Orlando leaned down and unlocked the shackles on Glen's legs. Glen shook one, then the other.

"Move along," Orlando said, and gestured with the gun to the edge of the water.

We walked while I frantically consulted my mental store of useless information. Wasn't there something I knew, anything that could get us out of this mess? Somehow, it seemed as if I should have been concentrating on collecting techniques in martial arts all these years instead of uselessly storing up the names of all the French Symbolist poets and how to get ketchup stains out of silk. As if on cue, Orlando broke the silence. "I have been wondering" he said, "how you figured out who I was in the first place?"

I looked over my shoulder at him. "If I tell you, will you let us go?"

He gave a sharp bark of laughter. "Right."

"Shakespeare," I said. "Orlando was the name of one of the sons of Sir Rowland de Boys in *As You Like It.*"

Orlando lifted his lips in a grim approximation of a smile. "Aren't you the clever girl?" he said. "Well, here's a little more Shakespeare. 'What fates impose, that men must needs abide; It boots not to resist both wind and tide.'"

"*Henry the Sixth, Part III,*" I said promptly. "What do I win?"

"An encounter with the tide itself," said Orlando. "Hold it right here." Glen and I came to a halt and looked bleakly at each other. We were under the pilings, nearly ankle deep in mud, and the icy, cloudy water of the bay was lapping near our feet.

"Sit down," said Orlando, and with a few yanks, he managed to get us arranged next to a splintery wood piling. He took a length of cord from his windbreaker and handed it to me. "Tie the little Irishman right up to the piling," he said to me. "And make it snug. I'll be checking on you." My hands were stiff and growing more numb by the moment from the cold, but I did as he ordered, looping the cord around Glen's torso and the piling. Then Orlando gestured me to sit on the other side of the piling. I felt the mud and water seep through my skirt. My mind drifted a minute as I wondered if I'd be able to get the smell off these clothes before I was jerked back to reality. I should be so lucky to have laundry problems ever again. Awkwardly, with the gun in one hand, he began wrapping the cord around me. I felt it bite into my arms, and for a moment the accompanying rush of blood felt wonderfully warm. Then, my arms began to ache. Orlando leaned in close to my ankles and began looping the cord around them. In one instant, I saw the gun droop and point toward the mud. I raised both feet and kicked hard at his face. He gave a shout, staggered back, scrambled for a foot hold on the muddy ground, and fell smack against a piling sticking out of the mud. As he did, there was a flash of light, a terrible noise, and a jolt of pain in my arm. And then, quiet.

I heard Glen breathing hard, and then his voice,

"Jaysus, Mary, and Joseph, Maggie, have you killed him?"

"I wish," I said grimly. "I think he's just knocked out. He'll wake up in a minute and he'll be pissed."

"I'm not sure we've improved our situation," said Glen.

"Well, you got the gag off," I said bitterly. "At least we can chat to the end."

"Are you ever serious, Maggie?" asked Glen.

I bit my lip as, all of a sudden, the ache in my arm seemed to deepen.

"Glen," I said, "can you look over at my arm a minute?"

I heard him struggle against the cord. "Maggie, you're bleeding."

"Yeah, I seem to be," I said. "I don't think it's serious. It just hurts like hell."

"Help!" I yelled.

"Shh, Maggie," said Glen. "You'll rouse the bloody bastard."

The light was fading fast.

"Tide's rising," observed Glen, in a whisper.

"So since we're in all this trouble," I whispered back, "why don't you distract me from the thought of my kids growing up without a mom and your kids growing up without a dad, and tell me what the hell this is all about." I felt my voice thicken and the pinpricks of tears starting in my eyes. Moon and Michael had warned me away from all this, I was irresponsible beyond belief, and my kids would grow up without a mom. How could I have been so arrogant?

"Ah, Maggie," said Glen. "Maybe my dear Corinne and your Michael will fall in love and give our youngsters a full complement of parents."

"My mother-in-law would love that," I said. "At long last, a nice Catholic wife for her precious son." I gave an anxious glance over to Orlando. Still not stirring.

"So tell me the story," I said, "before the tide comes in all the way, and we either drown or freeze to death. Or that son of a bitch Orlando wakes up and just shoots us."

"I think you know some of it," said Glen.

"I think I do," I said. "Skunkworks is a drug smuggling operation—but I can't figure out why."

"It's a subsidy," said Glen. "Orlando and his partners smuggle all sorts of drugs, but they use most of the money they make on the hard-core street stuff to distribute any promising new AIDS drug. And then they sell it at a premium to AIDS patients."

"Geez, don't the insurance companies pay for that stuff?" I asked.

"God, are you naive," said Glen. "Comes of having a husband with a great insurance plan, I imagine. They're smuggling stuff to late-stage AIDS patients, the ones who aren't responding to conventional therapies. And a lot of this stuff is very experimental. There's a small amount of it available in highly controlled clinical trials, and you've got to get in queue to get access to any of it. Orlando was a natural at this, because he's supported himself all these years with dope dealing gigs wherever he's been. And now he's got partners who help him run little kitchen-table labs all over the world, shipping this stuff in."

"But he wasn't doing this out of the goodness of his heart? Wasn't Skunkworks a nonprofit?" I asked.

Glen snorted. "Skunkworks was a nonprofit on paper. It was just a cover. Orlando and his retail pals were making big, big money on this deal. They're selling to people who cash in their life insurance to buy these drugs."

"And do they work?"

"Long-term, I have no idea. But in the short term, several people seem to buying a reprieve."

I thought about Joe Connolly's rapid comeback and remembered the cylinder I'd fished out of the trash can.

"And how did Quentin get involved?"

"He owed Orlando a couple of favors from the old days. And for all of Quentin being a self-centered SOB himself, he did have a lot of compassion for people with AIDS. And besides, all Orlando was asking him to do was run his damn little drawings with his communication codes in them."

"What was all that about?"

"You mean Jorge, the boy wonder, didn't explain everything to you? I couldn't believe how much that kid figured out."

"Yeah," I said, "he's a smart kid. Maybe he can do both our jobs now that we're out of the picture."

"Fine," said Glen. "Anyway, the codes were just a distribution system, to let anyone in the city who was in Orlando's underground know when a new shipment was coming in."

"In the pot handles?"

Glen sighed. "In the pot handles."

"And why couldn't they use a phone tree or e-mail to let people know?"

"Too traceable," I guess.

"And was Quentin paid for his part in this?"

"He was," said Glen. "And with Claire keeping him on a short string, the cash came in handy. Plus, he liked having access to the bonus—hash on hand, whenever he wanted it. He was covering all his bases. Even with all the precautions he took, Quentin must have worried he'd turn up HIV-positive one day."

We sat in silence and listened to the fog horns. The water was rising little by little.

"Glen," I said, "maybe Orlando will drown before he wakes up."

"I wouldn't be going to the races on it—he's face up."

"And you," I said, "what did you get out of it?"

"Nothing—yet," he said.

"What do you mean?" I asked.

"I just supported the system because I wanted it to be there when I needed it."

I swallowed. "You're HIV-positive?" I asked.

"I am," he said. "And I will do—would have done—anything, anything to stay alive for Corinne and the little ones."

"And that's why you killed Quentin?"

"It is. He finally began to understand the scope of the thing Orlando had going—and that people were spending their last pennies for these drugs. He was putting you and that young photographer on it to break the story."

"And you didn't want him to?"

"Absolutely not. I went to his flat to try to talk to him. He was cold as ice to me. He really had nothing to lose. He could claim to be an innocent dupe, and he'd bring the whole structure crashing down—and look like an investigative hero." Glen's voice broke.

"I begged him to think it over. And he refused. I didn't mean to kill him, but he turned back to his desk, ignoring me, getting his notes in order for you, so I picked up the walking stick and just smashed at him."

"You connected," I said. "Beginner's luck."

"Christ, that's not funny a bit, Maggie."

"I know, I'm sorry. It's gallows humor. Quentin stopped being a hero to me long ago, but of course, he didn't deserve to die."

"No, he didn't. But neither do I."

"And that's how you saw it—life or death? People live for years now, with the drugs that are available."

"Some do," said Glen. "But I saw Quentin doing just what he did at Oxford all those years ago—walking away from a mess he'd had a hand in."

"Then what?"

"I went crazy after I hit him. I knew he was dead. But I remembered that he kept a few cylinders of the latest drug around, and I thought I'd better find it. I went in the kitchen and began rummaging in the pots and pans."

"Making a terrible noise," I said.

"Right," said Glen. "So I just hit the play button on the stereo and some of Stuart's dreadful metal music came on and I hoped it would completely drown out what I was doing."

"I knew it," I said. "I knew Quentin wouldn't listen to that stuff."

Orlando groaned, and Glen and I both stiffened. He fell silent again, and I let my breath out.

"The water's getting higher," said Glen.

I started to reply, when faintly, I heard the most magical sound on earth, someone calling my name.

"Listen," I said to Glen. And then, I began to shout, "We're here, we're over here." The sound of a barking dog and heavy boots clomping in and out of the muck came closer, and in a minute, my own beloved Raider, German Shepherd extraordinaire, was covering my face with dog kisses.

In a minute, Michael was there, shouting, kneeling at my side, and crying, with John Moon and a bunch of other cops right behind him.

"See what I told you?" I said to Glen, as Michael hugged me, mud, blood, tears, and all. "Italian men are so emotional."

A NICE LONG RUN

I thought I might ask the guy at the Alta Bates Hospital parking garage for a discount. After all, it was my second trip of the evening. But Michael insisted on screeching up to the emergency entrance so that Glen and I could get checked out. John Moon arrived half an hour later, looking ready to arrest anyone who crossed his path.

Glen cleaned up quite nicely, and after a very good-looking young doctor (Indian, recommended a new Berkeley source for *papadam,* that crispy bread my kids love) stitched up the little tear in my arm created by Orlando's misfire, I was just fine also. When I stopped babbling long enough to let Michael get a word in, he explained how they'd tracked me down. Turned out that Joe Connolly was feeling so great he'd called the house to thank the kids for the plant. Michael answered, knew when I'd left Alta Bates, and began to worry when I didn't turn up. Especially after Anya started leaking the news about the poison bouquet. He called Moon, whose office paged him and dispatched a Berkeley black and white to Alta Bates to begin retracing my trip home.

"I knew if the traffic was heavy, you'd sneak off to that frontage road, even though I've told you a thousand times I think it's dangerous to drive it at night by yourself," said Michael.

"It never occurred to me that she'd actually listen to you," Moon weighed in. And then they discovered the car.

"But how did you find us?" I asked.

Moon said, "And that's why you leave detecting to the police. It was clear you'd left the car in a hurry; your handbag was on the front seat. The officers simply found the tracks left by the van and followed them off the road." He gave me a grudging smile. "We are, after all, detectives."

"If you'd been better detectives," I retorted, "I wouldn't have been in that mess."

"Oh, we're fine detectives," said Moon, "just a few minutes behind the nosy girl sleuth."

"What do you mean?"

"Did you really think you were the only one who would consider removing the handles from the pots?" he asked. "We did the same thing, but we were trying to tie up some loose ends before we made an arrest."

I sniffed, "Well, one of your loose ends almost killed me."

Moon sighed and turned to Michael. "Isn't there some nice convent where you can take her and keep her locked up?"

It was clearly time to change the subject, "And Raider?" I asked.

"I brought him along for company," said Michael. "I was frantic and didn't want to say anything to the kids. Raider was there to keep me calm."

"The dog must have scented you," said Moon.

"Anyway," continued Michael, "He led us directly to you."

An emergency room nurse walked in, a collection of pill bottles in hand.

"These for pain, these to knock out any infection, these to sleep, in case you need them."

Suddenly, a wave of exhaustion swept me, head to toe, and I thought I might slip right off the table. "I won't need anything to sleep," I said.

"Good," she said. "If you can pry your little friend away from Dr. Singh, you can all go home."

Disregarding Michael's advice, Anya had arrived at the hospital with the boys, and true to form, was flirting with the ER doc while the boys roamed around the waiting room bragging to anyone who would listen that their mom was involved in a shootout.

Over the next several days, Michael threatened, begged, bribed, and otherwise pressured me to confess to the error of my ways. I did, more or less. He led the boys in a little cheer every morning at breakfast: "No more detecting! No more detecting!" Josh and Zach thought it was hysterical. I more or less promised. After all, how many dead bodies are likely to turn up in the life of a suburban housewife, or even the life of a media mogul? It's not as if I were a reporter on the police beat, after all.

And the moral test I thought I'd have to face, to tell or not to tell about Glen's confession, never even came up. Glen spilled the beans to John Moon that night in the emergency room. His remorse began to melt both my fury at him for endangering me and my family and my horror at what he had done. In a way, Quentin's chilly focus on looking out for himself is what doomed him.

I talked with Glen after he was out on bail.

"Here's what I don't get," I said.

Glen snorted. "Hard to believe there's much you missed, Maggie."

I persisted. "Why set up this elaborate charade—sending Calvin and me out on this fake story?"

"It wasn't a charade," he said. "If Quentin had called the police on Rowland, he'd still have been in it up to his neck. But commissioning the story gave him a great cover; he could claim he'd played along just to expose the scam, and then assigned the story to gather investigative evidence."

"He was using me like that?" I said indignantly.

Glen laughed. "Quentin used everybody, Maggie, surely you figured that out. This way, he got the financial benefit of playing along and the glory when he exposed the whole mess."

I was quiet for a minute, letting go of the last of my feelings for Quentin.

"Still," said Glen, "I did the unforgivable. And then it just got worse and worse. Every day at work, there you were nosing around and coming closer to the truth."

I couldn't help but feel pleased. "Yes, I was, wasn't I? And all those threatening pranks? My car? The bouquet?"

"Teamwork, I'm afraid," said Glen. "Greg Bender, Joe Connolly, John Orlando; all of us were collaborators. Until the end, when Orlando thought I was going to crack. Then he just wanted to get rid of you—and me. He'd already grabbed me when he talked to Joe Connolly in the hospital and knew where you were."

"You've got lousy taste in co-conspirators," I said.

In the end, I couldn't help but see Glen as a guy who had a lot in common with me. He'd made a terrible mistake. I figure it takes a sinner to help a sinner—or maybe it takes a sinner's husband. So I put Michael to work on his behalf. Fortunately, though Michael himself wasn't spectacularly useful in the whole criminal law arena, he had plenty of friends who were. I'm a little troubled by how easily a serious crime can begin to seem less serious in the hands of a highly skilled attorney, but since it was Glen's life involved, I was willing to suppress those trepidations.

According to Michael, we're already down to manslaughter and, in his words, with Edgar the Invincible on the case, "we've not yet begun to fight."

"We?" I inquired archly, beginning to clear the breakfast dishes. "Are you planning to threaten the DA's office with a closely held trust or something?"

Michael reached out as I walked past and pulled me on to his lap. "I happen to be offering some counsel of worth, Miss Know-it-all," he said.

"I know," I said brightly. "I invited that nice Edgar out to lunch the other day. He brought me up to date."

Michael tightened his hold on me. "Maggie," he said, "don't you have enough to do at that damn magazine?" I did. I said so.

As for the story Quentin had planned for Calvin and me, we're working on it. Calvin's still feeling really annoyed he wasn't in on, as he calls it, "the big climax," so he's looking for opportunities to get into more mischief.

Orlando's in the clinker, awaiting trial. They found a passport and a one-way ticket to Belize City in his jacket, so the judge decided he was too much of a flight risk for bail. The other Skunkworks principals are under investigation. Much to my disappointment, it turned out Claire was a more or less innocent party in the whole deal. She was simply society do-gooding, and had no idea what Skunkworks was really up to. Stuart didn't know anything either, so he's in the clear. The remaining vials of BZT were retrieved and shipped over to the lab at the University of California, San Francisco med school for analysis. The pieces of the story are coming together, and we're hoping to run it in *Small Town* right after the New Year.

At Michael's firm, they invited him back on the executive committee. He turned them down.

"I think I like having a little more spare time for the kids," he said.

"How about for me?" I asked.

"Yeah," he countered, "more time to keep you under high-level surveillance." Things seem better between us, still a little fragile, but despite Michael's jokes about surveillance, I'm hoping he thinks I'm redeemable.

At least, that's what I reported to John Moon. We were having a drink at the silly, chichi martini bar that replaced Cock of the Walk.

"Redeemable," he said. "I don't know. If I were Michael, I think I'd be looking for a little more repentance. What about that?"

"Oh, I've repented," I said grimly. "Every day. I have no idea what possessed me...."

"To go detecting?" asked Moon.

"Oh, no, that was fun," I confessed. "I mean—"

"The affair?" he finished my sentence.

I nodded glumly. We fell silent.

Moon cleared his throat. "Well, look at me," he said, "asking nosy, personal questions, just like the infamous Maggie Fiori."

"Maybe it's catching," I said. "John," I hesitated. "You're a guy. Is Michael ever going to forgive me?"

He shrugged. "Remember my theory, Maggie. All marriages are puzzle boxes. Only you know that."

"Swell," I said.

"But I'll tell you how things seem to me. Michael is a much happier guy than he was six months ago."

"You mean he's not trying to kill people on the ice?"

"Oh, we're all trying to kill people on the ice," he said. "But I don't worry about what's going to happen off the ice any more."

I remembered Moon's questions about Michael's temper and felt remorseful all over again. I took a gulp of my drink.

"What is that odd thing you're drinking?" he asked.

"It's a theme martini," I said. "A hot tamale-tini. The olives are stuffed with hot peppers."

I deftly removed both olives from the toothpick with my tongue and felt my mouth catch fire. I chewed and swallowed quickly. "You know what they say," I managed to croak. "Marriage can be murder."

Moon snorted. "Being married to you could be murder," he countered.

Meanwhile, Joe Connolly is back at school, Andrea has invited Calvin home to Connecticut for Christmas, Jorge turned in his first story, and I've still got my job. Anya's dating that nice young doc from the ER. Uncle Alf's at yet another drying-out spa, so I figure my employment is secure until he's completely clean and sober. I'm hoping it will be a nice long run.

EPILOGUE: HAT TRICK

It was Family Night at Skate Oakland, and there we were, the whole *mishpucha*—Michael, Josh and Zach, Anya, her new beau, and me. Even Stuart had joined us. Anya looked lighter than air, freed of her clunky Doc Martens and gliding on the ice. Dr. Singh was slipping and sliding, and stopping to cling to the side rail every so often, following Anya like a duckling, ready to imprint. Stuart was spending more time off than on the ice, chatting up the cute guy who drives the Zamboni. Michael and Josh were streaking along the ice while I helped Zach get rid of the ankle-wobbles.

The lights blinked over the rink, and a disembodied voice came over the speaker.

"Hello, skaters," it said. "Time to dim the lights and invite all the romantics onto the ice. Moms and dads, come on down!"

Anya, Dr. Singh, Stuart, Zach, and I glided off the ice and reassembled in the bleachers. Josh and Michael sped up with a flourish and a little cascade of ice chips in the air.

"Mom, did you see me?" asked Josh. "Did you see how fast I was skating?"

"Like the wind," I said. "But even the wind's got to rest once in a while. Come sit for a few minutes."

Michael stayed on the ice, leaning on the rail. He dug into his back pocket and brought out his wallet.

"Who wants hot chocolate?"

I reached out my hand for the twenty-dollar bill he was waving. He handed it to Anya and looked back at me.

"Anya will get it, *cara*," he said. "I believe this dance is mine."

As if on cue, the lights dimmed and the sound system started up. The first notes of "The Skater's Waltz" tinkled out of the raspy speakers.

I joined Michael on the ice. He took my hand and led me slowly along the rail. Suddenly, my ankles felt almost as wobbly as Zach's. He slipped his arm around my waist and pulled me closer. "Relax. Longer glides," he urged. I leaned into him, caught his rhythm, and my ankles felt more secure. We picked up a little speed. We made a turn around the rink, and I began to enjoy myself.

"This is fun," I said.

"Ready to waltz?" he asked.

"Oh, I don't know," I protested, but in the time it took the words to get out of my mouth, he had pulled me into dance position and we were moving over the ice.

"Michael," I faltered.

"You're doing fine," he said.

"No, I want to ask you something."

"Just a second," he said. As we danced past Anya, Dr. Singh, Stuart, and the kids in the bleachers, he twirled me out and back again. I nearly stumbled, but recovered enough to come back to dance position and wave at the kids over his shoulders.

Josh gave me a thumbs-up.

"You're getting back in the swing," said Michael. "Now what do you want to ask me?"

"Do you think marriages are like puzzle boxes? That's what John Moon says."

"What do you mean?"

"That there's some secret way to make them work, and only the two people inside the marriage can figure it out."

Michael laughed. "That's one way to put it," he said. "Ready for a dip?"

As we drew close to where the kids were watching, he bent me backward. I fought a moment of panic, then relaxed and leaned back so far I felt the pom-pom on my silly hat brush the ice.

"Hey!" I said, exhilarated. "How was that?"

Michael grinned. "What a showboat," he whispered in my ear.

"So," I persisted. "A puzzle box?"

We skated in silence. "I don't know, Maggie. I think it's more like a hat trick."

"In hockey? Three goals in one game?"

"You've got to love your partner, you've got to like your partner, and then, you've got to trust them."

We took the turn, and Michael twirled me out on one arm and back again.

"Well," I said, "two out of three ain't bad."

He pulled me close. "Oh, we'll get back to three out of three," he said. "Hat tricks are happy accidents."

The morning after we went skating, I got out the little brown derby with the veil. I hadn't worn it since the day Quentin died. I tried it on and looked in the mirror. It wasn't quite me, not anymore. I packed that hat and the fawn cloche Quentin bought me into a hatbox and dropped it in the Goodwill bin at the supermarket. It's okay. I've got plenty of other hats.

ACKNOWLEDGMENTS

Writing is supposed to be a solitary pursuit, but I'm indebted to a small city of companions and cheerleaders. Whatever I got wrong was my fault; what I got right, I owe to my pals. The smartest, most supportive and loyal agent around, Amy Rennert. The best writing group in town: Eileen Bordy, Ronnie Caplane, Greg Ellis, Gloria Lenhart, Suzy Parker, Christine Schoefer. Friends who read and offered help, suggestions and corrections: Barbara Austin, Margret Elson, Scott Hafner, Kathy Halland, Maria Hjelm, Jonnie Jacobs, Michael Learned, Wendy Lichtman, Phyllis Peacock. Steve Tollefson, my longtime writing buddy, editor, and co-conspirator.

Thanks to Evan Young for many things, including the epilogue. Thanks to expert counsel: Ted Michon on shipping, Murray Winthrop and Bart Elmer on hockey, Inspector Bruce Fairbairn for SFPD titles. Editorial counsel came from many quarters, including Michael Castleman, Antoinette Ercolano, Donna Lemaster, and Ed Stackler, and manuscript assistance came from Susan D'Orazio and Kate Peterson. Thanks to Deke Castleman and 21st Century. Thanks to Jackie Jones for a handsome hardcover book, my website, and a beautiful friendship, and to Louise Kollenbaum for generous visual consulting. Hugs to David Skolnick, my business partner, who sent me to the mystery conference at Book Passage. I am blessed with an amen corner of family, fine writers and readers, one and all: Ken, Ben, and Kate Peterson, Larry and Pat Winthrop, and my sister, Laurie Winthrop, who thinks her full-time job is promoting me.

Maggie Fiori is an obnoxious know-it-all. Those of you who knew my nephew, Andrew Tuttle, had the privilege of knowing a non-obnoxious know-it-all. The memory of Andrew's omnivorous appetite for knowledge of all kinds—from sports ephemera to political strategy—may make Maggie a nicer person one day.

A new shout-out to Colleen Dunn Bates, Patty O'Sullivan, Jennifer Bastien, and all the crew at Prospect Park Books. They embraced my second mystery, *The Devil's Interval*, and re-issued (and re-edited) *Edited to Death* as a paperback and e-book. Thank you, new friends.

Finally, a toast to my parents, Vauneta Winthrop, who taught me to love books, and to Murray Winthrop, who introduced me to Dashiell Hammett.

ABOUT THE AUTHOR

Linda Lee Peterson is the author the Maggie Fiori mysteries, including *Edited to Death* and *The Devil's Interval*, as well as several nonfiction books. She is also the managing partner of Peterson Skolnick & Dodge, a creative services agency based in San Francisco, Philadelphia, and Portland, Oregon. A longtime resident of the San Francisco Bay Area, she was inspired to set her mysteries in the city that inspired Dashiell Hammett. Linda and her family now live in Portland, Oregon.